A DREAM BORN FROM TYRANNY

Athas, world of the dark sun. Ruled for thousands of years by power-mad sorcerer-kings, the cities of Athas have become vile centers of slavery and corruption. Only heroes of the greatest strength and bravest heart can stand against the might of these overlords. The Prism Pentad is a tale of such heroes. . . .

Sadira—the beautiful half-elven slave girl, caught between her desire to fight for her world and the seductive power offered to her by forbidden sorceries.

Nok—the halfling chieftan who leaves his lush forest home to search relentlessly for the woman who has stolen his magical staff.

Magnus—the elven windsinger, formed by the magic of the Pristine Tower into a creature of the New Races and raised by the elven chief, Faenaeyon.

PRISM PENTAD

Troy Denning

Book One
The Verdant Passage
October 1991

Book Two
The Crimson Legion
April 1992

Book Three
The Amber Enchantress
October 1992

Book Four
The Obsidian Oracle
June 1993

Book Five
The Cerulean Storm
September 1993

The Amber Enchantress

TROY DENNING

THE AMBER ENCHANTRESS

Random House and its affiliate companies have worldwide distribution rights in the book trade for English language products of TSR, Inc.

Distributed to the book and hobby trade in the United Kingdom by TSR Ltd.

Distributed to the toy and hobby trade by regional distributors.

Cover art by Brom.

DARK SUN and the TSR logo are trademarks owned by TSR, Inc.

First Printing: October 1992
Printed in the United States of America
Library of Congress Catalog Card Number: 91-66492

9 8 7 6 5 4 3 2

ISBN: 1-56076-236-5

TSR, Inc.   TSR, Ltd.
P.O. Box 756   120 Church End, Cherry Hinton
Lake Geneva, WI 53147   Cambridge CB1 3LB
U.S.A.   United Kingdom

Dedication:

To Bill, Anne, Matt, and Josh

Acknowledgements:

Many people contributed to the writing of this book and the creation of the series. I would like to thank you all. Without the efforts of the following people, especially, Athas might never have seen the light of the crimson sun: Mary Kirchoff and Tim Brown, who shaped the world as much as anyone; Brom, who gave us the look and the feel; Jim Lowder, for his inspiration and patience; Lloyd Holden of the AKF Martial Arts Academy in Janesville, WI for contributing his expertise to the fight scenes; Andria Hayday, for support and encouragement; and Jim Ward, for enthusiasm, support, and much more.

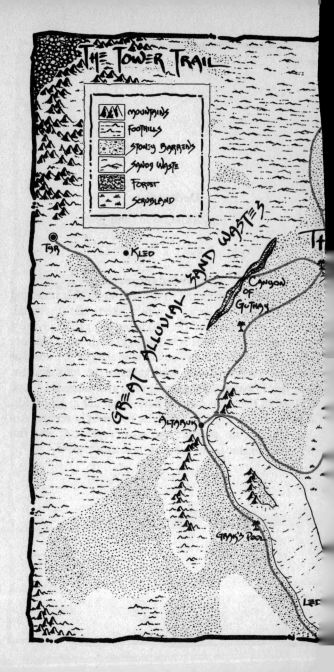

PROLOGUE

The gaunt figure of King Tithian I crept across his antechamber on all fours, his limbs splayed to the sides and moving in the disjointed rhythm of an insect. The lower mandible of his jaw worked constantly, as if gnawing a stalk of thornstem, and his glazed eyes remained fixed on the stones of the floor. The king reached a corner, then clawed his way up the wall until he stood more or less upright. He spent a few moments trying to pull himself higher, then abruptly fell back to the floor and continued his journey in a new direction.

Two disembodied heads followed the king across the room, hovering a yard off the ground and studying his actions with worried frowns. One was shriveled and ashen-skinned, with sunken features and cracked, leathery lips. The other was bloated and gross, with puffy cheeks, eyes swollen to narrow dark slits, and a mouthful of gray, broken teeth. Both wore their coarse hair in topknots. The bottoms of their necks had been stitched shut with thread.

The beast's mind has overpowered Tithian's, surmised

the bloated head, using the Way to mentally broadcast his thoughts. *I told you he wasn't ready for something so dangerous, Wyan.*

Liar. You said nothing, countered Wyan. *But it hardly matters, Sacha. If Tithian can't escape the kank's mind, he would be no good to us anyway.*

Though he realized the heads were conversing, Tithian did not understand the meaning of their words. Ten days ago, he had used the Way of the Unseen to establish a mental link with a kank, intending to spy on an adversary who would be riding it out of the city. When he had expanded the contact, the beast's bizarre senses had disoriented him, allowing the creature's natural essence to overpower his mind. Now, the most primitive part of Tithian's intellect believed him to be the kank: an insect twice the size of a man, with six canelike legs, a jacket of chitinous black armor, and a pair of bristly antennae on its head.

Tithian felt a strange rumble beneath his armpits, where, on a kank, a pair of drumlike membranes served as ears. The sounds rolled through his torso in muted tones that he dimly recognized as the voice of Sadira, one of the three people upon whom he was spying. As with Sacha and Wyan, the words seemed a meaningless garble.

The rational part of Tithian's mind, the tiny spark of intelligence that knew him to be a monarch instead of a kank, wanted to comprehend what was being said. It was for that reason that he had originally joined his mind to the beast's, and, despite his setback, the king remained determined to see his plan through.

Tithian focused his rational mind on the core of his being, that space where the three energies of the Way—spiritual, mental, and physical—converged in a tempest of mystical force. He visualized a cord of golden fire running from this nexus into his mind. An instant later, he felt an eerie tingle rise through his body. Though he knew it would fatigue him, the king continued to draw until even his fingers and toes burned with energy. If he wished to overpower the beast's instincts, he would need all the power he could marshal.

When he felt as though he would explode, Tithian used the energy to picture himself inside his own head: a gaunt, sharp-featured man with a hawkish nose, his long auburn hair encircled by the golden diadem of Tyr.

The insect immediately countered the maneuver, raising the image of a kank from the mucky gray terrain of the king's mind. The beast struck quickly, opening its mandibles and darting forward to seize its prey. Tithian leaped away and hit the ground rolling. By the time he returned to his feet, the creature was turning to attack again.

The king visualized a pair of wings growing from his back. His body tingled as more energy rose from his nexus, then the appendages appeared. The kank lunged, and Tithian flapped his new wings wildly. He rose off the murky ground, barely avoiding the pincers as they clacked shut beneath his feet.

Before the dim-witted creature realized where he had gone, the king lowered himself onto its back and grasped its antennae. The kank sprang into the air, trying to throw off its unwelcome rider. Tithian held tight, pulling hard on the bristly tendrils in his hands.

The beast returned to the ground squealing in agony and alarm. Its antennae were attached directly to the nerves in its head, and any attack against the crucial appendages was a devastating one. The kank tucked in all three of its left-side legs, attempting to roll over and crush its rider.

Tithian was ready. Again drawing energy from within himself, he visualized the terrain inside his mind turning from ground to fog. His stomach felt as though it had risen into his throat, then he and his mount found themselves tumbling through a gray haze. The king continued to pull on the kank's antennae steadily, asserting through the constant pressure that he was the beast's master. The kank struggled only a few more moments before resigning itself to Tithian's domination.

The king did not have to wait long to know that he had overpowered the creature's instincts. The kank had barely stopped struggling before its ear membranes resonated with a familiar voice. This time, with his own mind firmly in control of his perceptions, Tithian understood the words.

"What's wrong with your kank?" It was Rikus, one of the men accompanying Sadira.

"I don't know," Sadira answered. "It went mad and tried to throw me. I've never heard of such a thing."

Unable to distinguish between what was happening inside and outside its head, the kank had reacted physically to Tithian's attack. Hoping to soothe Sadira's concerns about her mount's behavior, Tithian lightly tapped the antennae of the insect trapped in his mind. Both it and the true creature, the one that Sadira was actually riding, started forward.

"Whatever upset it seems to have passed," observed Sadira's second companion, the nobleman Agis of Asticles. "Let's push on. Kled must be near, and I'm anxious to meet Er'Stali. From Rikus's stories, he's as learned as any sage in Tyr."

"I'm no judge of that," Rikus said. "All I know is that he's the only man alive who's read the *Book of the Kemalok Kings*."

"You're sure he's still in Kled?" asked Agis.

"Of course," Rikus assured his friend. "His knowledge of the book is all that remains of the dwarves' history. The whole village would die before giving him reason to leave—or letting something kill him."

Though the two men were only a few yards from Sadira's mount, Tithian saw them as little more than a blur. A kank could focus only upon nearby objects—customarily the rocky ground over which it walked. Everything else seemed part of a hazy curtain of shapes and colors, with even the slightest movement causing a flash of light to sparkle in its eyes.

Because a kank's range of vision did not include its rider, Tithian could not see Sadira at all. Still, he was far more aware of her presence than that of either Rikus or Agis. Through the kank's mind, he felt her weight on his back, spread along its entire length by the section of chitinous shell covering the beast's thorax. He could also smell her, for the insect's bristly antennae were loaded with the scent of sour human skin, carefully masked with the fragrance of silverthorn blossoms.

After the trio had ridden in silence for a few moments, Sadira asked, "Are you sure there'll be something in the *Book of Kings* to help us, Rikus?"

"I'm not sure, but it's our best chance," the gladiator grunted. He shrugged, and to Tithian it appeared that bronze lights were twinkling around his shoulders. "We'll never stop the Dragon unless we find a weak spot."

"Er'Stali's knowledge is our only hope," Agis said. He nodded in agreement with Rikus and bursts of black light appeared around his head. "If he can't help us, we may not be able to prevent Tithian from giving the Dragon his levy."

"Never!" answered Sadira. "I won't send a thousand people to such a gruesome death."

"Then what will you do, if the Dragon cannot be stopped?" demanded Rikus.

"Call all of Tyr to arms," Sadira answered. "We'll stand as one."

"Then we'll die as one," snapped Rikus. "Some evils can't be destroyed with force—I learned that in Urik."

"So you would surrender?" Sadira asked bitterly. "The man I remember from Tithian's gladiatorial pits would never have considered such a thing."

"Because he fought nothing but men and beasts—and if he lost to them, it was only his own life that was forfeit," Rikus countered, his voice booming sharply through the kank's—and Tithian's—body. "Now we have a greater responsibility, one that cannot be taken so lightly."

"That's true, Rikus," agreed Agis. "But neither can we sacrifice a thousand lives without a struggle. If we have even the faintest hope of saving them, we must try."

With that, the noble used a small switch to tap his mount between its antennae. The beast broke into a trot, its sticklike legs clattering over the rocky ground as it trotted toward Kled.

When it became clear that the conversation had come to an end, Tithian withdrew most of his attention from the beast's mind and focused it on his own antechamber.

"By Ral!" he cursed, his angry voice echoing off the stone walls. "I should have them all killed!"

"So we have told you many times," said Sacha, the bloated head.

"It isn't so difficult to arrange," added Wyan, a light of anticipation burning in his sunken eyes.

The two disembodied heads drifted around to face

Tithian, staying at eye level as he returned to his feet.

"What have they done to bring you to your senses?" asked Sacha.

"They know about the Dragon's visit," Tithian reported.

"Hardly surprising, when you let them plant agents in your palace," hissed Wyan.

"Better to suffer spies you know than those you don't," countered the king. "Besides, it's not what they've learned that angers me, but what they intend to do with the knowledge."

"Which is?"

"Deny the Dragon his levy," the king answered.

"Let them try," suggested Wyan, baring his yellow teeth. "They'll all die, and no one will hold you to blame."

"No," Tithian answered, shaking his head. "I've my own plans for the Dragon—and they don't include having him angered by such foolishness."

Tithian's chamberlain interrupted the discussion by stepping into the room. She was a blond woman, with a stately form that could not be hidden beneath her uniform of priceless chain mail.

"Excuse the intrusion, Mighty King," she said, bowing.

"Who summoned you, wench?" demanded Sacha.

"Leave us, or you'll pay a high price for your impudence!" snarled Wyan.

The chamberlain raised an eyebrow at the threat, then cast a steely gaze at the two heads. After a moment, she turned her attention to her king. "The halfling chieftain Nok requests the honor of an audience," she said.

Tithian recognized the name, for Nok had supplied the weapons that Rikus and Sadira had used to overthrow

Tyr's last monarch, the sorcerer-king Kalak. "What is the nature of his visit?"

"He refused to say," answered the chamberlain.

Tithian pondered the breach of courtesy for several moments, trying to decide whether the halfling had meant to insult him or simply did not understand civilized protocol. Finally, he said, "I'm unavailable for social calls until tomorrow evening."

"I'll suggest he return at that time," the chamberlain said, bowing.

Tithian dismissed her with a wave of his hand. He did not believe Nok had come so far to make a casual visit, but he never received visitors without knowing what they wished to discuss. It was not so much a habit of arrogance as one of political acumen. A man who thought about his conversations beforehand was less likely to say something he regretted later.

As the chamberlain stepped beneath the archway leading from the room, she reached for the sword on her belt. "I said to wait in the vestibule," she snapped, speaking to someone outside the room.

Before she could say anything else, a surprised scream erupted from her lips. A bloody splinter of wood sprouted from her body, shredding her chain mail as though it were cloth. She stumbled back toward the center of the room, gurgling in pain and feebly clutching at a burgundy-colored spear piercing her chest.

At the other end of the spear stood a halfling covered in greasy green paint and dressed in a cape of feathers. A crown of fronds encircled his tangled mass of hair, a golden ring hung in his nose, and a ball of obsidian dangled from a silver chain around his neck. Behind him were a dozen more halflings, adorned in simple breechcloths and carrying small bows with tiny, black-tipped arrows.

"An intruder and a murderer!" hissed Wyan, fixing his narrow eyes on the halfling leader.

"Kill him!" cried Sacha, licking his lips with a long red tongue.

The two heads split up to approach from different sides, but the king quickly waved them off. Even if he had not already guessed the halfling's identity, the weapon in the chieftain's hands would have warned Tithian to be careful. It was the Heartwood Spear, the magical javelin that Nok had loaned Rikus for the purpose of killing Kalak. In addition to penetrating any armor, the oak shaft would protect its wielder from the Way—which meant that Sacha and Wyan would be as ineffectual as gnats against him.

Turning his attention to the halfling, the king demanded, "How did you get past my sentries?"

"The same way I passed your chamberlain," answered the halfling, pulling his spear from the woman's body. She collapsed to the floor and did not move. "Do you truly believe your guards strong enough to prevent Nok from going where he wishes?"

"Of course not. But I did expect you to show me the courtesy of not murdering them," Tithian replied. Though it surprised him that the halflings had dared to kill his guards, it was that they had done it in such silence that amazed the king. Apparently, the legends regarding their hunting prowess were not exaggerations.

When Nok made no reply, Tithian said, "Now tell me why you invaded my privacy."

"The woman Sadira," the halfling said, scowling at the king's tone. "You must give her to me."

"And why *must* I do that?" Tithian demanded.

Nok swung the Heartwood Spear around and pressed it to Tithian's rib cage. The tip passed into the flesh with

unnatural ease, sending a small runnel of blood trickling
down the king's abdomen.

"Because I demand it!" the halfling hissed.

Tithian reached down and guided the spear gently
away. "You have much to learn about diplomacy," he said
evenly, meeting the halfling's scowl with steady eyes.
"But as it happens, Sadira is making a nuisance of herself. I'll let you have the woman—providing you capture
her."

"I would not trust you to do it for me," the halfling
said, regarding Tithian disdainfully. "Where is she?"

The king gave Nok a condescending smile. "In the desert. A hunter of your skill should have no trouble tracking her down."

ONE

The Closed Gates

"Er'Stali can't be disturbed," said the ancient dwarf, leaning over the balustrade atop Kled's gatehouse. "Get back on your kanks and return to Tyr."

Save for his great age, which had etched dozens of furrows into his brow and left his jowls sagging like a beard, the man appeared typical of the dwarven guards flanking him. He had a squat build, with dark hairless skin and a rocklike bearing. A ridge of thickened skull ran along the top of his head, and harsh, jutting features dominated his face.

"Who are you to speak for Er'Stali?" Sadira demanded. She placed both hands on the obsidian pommel of her cane, which was never far from her grasp.

"I am Lyanius, Kled's *uhrnomus*!" the old man bellowed.

"What's an *uhrnomus*?" Sadira asked, looking to Rikus for an explanation.

"The village founder," Rikus answered. With a hairless body that seemed nothing but knotted sinew, he looked to be a taller, more lithe version of the dwarves—and with

11

good reason. Rikus was a mul, a human-dwarf crossbreed who had inherited the best features of both races.

When Lyanius continued to stare silently down at them, Rikus went on to explain, "The *uhrnomus* speaks for his village. If he doesn't want us to see Er'Stali, then we won't."

"That's unacceptable," said Agis, speaking for the first time. The noble was a vigorous man, with a sturdy frame and handsome features. He had long black hair streaked with gray, a pensive brow set over brown eyes, and a square, firm jaw. "I didn't spend ten days in the desert to be turned away at the gate."

"The choice is Lyanius's, not ours," said Rikus.

"Perhaps I can change his mind," said Agis, fixing his eyes on the aged dwarf.

Rikus grabbed the noble's shoulder. "Lyanius may be stubborn, but I owe him a great deal. Don't even think of using the Way against him."

Agis pulled away indignantly. "Who do you take me for—Tithian?"

The noble returned his gaze to Lyanius. "Before you make your decision, won't you allow me to explain why we must speak to Er'Stali?"

"No," answered the *uhrnomus*.

"Has something happened to him?" Rikus demanded.

"What makes you think that?" demanded Lyanius, scowling.

"Because you won't let us see him," Rikus said, his voice growing more concerned. "He hasn't died, has he?"

Lyanius shook his head, though his eyes betrayed an unspoken concern. "No, he's alive—"

"But not well," Rikus concluded.

The old dwarf nodded.

"We'll disturb him as little as possible," Agis said. "Still, our need is great and we must speak—"

"I'm sorry," Lyanius said, holding his hand up to silence the noble. "I'll have water and food brought to the gate, so that you can begin your journey home freshly provisioned."

"There's more wrong here than he's saying," Sadira whispered to Rikus. "Even if Er'Stali's sick, that's no reason to keep us out of the village."

The mul nodded. "That's so, but what are we to do?"

As Sadira considered the problem, two more people appeared atop the gatehouse. The first was a dwarven male she did not know. He stood a full head taller than his fellows, with a lanky build and a crimson sun tattooed on his head. His rust-colored eyes burned with a fiery intensity, visible even from the bottom of the tower.

Sadira recognized the other figure, Rikus's former fighting partner from the arena. Neeva was a blonde human with emerald eyes, pale skin, and full red lips. She towered above the dwarves like a desert willow above a thicket of mulga bushes, with a hugely swollen belly that hung over the rooftop's low balustrade. Though she wore a light cloak over her back and fair shoulders, she had intentionally left her abdomen exposed to the sun's searing rays. Even the underside was burned to a deep red sheen, with pale pink strips where layers of skin had peeled away.

"Rikus!" Neeva called, temporarily ignoring Agis and Sadira. "How wonderful to see you!"

Rikus did not reply. Instead, he only stared at the underside of his ex-lover's swollen stomach, his mouth hanging agape and his black eyes betraying his distress.

Sadira tapped his arm with the tip of her cane. "Close your mouth," she whispered. "It won't do to seem jealous."

"I'm not jealous," Rikus hissed.

"Of course not," Sadira replied, a wry smile crossing her lips. "But it hardly matters to me. I don't resent your feelings for Neeva."

"Not that you could say anything if you did," Rikus said, casting a meaningful glance at Agis.

"Now is no time to discuss our relationship," the noble whispered. "The only thing that matters is convincing this Lyanius to let us see Er'Stali—and it occurs to me that you can persuade Neeva to support us."

Rikus frowned. "How?"

"You could start by saying hello," Sadira answered. "It might help if she doesn't think you're angry with her."

The mul looked back to the top of the gatehouse. "It's good to see you, too, Neeva," he said. "You're looking, uh—very hale."

"What I'm looking is fat and pregnant," Neeva laughed. "Now, what are you doing here? You didn't come all this way to wish me well."

"Tyr's in danger," Agis answered quickly.

"That's unfortunate for Tyr," said the red-eyed dwarf next to Neeva. "My wife is in no condition to fight."

"They can see that, Caelum," she said, laying a hand on the dwarf's arm. "Besides, I doubt they came all this way after a single sword arm."

"Neeva's correct, Caelum," said Agis. "If it comes down to a fight, a hundred warriors like her couldn't save Tyr."

"What do you mean?" asked Neeva, frowning.

"The Dragon's coming to the city," explained Rikus.

Neeva and the dwarves stared at the mul with blank expressions, as if he had spoken in a language they didn't comprehend.

After a pause of several moments, Agis added, "He's

demanded a sacrifice of a thousand lives—a levy we intend to deny. We're hoping Er'Stali can remember something from the *Book of the Kemalok Kings* that might help us defy the Dragon."

Looking at Rikus, Lyanius asked, "This Dragon, could it be the same one King Rkard spoke of?"

"I believe it is," the mul answered. To Sadira and Agis, he explained, "The last time I was here, the ghost of King Rkard appeared. Among other things, he told the dwarves that the lost city of their forefathers had been visited by the Dragon."

Rikus had hardly finished his explanation before Lyanius declared, "I must ask you to leave at once. You'll receive no help from Kled or any of its citizens."

"A thousand people will die!" Sadira objected.

"Better that than all of Kled," Lyanius answered. "If we help you, the Dragon will destroy us."

"He'll never know," said Agis. "We've taken measures to keep both our journey and its purpose secret."

The old man shook his head resolutely. "We cannot take the risk."

Sadira looked to Neeva. "You know better than anyone why we can't sacrifice a thousand blameless lives."

"The decision is the *uhrnomus*'s, not mine," answered Neeva, looking away.

"But the *uhrnomus* will listen to Caelum, and Caelum will listen to you," Rikus answered. "Help us—for the sake of Tyr."

"I can't ask these people to risk their lives for Tyr," Neeva answered, waving her arm toward the village. "I have no right."

"Forget about Tyr," Sadira said, pointing at Neeva's belly. "Do you want your child to live in terror of the Dragon?"

Neeva gave Sadira a resentful look. "Better that than to die in the womb," she said.

"Really?" Agis asked. "If you teach your child to hide from tyranny instead of resisting it, are you not teaching it to live in bondage?"

"That doesn't sound like the woman who helped kill Kalak," Sadira pressed. "If it is, tell us now and we'll stop wasting our time."

Neeva glared down at her old friends, biting her lip in frustration. "When you want something, is there anything you won't do to get it?"

"Not when what I want is to protect Tyr," Sadira answered. "But that has nothing to do with Agis's question. Will you teach your child to live in tyranny or freedom?"

Neeva fell silent for a moment, then dropped her gaze to her swollen belly. "You know the answer," she said, taking Caelum and Lyanius by their arms. "Excuse us for a while."

Neeva and the two dwarves were barely gone before Rikus turned around. "I'll stake the kanks out to graze," he said.

"Can you be so certain they'll let us see Er'Stali?" Agis asked.

The mul nodded. "Caelum can deny nothing to Neeva."

"But what about Lyanius?" asked Sadira. "He's the one she must win over."

"He has a good heart. In the end, he'll do the right thing—especially with his son arguing for it," Rikus answered.

"His son?" Agis asked.

"Caelum," Rikus explained. "He's the only one whose judgement Lyanius trusts."

With that, the mul started away, calling the kanks after

him. Although two mounts followed immediately, the one that Sadira had been riding lagged behind. The beast proved so stubborn that Rikus was finally forced to take it by the antennae.

"I wish I had his confidence," Agis said. The noble sat down, bracing his back against the sun-red bricks of Kled's village wall.

"Let's just hope that his faith is justified," Sadira said. She sat beside Agis, folding her heels under her haunches to use as a cushion. Although it would have pained most women to bend their legs so compactly, the position came to Sadira as naturally as settling into a chair. She was a human-elf crossbreed, with lithe, sinuous limbs and a supple frame typical of those born of such parentage. Her eyebrows were peaked and slender, hovering above pale eyes as clear and unclouded as a blue tourmaline. She had a small, full-lipped mouth and long amber hair tumbling over her shoulders in waves.

After making herself comfortable, Sadira opened her waterskin and drank. Even in the shade of the village wall, the temperature was blistering, with a feeble wind that seemed incapable of stirring up even the slightest whiff of fresh air. To one side of the village, the heat rose in shimmering waves off high bluffs of orange-streaked sandstone. On the other side, a giant sand dune reflected the sun's crimson light so brilliantly that it hurt to look in that direction.

A short while later, Rikus returned. Over his massive shoulders were slung the empty waterskins that had been tied to the kank harnesses. "No word from inside?"

"You might as well sit down," said Agis.

The mul shook his head. "I'll stand. It won't be long now."

Rikus was wrong. The sky faded from the brilliant

white of midday to the flaxen hues of early afternoon, and
still they heard nothing from Kled. Sadira fell into a lethargic torpor and could not keep her thoughts off the
cool well-water that would be available inside the village.
More than once she found herself cursing the stubborn
dwarves, and even began to daydream about casting a
spell that would allow her to sneak inside. She quickly
rejected this idea, however. Having warned Agis not to
employ the Way to influence the dwarves, she did not
doubt Rikus would also disapprove of using sorcery to
steal a drink of water.

Finally, as Sadira's mouth began to grow bitter with
thirst, the gate opened. Neeva stepped out alone. "Welcome to Kled." She held her arms toward Rikus, who had
stubbornly remained standing before the gate.

The mul stared into Neeva's eyes for a moment.
"Neeva, I've missed you."

"And I've missed you, Rikus," she answered, speaking
quietly.

The mul shrugged off his waterskins and moved forward, embracing her tightly. When Neeva hissed in pain,
he stepped away in alarm.

"I'm sorry," he said, staring at her stomach. "I didn't
mean to hurt you—or the child."

Neeva laid a hand on his arm. "You didn't," she said,
running her fingers over her sunburned belly. "It just
stung when you rubbed against me."

Sadira and Agis stepped to Rikus's side.

"Why don't you cover that thing up?" Sadira asked,
pointing at the red flesh of Neeva's abdomen.

"My husband wants me to leave it exposed."

"Why?" Sadira demanded. "Does he enjoy torturing
you?"

"The pain she bears is for our baby," said Caelum,

stepping from behind the gate. "If the child is to have the fire-eyes, the sun must kiss Neeva's womb from dawn until dusk."

"What, exactly, are fire-eyes?" Sadira asked.

Neeva pointed at Caelum's red eyes. "A sign of the sun's favor," she said. "Caelum wants our child to be a sun-cleric, like him."

"Let us hope you're successful," Agis said, speaking to Caelum. "Has your *uhrnomus* made a decision about our request?"

"My father believes it is wrong for a powerful city like Tyr to endanger a small village like Kled—"

"Tyr will extend its protection to your village," Agis quickly offered.

"What good will that do?" scoffed Caelum. "Aren't you here because Tyr can't protect itself against the Dragon?"

"That's true," Agis admitted.

"And that's why Caelum persuaded his father to grant your request," Neeva said, smiling warmly. "If it is in our power to help, we cannot stand idly by while the Dragon savages Tyr. That would make us not only cowards, but partly responsible for the deaths themselves."

Caelum nodded, then said, "You must promise that no one will know you spoke with Er'Stali."

"Done," Rikus said, retrieving their empty waterskins.

When Sadira and Agis also nodded, the dwarf motioned them past the gate. After explaining that Lyanius had returned to his duties, Caelum led the group into the village itself.

They moved quickly down a narrow avenue, flanked on both sides by the red flagstone walls of dozens of round huts. The structures stood barely as high as Sadira's chin, with no roofs to shade the busy inhabitants from the blazing sun. The sorceress could look down into the interior of each building and see that all were arranged in a similar fashion. Near the east wall was a round table with a trio of curved benches, while a set of stone beds stood near the west. Hanging close to the door of each family's hut were a battle axe, a short sword, and a spiked buckler—all forged from gleaming steel and freshly polished.

Sadira was about to comment on the priceless weaponry when they reached the village plaza, a circle of open ground paved with crimson sandstone. In the center stood a windmill, its sails slowly spinning in the hot breeze. With each rotation, the mill pumped a few gallons of cool, clear water into a covered cistern.

Despite her thirst, Sadira hardly noticed the well. Her attention was fixed on the far side of the plaza, where dozens of dwarves were sorting and polishing a small mountain of tarnished steel armor.

"By the moons!" Sadira gasped. On Athas, metal was more precious than water, and the mound of armor represented an unimaginable treasure. "Where did all that come from?"

"From Kemalok, of course," Neeva said. She gestured at the mountain of sand north of the village.

From what Rikus had told her earlier, Sadira knew that her friend referred to the ancient city of kings, which the dwarves were excavating beneath the dune. Although the mul had said that it was full of steel weapons and armor, the sorceress had not imagined it to be anything like this.

"Even at his wealthiest, Kalak himself would have envied that fortune," Sadira said.

"Which is why Lyanius didn't want to let us into the village," Agis surmised.

Caelum nodded. "Yes. You arrived at an inopportune

time," he said. "We brought the armor out of its vault only yesterday and were unprepared to receive visitors. I trust you'll keep what you see here to yourselves?"

"Of course they will," Neeva said peevishly. "Didn't I tell you that Sadira and Agis are as trustworthy as Rikus?"

"Please," Agis said, raising his hand. "Caelum's caution is understandable. If word of Kled's wealth spreads, the sorcerer-kings themselves will send armies to steal it."

"I'm glad you understand," Caelum said. He gestured at the waterskins hanging from Rikus's shoulders. "Leave those here, and I'll see that they're filled."

As the mul complied, he asked, "Does this mean Lyanius wasn't telling the truth about Er'Stali's health?"

Neeva shook her head. "I'm sorry, but no."

"A tribe of raiders attacked the village a few weeks ago," Caelum said. "Er'Stali insisted on helping us defend the gate, and he was wounded."

With that, the dwarf led the way up a narrow lane to a large hut covered by a makeshift roof of lizard hides. Neeva paused outside the door curtain and called inside to ask if Er'Stali would receive visitors.

"I'm working," answered a weak voice.

"We've come from Tyr," Sadira said. "We need your help."

A long sigh sounded from inside. "Come on, then."

"Caelum and I will see to your waterskins and provisions," Neeva said, holding the curtain aside for Sadira and her companions.

Before they could enter the hut, Caelum said, "Please don't stay long. Er'Stali's trying to set down all he can remember of the *Book of Kings*. Every minute is precious."

"Which is to say, I could die any time," the old man's

voice growled. He broke into a fit of coughing, then gasped, "Now, come in and ask me your questions— before it's too late."

Sadira stepped through the doorway. Pale sunlight shone through the hide roof, bathing the hut in a rosy glow. At the table hunched a skinny old man, swathed in ichor-stained bandages from neck to waist. He had a wispy white beard, gray eyes glazed with fatigue, and a face etched with deep lines of pain. On his forehead was a faded tattoo of a double-headed serpent. Both of the snake's mouths were filled by long, wicked-looking fangs.

Sadira recognized the mark as the Serpent of Lubar, the crest of a noble Urikite family. She knew the emblem from the personal standard of Maetan of Lubar, the Urikite general whom King Hamanu had sent to invade Tyr the year before. During the war, Maetan had stolen the *Book of the Kemalok Kings* from the dwarves, and Rikus had promised to recover it. Unfortunately, the book had not survived, but the mul had managed to kill Maetan and return to Kled with the only living person who had read it—Er'Stali.

The old man did not even look up as Sadira and the others entered his hut. Instead, he kept his attention focused on his table, using a wooden stylus to scratch at one of the dozens of diptychs scattered around the room. The clay tablets filled the air with a musty smell and were stacked everywhere: in his cabinet, on the benches next to Er'Stali, beside his bed, and all across the floor.

The old man held up a finger to keep them silent, then finished scoring his next thought onto the tablet. Finally, he looked up and squinted. "Who are you?"

Rikus stepped forward, to where Er'Stali's view of him would not be obscured. "They're friends of mine," the mul answered.

"Rikus!" Er'Stali gasped. "How good to see you again! What are you doing back in Kled?"

"We're hoping you might have the answer to a problem we face," the mul explained.

"Perhaps I do," the old man said, grimacing at some pain deep within his body. He dipped his stylus into the bowl of water, then cleaned the end on a cloth. "What problem is that?"

"We've learned that the Dragon will soon visit Tyr," said Agis. "Our king intends to sacrifice a thousand people to him."

Er'Stali's stylus slipped from his fingers and fell to the floor. "Then I suggest you let him," the old man said. "Better a thousand lives than the entire city."

"No," Sadira answered, shaking her head. "Tyr stands for freedom. If we yield to the Dragon's demand, we'll be no better than any other city."

"Can you remember anything from the *Book of the Ke- malok Kings* that might help us?" asked Rikus. "The Dragon must have a weakness."

"If Borys has any weaknesses, they were not described in the *Book of Kings*," Er'Stali snorted. Nevertheless, he rose and, bracing himself on the mul's arm, shuffled over to the tablets next to his bed.

"Borys?" asked Sadira. Rikus had mentioned the name to her, but had not identified it as that of the Dragon. "I thought Borys was the Thirteenth Champion—"

"Of Rajaat," Er'Stali finished, moving a stack of tablets aside. "Yes. He is also the Dragon." The old man looked up at Rikus. "You remember the story Rkard's specter told us, do you not?"

"Yes," Rikus said. He looked to his friends, then explained, "Er'Stali was reciting the story of the battle between Borys of Ebe and Rkard, the last of the dwarven kings. According to what Er'Stali had read, both Borys and Rkard died after the fight."

"But the ghost of King Rkard appeared to tell us the account was wrong. Borys and the Dragon returned years later to destroy the city," Er'Stali added. "Unfortunately, Rkard vanished before I could ask about the relationship between the two, but I have found an account that clarifies it."

The old man sat down on his bed, then laboriously searched through a pile of tablets until he found the one he wanted. "If the *Book of Kings* has any help for you, it will be here," he said. "It's the last story, set down by a scribe who returned to Kemalok long after Borys destroyed the city. As I recall, the hand was jittery and frail. Leaving the tale in the book of his ancestors may well have been his dying act."

Er'Stali read: "*The day came when Jo'orsh and Sa'ram returned to Kemalok and saw what Borys had done to the city of their forebears. Both men swore to track down the butcher and destroy him. They set off for the mighty Citadel of Ebe with all their retainers and squires. When they reached his stronghold, however, they found it long abandoned, occupied now only by a handful of wraiths patiently awaiting the return of their master. These, Jo'orsh interrogated with the Way of the Unseen, learning that Borys had mysteriously lifted the siege of Kemalok just when it appeared it would succeed. He had sent his army back to the Citadel of Ebe and left for the Pristine Tower, the stronghold of Rajaat himself, to meet the other champions.*"

Er'Stali looked up from his tablet to add an explanatory note. "The *Book of Kings* did not name all of these champions, but from what I can tell, each was to annihilate an entire race, much as Borys tried to destroy the dwarves. I have seen references to Albeorn, Slayer of Elves, and Gallard, Bane of the Gnomes."

"Gnomes?" asked Rikus.

"The book doesn't say what they are," answered Er'Stali. The old man looked back to the tablet, then continued reading. "*Jo'orsh and Sa'ram left the Citadel of Ebe and traveled with their retainers into the wild lands beyond the Great Lake of Salt until they sighted a spire of white rock in the distance. Here, all manner of horrid guardians appeared. They left their squires and retainers in a safe place, then continued to the white mountain alone. When they entered the Pristine Tower, they found that, like the Citadel of Ebe, it was abandoned, save for the shadow giants—*"

Sadira noticed Rikus's face go pale, so she asked, "What do you know of these shadows?"

The mul shrugged. "Maybe nothing, but during the war with Urik, Maetan sometimes summoned a shadow-giant that he called Umbra," the mul said. "The thing wiped out an entire company by himself."

As Rikus spoke, Er'Stali began to wheeze. He feebly clutched at his bandages, as if they were squeezing his ribs and making it difficult to breath.

"I'll get Caelum," Rikus said, starting for the door.

"No," Er'Stali croaked, waving him back. "He's done all he can today."

Fearing that the stress of their visit had weakened the old man, Sadira said, "Perhaps we should let you rest and come back later."

Er'Stali shook his head, uttering, "Later, I might be dead—just give me a minute to catch my breath."

They waited several moments for the old man to regain control of his breathing. Finally, pausing at short intervals to gasp for air, he began to read again.

"*Here Sa'ram met the shadows, whom he bribed with*

obsidian. They told him that Rajaat and his champions had argued over the annihilation of the magical races, then fought a terrible battle against each other. By the time it had ended, Rajaat ruled the Pristine Tower no more. He was taken to the Steeple of Crystals and forced to use its arcane artifacts to make Borys into the Dragon."

"To make Borys into the Dragon?" Rikus gasped.

Er'Stali nodded. "Now you know all the *Book of Kings* says about the Dragon."

"It's not much help," said Rikus.

"What happened to Rajaat and the other champions after Borys became the Dragon?" asked Agis.

"The book did not say," Er'Stali answered, wearily. "Jo'orsh and Sa'ram left the tower and sent their squires home. They were never seen again, but, obviously, they did not slay Borys."

"That's all?" asked Agis, incredulous. "The champions helped Borys become the Dragon, then disappeared without resuming their attacks on the other races?"

Er'Stali shrugged. "Who can say? You already know that after Rajaat's fall, Borys returned as the Dragon to attack Kemalok. It also seems that Gallard destroyed the gnomes—I have never seen one, have you?" When Agis shook his head, the old man continued. "Perhaps the other champions fell against Rajaat, or perhaps they were too weak to fight any longer. All I can say is that the book ends with the disappearance of Jo'orsh and Sa'ram."

The old man returned the tablet to its place.

Rikus turned to Sadira and Agis. "I'm sorry," said the mul. "It was a wasted trip."

Sadira frowned. "How can you say that?" she demanded. "We don't have the answers we need, but we know where to look."

"The Pristine Tower?" queried Rikus.

Sadira nodded. "If we are to learn more of Borys, we will learn it there."

"Don't be ridiculous," said Agis. "Even if we knew where to find it, we can't be sure the place still stands."

"The Pristine Tower still stands, far beyond Nibenay," said Er'Stali. "The elves know where."

"What makes you so certain?" asked Rikus.

"Because the shadow-giant you mentioned came from there," Er'Stali explained. "In exchange for Umbra's services, Maetan hired a tribe of elves each year to lead a caravan loaded with obsidian balls to the Pristine Tower. The caravan drivers never returned, but Umbra always appeared when Maetan summoned him. I assume the obsidian reached the tower."

Sadira gave Agis a haughty smile. "You see?" she asked. "We'll go to Nibenay and hire a guide in the Elven Market."

"The journey could take a month, even longer!" Rikus objected.

"Which is why we must hurry," Sadira countered. "We don't know how soon the Dragon will come to Tyr, and it would be best if we returned to the city as quickly as possible."

"And what do you hope to accomplish at the tower?" Agis demanded.

"What we failed to accomplish here," Sadira answered. "To learn enough about the Dragon to defy him. Besides, if we're lucky, we might even find some relics in the Steeple of Crystals that can help us."

"Forgive me for saying so," said Agis, "but I suspect that's the real reason you want to go to the Pristine Tower."

Sadira frowned. "What do you mean?"

"He means that when you smell magic, nothing else

matters," Rikus said. "Not even Tyr."

"That's not true!" Sadira retorted. "I love Tyr more than my own life!"

The mul shook his head. "It's magic you love," he said, pointing at the cane in Sadira's hand. "Otherwise, you'd have returned Nok's staff by now."

"We'll need it to deal with the Dragon," the sorceress countered angrily. "And if you had kept the Heartwood Spear—"

"I promised to return it to Nok," Rikus interrupted, his tone sullen and final. "Just as you promised to return the staff."

"And I will keep that promise—when Tyr is safe from the Dragon," Sadira said. She moved to the door and flung the curtain open. "Now, when do we leave for the Pristine Tower?"

TWO

Separate Ways

Upon cresting the scarlet dune, the kank lurched to a halt. The beast twisted its blocky head from side to side, searching for a route down that Sadira saw it would not find. The wind had scoured the crest into a sheer face that dropped more than a dozen yards to the steep slip face below.

In the valley between Sadira's dune and the next one, the hard-packed sand of a caravan road snaked its way toward the mountains of the Tyr Valley. In the distance, just coming around an outcropping of yellow sandstone, were the dark specks of a caravan's outriders.

Sadira looked over her shoulder, to where the kanks of Rikus and Agis were continuing to struggle up the slope. "The way's blocked by a scarp here," she called, waving her hand toward the west. "The descent looks easier over there."

After the two men signaled their acknowledgement, Sadira returned her attention to her own mount. When she tapped its antenna to make it turn left, the kank merely fixed one globular eye on her face and did not move.

The sorceress frowned at the strange look, wondering if the beast could sense the disquiet in her heart.

It had been two days since she and her companions had left Kled, and the sorceress had spent most of that time asking herself why Neeva's pregnancy disturbed her so. Her friend's condition made Sadira feel as though the world had become a prison, as if someone were forcing her into subtle bondage more inescapable than any she had known in Tithian's slave pits.

The sorceress knew such feelings had no basis, for she was not the one who would soon be entwined by the chains of parenthood. She suspected her uneasiness had more to do with her own family history than with Neeva's child.

In the days before Tyr's liberation, Sadira's mother, an amber-haired woman named Barakah, had supported herself through one of the city's few illegal occupations. King Kalak had declared it unlawful to buy or sell magical components in Tyr. Naturally, a thriving trade in snake scales, gum arabic, iron dust, lizard's tongue, and other hard-to-acquire items had sprung up in the notorious Elven Market. Barakah had made a living as runner between the secretive sorcerers of the Veiled Alliance and untrustworthy elven smugglers. She had also made the mistake of falling in love with an elf, a notorious rogue named Faenaeyon.

Shortly after Sadira had been conceived, Kalak's templars had raided the dingy shop where Faenaeyon traded. The elf had escaped into the desert, leaving the pregnant Barakah behind to be caught and sold into slavery. A few months later, Sadira had been born in Tithian's pits, and that was where she had been raised.

Given this history, it was no wonder that Sadira did not trust the bonds of family love. Neeva might be happy living the rest of her life with Caelum and their child, but such domestic bliss was unthinkable for the half-elf. Deep inside, she would always be expecting the man to abandon her, as Faenaeyon had abandoned her mother. For Sadira, it was better to love two men at once. That way, she would never need either one so much that his departure would destroy her.

Sadira's thoughts came to an end when the kank began clacking its mandibles, then tried to back away from the edge of the bluff. When the sorceress tried to make it turn left instead, the beast froze in its tracks.

From the sands beneath the beast's feet rose a sigh, so deep and quiet that Sadira did not hear it so much as feel it in her stomach. The ground shuddered, then the kank squealed in alarm. The sorceress felt herself falling.

Sadira screamed and leaped from her bone saddle. She landed at the kank's side in a choking cascade of sand. She and the beast tumbled down the steep slope head over heels, a blood-colored cloud of grit billowing around them. In the whorl of sand, legs, and antennae, the sorceress lost all sense of direction. It was all she could do to hold onto her cane.

The half-elf glimpsed the kank's gray body crashing down upon her, sticklike legs flailing madly in the air. She cried out in alarm and kicked at its carapace with both feet. A painful jolt shot through her body and she rolled away from the massive beast, descending the rest of the slope in a wild series of backward somersaults.

Sadira came to a rest in a tangle of hair and limbs, buried to the waist and spitting bitter grit. The kank slid to a stop within a mandible's reach of her head, and the roar of avalanching sand continued to sound from above. Fearing she would be buried alive, the sorceress pointed her cane at the descending wall of sand.

"Nok!" she cried, speaking the word that activated the cane's magic.

A purple light glimmered deep within the weapon's obsidian pommel. Sadira felt an eerie tingle in her stomach, then started to grow queasy. Beside her, the kank hissed in alarm as it, too, felt a cold hand reach inside it and draw away a portion of its life-force. Normal sorcery drew the energy for its spells from plants, but the cane utilized a more powerful kind of wizardry, one that drew its power from the life spirits of animals.

"Mountainrock!" she cried.

The sorceress moved her arm across the slip face. A vaporous wave of energy issued from the cane's tip. It settled over the slope like a net, catching the cascade in its golden light and bringing the avalanche to a quick halt. Crackling and hissing, the yellow haze lingered on the surface for several moments. Finally, it began to drain away, leaving a sheet of sandstone in its wake. By the time the fog was entirely gone, the unstable dune looming above had become a butte of solid rock.

Sadira breathed a sigh of relief and began digging herself out. The kank also began to claw itself free. With its six legs, it finished the task much more quickly than the sorceress, then dropped to its belly and lay trembling with its antennae pressed back against its head. It closed its formidable mandibles and plunged them deep into the ground, splaying its legs out to the side in a display of total submission.

"You don't have to be afraid," Sadira said, finally pulling herself free. "The spell is permanent."

From above, Rikus yelled, "Sadira, are you hurt?"

The mul came plunging down the rocky slope, his tough hide scoured red from sliding over the sandstone. In his hand he held the Scourge of Rkard, a magical sword that Lyanius had given him during the war with Urik. Behind Rikus followed Agis, his expensive wool burnoose hanging from his shoulders in tatters.

As soon as they reached the bottom of the butte, Rikus pointed toward the caravan Sadira had seen earlier. "Did they cause the avalanche?" he demanded.

Sadira shook her head. "The bluff just collapsed," she said. "Put your sword away. We don't want the drivers to think we're raiders."

As the mul complied with her request, Sadira turned her attention to the approaching caravan. The entourage had come close enough for the sorceress to see that its members were mounted on inixes. Most of the fifteen-foot lizards carried ingots of raw iron on their broad backs, though several were burdened with a rider's howdah instead. As they trundled along, their serpentine tails swished back and forth, sweeping up a small cloud of sand that kept the next beast in line from following too closely. They had long horny beaks, with pincerlike jaws that looked powerful enough to clip a man in half with a single snap.

"I wonder if they're bound for Nibenay?" Sadira asked.

Rikus and Agis gave each other a forbearing look. Since leaving Kled, they had been trying to talk Sadira out of going to the Pristine Tower.

"I thought we'd decided against that plan," Agis said, his tone overly patient and paternalistic.

"You decided," countered Sadira, turning toward her kank. The beast still lay in the sand trembling, but did not shy from her approach.

"Don't be a fool," growled Rikus. "Even if we find something to help us, we have little chance of returning in time to help Tyr."

"And we have even less chance of stopping the Dragon with what we know now," Sadira answered, climbing onto her mount's back. "Do you two have a better idea?"

Rikus looked to Agis, and the nobleman said, "Yes. There are many sorcerers and mindbenders in Tyr. Perhaps together we can find the strength to defy the Dragon."

"And if not, we can oversee the filling of the levy," added Rikus.

"You mean give up," Sadira said bitterly.

"I mean deal with the reality," said Rikus. "Thousands of people perished when I attacked Urik, and their deaths accomplished nothing except to annoy King Hamanu. If an entire army is only a minor irritant to a sorcerer-king, I don't see how we can stop the Dragon."

"What are you suggesting?" Agis demanded.

"That we limit ourselves to what is possible," Rikus answered. "Unless we stop him, Tithian will send only the poor to the Dragon. If we return to Tyr, at least we can be sure he fills the levy fairly."

"Fairly?" Sadira shrieked, forgetting herself. The kank began to shudder more violently. "How can you be fair about sending someone to his death?"

"You can't," Agis admitted, biting his thin lips. "Let us hope it won't come to that. A single person using magic or the Way can often succeed where a hundred strong men have failed. Perhaps a hundred sorcerers or mindbenders can succeed where Rikus's army could not."

"And if you fail, you'll destroy the entire city," the mul countered. "It would be better to go to the Pristine Tower than to fight the Dragon. If we don't fight, only a thousand will die, instead of all."

Agis considered the mul's words, then offered a compromise. "I'll organize a council of the most powerful sorcerers and mindbenders in the city," he said. "If they cannot develop a plan for defying the Dragon, we'll do as you suggest."

"A committee isn't going to defeat the Dragon," Sadira growled. "For that, you need power and knowledge."

"Perhaps there is more of both in Tyr than we realize," the noble countered. He turned to Rikus. "What do you say?"

"How will we choose those who are to die?" the mul asked.

"You're assuming that my plan will fail, and it won't," Agis said. "But if it comes to that, we'll do our best to ease the burden. We'll exclude the last bearers of a household name and the parents of young children—"

"So people like Rikus and me are dispensable, but people like you aren't?" Sadira demanded.

Agis frowned. "That's not what I said."

"But it's what you meant," Sadira spat. "How often have you said you need a child so the Asticles name won't die?"

Rikus glowered at Agis. "You asked Sadira to bear a child?"

"That's between Sadira and me," Agis replied.

"Hardly!" Rikus roared. "I love her, too!"

"Not that it has anything to do with the present situation, but the time has come for her to choose between us," the noble countered, not flinching in the face of Rikus's anger. "We should all be getting on with our lives."

"What makes you think Sadira will choose you?" the mul demanded.

Sadira awaited Agis's answer with a growing sense of outrage, angered by his assumption that only Rikus stood between Agis and his wish that she bear him a child.

"Why should she choose you?" Rikus demanded again, this time in a menacing voice.

"Because you're a mul," the noble answered, anger and pity clashing on the patrician features of his face. "You can't give her children."

"Sadira's life is full without children. She has Tyr to think of," Rikus said, looking toward the half-elf. "Isn't that right?"

Sadira did not answer. Instead, she tapped the inside of her kank's antennae. As the beast rose to its feet, Rikus and Agis moved to her flanks.

"What are you doing?" demanded Rikus.

"I'm not chattel, to be taken by the winner of some childish contest," Sadira said.

"Of course not," said Agis. "We didn't mean to imply that you were. But the time is coming when we must settle our lives. It was well enough to put off painful decisions when we didn't know if we would live to see tomorrow, but—"

"That has not changed," Sadira interrupted angrily. "Or have you forgotten the Dragon?"

"The Dragon is something we'll always have to live with," said Rikus. "After wandering Athas for thousands of years, he's not going to disappear just because Tyr has been liberated."

"Not if we refuse to challenge him," said Sadira. "I'm going to the Pristine Tower to learn how that can best be done."

Rikus and Agis gave each other resigned looks.

"I'll go with her," Rikus said. "She'll need a strong arm."

"My arm is strong enough," countered Agis, glaring at the mul. "And my skill with the Way will prove more useful than your fighting talents."

"I'm going alone," Sadira declared, trying hard to speak in a reasonable tone. Though she was upset at being argued over like contested property, the sorceress also realized that their best chance of helping Tyr lay in splitting up.

"It's too dangerous!" Rikus objected.

"If you're determined to do this thing, one of us should go with you—"

"No," Sadira said, shaking her head. "In our own ways, we're all right." She looked from Rikus to Agis. "As Rikus says, Tyr should prepare for the worst—and only he is popular enough to ask the citizens for the sacrifices that may be necessary. At the same time, Agis, someone should take an inventory of what Tyr can do to defend itself. Only you are smart enough to make people say honestly what they can or can't do."

"And you?" asked Rikus.

"I'm the only expendable one," Sadira said. "And our situation is desperate. We can't afford to ignore the possibility that the Pristine Tower holds some secret that may be of use to us."

With that, Sadira passed her hand over the kank's antennae, urging the beast toward the approaching caravan. "I'll return as soon as I can," she called over her shoulder. "Let us hope my journey won't be in vain."

* * * * *

Clutching the handle of her steel dagger, Rhayn slipped around the corner and stopped to examine the path ahead. She had entered a crooked alleyway that ran between two rows of mud-brick tenements, weatherworn and on the brink of collapse. In any other city, the lane would have been packed with starving paupers and thirsty beggars, hiding from the scorching sun in the shadows of the tall buildings. In Tyr, however, no person needed to suffer such indignities unless he were too lazy to work, for there was plenty of food and water on the relief farms outside the city. Still, a handful of derelicts, most lingering at various points along the path from drunkenness to death, lay in the stifling closeness of the lane.

Rhayn started down the alley, which stank of stale wine, unwashed bodies, urine, and a dozen things even more vile. She kept her new dagger in plain sight, lest any of the derelicts be foolish enough to accost her. It was not common for an elf, even a woman, to be frightened in the worst quarters of a city. But it was one of the contradictions of Tyr that, as the fortunes of the poor improved, those who remained behind grew more desperate. Already, returning from lucrative forays into Shadow Square, two members of Rhayn's tribe had been set upon by cutthroats. They had escaped with their lives only by dropping their booty and fleeing as fast as their long legs would carry them.

As Rhayn passed a bloated half-giant wearing a tunic emblazoned with the star of the last king, a man's voice cried out behind her. "That's the trollop!"

Rhayn looked back and cursed. Standing at the end of the lane was a thick-waisted wine vendor with a bandaged head and an empty dagger scabbard on his belt. Next to him were a pair of black-robed templars, each carrying one of the obsidian-bladed partizans that served as the emblem of the New King's Guard.

"You have no doubt that she's the one?" asked one of the templars, a powerful-looking man with a tail of red hair.

Rhayn had no need to hear the wine merchant's answer

to know he would be sure. Even across the distance separating them, he would have no trouble identifying her as the woman with whom he had just shared two flasks of good port. Although short for an elf, she stood a head and a half taller than most men of full human blood, with close-cropped hair and keenly pointed ears. Her build was typical of her race, lean and willowy, save that her figure was rounder and more inviting than that of most elven women. Beneath her arched brows, she had almond-shaped eyes as brilliant and deeply colored as sapphires, a regal nose, and a pouting mouth with thick savory lips. The same striking beauty that had originally attracted the vendor to her would leave no doubt in his mind about her identity now.

Employing the favorite defense of her people, she turned and ran.

"You there, stop!" cried the second templar, a blond-haired half-elf.

Rhayn paid him no attention, confident that her long legs would carry her safely away from the guardsmen. Normally, she would not have dared to flee, for most templars could have called upon their king's sorcery to stop her. It was common knowledge, however, that King Tithian of Tyr was a weak ruler with no magic to bestow upon his servants. That was one of the reasons her tribe had come to the city.

Rhayn reached the end of the alley before the merchant and his escorts had taken more than a dozen steps. She turned down a bustling avenue lined by two- and three-story buildings. The first story of each building contained a small shop with a broad door and a pass-through counter opening onto the street. Out of each shop peered a sly elven merchant, peddling goods his tribe had no doubt stolen earlier from an honest caravan in the desert wastes.

"Stand aside or die!" Rhayn yelled, brandishing her new dagger at the mob of pedestrians.

As she pushed her way into the throng, a chorus of startled cries and angry shouts rang out as men and women of all races hurriedly stepped aside. Despite her threat, Rhayn stopped short of stabbing those who didn't move quickly enough. While she doubted that the templars would conduct a thorough search of the quarter over the relatively minor matter of a stolen dagger, the elf suspected they would view a string of knife attacks in quite another light.

Instead of using the dagger to clear the pedestrians out of her way, Rhayn sent them sprawling with a hardy shove or well-placed kick. Soon, a long trail of cursing people lay in the street behind her. When the elf peered over her shoulder, there was still no sign of the templars or the wine merchant.

The avenue turned sharply to the left, obscuring the alley from which she had just run. Confident that her pursuers could not follow her through the swarming crowd in the street, Rhayn slowed to a walk. She pulled the tail of her low-cut tunic from its snakeskin belt, then slipped her dagger beneath the strap and dropped her smock back over it. The metal blade felt hot and dangerous against her taut stomach, stirring a tingle of excitement deep within her body. The dagger was the first steel weapon she had ever owned, and the feel of its smooth surface against her bare skin gave her a heady sense of power that sent an exultant smile creeping across her sultry lips.

Rhayn came to a small shop where a black-haired elf was leaning over the counter, talking to a pair of human boys. In his hand, the elf held a half-dozen pebbles, each glowing in a different color of the rainbow.

"The scarlet one is for love," he was saying. "If you leave it under your tongue for three full days—"

"You'll choke on it when you fall asleep," said the oldest human, a square-jawed youth with doubtful eyes.

"Not so," countered the elf, whom Rhayn recognized as Huyar, a long-brother of hers. "You'll never swallow one of these magical stones. But if you do as I say, you will steal the heart of any woman you desire."

As Rhayn stepped into the shop, Huyar's pale brown eyes darted in her direction, lingering over her curves with a salacious glint. Once the two boys followed his gaze, the elf continued his pitch. "As a matter of fact, I used the scarlet rock to win the heart of this beauty here," he said, reaching out to embrace Rhayn. "Isn't that true?"

Rhayn allowed Huyar's arms to encircle her, looking into his eyes dreamily. "It is, my dear."

Rhayn was lying, of course. Whatever Huyar was to her, he was not her lover. They shared the same father, but that meant little to either one of them—save that tribal tradition forbade them from bearing children together. Among the Sun Runners, as among most elves, only children of the same mother considered themselves to be true siblings. Those who had only a father in common looked upon each other as rivals, competing vigorously for affection and inheritance. Between Rhayn and Huyar, the strife was more fervent than normal, for their father happened to be the chief, Faenaeyon.

Nevertheless, they were members of the same tribe and, as such, would always stand together against any outsider. If, in this instance, that meant letting Huyar grope her in order to sell some worthless stones to a pair of young culls, she would do it.

As Huyar pulled Rhayn close, the tip of her new dagger pricked her in the lower abdomen. She did not cry out, but Huyar looked down with a raised brow. "What's that I feel?" he whispered.

"Nothing to concern you," Rhayn answered, pretending to kiss his ear.

"But perhaps it would be of interest to our father?"

Rhayn had to resist the impulse to bite off the lobe of her long-brother's ear. She had hoped to sneak the dagger into her bed-satchel without anyone noticing. If Faenaeyon learned that she had returned with a prize, he would demand it as a gift. Despite what it might mean to her inheritance, Rhayn had no intention of giving it to him.

"I must get out of sight," Rhayn whispered, disengaging herself from Huyar's arms.

She gave the two boys a lingering smile, then stepped away from the counter. Immediately, the younger one asked, "What do you want for the stones?"

Huyar, never very artful, was quick to move in for the kill. "How many coins are there in your purse?"

At the back of the shop, Rhayn slipped through the curtain of snake scales that separated the bartering floor from the storage area. Her father sat in his usual place, upon an undersized leather chair with his feet propped on a keg of fermented kank-nectar. Even for an elf, Faenaeyon was a big man, with heavily muscled limbs and a huge barrel of a chest. He wore his silver hair drawn back in an unruly tail that left his sharp-tipped, dirt-crusted ears exposed to full view.

At one time, he had probably been strikingly handsome, for his long, thin features were well-defined and of even proportion. Now, he appeared every bit as cruel and dangerous as he was. He kept his slender jaw tightly

clenched at all times, and his narrow lips were forever
twisted into a mistrustful sneer. His nostrils flared constantly, as if testing the air for the scent of enemies, and
the flesh of his cheeks was pallid and dead-looking. Even
his inert gray eyes, framed above by daggerlike brows
and below by black circles of exhaustion, burned with a
demented light that never failed to give Rhayn an uneasy
feeling.

"How did you fare?" Faenaeyon asked, not bothering
to focus his vacant gaze on his daughter.

Rhayn went to her father's side and kissed his cheek.
He smelled of stale belches and sour broy. "Not as well as
I would have liked," she answered, slipping a silver coin
into his hand. "But here."

For the first time since Rhayn had entered the dark
room, her father's eyes moved, focusing on the glittering
coin. He tossed it into the air to test its weight, then complained, "A daughter of mine should be able to do better
than this."

"Next time, Tada," she answered, using the elven term
for any male whose blood ran in one's veins.

The dagger blade beneath Rhayn's smock seemed to
grow warmer, and she felt a trickle of blood running
down her abdomen. Huyar's embrace had cut her with
the tip of the weapon.

Faenaeyon studied his daughter for a moment, then
grunted and slipped the coin into the one of the purses
hanging from his belt. Rhayn breathed a silent sigh of
relief and moved toward the bone ladder at the back of
the room. In a moment, she would be safely away from
her father, in the large common room where the tribe was
camped.

As Rhayn stepped onto the first rung, Huyar cried out
from the other side of the curtain. "What do you want

here, templars?"

Instantly, Faenaeyon was on his feet, in one hand clenching a bone sword and in the other an obsidian dagger.

"In the name of Tithian the First, stand aside," ordered a man.

"Wait here," countered Huyar. "You can discuss your business with our chief."

"I said stand aside!" repeated the templar.

There was the sound of a scuffle, and Faenaeyon stepped toward the bartering floor. Rhayn motioned for her father to stay where he was, then dropped off the ladder.

"What is it?" demanded the chief.

"They want me," Rhayn said.

He shoved her toward the bartering floor. "Don't let them come back here!" he said, motioning at the mounds of stolen goods filling the storeroom. "If they see this, it'll cost a fortune to bribe them off!"

"Don't worry," Rhayn said.

Her voice was tinged with shock and anger, but not at her father. After fleeing the alley, she had left the fat merchant and the templars so far behind that they could not have seen her enter the shop with their own eyes. Instead, one of the pedestrians outside had to have told them where she had gone. In any other city, such a thing would never have happened. The throngs would have feigned ignorance, as determined not to help a templar as they were anxious to keep their presence in the Elven Market secret. But, as Rhayn was still learning, Tyr was not like any other city. King Tithian was a popular ruler, and unfortunately the people here were eager to aid his officials.

As Rhayn stepped from behind the curtain, the

templars shoved Huyar with the shafts of their partizans and sent him reeling toward the storeroom.

"Is there a problem?" Rhayn asked, catching her longbrother. As she steadied him, she saw that a small crowd had gathered in the street outside. The men and women were watching the confrontation with amusement, occasionally voicing encouragement to the wine merchant and his escorts.

The fat man glared at Rhayn. "I want my dagger back!"

"It's my dagger now," Rhayn said. Her voice was even, but she was furious inside. Her father had, no doubt, heard the merchant's demand. Now she would have to defy the chief in order to keep the weapon.

Rhayn turned toward the templars and slowly lifted her tunic, revealing the steel blade and, not by accident, a long expanse of tightly muscled stomach. Giving the king's officers an inviting smile, she pulled the dagger from its hiding place and held it aloft. Whatever happened next, she wanted to make sure the half-elf and his partner had no excuse to search the rest of the shop.

The wine merchant snatched at the weapon. Huyar grabbed his wrist in mid-flight and whipped the arm back against the elbow, at the same time kicking the man's feet out from beneath him. The fat vendor landed flat on his back, wheezing for breath and holding his sore arm.

The templars leveled their partizans at Huyar. When the elven warrior made no further move to injure the vendor, they did not strike.

"Rhayn said it's her dagger," said Huyar, his eyes fixed on the fat vendor's face.

"Stealing don't make it so," gasped the merchant.

"I didn't steal it. You promised it to me," said Rhayn, finally letting her tunic fall back over her stomach. "Or have you forgotten?" she added in a suggestive voice.

The crowd outside chuckled and the merchant's face reddened, but he would not be embarrassed out of the weapon. "She didn't deliver!" he complained, looking at the two templars.

"Deliver what?" demanded Rhayn's father, slipping from the back room. He kept one hand hidden on the other side of the curtain. "Are you calling my daughter a harlot?"

The half-elf templar shifted his partizan toward the chief. Rhayn and Huyar glanced at each other with exaggerated agitation, supporting their father's bluff.

The merchant's eyes darted to the hidden hand, but his double chin remained set in determination. "We had an arrangement," he said, glancing at the templars for support.

"Our arrangement was that you'd give me your dagger, and now I have it," said Rhayn.

"I doubt the wound on his head was part of your arrangement," said the half-elf. "You robbed him."

The crowd outside murmured approval of the templar's determination, but Rhayn did not attribute any such nobility to him. To her, the man's actions suggested that he wanted a bribe, and she had no doubt that her father would gladly pay it—then steal it back later.

"The fat oaf deserves his bandage," Rhayn said. "I had to smash a flask over his head to keep his grubby hands off me." She gave the vendor a spiteful glare, then smiled at the half-elven templar. "Still, I can see why you are suspicious. What will it take to convince you of my innocence?"

"All the purses of your tribe don't have enough gold to bribe one of King Tithian's templars—if that's what you're asking," said the red-haired man.

Rhayn and Huyar glanced at each other with furrowed brows, unsure of how to proceed. In their experience, templars could always be bribed—usually for a modest price.

It was Faenaeyon who came up with their next ploy. "Did I mention that I have another daughter?" the big elf asked. "You may have heard of her—Sadira of Tyr?"

"If you say so," the half-elf answered, rolling his eyes. "And you might be my father as well. It still wouldn't matter."

The templar shifted his partizan to Rhayn's chest, then motioned at the dagger in her hand. "Give that back to the wine vendor," he said. "You won't be needing it where you're going."

A woman in the crowd yelled, "That's right! Let these elves know what happens when they rob the free citizens of Tyr!"

"To the iron mines with her!" cried another.

Rhayn looked to her father. "Maybe we could buy the dagger?" she suggested. If the templars couldn't be bribed, perhaps the wine vendor could.

Faenaeyon only scowled at her in return. "What else have you been holding back?" he demanded, gesturing at the dagger. He glared at the templars for a moment, then looked back to Rhayn with a silvery light gleaming in his eyes. "You're trying to dupe me!" he yelled. "You're in this with them!"

Rhayn scowled. She had heard her father make such accusations before, when he was well into his cups, but never at such a critical moment.

"Think of what you're saying!" Huyar exclaimed. "No Sun Runner would side with an outsider!"

"If she keeps the dagger from me, what else has she hidden?" hissed Faenaeyon. He raised his arm as though he were lifting something on the other side of the curtain.

"Stop!" ordered the red-haired templar.

"This is between me and my daughter," the chief growled, pulling his sword from behind the curtain.

"Your daughter is Tithian's prisoner now," the templar said, pushing his partizan toward Faenaeyon. "If you try to harm her, I'll kill—"

In a blinding fast kick, Huyar planted the sole of his foot square in the fellow's chest. As the templar stumbled back, Faenaeyon's bone sword flashed past his son's ear, striking the Tyrian's neck with a sharp crack.

Huyar wasted no time pondering how close the chief had come to killing him instead of the templar. He dove at the half-elf guarding Rhayn. The Tyrian started to bring his weapon around to defend himself, then saw Rhayn still clutching the disputed dagger and hesitated. In that moment, he was lost. Huyar struck simultaneously with three fingers to the larynx and a kick to the knees. The half-elf dropped his partizan and fell to the floor, grasping at his throat.

As the second templar fell, the wine vendor turned to flee. Rhayn leaped after him, burying the dagger's blade deep into his back. The fat man dropped, his death scream upon his lips.

Shrieks of terror and shock rose from the crowd outside. Men and women began to run, fearing the mad elves would come after them next. Cries of "Murder!" and "Call the King's Guard!" rang down the street.

Rhayn slammed the door to the shop, and Huyar used a stolen partizan to knock out the poles supporting the counter awning. The wooden shutters slammed into place with a loud bang, closing out the confusion in the streets.

Rhayn looked to her father and found him standing in

the center of the room, clenching his sword and staring at her with narrowed eyes.

"Tada, were you really going to kill me?" she asked.

Faenaeyon scowled and held out his free hand. "Give me that dagger."

THREE

Caravan Dancers

Over the melody of the ryl pipes came a strange trill, a feral call almost indistinguishable from the song. The sound was hauntingly familiar, enough so that it weakened the music's spell and released the sorceress from the ecstasy that had seized her. As Sadira's pivoting hips slowed and her rocking shoulders wavered to a stop, she focused her drink-blurred eyes on the face of a nearby musician.

"D'you hear that?" she asked, her slurred words barely audible over the bracing cadence of his finger drums.

"Dance," he said.

"No," Sadira replied, struggling to fight back the compelling waves of music that filled her head. "Something's out there. We could be in danger."

The man, a nikaal with dust-covered scales and a black mop of hair, cocked his reptilian head about at odd angles, turning his recessed earslits in all directions. When he heard nothing unusual, he repeated his command. "Dance."

Sadira stepped away from the dancing ring, where

women of many races—nikaal, human, tarek, even dwarves—were leaping about a sour-smelling fire of dried inix dung. The men stood gathered around the circle, either playing instruments or simply watching the dancing women with eager eyes. They were all dressed in Nibenese fashion, with a colorful length of cloth wrapped around the waist, then passed diagonally over the upper body. To Sadira, it looked as though the saramis might come unwound at any moment, but so far the robes had stayed in place even through the wildest gyrations of the dancers.

Once she escaped the dancing ring, Sadira turned to examine the rest of the campsite, searching for the haunting sound that had interrupted her trance. The caravan had stopped in the ruins of a toppled tower, a circular basin half-filled with sand and lit by the flaxen light of the two Athasian moons. The small compound was surrounded on all sides by what had once been the tower's foundation, a jagged wall that still rose anywhere from a few feet to a few yards above the ground. Atop the ancient wall stood a half-dozen sentries, their eyes fixed on the dark sands outside camp. The sentries showed no sign of alarm, or even of curiosity. Sadira began to wonder if she had imagined the sound.

Hoping she would hear the trill again if she moved away from the music, the sorceress retrieved her cane and walked over to a large cask a few yards away. Next to the keg stood Captain Milo, an attractive, dark-skinned man with a well-kept beard and a rakish smile. With Milo was his drive master, Osa, a female mul as hairless and as powerfully built as Rikus. She had a square face, with thin lips, enigmatic gray eyes, and a scar-laced scalp that suggested she had spent more than a few years in the gladiatorial ring. On the sides of her head were small holes, surrounded by lumps of fire-branded flesh that had once been ears.

The captain filled a mug and handed it to the sorceress. "You dance well, Lorelei," he said, using the name Sadira had given when she joined the caravan.

"It's hard not to, once you're out there," the half-elf answered, noticing that the mul woman was watching her lips. "They're playing more than music on those instruments."

"The music is enchanting," the captain agreed, giving her a noncommittal smile. "And I am happy that you partook of it. Most passengers do not understand. They think the women dance for the men's pleasure, not their own."

"I dance for both," Sadira replied, giving him a crooked smile. "What's the harm if I dance and a man watches? There are more dangerous things to do with an evening, and whose business is it, anyway?"

"Perhaps the business of one of the gentlemen who was with you when we met," Milo suggested. "I was under the impression that one of them was your . . . " he hesitated, looking for the right word, then said, "your special companion."

"Both of them were," Sadira said, enjoying the astonishment her answer brought to the faces of the captain and his assistant. Smiling to herself, she took a long drink from her mug. The broy was warm and spiced with a pungent herb that disguised its underlying sourness, as well as enhanced its enrapturing powers. "They're both my lovers, but no man is master to me," she said.

"Nibenay is a long distance to travel just to escape men who have no claim on you," observed Osa, speaking with the thick tongue of one who could not hear her own words.

"I travel not to escape someone, but on an errand," Sadira said, realizing that her hosts' questions were more than casual inquiries. "Why are you so interested in my reason for traveling to Nibenay?"

"We must know the cargo we carry—"

"Lorelei is not cargo," Milo said reproachfully. He gave Sadira a friendly smile. "What Osa means is that we're concerned for your welfare. Nibenay is not like Tyr. Lone women are always in great danger there. Perhaps you should stay with us in the compound of House Beshap."

From the way Osa frowned, Sadira guessed that there was more to this invitation than simple kindness—and more to their relationship than that of captain and drive master.

"Thanks, but no," Sadira said. "I'll be safe enough."

The captain did not look discouraged. "Then you know someone in Nibenay?"

"I can take care of myself," Sadira answered. She lifted her mug to her lips and looked away, hoping to forestall any more questions.

Milo waited for her to empty the vessel, then said, "You really must allow me to be your guide." He took Sadira's mug, drawing a frown from Osa, and started to refill it. "It would be my pleasure."

"Thanks, but no," Sadira said, holding out a restraining hand.

"To which, my guide services or my broy?"

"To both," Sadira answered. "I've had enough to drink. Besides, that's not why I came over. I heard something earlier—a trill, somewhere out in the sands."

"Hungry lirr," Osa said. "I see pack at dusk."

"All the same, have a look," Milo ordered.

"Guards have ears, not me—"

"Do it," the captain insisted.

"Yes, Captain!" Osa snapped, reaching beneath her sarami and withdrawing a curved blade of bone. She set her square jaw and glowered at Sadira briefly, then looked back to Milo. "Three wives enough," she growled, glaring at him fiercely. With that, she stalked over to the wall.

"Three wives?" Sadira asked, watching the mul woman climb out of the campsite.

Milo's swarthy skin deepened to a darker shade. "Two of them stay in Nibenay."

"And the third?" Sadira asked, looking toward Osa.

"What a man won't do to keep a good drive master," the captain said wistfully.

After Osa had disappeared into the darkness, Sadira said, "I was serious about that whistle, you know. I couldn't quite place the sound, but I know I've heard it before—and it was no lirr."

"Perhaps it's raiders," said Milo. "If so, they'll be sorry they picked this caravan. Osa may not be my most beautiful wife, but she's by far the best fighter employed by House Beshap."

Sadira gripped the pommel of her cane more tightly. "Do you think we're likely to be attacked?" she asked apprehensively.

"It has happened many times before. The desert is full of elves and other thieves," the captain said, shrugging nonchalantly.

When he made no move to silence the camp, Sadira asked, "Aren't you going to prepare for battle?"

"No. The drivers need their music," Milo said. "Besides, if we had to stop dancing every time someone heard a strange sound in the desert, we would be a sad caravan indeed." He returned his gaze to the whirling figures, letting his head bob to the beat of the finger drums. "About your visit to Nibenay," he said, still watching the dancers. "I wish you'd reconsider and stay at House Beshap. If one of the sorcerer-king's agents should happen to see you dance, you would never be allowed to leave the city."

Sadira was tempted to accept the offer, for few places in any city were as secure as a merchant house's compound. Nevertheless, she wanted no watchful eyes, friendly or otherwise, tracking her movements while she was in Nibenay. "I won't be staying long," she replied firmly, "and my acquaintances will look after me while I'm there."

"You mean those who wear the veil?" the captain asked.

Under her breath, Sadira cursed. Although she had not given him much of a hint, the captain had guessed her plan accurately. Upon entering Nibenay, she intended to contact the Veiled Alliance, hoping that the secret league of sorcerers would provision her and help find a reliable elf—if such a thing existed—to guide her to the Pristine Tower.

Sadira forced a laugh from her throat, trying to sound both amused and surprised. "What makes you say a thing like that?"

Milo studied her for a moment, then motioned at the sorceress's cane. "That does," he said. "You carry a fine steel dagger on your hip, yet hardly seem aware of it, while you treat your cane as a warrior would a fine sword. If you walked with a limp, such a thing might be understandable, but one who dances as you do needs no crutch. Therefore, your cane must be a magical weapon, and you must be a sorceress."

"Very observant, but you're wrong," she said, wishing her mind were not so clouded by broy. "The cane's value is sentimental. It belonged to my mother."

Milo smiled politely. "Was she a sorceress, too?"

Sadira scowled, wondering if Milo intended to abandon her here. Like most common people, caravan drivers seldom tolerated the presence of a sorcerer, blaming all spellcasters for the magical abuses that had reduced Athas to a wasteland. "If you're so sure I'm a sorceress, why have you brought me so far?" Sadira asked.

"Because you've paid for your passage, and I am an honest man," Milo answered. "Besides, I know the difference between defilers and honest sorcerers. If you were the type who ruined the land to cast a spell, you would not be going to visit the Veiled Alliance."

The captain's reasoning was logical. Although Sadira had never contacted any Veiled Alliance outside of Tyr, she had heard enough about the different societies to know none of them tolerated defilers. In spite of Milo's reassurances, though, Sadira still thought it wiser not to admit her identity.

"Perhaps you are the sorcerer," she said. "You certainly seem to know more about the Veiled Alliance than I do."

"Not because I am a sorcerer, but because one of my wives dabbles in the art," Milo said. He leaned closer to Sadira and, in a hushed voice, added, "She has been trying to contact those who wear the veil for many months. I was hoping you might assist her."

"I'm sorry, I really wouldn't know—"

Sadira stopped in midsentence, for again she heard the strange trill ringing above the ryl pipes. This time, being farther away from the music, she recognized the sound as the dulcet chirping of a singing spider. The half-elf had heard the sound only once before: on the other side of the Ringing Mountains, in the halfling forest.

Milo frowned at the sorceress. "What's wrong?"

"Didn't you hear that chirping?"

The captain nodded. "A bird of some sort. I don't recognize what kind, but—"

"It wasn't a bird," Sadira interrupted. "It was a spider."

"A spider that chirps—and that loud?" the captain replied, disbelievingly. "You were right—you have had too much broy."

"No," Sadira insisted, laying her cane in the crook of her arm. "These spiders are huge. The halflings of the Ringing Mountains hunt them for food—"

"We're a long way from the mountains," said Milo.

Sadira had to agree. The spiders were gentle creatures that made their homes in trees and fed themselves on puffy fungus that covered the forest floor. It did not seem likely that they could survive a trip into the desert, where there were neither many trees nor any fungus. Yet the sorceress felt certain the chirping was very close to the sound the beasts made when they rubbed their spine-covered legs together.

"If it isn't the spiders, it's someone imitating them—and doing very well at it," Sadira said.

"Like who?"

"It can only be halflings," the sorceress said. "Their normal language is half bird-squeaks and squawks. What I heard is probably a dialect they use to hunt the spiders."

"Halflings don't come into the desert."

"These have," Sadira said. "You'd better prepare for battle."

The captain rolled his eyes. "Please. The sentries have seen nothing—"

"And they won't, until it's too late," Sadira countered. When Milo still made no move to stop the dancing, the sorceress said, "Come with me. I'll show you."

With that, Sadira walked over to the wall. Milo followed a step behind, reaching beneath his wrap to draw an obsidian sword with a thick, curved blade. The pair climbed out of the campsite, then dropped into the dark sands outside the ancient foundation. The two moons lit the crests of the surrounding dunes in a shimmering yellow glow, leaving the troughs bathed in impenetrable purple shadows. Like a range of snorting hillocks, the silhouettes of the inixes loomed a short distance to the west. A gentle breeze blew from their direction, carrying on its breath the mordant smell of their reptilian bodies.

Sadira's kank was staked a few yards apart from the rest of the caravan mounts, isolated from the larger beasts to keep it from being inadvertently trampled. Like the inixes, her mount still carried its cargo—her personal belongings and a waterskin which was strapped to its harness—in case the caravan had to leave in a hurry. A dozen spear-carrying sentries prowled among the animals, watching for elves or predators that had snuck into the area hoping to find an easy meal.

Milo started toward the animals, but Sadira caught his arm and led him in the opposite direction. "Halflings are hunters," she explained. "They'll approach from downwind, where the inixes can't smell them."

"Lead the way. They're your halflings."

Sadira took him around the north side of the foundation, to a short stretch of moonlit cobblestones—all that remained of the ancient road the tower had once guarded. The lane ran a dozen yards north before being swallowed by the endless sands of the desert. The half-elf paused here, listening for signs of the halflings, then dashed into the sands across the road. Milo followed a few steps behind, easily keeping up with her in spite of his awkward robe.

Sadira guided them into a dark trough and waited. Soon, her elven vision began to function, lighting the night up in a vivid array of colorful shapes. The special eyesight was one of the few inheritances she valued from her father. When no other light source was present, it allowed her to see in the dark by perceiving the ambient heat that all things emitted.

Sadira instructed Milo to grip the tip of her cane, then set off through the pink-glowing sands. She had to stay in the dark troughs and not look at the glittering crests of the dunes. Even the weak light of the moons would wash out her elven vision, rendering her as sightless as a man staring into the crimson sun. Still, by staying in the shadows, she would have the advantage over any halflings they happened upon. The little men did not share the gift of elven vision and were as unseeing in the dark as humans.

Despite his own blindness, Milo easily kept pace with Sadira. Within a few minutes, they had snuck a hundred yards into the sands, and the half-elf stopped at the base of a large dune. To their right was a small expanse of rocky, moonlit scrubland, with even higher dunes on the far side. In order to proceed any farther, they would have to cross the open area or climb over the mound ahead. Sadira elected to wait here, for any halflings approaching camp from this general area would face the same obstacles.

"Do you see something?" whispered Milo.

Sadira shook her head, then remembered he could not see the gesture in the dark. "No," she said. "It's better to hide. If the halflings hear us moving about, we'll never find them."

They waited several minutes, the music of the ryl pipes

drifting to them on the wind. Sadira's body responded to the melody of its own accord, and she could only keep from swaying to its rhythm through a conscious act of will. Milo did not show as much restraint as she did, letting his head bob in time to the insistent beat.

At last, a short trill sounded from the other side of the moonlit expanse. It was answered immediately by another, and then a third.

"Do you hear that?"

"Yes," Milo replied.

"Come with me," Sadira said, concluding that her quarry was approaching camp somewhere beyond the open expanse.

The sorceress stepped onto the edge of the scrubland, then waited while the moonlight washed out her elven vision. The sweet smell of newly cropped tinchweed was mixed with the sour odor of fresh inix dung, and the sorceress guessed that this was where the drivers had grazed their mounts at dusk. The halflings had probably been here even then, watching in silence—no doubt looking for her and the cane that she had neglected to return to Nok. It was an unfortunate time for the halfling chieftain to decide that he wanted his weapon back, for she had no intention of giving it to him.

After Sadira's sight returned to normal, she started across the brush-flecked field at a sprint with Milo close behind. They were about halfway across when a loud trill sounded from the shadows just ahead. Sadira halted, realizing that the halflings were even closer than she had thought.

Milo continued past her, whispering, "Let's catch him!"

A thick-tongued voice cried out from ahead. "No, Milo!"

"Osa?" he gasped. A strident chirp sounded from ahead of the captain. He stopped abruptly and raised his sword, crying, "By Ral's light!"

As Sadira moved forward to see what was wrong, the tip of a barbed spear burst through Milo's back. When the sorceress reached his side, she saw that a halfling had risen from the center of a spinifex bush and attacked. The warrior's eyes were gleaming yellow as he pushed his small spear further into Milo's body.

Screaming in anger, the sorceress brought the obsidian pommel of her cane down on the halfling's tangled mess of hair. It struck with a sharp crack, and the halfling collapsed in a heap.

Milo dropped his sword and stared at the spear in his stomach with disbelieving eyes. As the captain pitched onto his face, something rustled behind Sadira. She spun around and saw a halfling crawling toward her on his belly. The sorceress did not give him a chance to stand. She leaped to the warrior's side and smashed his head again and again with her cane.

Sadira heard a set of heavy footsteps, then looked around to see Osa's bulky form rushing toward her. The mul was limping badly, and the sorceress could see the shaft of a barbed spear protruding from the woman's thigh.

Osa stopped at Milo's side and felt his pulse. When she detected no heartbeat, the mul kissed him in a last farewell, then snatched up his sword and looked to the sorceress. "Go!" she said, nodding toward the dune from which her husband and Sadira had come.

"I'm sorry about—"

Sadira did not have a chance to finish her apology, for Osa leaped to her feet and resumed her sprint across the moonlit field. The sorceress ran after the limping mul, but could not keep up even at her best pace.

As they approached the shadows where Sadira and Milo had hidden, several trills sounded ahead. Sadira stopped immediately, realizing a group of halflings was lurking in the darkness. Osa continued on, oblivious to the sounds.

The sorceress pointed the palm of one hand toward the ground, spreading her fingers apart. Shutting out all other thoughts, she focused her mind on her hand, summoning the energy for a spell. The air beneath her palm shimmered, then power began to rise from the ground into Sadira's body. As soon as she felt the surge weaken, the half-elf closed her fist and cut off the flow. If she had pulled more energy into her body, she would have killed the plants from which she drew it, defiling the soil and rendering it barren for ages to come. By stopping when she had, however, the sorceress had caused no permanent damage to the land. Within a day, the shrubs would recover their lost life-force and continue to grow as if they had never been tapped.

By the time Sadira had gathered the power for her spell, a small group of halflings had moved to the edge of the field. Osa raised her sword and they raised their spears. Sadira grabbed a handful of pebbles from the ground and, uttering her incantation, threw them toward the warriors.

The stones shot past Osa with a loud clap of thunder. Each missile struck a target square in the chest, knocking the halfling off his feet and sending him sprawling to the ground in a spray of blood.

The sorceress had no chance to gloat over her victory, for another halfling cried out behind her. Sadira hazarded a glance over her shoulder and saw the silhouette of a warrior gesturing in her direction. Wasting no more time, the half-elf rushed to Osa's side and pulled the mul into the sands. Together, they ran into the shadows of the large dune and stopped there to see what the halflings would do next.

"You throw rocks?" Osa asked, her eyes fixed on the halflings that the magical stones had killed.

Sadira nodded, wondering whether it would be better to sneak or run back to the campsite. Either way, there was no doubt that they should stay in the shadowy troughs between the dunes. Like half-elves, muls could perceive ambient heat when there was not enough light to see otherwise.

As Sadira was considering the problem, dozens of trills sounded from the other side of the field. She looked toward the sounds, but could see nothing beyond the open expanse of moonlit ground. The half-elf stepped farther into the shadows and lifted her cane.

"That sound like army, not hunting party," said Osa, her thick voice too loud.

Although Sadira agreed with the mul's conclusion, she was too stunned to say so. It appeared an entire tribe of halflings had come down from the mountains. Realizing that the caravan's only hope of escape lay in her hands, Sadira lifted her cane. "Nok," she whispered, activating its magic.

She felt the weapon begin to draw its energy from her body, and a purple glow twinkled to life within the obsidian pommel. At the same time, dozens of halfling warriors charged into the field. Sadira pointed the tip of the cane at them.

Before the sorceress could utter the name of her spell, Osa grabbed her arm. "Leave," the mul ordered, dragging Sadira into the shadows. "We run."

Sadira tried to pull free, but the woman's grip was too

powerful. "Let me go!" the sorceress yelled. "I can kill half of them now!"

If she heard Sadira's protests, Osa gave no indication. Instead, still limping because of the javelin in her thigh, the mul dragged the sorceress into the darkness between the dunes. The halflings raced after the women, calling to each other in the chirping language of the forest spiders. Sadira wrapped the hem of her cloak over the cane pommel, masking the purple light that glimmered from its depths.

Even after Sadira's elven vision had begun to work again, Osa did not release her. Instead, the mul kept her hand on the sorceress's arm, leading the half-elf first into one dark trough and then down another. As they rushed past the walls of pink-glowing sand that enclosed them, Sadira was strangely conscious that the music in the campsite continued to play, its melody strained and worrisome.

Despite Osa's evasive maneuvers, the halflings had little trouble following, tracking the two women by the soft patter of their feet. Each time the mul led the way through an intersection, a few halflings went down the second trough, sealing off any possibility that their quarry could circle back toward the caravan. Soon, the dunes were filled with the trilling of halfling warriors, and Sadira knew that she, at least, would be exhausted long before they could evade their pursuers.

After Osa had led them down what seemed the hundredth side trough, Sadira heard the twang of a bow. The blue streak of a tiny arrow flashed past her head, and the sorceress cringed in fear. Though the dart itself would cause little injury, the last halfling arrow she had seen had been tipped with a powerful poison.

Another half-dozen bowstrings hummed, and more arrows flew toward Sadira and Osa. Fortunately, even half-ling archers were not very accurate when firing on a dead run, and the darts all hissed harmlessly into the sand. Still, Sadira was far from relieved. It would not be long, she knew, before one of the shafts found its mark.

"We've got to do something," Sadira hissed.

Knowing it was useless to call out to the earless mul, Sadira opted for direct action. As they approached the next intersection, the sorceress pumped her legs as fast as she could and slammed into the other woman's back. Osa sprawled headfirst into the sand dune, dragging the half-elf down and hissing in pain as she banged the jave-lin still protruding from her thigh.

Sadira rolled onto her back and faced the halflings. Her maneuver had confused the warriors only momentarily, and those in front were already moving toward the sound of her labored breathing. The sorceress pointed her cane at them, allowing the hem of her robe to slip off its glow-ing pommel. The halflings swung their spears and tiny arrows in the direction of the purple light.

The warriors loosed their weapons in the same instant Sadira cried the name of her spell, "Clear-river!"

With a loud roar, a stream of force rushed from the sor-ceress's cane. The invisible river hurled the spears and poison arrows back toward the halflings, then slammed headlong into the warriors themselves. The little men opened their mouths to scream, but their voices could not be heard above the raging torrent of magical energy. They stood against its current for only a moment, then were ripped from their feet and sent tumbling into the darkness.

A few moments later, after the river and its roar had finally died away, Sadira grew aware of Osa lying at her side. The mul woman was studying her with an expression that was equal parts awe and fear.

"Let's go," Sadira said, motioning toward the music from the camp.

Osa shook her head, her blank gaze fixed on the sorceress's cane.

"I won't hurt you," Sadira said, speaking slowly so the deaf woman could read her lips. "I want to help the caravan."

The expression returned to Osa's eyes. Seeming to collect her wits, she said, "No. I send sentries back before Milo die." The mul's eyes grew sad for just a moment, then she clenched her teeth and fought her emotions back. "Wait here for better time."

Sadira frowned in confusion, but nodded.

Osa smiled, then motioned at the steel dagger hanging on Sadira's hip. "Let me borrow."

The half-elf unsheathed her dagger and gave it to the mul woman. Osa immediately sat down and began cutting the barbed javelin from her wounded leg. Sadira turned away to stand guard, in case any of the halflings still scurrying through the dunes happened to stumble upon them.

A few minutes later, the distant melody of the ryl pipes grew louder and more inviting. The halflings fell silent, and the sorceress suddenly found herself shuffling toward camp. She tried to stop, but the song could not be denied. Her body swayed and rocked of its own accord, the music filling her head with colors and gripping rhythms that she could not chase away.

Osa came up beside Sadira and slipped the sorceress's steel dagger back into its sheath. "Now we go," she said, speaking with her usual thick-tongued loudness.

Through a rip in Osa's sarami, Sadira saw that the woman had removed the spear and bandaged the wound with a strip of cloth. The mul still moved with a slight limp, though it was much less pronounced than when the javelin had been embedded in her thigh.

Osa took the sorceress by the hand and, with a considerable exertion of strength, prevented her from dancing straight toward the music. Instead, she guided Sadira back through the dark furrows between the dunes.

As they came within sight of camp, Sadira saw that the halflings were also dancing toward the music. The short warriors were whirling through the air in a frantic swarm, hurtling spears or firing arrows toward the campsite. On the other side of the ancient walls stood the caravan drivers, swaying to the melody and shooting arrows into the savage horde that the ryl pipes had drawn out of the desert.

"We go around," Osa said, pointing to where the inixes and Sadira's kank were still tethered. As the sorceress had told Milo earlier, the halflings had indeed approached from downwind. The area on the other side of camp was completely free of enemy warriors.

Osa skirted the open sands and crossed the cobblestone road north of the tower, still dragging Sadira's squirming form by the hand. Although the sorceress appreciated the wisdom of drawing the little warriors into the open, she also saw that the results of the effort were far from certain. With their double-curved bows and the protection of the stone wall, the drivers had a distinct advantage over their charging foes. On the other hand, two dozen of their number already lay in the bottom of the sandy pit, and the rain of halfling shafts was taking a steady toll on those who remained standing. If many more of the caravan's archers fell, there would not be enough of them to keep the halflings from pouring over the wall.

Osa stopped near the inixes, a couple of dozen yards

from the tower. "Safe. No one mistake you for halfling," she said. "I go back for Milo."

Sadira's feet shuffled forward. Despite the situation, she found herself actually enjoying the compulsions of the music. She guessed that the ryl pipes relied on some manifestation of the Way. Although magic could be used to influence a target's thoughts, it seldom exerted such control over the raw emotions of so many. It was unfortunate that the ryl players could not use their powers to achieve a more physical effect on the halflings.

That was where she could help, the half-elf decided. As Sadira danced forward, she raised her cane into the air and spoke the word to activate it. Again, she felt it drawing its energy from deep within her body, and a purple light came to life within the pommel. When the sorceress reached the campsite, she would use Nok's own magic to chase off the warriors he had sent.

Before Sadira had taken two more steps, a complete silence suddenly descended over the area. Her body abruptly stopped dancing. She stumbled over her own feet and fell sprawling to the ground.

The sorceress started to rise, but stopped when a halfling's words shattered the silence. "Lay down your weapons," he ordered. Though it had been almost two years since she had heard the voice, Sadira immediately recognized it as that of Nok himself. "You will not save yourselves by fighting."

Realizing that there was only one way to rescue the caravan drivers, Sadira sprinted to her kank and undid its rope. She climbed onto its back and turned her mount away from camp, then lifted her cane above her head and cried, "Skyfire!" Three bolts of crimson flame shot from the tip of the rod, filling the sky with ruby light and casting a scarlet haze over the yellow moons.

Confident that Nok would correctly identify the source of the magical display, Sadira whipped her cane across the kank's antennae and launched the beast into a furious gallop.

The Ancient Bridge

Had her throat not been so parched, Sadira would have screamed for joy. A short distance ahead, the red sands ended abruptly, dropping into a dark chasm stretching in both directions as far as she could see. On the other side of the gorge, the road climbed a scarp of brush-flecked ground, then faded out of sight against the olive hues of the morning horizon.

Between the dunes and the scarp hung a magnificent bridge, nearly a hundred yards long. Built from huge blocks of stone in seven different colors, the structure spanned the chasm in a great arch that resembled nothing quite so much as a man-made rainbow. Its roadway was paved with yellow cobblestones, save for a single black stripe where the edifice's massive keystones had been laid. To Sadira, the ancient trestle was as much an omen of good fortune as any harbinger of rain.

"Carry me to the other side, that's all I ask," the sorceress said, speaking to her kank in a croaking voice that even she barely understood.

Sadira tapped the creature's antennae with her cane,

urging it to greater speed, but the kank could not obey. Last night, the beast had begun their flight with a powerful, six-legged gallop that had set the sorceress's hair to waving in the wind. As she had hoped, Nok had followed immediately, leaving the caravan to mourn the death of its captain. At first, Sadira had been confident of escaping, for halflings were no match for a kank's speed. Yet, as the night wore on, the chief and his warriors had kept a steady pace, and she had never left them behind for long. By dawn, the gait of her exhausted mount had diminished to a jittery scramble that even she could have matched for a short distance. The halflings, showing no signs of tiring, had been slowly catching up to her ever since.

Sadira twisted around to look back. The effort sent waves of agony shooting through her hips, for the jarring ride had been almost as hard on the sorceress as it had on the kank. From the knees to the collarbone, her muscles burned with exhaustion. Her stomach had been aching for hours, and now it was seized by painful cramps that threatened to double her over at any moment. Even her head hurt, throbbing with a terrible ache caused by a dozen hours of mortal fear.

Behind her, Sadira saw that the halflings were moving up for the kill, pumping their knees hard in an effort to catch her before she reached the bridge. They were close enough that she could see they had pushed themselves beyond the point at which normal men would have collapsed. The warriors' faces were drained and gaunt, with their mouths hanging open and their sunken cheeks working like bellows. Their hair, usually bushy and wild, lay plastered against their skulls, dripping precious body water in the form of cloud-colored sweat.

Far behind the warriors came a single speck, moving at

what appeared a relaxed pace. Though the figure was too distant to see in detail, Sadira did not doubt it to be Nok. Even from this far away, the mere sight of him filled her with terror. The one who had created her cane and the Heartwood Spear was no person to offend.

Still, the sorceress did not regret keeping the cane. She had decided long ago to do whatever was necessary to keep Tyr free. So, after Kalak's death, Sadira had kept the cane. With it, she could defend her beloved home from many terrible threats, and the sorceress had been willing to risk her life for that privilege. Even now, with Nok closing in, she had no intention of returning the cane—at least not while she lived.

A halfling warrior hurled his bone javelin at Sadira. The spear fell short, but by less than a yard. The next one, she guessed, would clatter off the carapace covering her kank's abdomen. . . . There was little use picturing where the one after that might strike.

"What keeps them going?" Sadira muttered.

Even as she asked, she knew the answer to be Nok's magic. Otherwise, no halfling could have kept pace with a kank. Only elves could do such a thing.

The sorceress faced forward again and whipped her cane across her mount's antennae. If anything, the kank went slower.

The bridge still lay too far ahead. Sadira was just beginning to see the lichens growing on its massive stone blocks. By the time her kank actually set foot on it, she would be lying in the sand with a dozen barbed speartips in her body.

"Time for some magic of my own."

Bracing her cane beneath her leg, the sorceress reached into the satchel slung from the kank's harness. After a moment of searching, she extracted a pinch of yellow sulfur. She turned her free hand palm down and held it out, summoning the energy for a spell.

A javelin rattled against the kank's abdomen, and Sadira halted her mount, bringing it around to face the halflings. In trancelike unison, the warriors voiced a breathless war cry. Two of them broke stride to throw their spears. At the same time, Sadira flung the sulfur at her pursuers and uttered her incantation.

The javelins struck, hitting the kank in mid-thorax. One spear sliced past Sadira's thigh and bounced off the insect's carapace. The other sank deep into its middle leg socket, sending a violent shudder through its body.

In the same instant, a crackling wall of fire appeared between Sadira and the halflings. The flames, stretching many yards to both sides of the road, completely obscured the warriors from view.

Her heart pounding a little less forcefully, the sorceress picked up her cane again and tapped her mount's right antenna, signaling it to turn. As it obeyed, the rancid smell of kank flesh came to her nose. Sadira gagged and nearly retched, unused to the foul odor the beasts emitted when they were injured. Now she understood why few creatures preyed on the giant insects.

A series of bloodcurdling screams sounded from the firewall. The sorceress looked back to see a half-dozen halflings rushing out of the flames. Their faces were contorted in agony, with flakes of charred skin falling from their bones and streamers of ash hanging off their heads. They stumbled a few steps forward, then hurled their spears in the sorceress's direction before collapsing into smoking heaps.

Sadira pressed her body flat against the kank's back, simultaneously urging it into a gallop. Three of the spears clattered off the beast's carapace and fell harmlessly away, and the others did not even reach it.

Spurred onward by the rattle of spears against its shell, the kank bolted forward in a lop-sided sprint, carrying its injured leg off the ground. Sadira dared to sit up and glance back. To her relief, no more halflings had been rash enough to charge through the firewall, but it would not be long before they began to pour around its ends.

The kank suddenly slowed. Fearing that it was about to collapse, Sadira looked forward again. To her relief, she saw that the beast had only swerved off the road, where the soft sand made running more difficult. She tapped the outside of its antenna to guide the pained beast back to the caravan path, confident she still had plenty of time to reach the far side of the chasm. The bridge was so close now that she could make out the individual cobblestones lining its roadway.

The kank did not obey. Instead, it veered further off course, then stumbled and fell, pitching Sadira from its back. She landed face-first, the air shooting from her lungs in a painful rush. She tumbled over and over, dropping her cane and entangling herself in the straps of her waterskin. Finally, the sorceress came to a rest half-buried in hot, rust-colored sand.

Less than ten paces away, the kank lay cowering on its belly, its antennae pressed flat against its head and the black spheres of its eyes staring vacantly into the sky. The beast's shell shook in violent spasms, its legs as limp as worn-out rope.

Grimacing in pain, Sadira pulled herself to her feet. She picked up her cane and retrieved her satchel from the kank's harness. "Sorry to leave you behind," she said, patting its carapace.

A sputtering hiss sounded from the direction of the halflings. When Sadira turned around, she saw that Nok had turned the center of her firewall to steam. From out of the white vapor rushed her pursuers, their spears poised to throw.

Shouldering her satchel and waterskin, Sadira ran for the bridge. She still had not recovered from her fall and found herself gasping for air, but, in her terror, did not let that slow her down.

As the sorceress ran up the gentle slope leading to the center of the arched bridge, the halflings went wild, shrieking and screeching at each other in their strange language. Spears clattered off the stones at her heels, falling just inches short of their target.

Sadira kept her eyes fixed on the crest of the bridge, concentrating only on using her longer stride to open the distance between herself and the weary halflings. By the time the sorceress reached the top of the arch, she had moved far enough ahead that the halflings were no longer throwing spears at her. She stopped and tossed her cane a dozen yards down the roadway. Next, she ripped her waterskin from her shoulder and tore it open, then withdrew a handful of clay from one of the pockets inside her satchel.

The halflings reached the edge of the bridge and started after her. Sadira ignored them and rushed from one side of the bridge to the other. At the same time, she poured the last of her water over the clay in her hand, dripping the resulting sludge across the bridge's black keystones.

Summoning the energy for a spell, Sadira backed away from the crest of the bridge. The lead halfling, who had already thrown his spear, reached the top of the arch and pulled his bone dagger. Sadira pointed at the line of sludge beneath his feet and uttered her incantation.

As the black stones changed to mud, the halfling

rushed after the sorceress. Cursing, Sadira unsheathed her own dagger, but kept backing down the bridge. When her spell turned the last of the bridge's keystones to mud, the entire structure would collapse, and she did not want to be on it when that happened.

The halfling stopped just short of an arm's length away from Sadira and circled her, looking for an opening. His fellows reached the crest of the bridge and began to wade through the deepening pit of mud. The warriors did not throw their javelins, for it was obvious the sorceress could not flee with one of their number so close.

Sadira lunged straight at the halfling with the dagger. He slashed his bone blade across her arm, opening a deep gash. The sorceress cried out, then used her superior reach to drive her steel blade deep into the warrior's throat.

Although blood poured from the halfling's mouth, his eyes did not seem to register the fact that he had been wounded. He struck again, this time driving his dagger into Sadira's upper arm. She screamed and opened her grip, stumbling away from the warrior. Once again he lashed out, this time harmlessly, and finally fell dead at the sorceress's feet.

Sadira turned and ran, blood streaming from her wounded arm. As she passed her cane, she stooped and picked it up with her uninjured hand. The halflings behind her did not hurl their spears, no doubt confident they would soon catch the injured half-elf.

The bridge trembled beneath her feet. The halflings began chattering in alarm, then Sadira heard several grunt with the effort of throwing their spears. Though still a short distance from the end of the bridge, the sorceress dove forward.

A tremendous crash sounded behind her. Sadira felt

the air resonate against her belly, then smashed onto the stone roadway and rolled forward. Tendrils of fiery pain shot down her wounded arm, and the sorceress glimpsed halfling spears bouncing off the stones all about her.

When Sadira stopped rolling, she found herself at the edge of the bridge. Where the great edifice had once stood, there was only a plume of dust so thick that she could not see the far side of the chasm.

The sorceress collected her cane and satchel, then crawled off the last few feet of cobblestones, fearing that even the bridge pediments might collapse. For several moments, she lay on the ground breathing in shallow gasps, too shocked and exhausted to move.

After a while, Sadira sat up. She felt dizzy and weak, and her thoughts came slowly. When she examined her wounds, she saw that her cuts were bleeding profusely. Realizing that the more she bled, the more groggy she would become, the sorceress tried to rip two bandages from her dusty robe. She could not, for only her uninjured hand had the strength to tear the cloth. Sadira reached for her dagger, but found only an empty scabbard.

Of course. The blade was somewhere in the bottom of the chasm, still buried in the throat of the halfling she had used it to kill. Without the dagger, it would be difficult to survive in this wasteland for more than a few days.

Sadira chuckled at her own muddled thoughts. The loss of the knife was the least of her problems. If she didn't bandage her wounds soon, she would die in a matter of minutes, not days. Even if she stopped the bleeding, she would be too weak to walk more than a few miles. And if she was going to walk, she would need plenty of water—water that she had used to destroy the bridge.

Still, things had not turned out so badly. She had the cane, and that was what really mattered. If she could stop the bleeding, she might live a half-day longer and travel perhaps five miles. A half-day was not much time to find an oasis in strange ground, but it was possible.

Determined to make the most of the time she had left, Sadira took off her belt and wrapped it around her savaged arm. The sorceress tightened it until the flow of blood stopped, then fastened it in place. She took her cane and stood, peering up the steep slope ahead of her. Both sides of the road were flecked with all manner of gnarled cacti, some as tall as trees and others creeping over small circles of rocky ground like thorn-rugs.

It was then that she remembered Nok.

In the halfling forest, she had seen him step off a high pyramid and drift to the ground like a leaf. If he could do that, he could float over the chasm. Sadira looked across its gaping depths.

The dust had dispersed and she could see to the other side. To her relief, no one hovered above the canyon, but standing on the opposite rim were two dozen halfling warriors. Behind them, on a slope of rust-colored sand, stood Nok. From his shoulders fluttered a cape of colored feathers, and around each ear hung a band of hammered silver, glimmering scarlet in the crimson sunlight. In one hand he gripped a double-tipped lance that Sadira recognized as the Heartwood Spear. He held the other hand before him, supporting a small globe of obsidian. From inside the orb glowed a ghostly green light.

"Why flee, Sadira?" asked the chieftain. Though they were separated by the width of the chasm, his voice came to the sorceress as though he stood at her side. In it, there was no hint of kindness or forgiveness. "You know you cannot escape me."

Nok hefted the Heartwood Spear and threw it in Sadira's direction. The shaft sailed across the chasm as though it were a bird. The sorceress screamed and backed away, but the lance did not come near her. Instead, it struck a few feet below the canyon rim, sinking deep into the stone.

"Leave me alone," Sadira called. "I have killed too many halflings already. I'll kill more if you force me."

Nok laughed, the sound pitiless and cold. "Their lives belong to the forest," he said. "As does yours. Or have you forgotten your pledge?"

Sadira had not forgotten. After journeying deep into the halfling forest, she and her friends had fallen prey to a party of warriors they had never even seen. The group had awakened on Nok's Feast Stones, only to discover that the chieftain and his advisors were preparing to eat them alive. The sorceress and her companions had survived only by swearing their lives to the forest—which was the same as pledging them to Nok himself.

"It was pledge or die," Sadira objected.

"Still, you pledged," Nok said.

With the hand holding the obsidian ball, the chieftain gestured at the Heartwood Spear. A tendril of emerald light left the globe and drifted across the canyon. When it touched the lance, a layer of scaly bark grew over the entire length of the weapon. Before Sadira's eyes, the spear grew into an oak tree, stretching more than a quarter of the way across the chasm in a matter of moments.

"I beg you, let me keep the cane a while longer," the sorceress said. "The Dragon has threatened Tyr. I'm going to his birthplace, hoping to discover some way to kill him."

"No! If you kill the Dragon, who will protect Athas from you?" demanded the halfling. "You'll return the staff, as you promised. . . . Now!"

"I can't do that," Sadira answered quietly. Her gaze was fixed on the oak tree. It had grown impossibly large, with thick, leaf-burdened branches sprouting in every direction.

"You have no choice," Nok answered.

The oak tree had almost grown across the chasm now, and Nok's warriors were standing at the far rim waiting to come across. Sadira fixed her eyes on the chieftain. At this distance, he seemed no more than a child's doll.

"If I return the cane, will you protect Tyr from the Dragon?" Sadira asked.

"No," the halfling answered. "The levy must be paid, or the Dragon will hunt in the forest."

"And what about the people of Tyr?" Sadira demanded. "They're as important as your trees!"

Grasping her cane in the crook of her wounded arm, Sadira turned the palm of the other toward the ground. With all the gnarled cacti hugging the slopes of the scarp above, the energy rushed into her body in a flood. This time, when she felt the surge begin to weaken, she did not close her fist. To counter Nok's magic, she would need all the life-force she could summon. She spread her fingers wide and pulled harder, drawing every last bit of power she could from the plants within her reach.

"It does no good to kill these warriors," Nok said, waving his hand at the halflings before him. "You'll only tire yourself."

"You don't even care for your own people!" Sadira hissed, angered by Nok's callousness.

Even had the sorceress been uninjured and fresh, the halfling would have been more than her match in personal combat. Yet, he chose to send his men to their deaths solely to wear her down. Could it be that he feared her, or perhaps the cane she held in her blood-soaked hand? As unlikely as it seemed, the sorceress clung to that hope.

"What about your warriors?" Sadira demanded. "Aren't their lives worth saving?"

"No," Nok answered flatly.

Sadira kept her hand open. One after the other, the cacti drooped, then browned and withered. Within moments, they all shriveled into empty husks and tumbled to the ground. The sorceress continued to pull, sucking the life from their roots, from the seeds lying dormant in the sand, even from the lichens clinging to the rocks. Even then, she did not stop, until the soil itself turned black and lifeless.

Nok watched with dispassionate eyes. Only the tree he had created from the Heartwood Spear survived Sadira's desecration, though even its lobed leaves were wilted and drooping.

The tree finally reached the far rim of the canyon. Nok's remaining warriors leaped onto the trunk and rushed forward. The sorceress reached into her satchel and withdrew a tiny glass rod, then went to the edge of the canyon and kneeled beside the great oak.

"I was mistaken to entrust you with the cane," Nok said. "The forest would have been safer had Kalak become a dragon."

"Call them back!" Sadira yelled, giving the chieftain one last chance to save his warriors.

When Nok did not, she laid the glass rod on the oak and stepped away, speaking her incantation. A clap of thunder roared off the walls of the abyss, and a bolt of white energy flashed down the length of the bole. The halflings disappeared in puffs of greasy smoke. The great tree split down the center, belching fire and acrid fumes, then the leaves fell away with a sad murmur. A groan echoed through the canyon as the weight of the oak's tremendous branches twisted the two halves of the trunk away from each other. Finally, the tree wrenched free and tumbled into the abyss, its roots pulling a spray of rock and earth down after it.

Sadira sank down upon the earth she had blackened. It smelled of soot and something mordant, not decay or death, but the absence of life. For a hundred yards in each direction, the soil had turned as black as a cave, and there was not a living plant in sight. The corrupted ground wafted over her like ash, coating her with an inky stain of grit.

A lump of bile formed in the sorceress's stomach, threatening to rise into her throat and choke her. Had her mentor Ktandeo been alive to see what she had done, the old man would have tried to kill her with his own hands. To his eyes, she had committed a vile act from which there could be no redemption. It did not matter that she had done it for the sake of Tyr, or even to save the lives of a thousand people who would be sacrificed to the Dragon. She had become a defiler, and nothing under the two moons could make her anything else.

But Sadira had not always listened to Ktandeo in life, and, just because he was dead, she felt no greater compulsion to heed his words now. All sorcerers drew their energy from some form of life, usually plants. To her, the difference between defilers and other wizards was only one of degree: most sorcerers stopped short of ruining the soil when they drew energy for a spell, but defilers did not. Sadira did not believe that it was always wrong to defile the land, not when something good could be accomplished by doing so. To her, an acre or two of ground was a small loss in comparison to her life—and an insignificant price to pay for the chance to save a thousand lives.

Across the valley, Nok stepped off the side of the dune into midair. He floated toward Sadira leisurely, his only visible weapon the obsidian ball dangling from his neck. Sadira picked up her cane and rose, determined to meet Nok with the few tools she had.

The chieftain wasted little time in making his attack. Before he was halfway across the chasm, he fixed his black eyes on the sorceress's face. In the next instant, Sadira smelled wet, musky leaves and ripe, sweet-scented fruits. Her ears rang with the raucous cries of jungle birds and the steady drone of insects, while the air felt moist and humid against her skin. All around her, she saw towering hardwood trees with waxy red leaves, slanting over her head and casting shadows so thick it seemed like dusk.

Sadira's stomach knotted in panic. Nok had attacked with the Way, and she could not hope to fight him mind-to-mind.

A huge, batlike beast soared out of the forest shadows. Beneath its red eyes and square ears, a hideous pug-nosed muzzle gaped open to reveal a mouthful of fangs, all dripping yellow bile. At the elbows of its wings were four long fingers, each ending in a claw coated in filth.

Sadira forced herself to swallow her panic. Agis had shown her how to fight mental attacks, so she was far from defenseless. As the beast soared down upon her, Sadira pictured her good arm becoming an X-shaped blade, each edge as sharp as a razor. She thrust it upward, at the same time ducking her body out of the creature's path. The bat-thing swerved, narrowly avoiding the wicked blades.

"No!" Sadira yelled, lashing out.

Her arm was nearly ripped from its socket as it sliced

through the beast's wing. The impact swept her from her feet, and the bat-thing crashed to the ground nearby.

The forest vanished from Sadira's mind. She found herself lying on the blackened rocks of the canyon rim. Nok lay a few feet away, face-down, with his left arm twisted awkwardly behind his back.

The sorceress leaped to her feet immediately, activating her cane by calling Nok's name. The pommel began to glow with its familiar purple light, and she felt the customary tingle of life-force being drawn from her body.

The chieftain rolled onto his back. His left arm hung useless at his side, but in his right hand he held his own obsidian ball. "Do not think to kill me with my own magic," Nok said, glaring at Sadira.

As he spoke, an emerald light glimmered deep within the globe he held. The sorceress's life-force began to drain away more rapidly. Her stomach grew queasy and her head swam. A cold shudder ran through her body, then her knees began to tremble and she knew unconsciousness was only a moment away.

The sorceress stepped toward Nok and swung the pommel of her cane at the globe in his hand. "Dawnfire," she whispered.

Nok raised his arm to block the attack, and the two balls of obsidian met with a sharp crack. Brilliant lights flashed all the colors of the rainbow, momentarily blinding Sadira. Peals of thunder roared through the air, striking the far side of the canyon with such force that they sent tons of boulders clattering down into the chasm. At the same time, a tremendous shockwave hit the sorceress's chest, hurling her backward through the air.

As Sadira slammed into the rocky ground, Nok's voice rang out in a harrowing cry. The sorceress pushed herself to her elbows, lifting the cane to attack.

A horrified scream erupted from her throat. Only a few inches from her hand, the cane ended in a scorched stump, with a single shard of its obsidian pommel still buried in the shaft. For a long time, the sorceress stared at the stub in speechless dismay, her heart filled with a terrible sense of loss.

The cane had been almost as important to her as her own life. With it, she had been strong enough to defend all of Tyr, and powerful enough to face the unknown perils of the Pristine Tower. Now she had only her own magic and vigor to rely upon—and she did not know if those two things would be enough.

Sadira looked past the end of the cane to where Nok had fallen. In the chieftain's place was a jagged crater, coated with soot and deep enough that the sorceress could not see the bottom. From this hole poured a thick plume of smoke, as black as obsidian and shaped like a great oak tree. Rising with the inky fumes were long ribbons of watery color: green and purple, but also red, blue, yellow, and a dozen others. The branches of the vaporous tree were gently waving, as if stirred by an unfelt breeze, and they were hissing Sadira's name.

FIVE

A Bargain

"You over there!" called a man's voice. "Wake up!"

The words came to Sadira across the chasm, echoing through her head with agonizing clarity. The voice was deep, with a glib quality that nettled the sorceress's sensibilities and kindled an immediate distaste for the speaker.

"Are you alive?"

Sadira opened her eyes and found herself staring into the blazing orb of the sun. Terrible, sharp pangs stabbed through her eyes, and her vision disintegrated in a spray of crimson light. She squeezed her eyelids shut again, but the pain did not fade.

The sorceress's head was not all that hurt. Her arm throbbed with dull agony, and her back ached along her entire spine. Her face stung as though someone had just slapped her, and the skin felt brittle and tight. From the thighs down, her legs prickled with the torment of a thousand needles stuck an inch into her flesh. Even her throat and tongue hurt, swollen as they were from the lack of water.

Sadira turned her head to the side and raised her

eyelids again, this time forcing herself to keep them open. To her pained eyes, the other side of the canyon remained a blur. Nevertheless, she could tell that there was a group of people, probably a caravan of some sort, standing near the pediments of the bridge she had destroyed.

Ignoring them, the sorceress focused her attention on her own situation. She still lay where she had collapsed after the battle with Nok, in the filthy soot she had created by defiling the land. Her wounded arm had turned dark purple, and was swollen to the size of her shoulder. The cuts themselves, crusted with blood and foul black dirt, were already inflamed and oozing.

When Sadira's eyes fell below her waist, a gasp of horror rose to her parched throat. Several woody vines had sprouted from the crater where Nok had perished. They were grotesque gnarled things, coiled in a tangled mass and covered with grimy black leaves shaped like those of an oak tree. The plants had crept across the rocky ground to where she lay, entwining her legs in their tendrils and sinking their barbed thorns deep into her flesh.

Sadira shook her head, hoping this was a nightmare. She had not been chased by a tribe of halflings, the sorceress told herself. She had not killed Nok, and her cane had not been destroyed. Soon, she would awaken in Milo's camp and discover it had all been an hallucination brought about by the strange spice in the Nibenese broy.

"Hey, over here!" called the glib voice.

Sadira looked across the canyon again. This time, her vision was clear, and she saw a tall, lean shape with silver hair. Behind him, scattered over the hardpacked sands of the caravan trail, were a hundred more tall figures. Dozens of kanks were milling about both sides of the road, foraging on the clumps of golden salt brush strewn here and there in the red sands.

"Elves," Sadira hissed in a disgusted voice. "This is worse than a nightmare."

Ignoring the elf who had called to her, Sadira found the end of a vine and pulled, ripping a half-dozen barbs from her skin. She regretted her action instantly. The rest of the plants recoiled, planting their barbs more deeply and setting her legs ablaze with pain.

The vines retreated toward the crater, dragging the sorceress along with them. Screaming, Sadira tried to kick free, but her struggles only set the barbs more deeply. She clutched at a soot-covered rock and managed to hold herself motionless. The vines continued to retract, ripping long gouges in her flesh, and finally she let go.

Black fume hissed from the crater, carrying the sorceress's name on its breath: "Sadira."

"Nok?" she screeched.

The sorceress reached back and grabbed her satchel, barely managing to catch it before passing out of reach. Pinning the cloth sack beneath her swollen arm, she reached inside and fumbled around until she found a gummy yellow ball. She tossed the bag aside and turned her palm toward the ground.

It took precious moments to collect the energy she needed, for all the plants within her normal range were dead. She had to reach out beyond the blackened area, to the cacti that had barely felt her touch earlier. Even when the sorceress found what she needed, the life-force did not flow smoothly through the corrupted ground. She had to concentrate hard to keep it from dissipating into the starved soil.

By the time Sadira had collected the power she needed, the vines had pulled her to within a few yards of the hole. In the hissing black breath that came from the crater, she smelled the musty decay of the forest. Sadira threw the yellow ball into the hole and spoke the words of her spell, hoping she would survive what happened next.

For a moment, the sorceress continued to slide toward the crater, scratching and clawing at the filthy rocks in a vain attempt to stop the movement. Then a tremendous roar sounded from the hole and a cone of fire shot into the sky. Tongues of flame arced over Sadira's head, lapping at the ground near her satchel and casting an orange glare over the rocks at her side. Searing heat scorched her back and the smell of singed hair filled her nostrils. The sorceress did not complain, for the grip of the vines relaxed, and she no longer felt herself being pulled toward the crater.

A rousing cheer drifted from the far side of the chasm, as though she had put on the show for the enjoyment of the elves. Sadira looked across the canyon and saw them waving their lances in the air.

"Filthy thieves," the sorceress whispered.

She turned around and faced the crater. The smoke of her fireball still rose from the hole in black wisps, carrying with it a few charred oak leaves. Most of the vines had been reduced to lines of ash, although a twisted mass of blackened fibers were still draped over Sadira's legs.

Hissing in pain, the sorceress began pulling the thorns of these vines from her flesh. When she was at last free, Sadira struggled to her feet and grabbed her satchel. She turned and staggered away as fast as she could.

"Hey, woman! Where are you going?" called the elf. "Isn't this your kank over here?"

Sadira ignored him and continued onward. The last time she had listened to an elf had been before Tyr's liberation, when a slick-tongued rogue named Radurak had offered to help her escape a pair of the king's guards. In the end, he had stolen her spellbook and sold her into slavery. She did not see any reason to think this occasion would be any different.

"Stop!" the elf cried, his voice echoing down the length of the canyon. "We just want to help." He did not sound like he wanted to help. To Sadira, he sounded angry.

When Sadira did not obey, the elf made his final plea. "It won't cost anything!"

The sorceress paid him no attention, for although they often claimed otherwise, elves never helped anyone for free. She continued up the road a few more steps, then stumbled and fell to her knees.

"Woman!" the elf yelled, no longer trying to conceal his irritation. "We can see what happened. Halfling tracks all over, a carrier drone with a spear in her thorax, your legs torn to shreds, your arm the color of a hatchling queen. You need help—and soon."

Sadira looked toward the elf and squinted, amazed at his eyesight. She could barely tell the color of his hair, yet he could see her clearly enough to detail her wounds. She had heard that the vision of full-blooded elves was keen, but she had not guessed it was this good.

When the sorceress made no move to rise or to answer, the elf continued, "I'll save you if you bring me across!"

Sadira frowned, wondering how the elf knew she could. When she looked around, however, the answer was clear. From the swath of land she had blackened, it was obvious that, in her efforts to escape the halflings, she had used at least one powerful spell to destroy the bridge. It would not be unreasonable for the elves to assume that a sorceress of such power could levitate one of their number across the canyon.

After a few moments of thought, Sadira decided to accept the offer. It was certainly possible that the elf would betray his word and try to take advantage of her, but that hardly mattered at the moment. Whatever his intentions, he was right about one thing: without help, she would soon die. The sorceress rose and started to leave the blackened area.

"What's the matter with you?" screamed the angry elf. "Don't you speak the trade language?"

Sadira did not even to try to shout an explanation, for she knew the words would not escape her swollen throat. Instead, she waved her arm in the direction she was going, pointing to an area where plenty of cacti still rose from between the stones.

The elf and his tribe finally understood. As she stumbled forward, they mirrored her progress, moving along the dunes rimming the opposite side of the canyon. It took Sadira several minutes to travel the short distance to undefiled ground, but eventually she reached a place where the plant life showed no sign of the destruction she had caused.

Sadira put her satchel on the ground, then withdrew a small parchment and rolled it up. Holding the tube to her lips, she cast one of her simplest spells.

"Tie a line to an arrow and shoot it across the canyon," she whispered, her parched throat aching from even that small exertion.

The elf looked from Sadira to where the voice had sounded at his side, then spoke to his companions. One of them quickly returned with an arrow attached to a coil of twine and fired it across the chasm. The shaft clattered to the ground a few yards away. Sadira quickly retrieved it before the string, which was settling into the canyon, dragged it away. The sorceress looped the line of braided plant fibers around a rock.

That done, she lifted her parchment tube to her lips

again. "Hold your end of the line," she whispered. "And bring water."

The elf nodded, then sent two companions back to the kank herd. A short time later, they returned with a ceramic jug and gave it to the speaker. Sadira found it peculiar that they would carry something as precious as water in a vessel that could be so easily broken, but she quickly put her misgivings aside as she pondered the size of the jar. It was so big that the elf had to use both hands to carry it. Apparently, he intended to be sure she had plenty to drink.

"I'm ready!" he yelled.

Sadira prepared for her next spell, making a small loop out of a piece of leather string. This she tossed in the elf's direction as she spoke her mystic phrase. The loop vanished, and the elf rose off the ground. Sadira went to the line and pulled, bringing him across the chasm as though he weighed nothing at all.

The elf arrived, an overbearing grin on his face. He was a huge man, standing fully two heads taller than Sadira. The light burnoose covering his frame did not conceal his barreled chest, and the thick forearms extending from the sleeves of the robe were heavily muscled. His silver hair hung over his back in an unruly tail that left his sharp-tipped ears completely exposed. Even by the standards of his race, the man's features were singularly gaunt and keen, with high spiked brows, a nose as thin as a dagger blade, and a pointed chin. The sorceress wondered if he were ill, for his flesh was pallid and his gray eyes framed by dark circles of exhaustion.

As the elf stepped onto solid ground, a large purse of metal coins jingled under his robes. To Sadira, it sounded as though he were carrying a considerable fortune on his person. A distrustful light flashed in the elf's eyes, and she realized that her expression had betrayed her astonishment. She quickly lowered her brow.

"Thanks for your aid," she said, hoping her smile would not betray how ill-at-ease she felt in the elf's presence.

He returned her gesture, though his smile seemed far from sincere. "My tribesmen are your servants," he said, bowing so deeply that water sloshed from the jug's mouth. The elf's gray eyes bugged out. "By the sun, I am careless!"

He tried to catch what he had spilled by swinging the bottom of the vessel downward and shoving the mouth under the stream of falling liquid. The elf succeeded only in striking a stone, knocking a large hole in the jug and splashing its contents over the ground. Sadira leaped forward and scratched at the wet sand in a vain attempt to salvage a few gulps of water.

The sorceress succeeded only in scraping the skin from her knuckles. She looked up at the elf. "You did that on purpose!" she rasped, barely able to squeeze the words from her aching throat.

The elf looked hurt. "Why would I do such a thing?" he asked. "Water is too precious. I might as well throw my silver into the canyon!" He waved his free arm at the chasm.

"You might as well throw yourself in," Sadira commented sourly, snatching the jug from his hands. "I'm well versed in the ways of elves. You want something from me, and until you get it, you'll keep having 'accidents' with the water I need."

The elf frowned. "Is that any way to speak to your savior?"

"You haven't saved me yet," Sadira answered. She held the jug to her cracked lips and tipped her head back. A few dregs of water, drops clinging to the interior walls, trickled down her throat.

"But I shall," the elf said. He went to the canyon edge. "We have plenty of water over there."

"And how will you bring it over here?" Sadira asked, throwing the ruined jug into the abyss.

He gave her a gray-toothed grin. "Perhaps you could bring over one of my warriors?"

"And then another, and another after that, until I've brought the whole tribe over," Sadira concluded.

The elf nodded. "That would be kind of you."

"Forget it," Sadira said. "You're the only one I had the strength to bring over today. If you hadn't wasted the water, it might have been possible for me to bring the rest of the tribe over tomorrow."

"Come now, surely you can—"

"I can't use that spell again until tomorrow," Sadira said, twisting her cracked lips into a sardonic smile. "But as you can see, I'll be dead before then."

The elf's grin vanished. "I'm trapped here?"

"Not at all," Sadira said, gesturing across the chasm. "You're free to leave when you like."

The elf studied the sorceress with a mistrustful scowl, then stepped away from the rim and hopped into the air. When he dropped back to the ground, he smiled and wagged a long finger at her. "You are a brave woman to make jokes at a time like this," he said, kneeling at her side. "Let me look at your wounds."

Sadira allowed him to examine her shredded legs.

"These are not so bad," he said, indicating the thorn wounds. He shifted his attention to her arm. "But this . . ." He let the sentence trail off, shaking his head.

The elf suddenly reached up and, pushing away Sadira's interfering hand, undid the belt she had tied around her arm. The whole limb erupted into agony as circulation returned to it, and blood began to ooze from its cuts. Screaming in pain, Sadira shoved her tormentor away.

"Give me my belt," she commanded, holding out her hand.

"Your arm must have blood or it will die," the elf responded. He rose and threw the leather strap into the canyon.

"What good is it to have a live arm, if I bleed to death in an hour?" Sadira demanded.

"What good is it to live an hour, if your arm will kill you in a week?" the elf countered. He studied the sorceress's savaged arm for a while longer, then asked, "Are you sure you can't bring just one more person over the canyon?"

"I'm sure," Sadira lied. Despite her thirst and her injuries, the sorceress thought it wisest to complete her negotiations before using any more magic.

"Pity," said the elf, pulling off his burnoose. Beneath it, he wore a wide belt from which hung several heavy purses, a sheath containing a steel dagger, and his breechcloth. "In my tribe there is a windsinger who has healing powers. Perhaps I should have sent him over first."

"But that wouldn't have been prudent business," Sadira finished for him.

"I didn't realize your situation was so desperate," the elf said, shrugging.

He stepped toward her, holding his huge burnoose by the sleeves and shaking it out. Unsure of his intentions, Sadira reached for her satchel. Her tormentor quickly moved to stop her, placing a huge foot on the sack.

"Why so afraid?" he asked, his lip turned up in a sneer that he may or may not have intended to be a smile. With exaggerated gentility, he placed the burnoose over her shoulders, covering the skin that was left exposed by her own tattered cape, and pulling the hood up over her head. "We must keep the sun off. You will live longer."

"So I can bring your tribe across the canyon?"

"We only want to help, little one." The elf cast a sad glance across the chasm. "Of course, I could do much more if my people were with us."

The sorceress studied the elf for several moments. His sinewy body was fairly laced with knife scars, and there were other, more gruesome blemishes. If he had survived so many injuries, she suspected, the elf was telling the truth about his healer.

Even knowing that, however, Sadira hesitated to strike a deal. The enchantment she would have to employ was a complicated one that demanded more energy than she could summon without destroying another swath of land, and she was not sure she was prepared to commit such an act again. Her mentor had often chastised her for stretching her powers of sorcery to their limits, but until the fight with Nok, Sadira had never resorted to an intentional and massive degradation of the land.

Though the sorceress believed she had been justified in saving herself then, the present issue was less clear. Nok had been an imminent danger, but the threat now was not as immediate. If she resorted to defiler magic to save herself from eventual death, would she use it out of simple convenience the next time?

Yet, her only other choice was to die. Considering the difficulties and hardships she would undergo during the search for the Pristine Tower, and the dim likelihood of surviving without her magical cane, it might be best to accept her fate now. But if she did, a thousand Tyrian citizens would die with her, and a thousand more each time the Dragon returned. Tyr would be no different than it had been during Kalak's reign.

Sadira could not let that happen.

She met the elf's gaze. "What will you do if I can't bring your tribe across?"

The elf pointed westward. "A path descends into the Canyon of Guthay from both sides," he said. "It is only three days' run, but the beasts that live in the bottom have a taste for our kanks."

Remembering the foul smell her mount had emitted upon being wounded, Sadira made a sour face. "Nothing could eat a kank."

"Every creature is food for some other," the elf said. "That is the law of the desert."

Satisfied that there was no way to bring the windsinger across the chasm without casting her spell, Sadira decided to strike the best bargain she could in return for her service. "Your healer will look after me until I am well."

"Done," the elf said.

Sadira held up her hand. "You will supply me with plenty of food and water."

He nodded. "Of course—we are good hosts."

"And you'll escort me to the Pristine Tower."

The elf studied her for several moments. Finally, he said, "You are cunning. I like that."

Sadira scowled at the flattery. "What is your answer? Will you take me there or not?"

"No, of course not," said the elf, grinning smugly. "We both know that if I agree to such a thing, you cannot trust me to keep any other promise."

A terrible thought occurred to Sadira. "Why not?" she demanded. "The tower's real, isn't it?"

"It's real enough," the elf answered, raising a peaked eyebrow at Sadira's question. "But only a fool—"

"Then you must take me there," Sadira interrupted, breathing easier. "Unless you prefer to risk your kanks in the chasm."

"I would drive my kanks off the canyon rim before willingly coming within sight of the Pristine Tower," countered the elf. "Why does one of such beauty wish to visit it?"

"That's my business," Sadira answered. "Why are you so afraid of it?"

"If you don't know, you have no business going there," the elf replied evasively. He looked across the chasm to his waiting tribe. "But I'll take you to Nibenay. With luck and enough silver, you'll find a guide there."

Sadira nodded, convinced that she would strike no better bargain with the elf. "I'll need my spellbook," she said, motioning at her satchel. "And a couple of hours of quiet."

"In that case, we'd better cover your wounds," the elf said, ripping a pair of strips from the hem of Sadira's tattered cape.

By the time the sun had begun to descend toward the jagged peaks in the west, Sadira was ready to cast her spell. Whispering in a parched voice, she told the elf to have his tribe line up near the rim of the canyon. They should be ready to move quickly when she gave the word.

After the elf had relayed her instructions, Sadira turned her palm toward the ground. Before summoning the energy she needed, however, she turned to him and said, "After I finish, there'll be nothing but ash and rock on this hillside. If the desecration angers your tribe, I trust they'll be wise enough not to show it."

"The desert is vast, and there is plenty of forage elsewhere," he replied. "Besides, my tribe understands sorcery. My own daughter dabbles in the art."

"Good," Sadira said. "I'd hate to do to you what I did to the halflings."

The elf narrowed his eyes. "Among friends, there is no need for threats."

"Among friends, I wouldn't make them."

Sadira spread her fingers and summoned the energy she needed. The hillside was quickly covered with withered, blackened cacti. Not wishing to see the damage she caused, the sorceress closed her eyes and focused her thoughts only on drawing every last bit of energy from the ground. When she had cast the spell to destroy Nok's bridge, she had been too angry and frightened to notice her emotions. This time, she had no such insulation. She just felt dirty.

At last, the flow ceased. Sadira was at once exhausted and invigorated, her body prickling with stolen life-force. She opened her eyes and pointed her finger at the far side of the canyon, speaking the words of the spell. In front of the elf tribe, a dark circle appeared in the emptiness over the canyon.

"Tell them to jump," Sadira gasped. She backed away from the canyon rim and collapsed to her haunches, clutching her satchel to her breast. Her vision was swimming with black dots, and she felt as though she might retch at any moment.

"How do I know this isn't a trick?" the elf demanded.

Sadira looked up and waved her hand at the blackened scarp. "Do you think I would have done this just to kill a few elves?" she rasped. "The portal won't last long. Tell them to jump!"

The elf did as she asked and the first warrior stepped into the black circle. When he appeared on Sadira's side of the canyon, a great cheer rose from the rest of the tribe. Within moments, they were driving their reluctant kanks

into the black circle, then, as the terrified beasts emerged
on the other side of the abyss, chasing them up the scarp.
The elf came and stood next to Sadira, who watched the
procession through drooping eyelids, too exhausted to
ask which was the windsinger.

Some time later, the sorceress felt her satchel being
pulled from her arms. Her eyes popped open and Sadira
found herself staring at a tall woman with close-cropped
red hair. The elf was strikingly beautiful, with a regal
nose, pouting mouth, and almond-shaped eyes as deep
and brilliant as sapphires. Cords of sinuous muscle covered her long legs and lanky arms, and the waist of her
slender body was unbelievably thin and wasplike.

Standing next to her was a massive creature of one of
the New Races. He had two legs and two arms, but there
ended his resemblance to anything faintly elven. His
knobby hide was mottled and faintly reptilian in appearance. Before Sadira's eyes, it was changing from the rusty
red hue of the sands across the valley to the inky black
pigment of the defiled lands. The man-beast's limbs were
as thick and round as faro trees, and knotted with wide
bands of muscle. For feet, he had huge pads with three
bulbous toes, each sporting an ivory-white claw. His
hands were his largest single feature, with four bolelike
fingers and a stumpy thumb.

The thing's face was all muzzle, his enormous smiling
mouth filled top and bottom with needlelike teeth. His
eyes were set on opposite sides of his head, so that they
could look straight ahead or to opposite sides as he chose.
Directly behind these giant orbs were a pair of eloquent
ears, triangular in shape and currently turned to the sides
in an expression of solace.

"I am the windsinger Magnus," he said, speaking in a
surprisingly gentle voice. He waved a cumbersome hand

at the elven woman next to him. "This is Rhayn, daughter to Chief Faenaeyon."

"Faenaeyon!" Sadira croaked, searching for the tall elf whom she had first brought across.

Magnus's ears turned forward in curiosity. "I assumed you two had introduced yourselves," he said.

"My father's name means something to you?" demanded Rhayn, studying Sadira's face more closely.

The sorceress shook her head. "I've heard the name before, but it was probably someone else."

"Unlikely," said Rhayn. "Elves are named for the first interesting thing they do after learning to run. In our tongue, Faenaeyon means 'faster than the lion.' How many children do you suppose survive to bear such a name?"

"Not many," Sadira conceded. As she realized that she had probably just met the father who had abandoned her into slavery, the sorceress had a sinking feeling in her stomach.

"So, what have you heard about Faenaeyon?" Rhayn asked.

"Before sorcery was permitted in Tyr, he was known as someone who sold spell ingredients," Sadira said, deciding it would be wiser to keep her secret.

"That would describe half the elves in the city," Rhayn said.

When Sadira offered no further explanation, the elf gave Magnus a doubting look, then took a large waterskin off her lean shoulder and passed it to Sadira. From the vessel's lack of seams and bulbous shape, the sorceress guessed it had once been the stomach or bladder of some desert beast. She opened the neck and drank deeply of the rank water, hardly able to take her eyes off her father's face.

Sadira was surprised at the emotions she felt. To be sure, there was anger and hatred. A large part of her wanted to strike him down and, after revealing her identity, leave him in the scorching sun to die alone and maimed. Another part of her, less murderous but just as vindictive, wanted to tell him how she and her mother had suffered over the years, and, by blinding and deafening him, inflict some measure of agony in return for that they had endured.

The third aspect of Sadira's feelings confused her the most. Part of her didn't hate her father at all. Deep inside, she was amazed to see him standing before her. Until now, he had always been a distant abstraction, an enigma whose thoughtless cruelty had caused her a lifetime of pain. Now Sadira was merely curious about him. She wanted to know what kind of a man he was, and whether he had ever tried to find out what had happened to Barakah and his unborn child.

After several moments of allowing the tepid water from Rhayn's waterskin run to down her throat, Sadira finally removed the neck from her mouth. "My thanks," she said, handing it back to the woman who, she realized, was her half-sister.

Magnus kneeled at the sorceress's side. "Allow me to see to these wounds before we resume the run."

As the windsinger's thick fingers began fumbling at the bandages on the sorceress's arm, Faenaeyon opened her satchel and began to look through it.

Sadira was on her feet immediately, the palm of her good hand facing the ground and ready to draw the energy for a spell. "Close it!" she demanded.

Cringing, Rhayn stepped away from Sadira's side. "Don't try to stop him," she warned, half-whispering. "It's not worth it."

"Put my satchel down!" Sadira insisted, stepping toward her father.

The elf continued to paw through the sack, hardly looking up. "Why? Are you hiding something from me?"

"We had an agreement," Sadira said. "I told you what would happen if you didn't honor it."

Faenaeyon pulled her purse from the satchel. "I said my tribe would take you to Nibenay," he sneered. "I didn't say how much I'd charge."

He tossed Sadira's satchel at her feet, then turned away with her coin purse still in his hand. The sorceress started after her father, already drawing the power for the spell that would kill him.

Magnus wrapped a huge arm around Sadira's waist and lifted her off the ground, at the same time closing his fist around her hand. "Are you as mad as he is?"

Silver Spring Oasis

Faenaeyon strode into the lush field, using his bone sword to beat a swath through thickets of tart-smelling ashbrush. When he closed to within fifty paces of the mud-brick fort, he stopped. "Toramund!" he boomed. "What have you done to me?"

An armored elf leaned out of the gate tower. Though the distance was too great to see him well, Sadira could tell that he wore a leather helmet with a nose guard and broad cheek plates. In his hand, he held a curved sword with a blade of kank-shell.

"Take your Sun Runners and be gone, Faenaeyon," he yelled back. "All ye'll get from the Silver Spring is a belly full of arrows."

To give weight to Toramund's words, the elves standing along the walls flexed their bows, each pointing an arrow at Faenaeyon's chest. The Sun Runners, men and women alike, responded by nocking their own arrows. Sadira guessed that Toramund had about fifty elves on the walls, while her father had at least twice that number outside the fort.

Despite the looming threat of battle, Faenaeyon showed no sign of backing off. Instead, he ran a contemptuous gaze over the enemy warriors, as if challenging them to fire at him.

The sorceress turned to Magnus, who was mounted on a kank at her side. Since she had joined the Sun Runners, the windsinger had been her constant companion, healing her wounds and watching after her safety. "What's all this about?"

"Silver," the windsinger answered, focusing his black orbs on the small fort. It had obviously just been erected, for none of the mud bricks showed any sign of erosion and the highest rows were still black with dampness. "The Silver Hands claim this spring as their own and demand a silver coin from anyone who wishes to water his beasts here."

Sadira grimaced. It had been only a few days since she had helped the Sun Runners across the Canyon of Guthay, but already she could imagine how Faenaeyon would respond to such an outrageous price. "What happened the last time you were here?"

"There are more Sun Runners than Silver Hands," Magnus answered, twitching his ears.

"So you watered without paying," Sadira concluded.

"No," answered Rhayn, giving the half-elf a sheepish grin. "We robbed them."

Rhayn stood on the opposite side of Sadira's kank, near the leg that had been wounded by the halfling spear. The elf's skin glistened with sweat from the morning run, and a lanky infant dozed in a sling on her back. Although the child was Rhayn's, Sadira did not know who had fathered him—or his four older siblings. The elf woman treated more than a dozen men as a city woman might her husband, despite the fact that many of them made camp with meeker women who seemed half slave and half wife.

"Apparently the Silver Hands have decided to build a fort rather than suffer the indignity of another robbery," said Magnus, his ears turned forward in a thoughtful manner. "Rather far-sighted, don't you think?"

Back in the ashbrush field, Faenaeyon stopped glaring at the enemy warriors and returned his attention to their chief. "Open your gates, Toramund," he yelled. "My warriors and beasts thirst for your water, and my purses hunger for your coins."

Faenaeyon grabbed the purse he had taken from Sadira, the lightest of the five on his belt, and shook it for emphasis. A few Sun Runners laughed at his boldness, but many others cast nervous glances at each other.

"Does he want to start a fight?" asked Sadira. "Why doesn't he strike a deal?"

"Elves are too smart for that," Rhayn answered, looking at Sadira as though she were a child.

"Elven tribes know better than to trust each other," Magnus explained more patiently. "It's the great downfall of our otherwise noble race."

Sadira wanted to ask what was noble about an elf, but thought better of it and held her tongue.

After a short pause, Toramund responded to Faenaeyon's threat. "Take your rabble and be gone, before I lose patience!"

"Your goatyard won't save you," Faenaeyon countered. "I have a sorceress who can change bricks to dust with fewer words than I have already spoken."

"Rhayn? That trollop daughter of yours couldn't conjure light from a burning torch," Toramund scoffed.

Toramund reached into the depths of his tower and pulled forward a gray-haired man with a long beard. "Bademyr will make short work of Rhayn—and of your windsinger besides."

Faenaeyon's laugh echoed off the fortress walls, rolling back toward his own warriors in cruel waves. "It is not my daughter that I speak of—though you shall soon apologize to her," he cried. With a dramatic flare, he faced Sadira and said, "Destroy the fort, Lorelei."

"No," Sadira replied.

Her response brought a disbelieving murmur from the Sun Runners, and several warriors turned to stare with gaping mouths at the sorceress.

When Sadira made no move to cast a spell, Toramund mocked, "Your new sorceress must be powerful indeed, if you cannot control her. I'm so scared that I've made water in my boots. Perhaps you would like to drink that, Sun Runner?"

Faenaeyon paid the insult no attention. Instead, he glared at Sadira, his lips curled into an angry frown. He did not speak or move, but the mad light in his eyes made the message plain.

"Destroy the fort," urged Rhayn, a tone of desperation in her voice.

"It would be wise," agreed Magnus. "Without their fort, the Silver Hands will surrender. Faenaeyon will rob them, but there'll be no bloodshed. On the other hand, if the matter comes to blows, the fighting won't end until one tribe is destroyed."

"You can't trick me with your elven games," Sadira hissed. Speaking loudly enough for Faenaeyon to hear, she added, "I won't use my magic to help you steal."

"I hadn't thought a defiler would be so particular about her causes," observed Magnus.

The comment stung Sadira as no threat could have. "I only did what was necessary to save my life," she retorted.

"Then do it again," urged Magnus, glancing at Faenaeyon's angry form. "One of the lives you save will be your own."

"What do you care if one tribe of elves robs another?" Rhayn demanded. "You understand nothing! This is between the Sun Runners and the Silver Hands."

"Then your chief has no business bringing me into it," Sadira countered, her eyes locked on Faenaeyon's.

Magnus leaned his massive body close to Sadira. "What you say might be true if your were in Tyr, but you are not," he whispered. "You are with the Sun Runners, and here Faenaeyon's word is the only custom or law—as rapacious as it may seem. If he says to destroy the fort, you must—or a hundred warriors will leap to kill you when he gives the order."

The windsinger's harangue only hardened Sadira's resolve. "I won't help you," she called, speaking directly to Faenaeyon.

Narrowing his eyes, the chief started toward her. The Silver Hands yelled jeers and insults, mocking the bravery of the Sun Runners and their chief's ability to lead his tribe. One of the warriors raised his bow to fire at Faenaeyon's back.

"Look out!" Sadira yelled, her words echoed by a half-dozen warriors.

The bowstring snapped as the chief started to turn around. Before he could react, the shaft sank deep into his hip. Faenaeyon stumbled and nearly fell, then caught himself. As his own warriors began to draw their bowstrings back, he raised a hand.

"Hold your shafts!" he commanded.

The Sun Runners obeyed, though they kept their arrows nocked. Nodding his approval at their discipline, Faenaeyon stood with his back to the Silver Hands, challenging them to fire again.

Sadira resisted the temptation to reach for her spell ingredients. Faenaeyon had started this trouble on his own, and she was determined not to be dragged into it.

Inside the stockade, Toramund looked down the wall and bellowed, "Who did that? I gave no order to attack!" Several Silver Hand warriors responded by knocking a young woman off the wall.

After standing with his back to the Silver Hands for several moments, Faenaeyon reached around and tore the arrow from his hip. He tossed the shaft aside with a casual flick of his wrist, then continued toward Sadira. Although he bled profusely and walked with a limp, the chief's angry face showed no sign of distress.

"Doesn't he suffer pain?" Sadira gasped, leaving her hand in her satchel.

"No," said Rhayn, edging away from the sorceress. "He never feels anything except greed or anger. Right now, I fear it's anger."

To the other side of Sadira, Magnus tapped his kank's antennae, also moving away. "If you wish to survive, don't make the mistake of thinking he can be reasoned with."

Sadira began to doubt her wisdom in defying Faenaeyon. She could not believe he truly felt no pain. Yet, it was becoming clear he lacked the feelings that controlled the behavior of most men, such as fear and compassion. He saw the world only as a source of silver.

Faenaeyon stopped in front of Sadira, his sword still unsheathed. Though the sorceress remained mounted on her kank, her father stood so tall that he looked her straight in the eye.

"Destroy the fort," he ordered, raising his sword just enough to menace her.

Sadira dropped her gaze to the weapon. "If you lift that against me, it'll be the coins in your purse that I destroy, not the bricks of the fort."

She put one hand into her satchel and grasped a cold cinder, then turned down the palm of the other and began drawing energy for a spell. "How much is my death worth to you? A hundred coins?"

Faenaeyon's eyes widened. He glanced at the shimmering stream of energy rising into Sadira's hand, then lowered his weapon. "I'll deal with you later," he said. He turned back toward the fort and pointed his sword at the elves manning it. "Their deaths will be upon your head."

"Perhaps, if the Sun Runners needed water and I refused to help," Sadira countered. "But your tribe can reach the next oasis easily. Half your waterskins remain full."

"It's not water I want," Faenaeyon responded. The chief glanced over his shoulder and nodded at his warriors.

As they drew their bowstrings back, Sadira pulled her hand from the satchel, the cinder concealed in her fingers. "Not even an elf would start a battle like this over silver."

"I am no ordinary elf," he said, lowering his sword.

The strum of a hundred bowstrings rumbled down the line and Faenaeyon's warriors launched their shafts into the air. Toramund screamed a command in response, and the Silver Hands loosed their own arrows.

Sadira flung the cinder into the air, crying out her incantation. A fiery band flashed across the sky, intercepting the two flights of arrows over the field of ashbrush. An instant later, all that remained of the shafts was a dark cloud of soot and the dark specks of errant arrowheads falling harmlessly to earth.

Faenaeyon glanced back at Sadira, the features of his pallid face contorted into a furious scowl. "It is one thing not to help, and another to interfere. Don't do it again!"

Sadira barely heard him, for the ashbrush in front of the gate tower was turning black and shriveling. She looked up and saw that the old man next to Toramund was preparing to cast a spell, and his beady eyes were looking the direction of her and Faenaeyon.

"Get down!" Sadira yelled.

The sorceress urged her kank forward, using its mandibles to push her father to the ground. She had barely leaped from the saddle before she heard the sizzle of a fireball streaking from the tower. It passed above the kank's back and, leaving the stench of burning sulfur in its wake, crashed to earth a short distance away. There it remained for a moment, sputtering and hissing, before it finally erupted.

A wave of heat rolled overhead, igniting a half-dozen dry bushes and singing Sadira's hair. Her kank bolted, and then she heard Faenaeyon's warriors screaming his name.

The sorceress lifted her head and looked toward her father. If Faenaeyon was seriously injured, she knew more bloodshed would be unavoidable. When he didn't move, she asked, "Are you hurt?"

"I am angry," the elf hissed, rising.

Breathing a sigh of relief, Sadira looked upon the field ahead. A wide expanse in front of the gate tower had been reduced to barren and blackened soil. A bewildered iguana clattered across the naked rocks, scurrying for the withered brush at the edge of the desecrated tract. There was no other sign of life in the area.

A terrible sense of loathing and hatred came over the half-elf, and she shifted her gaze to the gate tower. There stood Toramund's sorcerer, grinning smugly and showing no remorse for the desecration he had committed.

"Go away, Faenaeyon," yelled Toramund, laying a hand on the sorcerer's shoulder. "Or Bademyr will finish what he began."

Before Faenaeyon could respond, Sadira rose and took his arm. "Do as I say, and you shall have your silver," she whispered, turning her father around.

"You've changed your mind?" the elf asked, allowing the sorceress to guide him away from the fortress.

"I have," Sadira answered. To prevent Bademyr from noticing that she was drawing the energy for a spell, she kept her back to the Silver Hands. "But you must kill the defiler and no one else."

"Done," the elf agreed.

Long before she had destroyed any ashbrush, Sadira cut off the flow of energy into her body—unlike Bademyr, she did not defile lightly. She scraped a handful of red silt off the rocks at her feet, then spun around and held her fist out toward the gate tower. She cast her spell, letting the dust slip from her fingers. The fortress bricks began crumbling away. An instant later, the entire structure stood on the brink of collapse.

Sadira closed her hand, temporarily halting the destruction. "Silver Hands!" she yelled. "Leave the walls at once, or you'll fall with them."

The elves quickly availed themselves of Sadira's advice, save for the small group in the gate tower. There, Toramund looked to his own sorcerer. "Stop her!" he yelled.

As Bademyr reached for his spell components, Sadira opened her hand and slowly let dust grains slip from between her fingers. To either side of the tower, sections of wall began to fall. Toramund grabbed his sorcerer by the shoulders, then shoved the old man over the railing.

"Our agreement has come to an end," he yelled, lingering on the tower just long enough to watch Bademyr hit the ground.

As Toramund and the last of the Silver Hands fled the gate tower, Faenaeyon waved his warriors forward, yelling, "Silver Hands, gather your coins and your daughters! The Sun Runners shall have them all!"

Sadira remained where she was, watching the injured sorcerer struggle to crawl out of the path of the approaching Sun Runners. The sorceress was surprised by her feelings toward the defiler. She had asked Faenaeyon to kill him, not because she was angry about the attempt on her life, but because he had desecrated the field.

It was not lost on the half-elf that she had destroyed a much larger area just three days ago. But she had resorted to desperate measures only to protect herself from Nok. Bademyr, on the other hand, had committed his offense with seeming indifference, and for a dubious purpose. Sadira knew that Ktandeo would have found her action as morally indefensible as that of the Silver Hands' sorcerer. But to her, there was a difference between using defiler magic to save life and to take it.

Sadira watched Faenaeyon approach the gate. Although the rest of the Sun Runners had rushed past the injured defiler, the chief went over to Bademyr. He leaned over and spoke to the sorcerer, then sheathed his sword and picked up the old man. Bademyr's head nodded in thanks, and Faenaeyon carried him back toward Sadira and the young elves who had stayed behind to watch the tribe's kanks.

After moving into the circle of defiled ground, where he had a clear view of Sadira, the chief stopped and threw his burden down. The old man cried out, then held out

his hand to summon the energy for a spell. By the time
Faenaeyon had pulled his sword from its scabbard, more
ashbrush had begun to wither at the edges of the blackened circle.

The chief brought his blade down, lopping off the sorcerer's head. A dazzling ribbon of green and gold radiance shot from the severed neck, filling the air with a
deafening skirl. Crying out in surprise, Faenaeyon leaped
back and watched the sparkling lights streak into the sky.
Once they had disappeared from view, he sheathed his
sword and rushed into the village.

Rhayn came and stood next to the sorceress. The defiler's fireball had frightened her infant, but the elven
mother seemed oblivious to her child's sobs. Sadira
stepped around to her sister's back to comfort the baby.
He was crying so hard that his arched eyebrows were almost flat, and his pointed ears had turned as crimson as
the sun.

"Hush, little one," Sadira cooed, speaking to the child
as he was customarily addressed. From what Sadira had
seen, elven children were not named until they could run
alongside their parents. Of the four other juveniles who
spent their nights at Rhayn's camp, she had heard only
the oldest called by name.

When the infant didn't stop crying, Sadira asked her
sister, "Shall I hold him?"

Rhayn turned around, moving the child out of sight.
"Don't comfort him," the mother said. "It'll be better if
he learns to be brave."

Though Sadira doubted that comforting a frightened
infant would make him fainthearted as an adult, she de-
ferred to her sister's wishes. "Elves are hard parents," she
observed.

"The desert is a hard place," answered Rhayn.

"Though I see you must have also led a hard life—or been raised by a fool. Only a brave woman or a stupid one would have defied my father as you did."

"At heart, Faenaeyon is spineless," Sadira answered. "He's no different than any other tyrant."

"My father is no coward!" snapped Rhayn, her deep blue eyes burning with indignation. She studied Sadira for a moment, then the anger faded. "And he was not always a tyrant," she said. "Once, he was a great chief who showered his warriors with silver and his enemies with blood."

"If you say so," Sadira answered, shrugging. "It means nothing to me."

"You're wrong," said Rhayn. She took Sadira by the arm and led her toward Magnus, who had gone to chase down the sorceress's kank. "Faenaeyon will overlook your defiance, for your powers are useful, and, in the end, you did what he wanted you to. But you're also dangerous to him. When you threatened his fortune, you threatened his hold over the tribe. He won't tolerate such a risk for long."

Sadira studied Rhayn for several moments, wondering what had moved the elf to share this warning with her. Finally, the sorceress said, "My thanks. I'll take my leave as soon as we find another caravan traveling toward Nibenay."

"Don't be a fool!" Rhayn hissed. She glanced around to make sure they were out of earshot of the rest of the tribe. "Even if we see another caravan, Faenaeyon will never let you join it!"

Sadira scowled. "What are you saying?"

Rhayn shook her head. "Are you really so naive?" she asked. "You have become Faenaeyon's sword. As long as you serve him well, he'll take care to keep you sharp. But when you become so heavy that your edge is dangerous, he'll shorten your blade or destroy you altogether. Don't think that he'll let you fall into someone else's hands. There's too great a danger that you'll be used against him someday."

"I don't believe that," Sadira said. "He promised to take me to Nibenay, and so far he's keeping that promise."

"You shall see Nibenay," Rhayn said. "Do not despair of that. But when you leave, it will be with the Sun Runners—or not at all."

Rhayn paused to let Sadira consider the warning. After a few moments, she said, "There is an alternative."

The sorceress raised a brow. "And what is that?"

"All Sun Runners remember when Faenaeyon was a great chief, and that's why so many tolerate him now," Rhayn said. She lowered her voice to a conspiratorial whisper. "But there are those of us who are tired of living in fear and having every coin we earn stolen by him."

"I don't see what that has to do with me," Sadira said.

"Nothing and everything," answered Rhayn. "That's the beauty of it. Even if we wished to see Faenaeyon hurt, which we don't, we couldn't kill him. Too many of the old warriors remember when he was young, and they would never stand for his assassination."

"What do you want from me?" the sorceress asked, deciding to cut directly to the point.

"If you could incapacitate my father, the tribe would have to select a new leader," Rhayn said.

"You, of course," concluded Sadira.

"Perhaps." Rhayn shrugged. "But the important thing is, there'll be no trouble between those who support Faenaeyon and those who don't."

"Because you'll blame me," Sadira said. Over the last

two days, she had begun to feel a certain fondness for Rhayn, and thought that the same had been true for the elf. Now, it was clear that her sister had only been preparing her as a scapegoat.

"It will come to that only if someone figures out what you did," Rhayn said, not even trying to deny the treachery in her plan. "Even then, you should be safe enough. You and I won't make our move for a week, until we're near Nibenay. By the time anyone realizes what's happened, you'll be in the city—free of us and Faenaeyon."

Sadira studied the elf for a moment, then shook her head in disbelief. "You must take me for a fool," she said.

"Not at all," the elf said. "I know you to be a cunning woman—cunning enough to know that if you want to leave the Sun Runners alive, this is your only hope."

"I'll take my chances with Faenaeyon," Sadira replied coldly.

"The mistake you are making is a fatal one," Rhayn hissed. She spun around and stalked off, her infant sobbing more loudly than ever.

As Rhayn left, Magnus came over, leading his kank and Sadira's behind him. "You must delight in danger," the windsinger observed, watching Rhayn leave. "A stranger among lirrs does not usually give two of the beasts such good reasons to eat her."

"I have faced worse than elves," Sadira replied. "But how do you know what passed between Rhayn and me?"

Magnus tilted his ears forward. "When someone speaks, I seldom miss a word," he said, waving the huge appendages back and forth. "It's the curse of my heritage."

"Which is?" she asked. When the windsinger did not answer, she pressed the question. "I've never met anyone like you. What, exactly, are you?"

"An elf, of course," The windsinger said, flattening his ears. He started walking, taking his mount and Sadira's to join the rest of the tribe's kanks.

"You don't look like any elf I know," Sadira said, following the windsinger.

"My appearance makes no difference. I've been with the Sun Runners all my life," Magnus answered sharply. Then, more gently, he said, "Faenaeyon found me near the Pristine Tower, then took me in and raised me at his fire."

"The Pristine Tower!" Sadira gasped. "Could you take me there?"

"Not even if I wanted to. I was only a babe when Faenaeyon found me," the windsinger said, shaking his head. "Besides, no matter what you've told Faenaeyon, you don't want to go to that place."

"Why not?" Sadira asked.

"Because it's beset by New Beasts, creatures more horrid and vicious than those anywhere else on Athas." He stopped walking and looked down his long muzzle at the sorceress. "You couldn't survive a day in that place. No one could."

"Apparently, you did," Sadira observed. "And so did Faenaeyon."

"When he was young, Faenaeyon did many impossible things," Magnus said, resuming his stride. "And as for myself, the winds have always watched after me."

Realizing that she would learn nothing of the Pristine Tower's location from Magnus, Sadira switched the topic to something of more immediate interest. "If you were raised by Faenaeyon, then I doubt you're a part of Rhayn's plan," the sorceress said. "You could warn him of what she's doing."

"And why would you want me to do that?" asked

Magnus.

"Because he'd never take my word over hers," Sadira answered. "And I don't want to get blamed if she tries something before we reach Nibenay."

"Sorry," Magnus said. "I intend to keep her secret. Faenaeyon was a great chief when he was younger, but Rhayn's right about him now. It would be better for us all if you did as she asked."

SEVEN

The Dancing Gate

"Is that Nibenay?"

Sadira pointed at the plain below, to where a distant city of minarets sat huddled in the shade of a rocky butte.

"Of course," Faenaeyon answered, keeping his eyes focused on the hillside beneath his feet. He leaped over a spray of yellow cloudbrush, landing on a round boulder, then immediately launched himself toward a jumble of copper-colored stones. "Did I not promise to take you to the City of Spires?" he called.

"And now you have," the sorceress confirmed. She kept her hands tightly clutched on her kank's harness as it scuttled after her father's running figure. "Your obligation has been met. You don't have to escort me into the city."

Faenaeyon stopped and looked at her. "You'll need us to help you find a guide," he said, a silver glint in his eye. "Besides, Nibenay is a good place for elves to do business."

"I can take care—"

Sadira's objection was interrupted by a wild scream

120

from the hunters running ahead of the tribe.

"Tul'ks!"

Four terrified creatures sprang from a copse of silverbristle and bounded down the hill. They were larger than half-giants and as gaunt as elves, with stooped shoulders and white skulls uncovered by any sort of flesh. The tul'ks had bulging eyes, toothless jaws, and a set of oblong cavities where their noses should have been. Each wore a shabby tunic of tanned leather, secured about the waist with a snakeskin belt.

As they ran, the frightened manbeasts dragged their knuckles along the ground, using their gangling arms like an extra set of legs to keep themselves from stumbling. The Sun Runner hunters set off in pursuit, gleefully nocking arrows as they leaped from boulder to boulder.

"Stop your warriors!" Sadira said.

Faenaeyon gave the sorceress a look of disdain. "Why?"

"Because it's murder," she replied. "The tul'ks have done nothing to you."

One of the hunters loosed an arrow. The shaft sank deep into a tul'k's back. The manbeast stumbled and fell head over heels.

"They are beasts," the chief scoffed, grinning in amusement as he watched the injured tul'k regain his feet and try to flee.

"Beasts don't wear clothes," Sadira said. She thrust a hand into the satchel holding her spell components. "Call off your hunters, or I will."

"As you wish," Faenaeyon said. Turning toward the hunters, he boomed, "Let the tul'ks go!"

The elves came to a stop and looked back to Faenaeyon, their faces showing their confusion. "What did you say?" demanded one.

"He said to leave them alone," Sadira called. "They've caused you no harm."

The hunter looked from her back to Faenaeyon. "You want this?"

"I do," Faenaeyon said. As the tul'ks disappeared into the brush, the chief turned to Sadira. "You really shouldn't have stopped my hunters. By killing the tul'ks, we're doing them a mercy."

Sadira removed her hand from her satchel. "How can that be?"

"The tul'ks are descended from the Ruin Stalkers—a tribe of elves that disappeared three centuries ago." He stepped closer, watching Sadira with a roguish grin on his lips. "Do you want to know how they became tul'ks?"

"Probably not," the sorceress answered. "But tell me anyway."

"The Pristine Tower," Faenaeyon said. "They were searching for the treasures of the ancients." He looked in the direction the tul'ks had fled, then added, "You saw for yourself what became of them."

"What are you saying?" Sadira asked, suspicious of Faenaeyon's story.

The chief shrugged. "The elders don't claim to know exactly how it happened. The warriors might have fought between themselves, or they could have been attacked by a herd of wild erdlus," he said. "Or maybe they just stumbled across a wasp's nest. Whatever it was, everyone in the tribe was wounded, and they were changed into the beasts you saw."

"I don't believe you."

"Believe what you like," Faenaeyon countered. "But if you go to the Pristine Tower, take care not to spill your blood. If you cut yourself, even if you just scratch yourself, the magic of the place will change you into a beast more pitiful than the tul'ks. I've seen it happen."

Sadira started to sneer at his claim, then remembered what the windsinger had told her about his origins. "Was that when you found Magnus?"

Faenaeyon's eyes flashed, more in pain than anger. "Yes. What do you know about that?"

"Only what Magnus told me—that you found him there when he was a child."

"He was a newborn baby," the chief corrected.

"Tell me about it," Sadira said. "Perhaps it'll give me reason to heed your warning."

Faenaeyon nodded. "When I was a young warrior, the Sand Dancers attacked us and stole my sister, Celba. By the time I recovered from my wounds and tracked them across the Ivory Plain, my sister had grown weary of being a slave-wife and fled into the desert. Her husband and four of his brothers went after her, so Celba fled to the one place they wouldn't follow—the Pristine Tower. I found her pursuers camped in the lands just beyond sight of the tower."

"What did you do?" Sadira asked. She found herself more interested in Faenaeyon's dedication to his sister than in what had happened at the Pristine Tower. From the tale he had told so far, the chief did not sound like a man who would have abandoned a pregnant lover into slavery.

"I killed all five, of course," Faenaeyon answered. "Then I followed Celba into the wild lands. What I didn't know was that the Sand Dancers had gotten a child on her. When I found her, she was already giving birth."

"So Magnus is your nephew?" Sadira gasped.

The chief nodded. "Yes, but Celba didn't live to raise him. Because of the blood she had shed during labor, the magic of the tower changed her into a hideous, mindless

beast. She tried to devour her child, and to save Magnus I
killed her with my own sword."

"And Magnus was wounded, which is why he's—"

"Do you take my blade to be that slow?" Faenaeyon
demanded crossly. "Magnus was born as he is."

The chief fell silent and began a gentle trot toward Nibenay. Sadira spent a moment trying to reconcile the image she had always had of her father as a coward with the
tale of bravery she had just heard. When she could not,
she gave up and urged her mount after him.

As her kank came up behind Faenaeyon, she called, "If
you're telling me this because you want me to stay with
the tribe, it won't work."

Faenaeyon slowed, allowing Sadira to guide her mount
to his side. When he spoke, his voice was overly calm.
"What makes you think I want you to stay?"

"Don't you?" Sadira demanded.

The chief allowed a conniving smile to cross his lips,
but did not take his eyes off the ground over which he
ran. "We might come to an arrangement—"

"I doubt it," the sorceress spat. "My talents are not for
sale."

Faenaeyon shrugged. "That's unfortunate," he sighed.
"But it doesn't change what you'll find at the Pristine
Tower. Truly, it would be better if you stayed with us."

"Better for you, perhaps," Sadira answered. "But I've
promised to go there, and I will."

"Only a stupid fool would let her promise kill her,"
Faenaeyon answered, shaking his head. "There's a reason fear is stronger than duty."

Sadira wanted to ask if he had forsaken her mother because he was frightened, but restrained herself. To do so
would have been to reveal her true identity, and she still
thought it wise not to trust her father with that particular

secret.

Instead, she said, "Fear isn't always stronger than duty, even for an elf. You must have been afraid when you went after Celba."

"I was angry, not scared: No one steals from me!" Faenaeyon said, glancing at her with a frown. "If I had let them take my sister, they would have come back for my kanks and my silver."

"I should have known," Sadira said. If there was bitterness in her voice, it was because she felt naive for thinking her father had ever acted out of noble motives. "You elves live only for yourselves."

"Who else?" Faenaeyon asked. They reached the bottom of the hill and started across the flat plain, pushing their way through a thick growth of brittlebrush. "Life is too short to waste on illusions like duty and loyalty."

"What about love?" she asked. The sorceress was curious about Faenaeyon's feelings for her mother, and how, if he had known Sadira's true identity, would he have felt about her. "Is that an illusion?"

"If so, it is a good one," Faenaeyon said, grinning. The terrain here was less broken, so he could afford to look at Sadira more often. "I have loved many women."

"Used them, perhaps, but you didn't love them," Sadira said acidly. She did not know whether she was more angered by the elf's flippant use of the word love, or the implication that her mother had been one insignificant consort in a stream of many.

Faenaeyon frowned. "How would you know about my women?"

"If you feel no duty or loyalty to your women, you can't love them," Sadira countered, avoiding a direct answer to the question.

"Love is not bondage," the chief scoffed.

"I know that as well as you," Sadira countered. "But it's not self-indulgence, either. Did you even care for all the women you took as lovers?"

"Of course," the chief replied.

"Then prove it," Sadira said.

"And how do you expect me to do that?"

"Nothing too difficult. Just name them," Sadira replied, wondering what it would feel like to hear Faenaeyon speak her mother's name—or to hear him forget it.

"All of them?"

Sadira nodded. "If you cared for them all."

The chief shook his head. "I couldn't possibly," he said. "There've been too many."

"I thought as much," Sadira sneered. She tapped her kank's antennae, urging it into a gallop.

Faenaeyon quickly caught up to her. "There's no reason for haste," he said, loping along at her side. "We'll reach the city long before they close the gates for the night."

"Good," Sadira said, not slowing her mount.

They continued at that pace throughout the morning, eventually coming to a caravan track that led into the city. A spirited melody rose from the main gate and drifted out over the plains, welcoming the travelers to Nibenay. Many of the elves began to dance, trotting along the dusty road in a heel-and-toe quickstep. Some of the warriors kept the beat by pounding the flats of their blades against a kank's carapace. Even those fatigued by the morning's hard run joined in the revelry and rocked their shoulders to and fro.

Only Faenaeyon seemed to resent the greeting, continuing toward the city at the unrelenting pace Sadira had set earlier. "By the wind, I hate this place," he growled.

"The last time we were here, the guards demanded five silver coins to let us inside. No wonder they're glad to see us."

His gray eyes remained fixed on the gate, a high-pointed arch flanked by a pair of craggy minarets. On the terraces of these towers stood many Nibenese guards, each waving his bow over his head as he swayed to the music. Between the minarets, a buttressed porch extended from the city wall and overhung the gateway. A dozen musicians stood on this balcony, playing the huge drums, xylophones, and pipes that sent the melodies drifting into the silvery desert.

"I can get us inside for two coins," said Sadira.

"How you can you save me this money?"

"Sorcery," she answered.

Sadira gave him a knowing smile, hoping it would disguise the lie in her eyes. Her conversation with the chief had convinced her that Rhayn's warning earlier had not been entirely self-serving. Despite the casual manner in which he had accepted the sorceress's refusal to join the tribe, Faenaeyon clearly did not wish her to leave. As for her own feelings, Sadira's curiosity about her father was sated. If he was braver than she had imagined, he was no less self-centered, and she had no desire to know him better.

Faenaeyon nodded. "Good. Do it."

When he did not reach into any of his purses to extract the coins, Sadira held out her palm. "Have you forgotten?" she asked. "I gave all my coins to you at the canyon."

"In matters of money, I never forget," the chief said. Instead of reaching for his purse, he summoned his son Huyar forward. The warrior's relationship to Sadira showed only in his pale eyes, for his features were square and heavy for an elf. "Give her two silver, my son," Faenaeyon ordered.

"I would, willingly, but you have taken all my coins," answered Huyar.

Faenaeyon frowned. "I would expect one who hopes to replace me someday to be wise enough to hold a few coins back," the chief said, still waiting for his son to produce the money.

"I would never dishonor my tribe by disobeying my chief," Huyar said. The warrior scowled at Sadira, clearly blaming her for this setback with his father.

Resentment had become common for Huyar since the sorceress had ingratiated herself with Faenaeyon. Whenever she wanted something, the chief looked to his son to provide it. Sadira suspected that her father had no true fondness for Huyar, but pretended to favor the gullible warrior only because it made him more willing to do as Faenaeyon wished.

Glowering at his son, the chief opened the purse he had taken from Sadira and gave her two of her own coins. "Will you get them back for me?"

Sadira shook her head. "Think of it like this—you're not losing two silvers, you're saving three." She took the coins and slipped them into the pocket of her tattered cape. "I'll go ahead and cast my spell on one of the guards. Allow a quarter of an hour for it to work its enchantment. Then, when you reach the gate, be sure to speak to the same guard I did."

Faenaeyon looked suspicious. "Perhaps I should go with you."

Sadira had an answer ready to counter her father's concern. "It'll be easier to work my magic if I'm alone," she said. "I'll be waiting for you on the other side of the gate."

The chief's gray eyes dropped to the pocket where she had deposited the coins. He bit his lip, then nodded and looked away. "Two silver is not so much."

"You'll save more than that," Sadira said, leaning forward to tap the inside of her kank's antennae.

The beast slowly worked its way ahead of the tribe, two of its six legs striking the ground with each beat of the distant drums. A short time later, she passed between two argosies drawn up close to the city walls, one to either side of the road. A long line of Nibenese porters worked to unload each of the mighty fortress wagons, carrying heavy vessels and huge baskets into the dark shadows beneath the musicians' balcony. The great mekillots that drew the argosies, hill-sized lizards with a penchant for making snacks of unwary passersby, were turned away from the road.

Sadira slowed her kank to a walk and glanced over her shoulder. Her father's tribe was more than a hundred yards behind. It was approaching in its customary disarray, the warriors moving together in a confused, noisy mass while their sons and daughters tended to the difficult work of keeping the kanks from straying into the king's fields.

Sadira turned forward again and, as she passed into the shadows beneath the musicians' balcony, found a sharp-featured half-elf stepping into the road. He wore a long checkered scarf wrapped around his head and a yellow sarami swaddled over his body. In his hands he clutched a spear of blue-tinted agafari wood.

"Nibenay welcomes you," he called.

As he spoke, two guards forced their way past the bustling porters and crossed their spears to bar Sadira's path. She waved a hand over her mount's antennae, bringing it to a complete stop. The music from the balcony above reverberated through the stone ceiling, echoing off the walls in sonorous tones that were slightly less compelling than those drifting into the desert.

Sadira reached into her pocket and extracted one of the silver pieces Faenaeyon had given her. Holding it out for the man, she said, "If you overlook the baggage of the elf tribe following me, there will be nine more of these for you."

The guard opened his palm and bowed. "If that is true, my eyes will not see."

"Good," Sadira said.

She released the coin, and the guard signaled his fellows to let her pass. As she rode through the gateway, the sorceress felt confident she had at last escaped the elves. Faenaeyon would never pay a bribe of nine silver, and the guard would not allow the Sun Runners to pass through the gate until he received the coins he had been promised. With luck, the tribe would be turned away from the city altogether. Even if that was not the case, it would be delayed long enough for Sadira to lodge her mount. Then she would search out someone from the Veiled Alliance and ask for the secret organization's help in finding a guide to the Pristine Tower.

The gateway opened into a muggy, foul-smelling courtyard surrounded by a warren of mountainous towers and gloomy portals. To all sides, square doorways led into the bases of jagged minarets, reminding Sadira of nothing quite so much as the ancient mines that honeycombed the peaks west of Tyr. Huge sculpted faces, sometimes vaguely human and sometimes completely monstrous, covered every available surface.

From the corners of the buildings peered long-nosed giants with disapproving frowns and blank stares. Where there should have been windows were gaping, fang-filled mouths. Columns carved to look like stacked skulls supported the balconies and overhangs. Even the walls were masked by fat cherubic visages with gluttonous smiles, or by skeletal countenances of long-tusked fiends.

Between these looming buildings ran narrow, twisting lanes covered by vaulted ceilings of stone. Lines of Nibenese porters bustled down two of these dark tunnels, carrying their heavy loads to the emporium of some merchant house in the heart of the city.

Sadira directed her kank into what seemed to be the widest street. She had expected the shaded lane to be cool and pleasant. Instead, a stifling wind drifted down the tunnel, carrying with it the sour smell of too much humanity and the putrid scent of unkempt stables.

The sorceress urged her mount past a dozen Nibenese citizens and entered another courtyard, also encircled by sculpture-covered towers. Many of the doorways were larger than normal, with kanks and riders moving into and out of them. Sadira rode halfway through the plaza to an anonymous-looking livery, then dismounted and led her beast toward the door. She was greeted by an elderly, bald-headed man dressed in a grimy sarami.

"You wish to lodge your mount?" he asked.

"How much?"

"Three days boarding for a king's bit," he answered, referring to the ceramic coins most cities used as common currency. "We will feed it every night and water it every five."

Sadira nodded. "I'll pay when I return and my kank is in good health."

The old man shook his head. "That's not the way in Nibenay," he said. "You pay in advance—every day if you like. If you don't return before your money runs out, I sell your mount."

Sadira fished her second coin out of her pocket. "You can give me change?"

"I can," the man replied.

He snatched the coin and led her inside. The lowest floor of the gloomy building was a workshop, filled with slaves laboring to repair howdahs, carts, and even a massive argosy wheel. Sadira caught only a glimpse of this room before her guide took a torch from a wall sconce and led her up a dark ramp spiraling through the interior of the unlit building. The over-sweet stench of kank offal was terrible, and Sadira had to pinch her nose closed to keep from gagging.

Soon they reached the first of the dark animal pens. As they passed each gate, a kank stuck its mandibles through the bone bars and clacked them at the newcomer. Sadira's beast returned the gestures, keeping up a constant clatter as they slowly climbed the steep ramp.

Dozens of pens later, they reached one with an open gate. The bone grid was held aloft by a rope running through a wooden pulley and tied off to a bone stake in the wall. The old man allowed Sadira's mount to pass by the vacant pen, then stopped. He forced the beast to back into the stall by standing in front of it and tapping its right-hand antenna.

As the kank's head went under the gate, it stopped and began waving its antennae in agitation.

"Go on, stupid beast," the old man said.

He raised his hand and stepped toward the kank. Sadira saw an angry glint in the beast's eyes. "Careful!" she cried, pulling the old man back just in time to avoid the kank's snapping mandibles.

The beast started forward, but Sadira quickly stepped to its side and grabbed an antenna. She yanked on the stalk and forced it back into the pen.

"When I let go, drop the gate," she said, looking over her shoulder. The liveryman, who was staring at her kank with his mouth hanging agape, made no move to obey. "Do as I say!"

The old man snapped out of his shock and untied the gate rope. "I've run this livery for thirty years, and never has a carrier drone snapped at me," he said, keeping a suspicious eye fixed on the beast. "What's wrong with yours?"

"I don't know," Sadira said. "It did something like this once before, not long after my journey began, but has never been so violent."

The sorceress released the antenna and leaped out of the pen, barely clearing the threshold before the gate came crashing down. The kank threw itself at the bars. When they showed no sign of breaking, it retreated to the back of its stall, then slammed into the gate again. It repeated the actions over and over as Sadira watched, perplexed.

"I've never seen anything like this," the old man said, shaking his head in bewilderment. "I'll have to hire an elf to look at it."

"What for?"

"It could be diseased," he said, leading the way back down the tunnel. "If so, I'll have to kill and burn the drone. Otherwise, the sickness could spread, and every kank in my stable could die."

Sadira was immediately suspicious of his motives. "My mount had better be here when I come back," she warned.

"Can't promise that," he answered, not bothering to look at her. "And I'm keeping your whole silver. You'll have to pay for the elf."

"No!" Sadira protested.

"It's your kank," the old man said. "It's only fair that you pay the cost of examining it."

"How do I know you won't pocket my coin, sell the kank, and claim the beast was diseased?" Sadira demanded, outraged.

The old man stopped and pointed up the ramp. "You don't, but listen to that." The echoes of Sadira's mount banging itself against its gate continued to fill the corridor. "I'll give you the coin back, but you've got to take the kank with it. Do you think any other livery master will charge less?"

"I suppose not," Sadira admitted, wondering where she would find the money to feed herself until she contacted the Veiled Alliance—or to buy another kank, if it came to that.

The old man started down the ramp again. "Don't worry," he said. "I won't destroy your beast unless I must, and I'll get the best price I can from the elf who looks at it." When they reached the ground floor, the old man turned toward his workshop.

Deciding to see how well her plan to rid herself of the Sun Runners was working, Sadira retraced her steps into the dark lane from which she had approached the livery. She stopped in the shelter of its depths, then looked toward the gate. Her father had just arrived at the head of his tribe, and was approaching the sharp-featured half-elf to whom Sadira had given the silver coin. Faenaeyon smiled warmly and said something to the man.

The guard also smiled and held out his hand.

The chief scowled, then shoved the half-elf so hard that he came tumbling into the square. The gateman's assistants screamed the alarm and thrust their spears at Faenaeyon. The elf casually slapped the weapons from their hands, then stepped past the two men into the courtyard.

"Lorelei!" he screamed, his angry eyes searching the gloomy portals that lined the small plaza.

Sadira saw a company of guards beginning to pour from the gate tower, then smiled to herself and turned to leave.

EIGHT

Prince of Nibenay

An inky murk filled the chamber, so thick and dark that it seemed to brush over the kank's carapace like smoke. In the pitch blackness, not even the ground—the one thing the beast's weak eyes always kept in focus—was visible. To stay attuned to the creature's surroundings, Tithian had to rely entirely upon the insect's other senses. For the king's vision-oriented mind, the task was an onerous one.

Still, Tithian could tell that the earthy scent of mildew clung to the insect's antennae, as did a muskier smell that terrified the drone. Clutched in the kank's powerful mandibles was the old liveryman to whom Sadira had entrusted her mount. He smelled of sweat and blood, and drew his breath in shallow gasps.

The clatter of two dozen sticklike legs rose from the far side of the room and approached, reverberating through the kank's drumlike ears with a chilling quiver. When they reached the liveryman trapped between the kank's pincers, the legs stopped and fell silent. Then Tithian heard something else coming from the other side of the

136

cavernous room. This creature moved much more quietly, its feet whispering across the floor as though barely touching the slimy stones.

When the second arrival reached the old man's side, a pair of bulbous eyes appeared in the darkness. The orbs were golden yellow, with pupils as black and glassy as obsidian. Tithian could tell little else about the creature, for the gleam of the eyeballs was too faint to illuminate any more of its face.

"Make the kank speak, old man," demanded a man's voice, as quiet and as smooth as the frigid breath of night.

"The drone doesn't speak aloud, Mighty King," gasped the liveryman, weak and pained from having his ribs constricted by the kank's mandibles. "It talks to me, and I repeat its words."

The color of the eyes changed to scarlet, but the king did not speak. Instead, a harsher, chattering voice sounded from where the clattering legs had stopped. "If you came here thinking to dupe my father with sophistry, your death will be slow and painful." The speaker remained concealed in the darkness.

The liveryman began to tremble. "Please, Great Prince, I am only a prisoner," he said. "After it was lodged with me, the kank collapsed and acted like it was dead. When I opened its pen to dispose of it, the beast sprang past two of my assistants and seized me. I heard a man's voice in my mind, demanding that I show it the way to your palace. If you will allow me, I can prove that what I say is true."

The liveryman made his statement with brisk efficiency, for he had already repeated it to the gate guards, to their commander, and to a bare-breasted woman addressed as the Consort of the South Gate. In order to convince each of the officials to take his request for a royal

audience to the next level, the liveryman had asked them
to command the drone to do whatever they wished.
Tithian had used his control over the beast's mind to
make the kank respond appropriately.

Unfortunately, the last official, a naked matron calling
herself the Most High Concubine of the Palace Chambers, had proven even more difficult. To win her over,
Tithian had been forced to speak to her mentally, as he
had to the liveryman. The exertion had left him exhausted, for it was no easy matter to use the Way over such vast
distances.

When both the prince and his father remained silent,
the liveryman looked back to the yellow eyes. "Command the beast to do anything you wish," he said. "You
will see that it seems truly intelligent."

"There's a better way to see if you are lying," said the
king's voice.

He slipped past the old man and moved closer to the
kank's head, until the creature's antennae began to dance
in the Nibenese ruler's musty breath. The king's eyes
shined directly into those of the drone, and Tithian was
almost blinded by the golden luminescence. The light
shimmered and twinkled for several moments, forming a
series of ephemeral shapes as the sorcerer-king used the
Way to invade the kank's mind.

When the glow died away, Tithian found his attention
focused on a mass of slime-covered flesh, shaped like a
teardrop and banded with thick folds of skin. From one
end of its body rose a tube-shaped torso, with a pair of
corpulent arms ending in hooklike claws. The creature's
head was the only thing even remotely human, with a
heavy crown of gold sitting atop a fine-boned brow. He
had a broad nose with flaring nostrils and bloated lips
that did not quite conceal the curved fangs hanging from

his upper jaw. His eyes were bulbous and yellow, identical to those that the liveryman had addressed as the sorcerer-king of Nibenay.

The thing moved forward on six bandy legs, scuttling across the rippled sands of the kank's mind with surprising speed. It stopped at the base of a dune and dropped to its haunches, where it seemed to be waiting until a thought passed near enough to ambush.

Deciding the time had come to show himself, Tithian pictured himself rising from the sands. The creature remained motionless, watching with no sign of fear or curiosity as the king emerged. First came his golden diadem, then his long tail of auburn hair, his hawk-nosed face, and finally his gaunt torso.

"Who are you?" asked the creature, his nostrils flaring in suspicion.

"The King of Tyr," Tithian answered, straining to keep his body from being drawn back beneath the sands. "And you are the King of Nibenay?"

The king-beast did not answer. Instead, he demanded, "You wish to speak with me, Usurper?"

Tithian's face hardened at the other's derogatory tone. "We must discuss a matter that concerns both our cities."

"I'll judge what concerns Nibenay," the sorcerer-king spat.

"Of course," Tithian allowed, "but I'm sure this matter will interest you. Have you heard of the Pristine Tower?"

The sorcerer-king's eyes darkened to fiery scarlet. He scuttled forward, his corpulent arms half-raised. "What do you know of the tower?"

Tithian sank a few inches into the sands. "Enough to realize the Dragon would not want someone to visit it."

"Anyone foolish enough to go there would never

survive."

"This one might," Tithian corrected. "She's a powerful sorceress and is one of the people who killed Kalak."

"Sadira of Tyr," the creature hissed.

"You know her?" Tithian asked, surprised.

"I know of her," he answered. "Even if my spies did not inform me of what happens in Tyr, the caravan minstrels have made her name familiar to my slaves." The sorcerer-king frowned thoughtfully. "You must kill the sorceress at once."

Noting that the Nibenese ruler had not even asked why Sadira was going to the tower, Tithian asked, "What will she discover at the Pristine Tower?"

"In all likelihood, death—or something much worse," the king-beast answered. "But if she survives, she might find what she wants." He gave Tithian a distrustful look, then asked, "She is searching for a way to deny the Dragon his levy, is she not?"

"She is," Tithian answered.

"Then you must be certain she does not succeed," the other said. "If she challenges him, the Dragon will take his wrath out on all of Tyr. That will leave one less city to supply him with his levy, and he'll call upon the rest of us to make up the difference."

"Why does the Dragon need so many slaves?" Tithian pressed, determined to learn as much as he could from this conversation.

"That is not for me to say, or you to ask. Unless you wish your reign to be a short one, do not concern yourself with such questions," the Nibenese king warned. He pointed a corpulent arm at Tithian. "Just kill the sorceress at once."

Realizing he had learned all he would from his counterpart, Tithian said, "If Sadira were in Tyr, I would have done it already—but she is in Nibenay."

The eyes of the sorcerer-king narrowed. "My son will see that she never leaves the city," he said, his form shimmering as he brought the audience to an end. "But I will demand a dear price for this favor."

*   *   *   *   *

Sadira had never before seen anything like the man-beast clattering into the square. He seemed to be part human and part cilops. From the knees down, he resembled a giant centipede, with a flat body divided into twelve segments. Each section was supported by a pair of slender legs ending in hooked claws. From the knees up, he was remotely human, with his torso swaddled in a silk sarami and a black skullcap covering his shaved head. He had tiny ears located at the base of his jaw, bulbous eyes resembling those of a cilops, and a muzzle with cavernous nostrils that flared every time he drew a breath.

Sadira ducked into the sweltering darkness of the nearest alley and hoped the cilops-man would pass. She had no particular reason to hide from him, but she thought it wisest to avoid officials of the sorcerer-king—which this person obviously was. In front of him walked two half-giants, their loins swaddled in silken breechcloths and their arms cradling great clubs of blue agafari wood. Behind him came a pair of bare-breasted Nibenese templars, each wearing necklaces of colored beads and a yellow skirt decorated with a wide bejeweled belt.

As the official passed in front of Sadira's hiding place, his black eyes turned in her direction and seemed to linger on the place where she stood. The sorceress held her breath and did not move. Not even an elf's eyes could penetrate the alley's dark shadows while he was standing

in the light of day, but Sadira was less sure about the
manbeast's other senses. Judging from his large muzzle
and flaring nostrils, it certainly seemed possible that he
could smell her—though her scent would only be one
among a hundred odors coming from the squalid alley.

After what seemed an interminable length of time, the
official continued on. Sadira breathed a sigh of relief and
waited, not wanting to step from her hiding place until
the procession was out of sight.

The sorceress had spent the night shivering in the
city's crowded alleys with other vagrants, then had gone
to the Elven Market at dawn. She had assumed that her
best chance of contacting the Veiled Alliance lay in that
disreputable quarter, for it was there that sorcerers came
to purchase snake tongues, glowworms, powdered wych-
wood, and other ingredients vital to their magic. In Nibenay, as in most Athasian cities, the sorcerer-king jealously
guarded the right to use magic, reserving the precious
plant energy in his fields for himself and his agents.
Therefore, magic components had to be smuggled into
the city and sold secretly—just the sort of sneaky work at
which elves excelled. Unfortunately, Sadira had not managed to spy out any sorcerers. Therefore, she had decided
to try her luck in Sage's Square, where she had heard sorcerers sometimes came to hear wise men speak.

Once the manbeast and his escorts were out of sight,
Sadira slipped from the alley and entered the refreshing
coolness of Sage's Square. It was surrounded on all sides
by the city's largest merchant emporiums, though the
stately buildings were hardly visible through the grove of
blue-barked agafari trees that dominated the plaza. More
than fifty of the mighty hardwoods were scattered
throughout the park, their gnarled roots sunken into circles of unpaved ground. Their trunks did not rise so

much as flow into the air, marked as they were by deep creases and ribbonlike pleats that gave Sadira an impression of immeasurable age. A hundred feet above the ground, they spread their boughs out in great, sweeping fans, shading the entire square with a canopy of enormous turquoise leaves shaped like hearts.

Marveling at the beauty of the trees, Sadira worked her way through the grove until she came to a small crowd. The mob was gathered around two old men seated on the gnarled roots of one of the trees, neither wearing anything more than a breechcloth of plain hemp. Both were impossibly thin, with haggard faces and limbs that seemed nothing but leathery skin draped over bones as thin as canes.

"Only with an empty mind can you find your true self," said the first sage. Despite his great age, he appeared to be as limber as an elf, for he had folded his ankles beneath his buttocks at an angle that most humans would have found impossible. "Looking into a head filled with thoughts is like looking at your reflection in the waves of an oasis pond. You may see a face, but mistake it for one of the moons."

There was a short silence while the second sage formulated his reply. Finally, he said, "The heart is more important than the mind. If it is unstained, the mind will be pure; there is no need to empty it."

Sadira ran her hand across her lips and chin as if pondering the sage's words. If there were any members of Nibenay's Veiled Alliance in the audience, they would recognize the gesture as a request to meet. Sooner or later, someone would approach her to determine what she wanted.

Sadira listened to the wise men continue their debate for several minutes. Finally, she repeated her gesture, this time pretending to scratch her nose, and left. As she stepped away, a thin youth wearing a sarami of green hemp bumped into her.

"I thought you would never leave," he said, bowing low and running his own hand over his lips.

The young man stood a head shorter than the half-elf, with ginger-colored skin and warm brown eyes. His features were gentle and boyish, with the thin line of a mustache creasing his upper lip. He took Sadira's arm and led her toward a basin in the center of the grove, where a trickle of water spilled from the mouth of a stone mantis.

"What do you need?" the youth asked.

"Assistance," Sadira answered, wasting no time in getting to the point. She had only a few moments before the boy left, for the less time they spent together the less dangerous the meeting was for both of them. "I'm looking for someplace called the Pristine Tower, located in the desert to the east. I need supplies, a guide if you can supply one, and silver."

"You ask a great deal," the youth commented.

"It's in a good cause," Sadira said. "The secret of the Dragon's birth is hidden in the tower. I hope to uncover it."

"To what end?" the youth asked.

"The Dragon has demanded a thousand lives from the city of Tyr. I'm trying to save those lives—and perhaps many more from Nibenay and the other cities of Athas."

The youth stopped and studied Sadira for a few moments, his brow furrowed in thought. Finally, he said, "If that is truly your goal, I fear you are too late—at least this season."

"What do you mean?" Sadira asked.

"Once each year, the king sends his son into the desert with a thousand slaves," the boy said. "The prince and his retinue returned just a few days ago—without their charges, as always."

"He delivered the slaves to the Dragon?" Sadira asked.

"We don't know," the youth answered. He shrugged, then began weaving his way through the trees. "Our spies have never returned from these journeys. Your explanation sounds as reasonable as any."

"Then I don't have much time before the Dragon reaches Tyr," Sadira said.

"Perhaps four weeks," the Nibenese agreed. "Gulg lies directly between the two cities, so the Dragon will certainly stop there first. It's even possible that he will travel north to Urik or south to Balic before going to Tyr—"

"I doubt it," Sadira said. "I need your help now more than ever. Can I count on it?"

"The decision is not mine," the boy answered, turning to go. "But I will tell you this much. If my master believes you, I know he'll help."

Sadira caught the boy by the arm. "Then please tell your master that it is Sadira of Tyr who needs his assistance."

The young man's jaw dropped in astonishment. "Sadira?" he gasped. "The one who—"

"Yes," Sadira answered, touching her fingers to his lips. "And I am very much in need of your help."

The youth bowed to her. "I have heard the minstrels sing of your bravery and your beauty, but never did I expect to meet you in person," he said. "I wager you shall have all you need."

Sadira pulled the young man upright, blushing at his open adoration. "Please hurry," she answered. "Where shall I meet you, and when?"

"Call me Raka. We shall meet—"

He stopped speaking, for the crowd had suddenly

parted to allow a pair of half-giants through. Following close behind was the manbeast official Sadira had avoided earlier, his bulbous eyes sweeping the faces of everyone in the square.

In a terrified whisper, Raka hissed, "Prince Dhojakt!"

Sadira slipped her arm through the crook of Raka's elbow, pulling him close and fawning at him. The surprised youth stumbled and nearly fell, but Sadira caught him. Running a long finger under his chin, she gave him a beguiling smile. "Relax, my young sweet. Soon, you will know the thirty-six positions of love."

"I will?"

Dhojakt's gaze reached the pair and stopped. He started toward them, his bulbous eyes fixed on Sadira's amber hair. The sorceress's heart began to pound fiercely, for the prince was clearly searching for someone, and she had the sinking feeling it might be her.

The sorceress released Raka's arm and pushed him away. "Sorry, little boy," she said, flashing Prince Dhojakt a frankly wanton smile. "It seems I've found a deeper purse."

Without waiting to see how Raka would respond, she walked toward Dhojakt with a wildly exaggerated sway to her hips. "See something you like, Mighty One?"

Scowling, the half-giants positioned themselves between her and their master. Dhojakt's templars stepped forward to go after Raka, but Sadira's maneuver had already bought the youth several seconds—enough time, the sorceress hoped, for him to fade into the grove.

As the templars bustled past Sadira, the half-elf suggestively ran her eyes over the flabby torso of the nearest guard. Resisting the temptation to glance back and see if Raka had escaped, she laid a hand on the inside of the half-giant's thigh and fixed her gaze on Dhojakt.

The prince studied Sadira for several moments, his eyes never drifting from her face. Accustomed to dealing with all sorts of looks from men, the sorceress did not let the seductive smile leave her lips.

"Well?" she asked.

"Where are you from?" the prince demanded. When he drew his corpulent lips back to speak, Sadira noticed that in place of teeth, he had bony mandibles.

"Tyr," Sadira answered truthfully, realizing that her accent had probably already told him that much.

"How did you arrive here?"

"With an iron caravan." The sorceress ran a hand up her hip. "I earned my passage. The captain was pleased."

"No doubt," the prince sneered. He studied her for several moments more, his face vacant of any hint that he found her attractive or enticing. At last, he said, "You will come with me—Sadira of Tyr."

The sound of her name struck Sadira like a war-hammer. The sorceress immediately began to wonder how the prince had learned her identity, but could think of no reasonable answer. She knew that he had not used the Way to probe her mind, for Agis had practiced such invasions against her until she recognized them instinctively. Besides, it appeared that Dhojakt had been looking for her since the moment he entered the square, and that could only mean she had been betrayed. The Sun Runners, of course, were the obvious suspects—save that Sadira had no reason to believe they knew her true identity.

But now was not the time to wonder about such things. Ignoring the knot of panic forming in her stomach, she asked, "Where are we going?" The sorceress neither denied nor confirmed her name, for she knew that even if the prince was unsure of his identification, he would insist on interrogating her.

"To the Forbidden Palace," the prince answered, motioning one of the half-giants forward. "You will follow Ghurs."

The sorceress obeyed. Dhojakt was no doubt prepared for her to flee. It would be wiser to save her energies until later, when she could hope to take him by surprise.

Dhojakt's templars returned a few moments later. Between them was a frightened youth of Raka's age, also dressed in a sarami of green hemp. The boy threw himself to the ground at Sadira's feet. "Tell them I was not with you!" he begged.

Sadira glanced over her shoulder at the prince, preparing to summon the energy for a spell. The youth's plea, however, had not provided the distraction the sorceress needed. Dhojakt's eyes were fixed on her back, his thick lips twisted into a faintly amused sneer.

The templars grabbed the young man's shoulders and dragged him back to his feet. Keeping his eyes fixed on Sadira, the youth cried, "Please, say you do not know me!"

Sadira looked away. "They wouldn't believe me."

Although the sorceress suspected her words to be true, a pang of guilt shot through her breast. By doing as the youth asked, there was a slim chance she might have won his freedom. Unfortunately, if the templars realized they had captured the wrong person, they would probably resume their search for Raka. Sadira could not allow that to happen, for doing so would place Nibenay's Veiled Alliance at risk. Instead, she would try to save the boy later, when Raka had had plenty of time to disappear.

It did not appear Dhojakt would give her that chance. "We have no need of the youth," he said.

One of the templars pulled a dagger from her belt and

raised it to strike.

"No!" Sadira yelled, spinning around to face Dhojakt.

The prince motioned the templar to stop. "Obviously, this boy is not of the Veiled Alliance, or he would never have allowed himself to be captured alive," said Dhojakt. "Is there some other reason I should spare his life?"

"Is there any cause to take it?"

The prince smiled at her calmly. "I need no cause."

He nodded to the templar, signaling her to finish what she had begun.

Though she had no doubt Dhojakt expected her to attack, the sorceress turned her palm downward. Before she could summon the energy for a spell, a tremendous sizzle echoed through the square. A woman's voice screamed in agony, and the templar who had been preparing to kill the innocent youth fell to the ground. Her back was covered with a bubbling slime that had already dissolved the flesh clear to the bone.

The prince raised a hand and pointed across the square, to where Raka was peering from behind the trunk of an agafari tree. "There's the one we want," Dhojakt said. "After him!"

The uninjured templar and both half-giants obeyed the prince, sending astonished townsmen scurrying in all directions. Raka fled, and, closer to Sadira, so did the astonished youth who had been mistaken for the young sorcerer.

Sensing the time had come for her to escape as well, Sadira began to draw the energy for a spell. Dhojakt's claws clattered across the cobblestones and he was beside her almost instantly.

"Don't," the prince advised, his corpulent lips drawn back and his bony mouthparts dripping venom. "Before you die, my father wishes to hear how you learned of the

Pristine Tower."

"You know where I'm going?" Sadira gasped. Despite her shock, the sorceress did not cut off the flow of energy rising into her body.

"You have been warned," Dhojakt snapped. He reached out to grasp Sadira, at the same time lowering his gruesome mouth to her neck.

The sorceress leaped back. Her feet had barely touched the ground when a golden flare shot from the darkness of a distant alley. The streak blasted into the prince's temple, exploding into a ball of blazing embers that would have reduced a half-giant's head to a lump of charred bone.

The spell did not even scorch Dhojakt. The prince shook his head as though dazzled by the light, then scowled at the tunnel from which he had been attacked.

The attack stunned Sadira more than it had Dhojakt. It did not seem unusual that another member of the Veiled Alliance had been secretly watching her exchange with Raka, but the sorceress could hardly believe the unseen wizard had moved so quickly to defend her. The Tyrian Alliance would not have extended such protection to a stranger.

Nevertheless, Sadira was determined not to waste the bravery of the Nibenese. Judging from how easily the prince had resisted the previous spell thrown at him, the sorceress knew it would be futile to use magic to injure him. Instead, she could only hope to keep him detained long enough for her and her saviors to flee.

Dhojakt grasped her wrist and started toward the alley. "You shall pay for your brazenness!" he yelled.

Sadira plucked a thread from her robe. She laid the strand across his arm, simultaneously uttering an incantation. The filament lengthened, wrapping itself around

Dhojakt hundreds of times in the span of a single instant. From the head to the last segment of his centipedelike body, the prince was swaddled in a mesh of constricting fibers.

The sorceress pulled free and ran toward her rescuer's tunnel. She was only a few yards from her goal when she heard Dhojakt's voice. "Do you really think you'll escape Nibenay when I'm looking for you?"

Sadira looked over her shoulder. The prince was still entwined, but he had curled himself into a ball. With the claws of his many legs, he was furiously ripping apart the strands of her magical net—strands that should have been impervious to cutting or tearing for another hour.

"In the name of Ral!" she gasped. "Is there no magic that will stop you?"

The Bard's Quarter

Sadira fled into the alley, leaving Dhojakt in the square.
Once she had gained the sheltering darkness of the tunnel, she paused and called into the shadows.

"I owe you my life. Where to now?"

No one replied. From behind the sorceress came the sound of more clattering. She glanced back and saw that Dhojakt had freed his hands. He was pulling the magical mesh off his torso as if it were ordinary rope. He kept his nose turned in her direction, his nostrils flaring as he tested the air for her scent.

The sorceress moved deeper into the tunnel. "Hello?"

When her only answer was the distant sound of running feet, Sadira decided to waste no more time looking for her rescuer. She rushed into the darkness, not waiting even the single moment it would take for her elven vision to become active. A few steps later, she came to a corner and saw light streaming in from the right.

Sadira rushed around the corner and felt a huge, knobby hand grasp her by the wrist. A hulking form stepped away from the alley wall, silhouetting itself against the far end of the tunnel.

"Magnus!" Sadira gasped.

"I'm not going to hurt you," came the windsinger's reply.

A taller, more slender form stepped into view from the opposite wall. "You cost Faenaeyon a lot of silver, and he wants it back," said Rhayn, brandishing a bone dagger. "He's sent the whole tribe out to look for you."

Sadira cast a nervous glance back toward Sage's Square. Of course, she saw nothing but darkness, which only made her more fearful of the threat that would soon be coming after her. "Faenaeyon's not going to get his coins back, especially if we don't get out of here."

Sadira started to move forward, but Magnus pulled her back. Rhayn pressed the dagger to the sorceress's throat. "Not until we come to an agreement."

"You don't understand!" Sadira objected. "Prince Dhojakt will be—"

"I know all about Prince Dhojakt," hissed Rhayn. "Who do you think saved you from him?"

"You?" Sadira gasped.

Rhayn nodded. "My spells may not be as powerful as yours, but they serve their purpose," she said. "Now, as you pointed out just a moment ago, you owe me your life. I'll settle for a favor that costs you a great deal less."

"What do you want?" Sadira asked, listening for any sign that Dhojakt had entered the other end of the tunnel.

"Do you remember the matter we discussed at the Silver Spring?"

"The overthrow of Faenaeyon," Sadira responded.

Rhayn nodded. "Will you help me, or would you rather return to the prince? Answer quickly—I doubt you have much time to think matters over."

"I'll do it," Sadira answered. "Assuming you'll keep

me hidden from Dhojakt until I can make other arrangements."

Rhayn did not take her dagger from the sorceress's throat. "And you won't change your mind just because Faenaeyon's your father?"

"How do you know that?" Sadira asked.

Rhayn looked at Magnus, who wagged his large ears back and forth. "The same way we know why you're so keen to go to the Pristine Tower," the windsinger said. "You'll do as Rhayn asks?"

"Faenaeyon's blood may run in my veins, but he's no father to me," Sadira said. "I'll help you—if Dhojakt doesn't kill us first."

Rhayn nodded to Magnus, and the windsinger led Sadira out of the tunnel at a trot. Rhayn lingered behind and removed a vial of green liquid from her shoulder satchel. She opened the top and poured the entire contents over the floor where the trio had been standing, then joined the other two.

"Why'd you do that?" Sadira asked.

"Dhojakt knows your smell," explained the elf. "This will keep him from tracking you—and us."

With that, she motioned to Magnus, who led them through the city's alleys to a crumbling gateway opening into the Elven Market. This area of Nibenay had once been a vast palace. Its battered walls were still decorated with stone reliefs that depicted a jungle unlike anything Sadira had ever seen. On the ground, naked hunters armed with broad-tipped spears stalked all sorts of vicious animals, and sometimes even bare-breasted women, through a tangle of vines and blossoming trees. Above the warriors' heads, lethargic snakes hung draped over low branches, and inert lizards clung to smooth stretches of bark. In the canopy of the jungle, flitting from one branch to another, were all manner of birds, magnificently plumed and so plump it seemed impossible they could fly.

The reliefs could not have been a starker contrast to the pungent bazaar that now occupied the citadel's outer ward. With a total disregard for order, dozens of elven tribes had pitched their hemp pavilions and lizardskin marquees upon the courtyard. Wherever Sadira looked, leering elves were barking offers to sell everything from honey-boiled cactus to dwarven children.

With Magnus's immense bulk blazing a trail through the close-pressed throng, the trio steered their way through the mad bazaar as Sadira might the familiar halls of Agis's mansion. Finally, they passed beneath another gate, this one leading to what had once been the palace's inner courtyard, and the babble of the elven bazaar faded to a distant buzz.

The grounds of this small ward were so tightly packed with mud-brick shacks that Magnus could barely walk down the lane. On every second stoop sat a handsome man or comely woman, strumming dulcet notes on a lute or sitar, often accompanying the tune with the practiced voice of a vagabond troubadour.

Despite the sweet sounds, Sadira had to fight to keep from retching as they moved deeper into the ward. The sour aroma of stale broy poured from every doorway, and amorphous piles of rubbish filled the sweltering air with the stench of human refuse.

Magnus stopped in front of a small building decorated with human skulls and the skeleton of some six-legged rodent as large as a halfling. "This is the one."

"Watch Sadira," Rhayn said.

"Why are we here?" Sadira asked. "Isn't this the Bard's Quarter?"

"Very observant," Rhayn answered, stepping toward the door. "As for why we're here, you'll understand that soon enough."

Magnus took the sorceress's arm in his hand, and held it in a firm grip. "Don't worry," he said. "Rhayn knows what she's doing."

Despite the windsinger's reassurances, Sadira kept a careful watch in both directions. Bards were notorious assassins, as well versed in the arts of killing as they were in singing and poetry. From the stories she had heard, they would not hesitate to murder someone for the sole purpose of testing a new technique.

Rhayn returned just a few minutes later, accompanied by peculiar-looking half-elf with skin as white as bone and a star tattooed over one eye. In his hands, the minstrel carried a small wine cask, which he placed at Magnus's feet.

"One goblet and your troubles will be gone," he said, speaking to Rhayn.

"And the antidote?" Rhayn demanded, holding out her hand.

"The price was for the wine," the bard said, turning away. "The antidote is extra."

Rhayn reached for her dagger, but Magnus caught her arm and shook his head.

"A wise beast you have," said the minstrel, slowly turning around to sneer at Rhayn. "Only a fool would try to best a bard at his own art."

"I'm no beast," Magnus growled. "And Rhayn is no fool. The price she offered was for the antidote as well as the wine."

The bard glared at the windsinger, then switched to a brotherly smile. "Come now, my friend. We're only talking about another silver." He reached up to place an amicable hand on Magnus's shoulder.

The sudden switch from hostility to goodwill sent a cold shiver down Sadira's spine. She turned one palm toward the ground and plunged the other into her satchel, searching for the pocket that contained her sulfur balls. "Touch him and there'll be a scorched hole where you and your house once stood."

The bard quickly drew his hand away from the windsinger, and Sadira glimpsed a dark needle disappearing between two of his fingers.

"Very observant," the man said. He eyed the sorceress's hands for a moment, then slowly withdrew a bone vial from his pocket. It was decorated with what appeared to be musical notes. "This is enough to protect twenty of your tribesmen from the poison. Two drops before drinking will counteract any amount of wine, but you'll need twice that dose if you wait until after the poison has taken effect." He handed the vial to Rhayn, then passed an open palm over a closed fist. "Our business is done. You have nothing to fear if you do as I have explained."

With that, he went back into his house.

Magnus turned to Sadira. "I think you just saved my life. Thank you."

"You're welcome," the sorceress answered, confident that she had. She raised an eyebrow at the cask by his feet. "I thought you were only going to disable Faenaeyon?"

"Snakes have many kinds of venoms," Rhayn answered, motioning for the windsinger to pick up the keg. "Not all are fatal."

As they started out of the quarter, Sadira asked, "And exactly what do you want me to do?"

"Very little," she said. "Simply return to the tower

with us. We'll claim that we found you with this cask of
wine—"

"I told you before I won't take the blame," Sadira said.
"That's especially true now, since I don't know how long
I'll need to hide with the Sun Runners."

"No one will blame you—or anyone else," said Rhayn.
"It'll look like Faenaeyon drank himself into a stupor and
never recovered."

"And you expect me to believe this poison will affect
only your father?" Sadira asked.

"It'll have the same effect on anyone who drinks it, but
Faenaeyon is as selfish with his wine as he is with his
silver," Rhayn said. She held up the small bottle of antidote. "Besides, that's why I have this. If someone else
sneaks a swallow, I'll slip it to him before anyone realizes
he's been poisoned."

Sadira stopped and reached for the bone vial. "I'll keep
the antidote," she said. "If you betray me, I'll give it to
Faenaeyon—and your plan will be for naught."

"You've nothing to fear," Rhayn said, withdrawing the
vial.

Sadira continued to hold out her hand and did not
move. "I agreed to help you and I will—but not because
I'm a fool," she said. "It suits me to stay with the Sun
Runners for a time, but I won't involve myself in your
plot unless I have a safeguard."

"After what you did for Magnus, I would not let you
come to harm," said Rhayn.

"Surely, you don't expect me to believe that?"

"If I were you, I suppose I wouldn't," Rhayn sighed.
She handed the flask to Sadira. "But I warn you, if you
try to betray us, the tribe will accept my word and
Magnus's over anything you say."

"Of course," Sadira answered. She turned and briskly

led the way out of the Bard's Quarter, walking well ahead of her companions.

As the sorceress stepped through the gate leading into the Elven Market, she bumped into a young elf coming around the corner. The young warrior's jaw fell slack, and he stared at her as though looking at the king of Nibenay himself.

"I beg your pardon," Sadira said, moving to step around him.

The elf grabbed the collar of the blue smock the sorceress was wearing, reaching for his dagger with the other hand. Sadira stomped on the arch of his foot and pulled away, leaving a long strip of cloth in the astonished elf's hand.

"Leave me alone," she warned.

The elf pulled his dagger and cautiously limped toward her. "Who'd have thought I'd find you so close to camp?"

The young warrior's face, with its hooked nose and square jawline, seemed only remotely familiar to Sadira. "Are you a Sun Runner?" she asked.

"How many other tribes have you robbed?" the elf demanded. "Come with me. Faenaeyon wants to—"

The youth stopped speaking in midsentence and peered over Sadira's shoulder. "Magnus, Rhayn! What are you doing here?" he demanded. His gaze dropped to the heavy keg in the windsinger's hands. "Where did you get that?"

There followed an uncomfortable silence as Sadira waited for her companions to respond. When both Magnus and Rhayn seemed too stunned to answer, Sadira did it for them. "As you can see," she said, gesturing at her captors. "I've already been caught."

"With a cask from the Bard's Quarter?" the youth

demanded, pointing his dagger at the poisoned wine. "What fool did you intend to drink that?"

This time, not even Sadira could think of a reasonable answer. There was only one thing to do with a cask from the Bard's Quarter, and the young warrior certainly seemed to realize what that was. Even if the sorceress claimed that the wine had been intended for someone else, Faenaeyon would never drink it now.

Then Sadira thought of the antidote in her pocket. "There's nothing wrong with this wine," she said. "Maybe you'd like to share some with me?"

The warrior scowled at her. "I'm no fool."

"This wine is not poisoned, Gaefal, if that is what you are thinking," said Rhayn, picking up on Sadira's tactic. "I'll have some, too."

"How can you know this wine's safe to drink?" the youth demanded.

"Because she didn't get it here," said Magnus. "We saw her buy it from the Swift Wings."

"I saw no wine in the tent of the Swift Wings. And their camp is on the other side of the market," Gaefal said, waving the cloth he had ripped from Sadira's collar toward the far end of the courtyard. "Why let her come all the way to the Bard's Quarter if you saw her back there?"

As he realized the answer to his own question, the young warrior's jaw dropped. "You're lying," he gasped, backing away. "I don't know why, or what you're up to, but you're lying."

He turned and began to push his way into the crowd.

"Gaefal, come back!" yelled Magnus.

When the young warrior showed no sign of obeying, Rhayn pulled her dagger and threw it. The blade struck the boy squarely between the shoulder blades, sinking clear to the hilt. He cried out once, then sprawled face-first onto the cobblestones.

A few astonished cries rose from the crowd, then people scurried away as fast as they could. In the Elven Market, someone died every day. If this time it happened to be an elf, it was more a cause for relief than concern.

For a moment, the three stood outside the Bard's Quarter in absolute silence, staring at the boy's unmoving body. Finally, Magnus allowed the cask to slip from his thick fingers. "Rhayn!" he gasped. "In the name of the Silt Wind, what have you done?"

"Stopped him from giving us away, that's what," the elf answered. She pushed the windsinger toward the youth's inert body. "Now heal him, then we'll decide what to do."

Sadira started to follow Magnus, but Rhayn pointed at the cask. "Don't let that out of your sight," she said. "Someone will steal it."

The sorceress began to object, but when she thought of what would happen to the hapless thief who stole the keg of poisoned wine, Sadira saw the wisdom of Rhayn's command.

The windsinger's lyrical voice began to drift over the cobblestones, carried on a soft breeze. He was singing the same healing canticle he had used to mend Sadira's wounds. It was a calm, melancholy tune with an undertone of hope and kindness, and Magnus rendered it beautifully.

Before the sorceress had come to fully realize how angry she was at Rhayn for attacking the youth, she found all of her wrath fading away in the dulcet harmony of the healer's song. There was no room in her heart except for the emotions that the music demanded of her: sympathy for the young man's pain, and the desire to bear some of his suffering.

The song ended too soon. Sadira rolled the heavy keg over to Magnus and Rhayn. The windsinger kneeled on the ground, the injured elf's limp body cradled in one massive arm. To plug the hole in Gaefal's back, he had used the shred of cloth the young warrior had ripped from Sadira's collar.

"What's wrong?" Sadira asked. "Can't you heal him?"

The windsinger fixed his dark orbs on her face and slowly shook his head. "Even the winds of mist cannot bring a man back from the dead." He glanced up at Rhayn, who was staring at the boy with an expression of disbelief and horror. "You have gone too far," he said reproachfully.

"I didn't mean to kill him, but we couldn't let him return to camp and tell on us," Rhayn whispered. She ripped her eyes from the youth's face and studied the area. There were no onlookers, for wise pedestrians in this part of the city made it a point not to interfere in the business of others. Nevertheless, the three companions were quite noticeable. In avoiding the area, the passersby had created a conspicuous circle of emptiness around the body.

"We'd better leave," Rhayn said. "Sooner or later, a templar will come."

Magnus nodded and laid the body down on the street. He gave Rhayn's dagger back to her, then took the cask and started to leave.

"What about Gaefal?" Sadira asked, unable to believe Rhayn and the windsinger would leave the body lying in the street.

"We can't take him back to camp," Rhayn answered. With that, she turned to follow Magnus toward the center of the market.

Sadira stood over the body a while longer, wondering what courtesies Sun Runners normally showed their dead. Finally, she decided that, given what she knew of elves so far, it might well be customary to let them lie where they fell. She turned and went after her two companions.

When she caught up, Sadira said, "Rhayn, I want no part of helping you become chief if it means murdering innocent people."

Rhayn stopped and spun on the sorceress. "What does a defiler care about one elf's death?"

Hoping her eyes did not show how much Rhayn's question had hurt, Sadira retorted, "I may be a defiler, but I have never killed one of my own."

Rhayn grabbed Sadira by the arm. "You are not a Sun Runner," she hissed. "It doesn't matter to you whether one of us dies or we all do. You'll take the wine to my father."

"Don't be so sure," Sadira countered.

"Would you really want the Veiled Alliance to discover that the legendary Sadira of Tyr is a defiler?" Rhayn asked, releasing the sorceress's arm. "And to believe that she would betray them to the king of Nibenay?"

"It would be a simple thing for me to kill you," Sadira warned. "I should probably do that anyway, considering what you are saying."

"And would that not make you a murderer, too?" Rhayn asked. The elf studied Sadira for several moments, then gave her a conciliatory smile. "Let us do what we must and be done with each other," she said. "There is no reason for empty threats."

"My threat is not empty," Sadira said. "I'll help you with Faenaeyon, but only so long as it suits me to stay with the Sun Runners—and provided there are no more murders."

"Then we are agreed," Rhayn said. "As long as we both do what we have promised, neither of us need worry about the threats of the other."

TEN

Sweet Wine

Sadira rolled the cask toward the dark archway, followed closely by Magnus and Rhayn. They were entering the moldering tower where the Sun Runners had made camp. The building's ancient foundations had settled badly, and it seemed to the sorceress that the derelict structure remained upright only because it stood propped against the walls in one corner of the Elven Market.

Before crossing the threshold, the sorceress stopped and braced herself against the heavy barrel as if resting. Without raising her head, she whispered, "Won't Faenaeyon wonder how I could push this thing through the Elven Market?"

"Not as much as he'd wonder why we're carrying it for you," hissed Rhayn. The elf gave Sadira a rough shove, then barked, "Go on!"

With a great heave, the sorceress pushed the cask across the threshold. The shadows were thick with the musty smell of kank offal, and the constant tick-tick of nipping pincers echoed off the stone walls. As Sadira's eyes adjusted to the darkness, she saw that the round tower's first floor consisted of a single arcade. Most of the stilted pillars now teetered on the edge of collapse, and half of the double-tiered arches lay broken and scattered in the dust.

"Welcome back, my sweet," said Faenaeyon, speaking from the shelter of the darkness. "How nice to see you again."

To Sadira's surprise, the chief did not sound angry. "I wish I could say the same," she answered suspiciously.

The sorceress peered into the gloom and saw Faenaeyon leaning against one of the unsteady pillars. He stepped away from it and came toward her. Without acknowledging either Magnus or Rhayn, he pointed a dagger-length finger at the wine cask. "What have you there?"

"Nothing that concerns you," Sadira said. "And by searching for me, you have accomplished little except wasting your tribe's time. I don't have your silver."

Faenaeyon's eyes flashed in irritation, but he did not let the smile leave his lips. "Of course not," he answered. "And even if you did, you could not repay me for the ten coins it cost to bribe the gate-sergeant."

"Then what do you want with me?"

"I only wish to offer you a place to stay," the chief answered, waving a hand toward the curving staircase that ran up the tower's outside wall. "Nibenay is a dangerous place."

"So I have learned," Sadira said, rolling the cask toward the stairwell.

Although Faenaeyon's lack of hostility surprised her, Sadira did not believe for an instant that he viewed her as anything but a prisoner. His politeness only meant he wanted her to help him recover the coins he had lost—

and probably many more. If she did not respond to his courtesy, the sorceress knew, Faenaeyon would be fully prepared to resort to more direct means to enforce her cooperation.

Sadira reached the stairs and stooped down to pick up the cask.

"Let me help you with that," Faenaeyon said, moving to take the keg.

Following the advice Rhayn had given her not to yield the wine readily, Sadira pushed the elf away. "If I'm truly a guest, then you'll leave me to my wine."

Faenaeyon glanced at Rhayn and Magnus with an amused smirk, then gestured toward the stairs. "If that is what you wish," he said.

With a grunt, Sadira picked up the cask. Although she was not a weak woman, she managed to climb only a dozen stairs before her arms grew so fatigued that they began to tremble. She stopped and rested the keg on a step.

"Are you sure you don't want me to carry that for you?" Faenaeyon asked, coming up the stairs behind her.

The sorceress blocked his way.

"Perhaps Magnus, then?" he suggested.

"I can do it," Sadira snapped.

The chief scowled and backed away from the sorceress, growling, "What's wrong? Do you think we're going to steal it?"

"Yes," Sadira answered frankly.

Faenaeyon smiled broadly and deceitfully. "And risk our friendship?"

"I'm your prisoner, not your friend," Sadira said. "If we were friends, you'd return the purse you took from me."

"That was business," Faenaeyon said sharply. "As was

your little deception at the Dancing Gate."

Sadira lifted the cask and struggled up more steps, beginning to fear her father truly had no intention of stealing the keg from her. After another half-dozen stairs, Sadira had to put the cask down again. This time, she gave up trying to carry the heavy load and settled for rolling it up the steps one by one. Faenaeyon hovered a few feet behind, peering over the sorceress's shoulder, ready to catch the barrel if she happened to let it slip.

By the time she reached the second story, Sadira's breath was coming in heavy gasps.

"Welcome back to the camp of the Sun Runners," said Huyar.

The black-haired elf stood in a short passageway, which led to a jagged arrow loop that overlooked the streets outside the Elven Market. The flushed yellow light of the afternoon sky streamed in behind him, so that the sorceress could hardly separate his craggy features from the edges of the window-slit.

To the other side of the landing, the room opened into what had once been the foyer of someone's official chambers. Several stone benches hung from the walls, flanking the battered remains of a decorative fountain. At the back of the small parlor, an arched doorway opened into a much larger compartment, though the floor had long since collapsed into the arcade below.

Ignoring Huyar, Sadira rolled the cask toward the next set of stairs. As soon as there was space, Faenaeyon slipped past her and snatched the barrel.

"This is too heavy for you," he said, lifting the barrel as though it were empty.

Though she was relieved Faenaeyon had finally taken the wine, Sadira found herself vaguely disappointed that Rhayn had been so right about their father's gluttony.

"So much for friendship," she said.

"Friends share, do they not?"

Slipping the keg under one arm, the chief used his steel dagger to pry the stopper from the taphole, then sheathed the weapon and hefted the cask high over his head. The fruity wine sloshed from the opening and went down his throat in a red stream.

Rhayn and Magnus stepped from the first stairway and crossed to the second set of stairs, which led to the tower's third story. They did not tarry long enough to cast even a single glance in the chief's direction.

At last, Faenaeyon lowered the cask and closed his mouth. Though only a few seconds had passed since he started to drink, his eyes were already glazed. "Too sweet, but powerful," he said, holding the wine toward the sorceress. "Have some."

Sadira's heart leaped into her throat. From the speed with which the drug was taking effect, the sorceress feared she would not be able to sneak away and drink the antidote before falling into a stupor.

"Come," said Faenaeyon, squinting as though he were having trouble seeing Sadira.

Huyar pushed the sorceress forward. "Do not insult the chief by making him ask again," he said. "He does not often share his wine."

Faenaeyon tilted the cask, spilling a stream of poisoned wine over the sorceress's face. She stepped away. "I prefer to drink from a mug," she spat, using the sleeve of her tattered smock to wipe the red fluid from her lips.

Her comment drew laughter from both Faenaeyon and Huyar, then the chief waved his son toward the stairs. "Fetch her one," he said, "and be quick about it. My thirst is great, and I would not forgive myself if I finished all this wine before you returned with a mug for our guest."

Huyar hesitated to do as commanded. "Be careful," he said. "She may try to flee."

"If I wanted to escape, do you really think I would have allowed Rhayn and Magnus to bring me here?" Sadira demanded in an imperious tone. "I have cause of my own for returning to the Sun Runners."

Huyar narrowed his eyes. "What cause?"

"My reasons are not for you to know," Sadira answered, looking away. "Now fetch me a mug, while some of my wine remains."

"I'm not your servant," Huyar spat. Nevertheless, he stepped into the stairwell.

As the warrior climbed out of sight, Faenaeyon chuckled. "You should be more careful of Huyar's feelings," he said. "Someday, he'll be chief."

"I won't be with the Sun Runners that long," Sadira answered sharply.

"Don't be so sure," slurred the chief.

"What do you mean by that?" Sadira demanded in a sharp voice.

"Nothing at all," Faenaeyon answered. "Just that life can be as surprising as it is short."

"I suppose that's so—especially for elves," the sorceress said.

Under the pretense of looking out on the street below, she stepped into the arrow loop and turned her back to her father. The sorceress pretended to be interested in the pedestrians below, watching them swish along the lane in their bright saramis. Upon hearing Faenaeyon begin to gulp down more wine, she glanced over her shoulder to be sure his attention was entirely consumed by his drinking.

Sadira found the chief with his head tipped back and

the cask braced against his chin, wine rushing down his throat in a steady stream. She removed the antidote from her satchel and dabbed two generous drops onto her tongue.

The sorceress had barely slipped the bone vial back into its hiding place when Faenaeyon let a loud belch escape his lips. "The only thing I like more than wine is silver," he pronounced, setting the cask on the floor with a bang.

Sadira turned away from the arrow slit. Faenaeyon had slumped down beside a bench and wrapped one massive arm around the cask. "Why are you so fond of silver?" she asked. "After all, you can't drink it."

"A chief needs silver," Faenaeyon declared, his face grimly serious. "It's the measure of his power and of his warriors' respect for him."

Sadira shook her head at this superficial definition of leadership. "That's not true," she said, sitting on the bench at his side. "I've heard your warriors speak of you. They talk about your feats of bravery and your skill as a warrior—not how much silver there is in your purses."

Faenaeyon looked at her, his head cocked in surprise. "Truly?" he asked, his speech slightly slurred.

Sadira nodded. "I've heard it said that when Faenaeyon was young, nothing was impossible for him."

"That was so," Faenaeyon said, a wistful light in his gray eyes. "Nothing in the desert ran as fast as I did, and even the falcons had reason to fear my arrows." The chief stared into the air a moment longer, then the happiness slowly faded from his eyes. "And what do they say now?"

He seemed unable to look at Sadira as he asked the question.

"Nothing you could not change," she answered, ignoring for the moment that soon he would be beyond changing anything. "They say you claim for your own too much of what they've earned."

Almost unconsciously, Faenaeyon's fingers played over the hilt of his steel dagger. He nodded sadly, and Sadira wondered if Rhayn and Magnus might be acting prematurely in moving to replace him.

Her doubts came to a quick end. Faenaeyon jerked his hand away from his dagger and shoved her off the bench. "What do you know of our ways?" he demanded. "You're no Sun Runner—you're not even an elf!"

"You don't have to be an elf to know what makes a good chief—or a bad one, either," Sadira countered, picking herself up off the floor.

"Our friendship goes only so far," Faenaeyon warned, a cold light glimmering in his steely eyes. "Do not speak to me in such a manner."

"In what manner?" asked Huyar, stepping from the stairwell. In his hand, he held a grimy soapstone mug. "What has this woman said to anger you, my chief?"

"Only the truth," Sadira answered, keeping her eyes fixed on Faenaeyon.

Smirking at Sadira's recklessness, Huyar extended his empty hand to take the sorceress away. "I'll make certain she doesn't bother you."

Sadira jerked away. "If you touch me, it'll be the last time." Her reaction was deliberately extreme. She did not know how much longer she would need to stay with the Sun Runners, and she wanted to make it clear that her visit was on her own terms.

Huyar flung his mug aside and moved to grab Sadira with both hands. Faenaeyon was on his feet and between them more quickly than Rikus could have been.

"She might make good on her threat, and I don't want to have to avenge your death," the chief said, speaking with a drink-thickened tongue. "I've got plans for this woman."

Faenaeyon pushed Huyar toward the discarded mug. "Now hand me that cup," he said. "I promised this woman some wine."

Huyar did as his father commanded, and held the mug while Faenaeyon filled it. Then, with a final glare at Sadira, the warrior handed the vessel to her and stalked back up the stairs.

As soon as Huyar had ascended the stairs, Sadira asked, "What plans?"

Faenaeyon gave her a muddle-headed frown. "Huh?"

"You told Huyar you had plans for me," the sorceress said. "What are they?"

"Oh, those," the chief answered. "Don't worry. We'll earn lots of silver, and you can even keep your share— after you repay what you cost me at the gate."

The sorceress did not tell her father so, but she had plans of her own. Tomorrow morning, she would return briefly to Sage's Square to see if she could find Raka—or at least discover whether or not he had escaped Dhojakt's servants. If that failed, she would return to the camp of the Sun Runners, and use it as a base for trying to re-establish contact with the Veiled Alliance.

Sadira spent the rest of the afternoon watching Faenaeyon drink. It was impossible to tell how much of the chief's growing torpor was due to the bard's poison and how much to the wine itself, but it hardly mattered. He sank steadily into a stupor, growing less and less aware of the world around him. Occasionally, he remembered to offer the sorceress more drink, but she rarely accepted. Not anxious to test the limits of the antidote, the half-elf sipped only enough of the fruity liquid to make her father believe she was enjoying it as much as he. Finally, Faenaeyon slumped down against the wall, his long legs splayed before him and red wine dribbling off his pointed chin. Sadira put her mug aside and stopped drinking altogether.

Soon, the sky outside faded to dusky purple. The Sun Runners began returning to camp in small groups, usually carrying with them some small prize they had stolen from an unwitting victim. Upon reaching the second story, they looked more than a little surprised to see Sadira sitting on a bench near Faenaeyon's snoring form, but no one spoke to her. Instead, counting themselves lucky to have returned while their chief was oblivious to the world and could not claim their stolen goods, they snuck past as quietly as possible.

A little after dark, a boy descended the stairs with a wedge of faro bread and a skin of broy. "Rhayn thought you might be hungry," he said.

"Thanks," Sadira replied, accepting the food from him.

The boy glanced at the half-empty cask at Faenaeyon's side and licked his lips. "How's the wine?" he asked.

"Not bad," Sadira answered, giving him a sidelong glance. "Why don't you try some—unless you think Faenaeyon would object?"

"I'm not that thirsty," he answered, retreating to the arrow loop.

There, he took up his position as a sentry. Sure that the youth had come to watch her as well as the lane outside, Sadira finished her meal. To be sure the young guard did not get any ideas about sneaking a few swallows of wine from her mug, the sorceress drank the last of it, then lay down on the bench and covered herself with a cape. Within a few moments, she was fast asleep, for it had been a trying day and she needed rest.

Sadira woke to the sound of scurrying feet. The room was still black as obsidian, but with her elven vision, she saw the last of a long line of warriors descending to the ground floor. Behind them came Rhayn and Magnus, who stopped in Sadira's room.

"What's happening?" Sadira asked, quickly sitting upright.

"Huyar and some friends are going to look for his brother," Rhayn explained casually. "The foolish boy has not returned yet."

"Gaefal?"

Sadira mouthed the dead elf's name quietly, for the young sentry that had come down earlier still stood at his station. Rhayn nodded, and Magnus went over to the arrow loop.

"I'll take over," the windsinger said to the sentry.

The youth nodded eagerly, then started for the steps leading into the street. Rhayn caught him by the sleeve and redirected him upstairs. "One boy lost tonight is enough," she said. "Go and get some sleep."

Once the young warrior had reluctantly obeyed, Magnus produced an empty waterskin from beneath his tunic. He handed it to Rhayn, then picked up the cask and opened the taphole.

"What's that for?" Sadira asked.

"I doubt we'll need this, but it's best to be prepared," said Rhayn.

The elf held the skin steady while Magnus filled it. Once that was done, the windsinger smashed the cask at the chief's side.

"If anyone asks, Faenaeyon dropped it himself," Rhayn said, sealing the skin in her hands. "Now, go back to sleep."

"Keep a close eye on that wine," Sadira said.

"Someone may try to sneak a gulp."

"Not from my satchels," said Rhayn, going back upstairs.

This time, it took Sadira much longer to doze off. At last she slept, only to dream of murder and betrayal.

ELEVEN

Sudden Departure

Sadira felt someone pull away the cape she had been using as a blanket, then a rough hand began tugging at her smock. She opened her eyes to see Huyar bending over her, a crumpled wad of blood-soaked blue cloth clutched in his hand. Behind him stood a dozen elves, the green rays of dawn streaming over their shoulders. Two of the warriors held Gaefal's lifeless body suspended between them.

"What are you doing?" Sadira demanded, trying to sit up.

Huyar forced her back to the bench, then grabbed her smock and held the cloth next to it. The smell of stale blood came to the sorceress's nostrils.

A cold knot of dread formed in Sadira's stomach. "Get off me!" she yelled, pushing the elf's hand away.

"It's the same color!" Huyar screamed, thrusting the blood-crusted rag into Sadira's face.

"So what?" demanded Magnus. He forced his way through the elves behind Huyar and plucked the enraged warrior off Sadira. "Leave her alone."

"I found this cloth in the wound that killed my brother," Huyar explained, holding the rag up for Magnus to see.

Sadira grabbed her satchel and stood, fearing she might need her magic to defend herself.

Without putting Huyar down, the windsinger took the rag and held it up in front of one of his black eyes. "This cloth's so blood-stained it's impossible to say what color it is."

"There's blue around the edges," Huyar said. He pointed at Sadira's smock. "The same blue she wears now."

"I've seen a thousand tunics that color," Magnus said dismissively.

The windsinger started to slip the bloody cloth into his pocket, but Huyar snatched it back and stepped toward Sadira.

"Then let us see if this matches the shape of her torn collar," he said, unwadding the cloth.

"It does," Sadira answered, realizing she would only arouse suspicion by trying to keep Huyar from checking the rip. "I was passing by the Bard's Quarter when I saw that youth stagger from the gate," she said, pointing at Gaefal. "I stopped and bandaged his wound, but he died anyway."

"Rhayn and I found her not too far from there," Magnus said, his snaggle-toothed snout creased by what may have been an approving grin.

"I'm only sorry I didn't recognize him as a Sun Runner," Sadira added. "I would have told you about him sooner."

"What do you suppose Gaefal was doing in the Bard's Quarter?" Magnus asked, at last releasing Huyar. "Hasn't Faenaeyon always warned us to leave the bards alone?"

The windsinger's ploy almost worked. The warriors began discussing the reasons the youth might have had for entering such a dangerous place. Even Huyar fell into a thoughtful silence.

Unfortunately, the warrior reached the wrong conclusion. "There's only one reason Gaefal would have disobeyed his chief," the warrior said, glaring at Sadira. "He was chasing you, so you killed him."

"You don't know that to be true," said Magnus.

"I don't know it to be false," Huyar answered, stepping toward Sadira and reaching for his dagger. "And I won't take Lorelei's word for it."

Magnus grasped the elf's wrist and prevented him from drawing the weapon.

Sadira tugged on the empty sheath at her waist. "Have you ever seen a knife in my belt?" she asked. "I lost my dagger before I helped the Sun Runners get across the Canyon of Guthay. If I killed your brother, what did I use?"

"You're a sorceress," countered the elf. "You could have used magic."

"True, but that looks like a knife wound to me," said Rhayn, stepping out of the stairway. "Why do you insist on blaming Sadira?"

"Sadira?" Huyar repeated, confused. "What are you talking about?"

"Our guest," Rhayn explained. "Just before we captured her, Magnus overheard her talking to a boy from the Veiled Alliance. Her real name is Sadira—Sadira of Tyr."

Sadira cursed under her breath. She knew Rhayn was trying to keep Huyar off-balance and save her life, but the sorceress would have preferred it to be done without revealing her identity to the rest of the tribe.

Huyar stared at Sadira in shock, and a buzz of astonishment ran through the warriors gathered behind him. "You are Faenaeyon's daughter—the one who killed Kalak?"

"I am the daughter of Barakah of Tyr and your chief," Sadira allowed, glancing pensively at her slumbering father. "Though, after abandoning me into slavery, I'm not certain Faenaeyon has the right to claim me as daughter."

"What Faenaeyon claims is his," Huyar answered. "But that gives me no cause to believe you. Perhaps your friend from the Veiled Alliance had a dagger."

Back in Tyr, no Templar of the King's Justice would have accepted the elf's logic, but it was becoming increasingly clear to the sorceress that Huyar was not looking for the truth so much as a scapegoat.

"I didn't kill your brother, but I can see there's no use telling you that," Sadira said, slipping a hand into her satchel. "So attack me now, or let the matter drop."

"I'm no fool," Huyar said, casting an uneasy glance toward the sorceress's concealed hand. "But I won't let my brother's death go unavenged."

"No one's asking you to," said Rhayn. "But it's not for you to say who should be punished. Faenaeyon is chief—or have you forgotten?"

"I have not forgotten," Huyar said. He motioned at one of the elves standing over Gaefal's dead body. "Wake the chief, Jeila."

The warrior, a woman with tangled brown hair and three bone rings piercing one nostril, scowled at Huyar's back. Nevertheless, she went to the chief's side and, placing a cautionary hand over his dagger hilt, shook him by the shoulders. "Faenaeyon," she said softly. "We need you."

The chief uttered an indignant growl, and his eyelids rose to reveal a pair of glazed pupils. He struggled to focus on the woman's face, and for a moment it appeared he might overcome his stupor. Then he let out a loud groan, as though in terrible pain, and his pointed chin dropped back to his chest. His glassy eyes remained open and vacant.

"He's still drunk," Jeila reported.

Huyar shook his head and went to his father's side. "I don't think so," he said, placing a hand under the chief's shirt.

"Is he dead?" asked another warrior.

"No, but he's sick. His heart barely beats, and his skin is as cold as night," Huyar answered. Taking his hand away from his father, the elf looked at Sadira. "I wonder how many other tragedies your return to the Sun Runners will bring?"

"I'm not responsible for Faenaeyon's gluttony, if that's what you mean," Sadira retorted. "He stole the wine from me—or have you forgotten?"

"Huyar, say what you mean or be quiet," added Rhayn. "Only a coward implies what he is afraid to speak outright."

"She's right," agreed Magnus. "Sadira is Faenaeyon's guest, and you'd do well to remember that."

At first, Sadira thought the two were defending her because of the help she had provided, but a better explanation occurred to her. They were trying to undercut Huyar's influence with the rest of the tribe, so that it would be easier for Rhayn to maneuver herself into position as the new chief.

After glaring at Rhayn for a time, Huyar hissed, "I'm no coward. As for Faenaeyon's 'guest,' she has cast an enchantment on him."

"For what purpose, Huyar?" Sadira demanded, taking her defense into her own hands.

Huyar came toward her and did not stop until he was within a few inches of her face. "Yesterday, did you not tell me that you had reasons of your own for returning to us?"

"I said that," Sadira conceded.

"I think you came back to enchant Faenaeyon," Huyar concluded. "To force us to take you to the Pristine Tower."

Rhayn cast a sidelong glance at the chief's torpid form. "Whatever's wrong with Faenaeyon, he isn't enchanted," she said. "If you had any sense, you'd know that."

"What would you know?" countered the warrior. "You're no more than a trickster."

"I'm skilled enough to put you into your place," spat Rhayn. "Not that I'd need magic to do it."

Huyar stepped toward his long-sister, fists clenched in rage. Magnus slipped between the two, conveniently preventing Rhayn from having to make good on her threat. "We're members of the same tribe!" he growled. "Act like it."

Though Magnus pretended to be speaking to both of them, his black eyes were turned only toward Huyar.

Before Huyar could respond, a young warrior rushed into the chamber from the room above. "Templars are coming!"

Huyar motioned at the warriors standing by Gaefal's body. "Stall them, and see to the kanks," he said. As they rushed down the stairs, the elf looked to Sadira and snarled, "It wouldn't surprise me to learn you've brought this upon us, too."

"We should be getting the tribe out of this tower, not worrying about why the templars are here," Rhayn said, rushing up the stairway. "Let's go."

Huyar threw his brother's body over his shoulder, then ran up the stairs after her.

"Where are they going?" Sadira asked. "We'll be trapped."

Magnus shook his head. "Elves can always run," he said, starting to follow the other two Sun Runners.

"Wait!" Jeila called. "I can't get Faenaeyon to stand. We'll have to carry—"

A resonant thump shook the tower, interrupting the woman in midsentence. The noise was followed by a moment of eerie silence, then the cries of injured elves began to ring out from the floor below. Magnus rushed for the stairway.

"I'll see if I can help," he said. "Take Faenaeyon up to the others."

The windsinger had barely reached the threshold when the hum of a dozen bowstrings sounded from the stairs below. Magnus threw an arm up to protect his eyes, then grunted as a flight of arrows ticked into his thick hide. To Sadira's surprise, he did not fall. Instead, he slapped the shafts off his body, screaming madly—as a normal man might after being stung by a swarm of wasps.

The sorceress went to Jeila's side and slung one of Faenaeyon's arms over her shoulder. As they dragged the chief's limp form across the floor, the windsinger roared in anger. Sadira saw the tip of an agafari spear glance off his knobby elbow, then he plucked a shrieking templar off the floor and hurled her down the stairway. She crashed into a file of women that had been following close behind, and they all went tumbling down the steps. Magnus opened his great mouth and began a deep-toned ballad of war, making Sadira's heart pound and stirring the bloodlust in her spirit.

A deafening blast silenced the windsinger, sending his huge form sailing into the air. He crashed into the opposite side of the chamber and slammed his skull into the wall, then dropped to the floor amid a clatter of loosened stones. Despite the charred circle in the middle of his chest, Magnus shook his head to clear it, then braced his massive arms by his sides. Gathering his legs beneath him, he slowly pushed himself upward.

The windsinger was about halfway to his feet when his knees buckled. He crashed back to the floor and did not move, his chin resting on his chest and the black in his eyes fading to gray.

Once again, Nibenese voices and the slap of sandals on stone echoed from the stairway. Jeila slipped Faenaeyon's arm off her shoulder. "Come," she said, pulling the steel dirk from the chief's belt. "We must give the tribe time to escape." She handed her own dagger, made of simple bone, to the sorceress.

Sadira let the dagger drop to the floor. "Hold them for just a moment," she said, reaching for her spell ingredients. "I have a better way."

Jeila nodded and leaped to the stairway. She dodged a wild slash from the first templar's obsidian sword, then sliced open the arm holding it. The elf kicked her attacker back into the stairwell and, with her free hand, snatched up the falling sword.

As Jeila fought against the next pair of templars, Sadira shaped a lump of clear paraffin into a small cube. After summoning the energy for a spell, she tossed the wax over Jeila's shoulder and spoke her incantation. The paraffin burst into a fine mist and spread through the entire stairwell. An instant later, it congealed into a transparent gel and engulfed the templars.

The Nibenese women tried in vain to free themselves,

their arms and legs straining against the viscous mass in slow motion. Jeila stepped away and watched in amusement as the templars' faces turned purple with suffocation.

Wasting no time on such frivolities, Sadira went to Magnus's side and cast another spell. When the massive windsinger rose off the floor, she took him by the arm and tugged him to the stairway.

As she started up the steps, Sadira called, "Jeila, bring Faenaeyon, and hurry! That plug won't stop our enemies forever."

The elf slipped the dagger and sword into her belt, then grabbed the heavy chief under the shoulders and dragged him after Sadira. By the time they had ascended halfway up the stairway, both women were out of breath. Even though Magnus was floating in the air, it was no easy matter for a woman of Sadira's size to pull that much bulk up the steep pitch.

As they neared the top of the stairs, they heard a confused babble of elven voices coming from the room above. Jeila stopped and looked toward the noise. "Half the tribe should be gone by now," she panted. "Something's wrong."

"We won't find out what until we get there," Sadira gasped, continuing to climb.

As Jeila moved to follow, the clatter of claws on stone came from the bottom of the stairwell. Summoning the last of her strength, Sadira dragged Magnus upward at a run.

Jeila did not follow. Instead, she laid Faenaeyon down and began to descend. "I'll hold them below. You get help and come back for Faenaeyon," she said, drawing her sword and dagger.

"No!" Sadira yelled, stopping on the highest step. "It

doesn't sound like templars."

Her warning came too late. Dhojakt's head peered around the bend. Sadira's jaw fell open in astonishment, for he was covered with sticky slime from the crown of his black skull-cap to the bottom of his round chin. From the looks of it, he had forced his way through her magical mire with his strength alone—something not even a giant could have done.

Sadira shoved Magnus over the threshold, then began preparations for another spell. At the same time, Jeila launched herself at Dhojakt, slashing her sword at his neck and thrusting her dagger at his dark eyes.

The prince did not even bother to block the attacks. Instead, he simply turned his face away from the dagger and allowed the sword to strike his neck. Without causing even the tiniest wound in Dhojakt's skin, the obsidian blade shattered into dozens of chips. The steel dagger fared little better, glancing off his cheekbone and opening a small scratch beneath the eye.

Jeila landed just ahead of the prince, her eyes wide as saucers. She raised the dagger to attack again, but Dhojakt's arm shot out and three of his thin fingers pierced her throat. The dirk slipped from her grasp and she clutched at the prince's arm. He casually tossed the elf over his shoulder and scurried up the stairs.

As Dhojakt clattered over Faenaeyon's unconscious form, Sadira tossed a tube of carved wood onto the steps. She spoke a string of mystical words. With a sonorous rumble, the stairwell stretched to an impossible length. Suddenly the prince and her father were so far away they could barely be seen.

The sorceress turned away, already listening to the distant tick of Dhojakt's claws growing louder in the magical tunnel. She had delayed the prince for the time being, but Sadira knew it would be all too soon when he—and any of the templars who had followed him through her first trap—were upon her again.

The sorceress stepped onto the third story, where the stairwell opened into a round chamber. At one time, the room may have been divided into smaller compartments, for the stone baseplates of long-vanished walls still traversed the floor in various locations. Now it was a single large garret, littered with pottery shards, scraps of hemp cloth, and the bones of small animals.

The Sun Runners had tied a half-dozen ropes to the ceiling beams, but had not yet thrown the lines out the tower windows. Instead, the warriors were firing arrows at someone below. Sadira found Rhayn and Huyar standing together, on opposite sides of a doorway opening onto empty air. A pair of stone buttresses were all that remained of the balcony that had once hung outside.

As she approached, Sadira said, "Let's go! Dhojakt is less than a minute behind me."

"You first," said Huyar, waving Sadira ahead.

The sorceress peered outside and found herself looking down upon the avenue that bordered the outside wall of the Elven Market. Standing in the street directly below the tower was a company of Nibenese half-giants. To defend themselves from the Sun Runners' arrows, they were holding their wooden shields over their heads in a makeshift roof.

Sadira pulled a handful of powdered sulfur from her satchel. "Tell your warriors to put their bows away and drop their lines on my command," she said. "And have someone bring Magnus. I'll clear the way for our escape."

As Rhayn passed the instructions along, the sorceress turned to Huyar. "I need some water."

The elf ignored her and searched the room with a frown on his face. "What happened to Jeila and Faenaeyon?"

"Jeila's dead, and Faenaeyon's with the Nibenese."

Huyar clamped a hand over Sadira's arm. "You won't save yourself that way," he growled. "You're not leaving until Faenaeyon is safe."

"You left him downstairs, not me. I'm the one who tried to help him," Sadira said, jerking her arm away from the warrior. "And if you don't get me the water I need, I'll leave the Sun Runners here to face Dhojakt's wrath. It'd be easier if I didn't have to save your whole tribe as well as myself."

Huyar glared at her for a moment, then spun around and grabbed a skin from a nearby warrior. Sadira opened her hands and instructed him to pour water over the sulfur. When the powder had turned into yellowish muck, she flung it out the window and spoke the words of her spell.

Instead of falling to the ground, the mudball hung motionless in the air. A cloud of yellow mist began to form, spreading steadily outward. From the street below came the concerned murmurs of half-giants, along with their commanders' exhortations to stand firm. Sadira allowed the cloud to expand until it covered the entire company.

Rhayn came over, two huge satchels slung over her back and dragging Magnus's floating form behind her. "Hurry! Dhojakt's coming—with a company of templars behind him."

"Storm!" Sadira said, waving her hand outside.

With a peal of thunder and a flash of golden lightning, the cloud burst open. Fire rained down on the half-giants in a deluge of flame. The shields covering their heads dissolved into shrouds of fume, and in the next instant the air was heavy with the rancorous smell of burning flesh. The half-giants stumbled away, their bodies trailing smoke and their death screams ringing through the streets like howling wind.

Sadira waited an instant for the firestorm to die down, then yelled, "Drop your lines!"

A half-dozen ropes sailed out the windows. Almost before the ends hit the cobblestones, the first elves were dropping to the street below. Sadira moved toward the line dangling from the balcony door, but Huyar pushed her back.

"Not before the last Sun Runner has gone," he snapped, waving forward a powerful woman with a heavily lined brow.

Rather than hold things up by fighting over the matter, the sorceress stepped over to wait with Rhayn. Already, half of the tribe had left the chamber, carrying their personal satchels on their backs. Nevertheless, thinking it wise to be prepared for Dhojakt, Sadira scooped a handful of grit off the floor and prepared another spell.

Once that was done, Sadira looked across Magnus's body and asked, "Do you rehearse these sorts of escapes often?"

Rhayn shook her head, keeping a careful eye on the stairwell. "We never practice," she said. "We do this so often that there's no need."

Sadira heard Dhojakt's legs rattling. She cried out her incantation and threw the grit in her hand at the sound. A furious sandstorm rose at the mouth of the stairwell, blowing down the dark hole with such fury that the entire tower trembled. Although it was impossible to hear anyone screaming above the wind, the sorceress knew that those trapped in the squall's fury would be crying out in agony as the flesh was scoured from their bones by the abrasive, whirling sand.

"That should stop him!" Rhayn yelled.

The elf had barely spoken when Dhojakt stepped from the stairwell. The prince's expression showed no sign that he felt the sand raking over his skin. He held his body perfectly upright, as though the ferocious wind were no more than a breeze to him.

Sadira looked toward the ropes and saw that there were still several elves waiting to descend each of them. Even if she were able to push her way into line, she would never be able to reach the street before Dhojakt was once again upon her.

The prince's black eyes searched the room for a moment, then came to rest on the sorceress. When he moved toward her, a pair of elven warriors stepped to block his path—not so much for Sadira's benefit, she was sure, as to protect Huyar and the other elves who still had not descended the rope.

The warriors swung their bone swords, striking Dhojakt so hard that, even over the roar of Sadira's magical wind, the thud of their blows was audible. The blade of one weapon snapped at the hilt and went skittering across the floor, while the other bounced off as though it had struck stone.

The prince did not even slow down. Stepping between the two elves, he finished one with a punch to the heart, sinking his hand fist-deep into the warrior's chest. The other he killed more artfully, reaching up behind the tall elf's back and snaking a hand around to grab his chin. With a quick jerk of his arm, Dhojakt snapped his victim's neck, then threw the body aside and continued inexorably toward Sadira.

"Let *go*, Rhayn!" the sorceress yelled, taking Magnus's wrist and pulling the windsinger toward the doorway.

"Unless you want to learn to fly."

"I'll take my chances with you!" Rhayn answered, casting a frightened glance at Dhojakt.

Huyar and the other elves in front of the door scattered before Magnus's bulk. Sadira and Rhayn pushed the windsinger out of the tower, throwing themselves onto his immense chest. At first, they dropped rapidly, but their descent slowed after a few feet, and they sank toward the scorched street more or less under control.

"Just hold tight," Sadira advised. "We're going to be fine."

"I don't think so," Rhayn answered, looking toward the tower.

Sadira craned her neck and, to her dismay, saw that she and Rhayn were descending more slowly than the elves on the ropes. Already, Huyar had jumped onto a line and descended farther than they had.

That was not what concerned Rhayn most, however. Dhojakt stood in the doorway of the balcony, pointing a slender finger in their direction. He held his other hand turned palm down, and Sadira could barely make out the shimmer of magical energy rising into his body.

"No!" she cried. "Don't tell me he's a sorcerer!"

Rhayn had no chance to reply. Dhojakt uttered his incantation, then the magic Sadira had used to levitate Magnus failed. The windsinger plunged to the street below, with Sadira and Rhayn still clinging desperately to his arms.

Magnus crashed into the charred body of a dead half-giant. The sorceress heard the staccato cracking of the guard's ribs, then a brutal jolt rocked every bone in her body. The air left her lungs in an agonized scream, and her mind went numb with shock. She felt herself bounce off the windsinger, but barely noticed as she dropped back to the cobblestones at his side. There was a sick, mordant smell, a spray of black ash, and an explosion of unimaginable agony.

Sadira did not lose consciousness. She remained alert enough to see a pair of fleeing elves stoop to gather up Rhayn's form. Several more paused to grab Magnus and drag the heavy windsinger to safety. The task of helping the sorceress fell to one of the last stragglers, a pregnant elf with green eyes.

As she tried to lift Sadira, the woman gasped in pain and clutched at her swollen abdomen. "I can't lift you," she said, grasping the sorceress's wrists. "Maybe I can drag—"

"Go on," Sadira said, shaking her head. The sorceress knew that if she could not stand by herself, the pregnant elf would be risking her life with little chance of saving Sadira's. "I'll be fine."

The woman did not need to be told twice. Without saying anything more, she turned and ran out of sight.

Sadira pushed herself up to her knees. Her entire body protested in torment, but she did not stop. The sorceress gathered her legs beneath herself and rose to her feet. For a moment, Sadira actually remained upright.

Then a terrible burning ran through her legs, as though her veins were filled with fire instead of blood. She lost control of her muscles and collapsed back to the cobblestones.

Sadira did not allow herself even a moment of self-pity. Instead, she immediately resorted to pulling herself across the street with her hands alone. She did not dare look back, for fear that she would see Dhojakt swooping down like some bird of prey to snatch her away.

A few feet later, it was clear to the sorceress that she would never escape this way. Her only hope was to cast another enchantment and hope Dhojakt did not dispel it, too. The sorceress reached for her bag.

A sandaled foot pinned her arm to the street. "There's no time for that," said a familiar voice.

The sorceress looked up and saw Raka's boyish face bending over her. Though one side of his jaw was mottled with the scabs of a day-old burn, he looked more or less the same as he had when she last saw him.

"You escaped!" Sadira gasped, delighted.

"Yesterday, at least," the youth said, grabbing her under the arms. "Today, we may not be so lucky."

Sadira followed his gaze to the tower. Dhojakt was coming down the wall headfirst, easily clinging to the rocky cracks with the sharp claws of his two dozen legs.

The sight brought new vigor to the sorceress's legs. She managed to push herself up high enough to slip an arm over Raka's shoulder. The youth led her into one of the narrow lanes down which the Sun Runners had fled. Instead of following the elves deeper into the city, however, he ducked into the doorway of a half-collapsed hovel.

"What are you doing?" the sorceress asked.

"My master sent something along to hide us from the prince," he answered, pulling a small ceramic plate from his purse. "This will put him off our scent for a while and give us a chance to escape."

"Then you were looking for me," Sadira surmised. "I guess it makes sense that this is no chance meeting."

"Correct," Raka answered, laying the plate on the floor. "After you disappeared from Sage's Square, we set a watch on the gates of the Forbidden Palace. When Dhojakt left this morning with a company of templars and another of half-giants, we knew we'd find you by following him."

"Then the Alliance will help me?" Sadira asked hopefully.

"As much as we are able," Raka answered. He passed his hand over the plate and whispered a command word. The disk melted into the ground and faded from sight. "But not as much as you would like. We cannot take you to the Pristine Tower."

"Why not?" Sadira asked.

Raka took her arm and guided her through the ruins of the hovel. "Because we don't know where it is," he answered. "From what my master can learn, only the elves have visited it—and even then, just the most courageous have dared to attempt the journey. There might be no more than a dozen warriors in the Elven Market who know where to go. We'll try to help you find one, but time is running short. We've learned that the northern cities sent their levies to the Dragon many weeks ago, while the Oba of Gulg is gathering her slaves even as we speak. My master believes this means—"

"That the Dragon is going from north to south," Sadira surmised. "Tyr is after Gulg, leaving Balic for last."

Raka nodded, then helped the sorceress climb through the hovel's back wall. "You have perhaps three weeks left to stop him."

"Then I can't waste time searching for a guide," Sadira said, looking toward the tower where her father had been captured. "But I do know someone who can take me there—provided you'll help me get him back from the prince."

"We'll do our best," Raka promised.

The muffled rattle of Dhojakt's feet echoed through the hovel. Raka smiled and held his hand to his lips. An instant later, an enormous hiss sounded from the other side of the shack and a spray of green sparkles shot into the sky. Dhojakt roared in anger, then such a terrible stench filled the air that Sadira could not keep from retching.

"There," said Raka. "Now you'll be safe—at least long enough to leave this part of the city."

TWELVE

The Emporium

They found Faenaeyon crammed into a stall at the back of the emporium. He sat with his knees pulled to his chest, staring blankly at the cracked flagstones of the floor. One hand incessantly searched along his belt for his missing purses, and his haggard face was twisted into a scowl. With a long line of drool dripping from his pointed chin, he mumbled incoherent phrases and seemed completely oblivious to what was happening around him.

Clearly, the elf was in no shape to attempt escape, but the emporium agents had restrained him the same way as every other slave in the market. Around his neck, the chief wore a collar of coarse black rope. Spliced into this was a cord running a few feet back to the wall, where the other end was attached to a bone ring set between the stone blocks. From her own days in bondage, when she had slept with a similar rope around her neck, Sadira knew that even Magnus could not have snapped it. Nor could the line be easily cut, for it was braided from the hair of giants. The resulting cord was so tough and resilient that even steel blades would be dulled on it.

"I hope you're alert enough to know how being tethered feels," Sadira whispered, looking away from her father's pen.

Even had he been lucid, the sorceress doubted that her father would have recognized her. She had used henna root to dye her hair swarthy red, the bark of an ashbush to darken her skin, and black kohl to decorate her eyelids. She had also exchanged her customary blue smock for a green sarami.

As Sadira and Raka moved down the aisle, she paused several times in front of other slaves, as though evaluating their suitability for her home. The Slave Emporium of the Shom Merchant House was larger and more crowded than any Sadira had ever seen. It was a single cavernous gallery, lit by huge windows and buzzing with the drone of hundreds of bickering buyers and sales agents. The chamber's ceiling was high and shadowy, supported by hundreds of double-stacked arches and marble columns. These pillars were almost hidden beneath lush climbing vines loaded with aromatic blossoms.

Beneath each row of arches ran a wide aisle, flanked on either side by stalls barely large enough to hold the men and women lying in them. Along the back of the pens stood the high brick walls to which the slave ropes were attached.

As they reached the end of the aisle, Raka asked, "Is that the elf you seek?"

Sadira nodded, then led the way around a pillar so entwined with vines that its stone surface was not visible. "I saw no sign of templars or royal guards," she said.

"Nevertheless, they are here," the youth answered. "One of our agents tried to buy him this morning, but the price was outrageous. House Shom does not wish to sell this particular elf—no doubt because Dhojakt has concluded that he is your guide. The prince is using him as bait."

They passed a bony old man watering the gallery's vines from a huge bucket. He kept his eyes focused on his work, paying no attention to pleas for water coming from his fellow slaves.

"You're right, of course," Sadira answered, casting a wary eye toward the crowd ahead. For all she knew, half the sarami-clad women in it were templars, and the agents wearing the tabards of House Shom could just as readily have been royal guards. "It'd be too simple if all we had to do was buy him back."

They made their way up the aisle, to where Magnus and Huyar were studying the gangling arms and square heads of two tareks. Though the windsinger had used his magic to heal the injury he had suffered during yesterday's battle, he seemed tired and could not quite keep his massive body from swaying as he stood waiting. He wore a dark burnoose with the hood pulled over his head. The robe did little to hide his immense size, but at least it concealed the burn marks on his chest.

"Did you find him?" asked Huyar, who had not bothered with a disguise. If Dhojakt's agents were present, they would not be able to tell him from a warrior of any other tribe. "Has he recovered from his stupor?"

"We found him, but he's still sick," Sadira said. "Our agreement stands?"

"Of course," the elf answered. "Provided Faenaeyon returns to his senses and tells us where to find the Pristine Tower."

Sadira did not expect Huyar to keep his word, of course. The warrior would say anything to recover his father, but she knew he would not absolve her of Gaefal's death so easily. The sorceress was also keenly aware that once Faenaeyon returned to the tribe and was given the antidote, the final decision about going to the tower would rest in his hands.

Still, Huyar's promise and the fact that Sadira was the one who had rescued him could only help persuade the chief to take her to the Pristine Tower. He could still refuse—but the sorceress would deal with that possibility when it occurred. For now, what was important was rescuing the elf.

Sadira was more worried about the motives of Rhayn and Magnus for helping her. They were both cunning enough to realize that she intended to use the antidote to clear the chief's mind, yet they had agreed to her bargain as readily as anyone else. Perhaps, as Rhayn had claimed all along, they had no wish to see Faenaeyon come to any physical harm. Or perhaps they had a different scheme— such as using the wine they had secreted away to poison him again.

Whatever their plan, the sorceress did not want to concern herself with it. As long as the Sun Runners took her to the Pristine Tower, she did not care what happened to Faenaeyon—at least that was what she told herself.

Sadira turned to Raka. "The Alliance is ready to help?"

Before the youth could answer, a tremendous crash sounded from the other end of the emporium. Terrified screams echoed down the aisles. When Sadira looked toward the noise, she saw a plume of dust rising from a pile of debris that had once been an arch. Next to it stood the stump of a marble pillar, its clinging vines still smoking from the effects of a fire-based spell.

Raka smiled at Sadira. "The Alliance is already testing our enemy's response."

The gallery filled with alarmed cries and more than a few buyers moved to leave. A handful of Shom agents joined the stream, ignoring the pleas of the slaves they were leaving behind. Most vendors, however, remained at their posts, reassuring their shocked customers that it was much wiser to remain where they were and finish the deal. Those with exceptionally nervous patrons even managed to turn the event into a negotiating advantage, grabbing the arms of their frightened clients and making it clear they would not let go until a bargain had been struck.

A handful of guards bearing shields with House Shom's triple dragonfly rushed toward the collapsed arch, but no one else. "If Dhojakt's templars are here, they aren't showing themselves," Raka observed. "Tell me when you're ready for the next move."

Sadira looked to Huyar. "After today, I suspect House Shom will want to avenge itself on Faenaeyon's tribe," she said. "I hope you're right about how easy it will be to recover your kanks and leave the city."

"I didn't say they would be our own kanks we recovered," he answered. "As for leaving the city, our warriors should have left at dawn. When we meet Rhayn, she'll tell us where the tribe is gathering." He gave Magnus a spiteful glance, then added, "Unless she decided it would be easier to name herself chief by abandoning us here."

The windsinger scowled. "You know better," he snapped. "Faenaeyon's warriors would never stand for such a thing."

"Go on, Huyar," Sadira said, motioning him toward the door.

The elf did not obey. "I should stay with you," he said. "Faenaeyon is my father—"

"Someone must wait at the door, to keep a watch in

case Dhojakt is setting up an ambush outside," Sadira said. "And only an elf will look natural loitering out there. They'll think you're trying to pick pockets."

"If you insist," Huyar agreed. "But I warn you, if something happens to Faenaeyon—"

"He'll be no worse off than now," Magnus snapped, shoving the elf toward the exit.

Huyar glared at the windsinger, then turned and stalked off.

Raka left next, saying, "When you hear thunder, you'll know we've attacked. Wait a few moments after that before freeing your elf. Meet me in Sage's Square at first light, and I'll sneak you all out of the city."

After the youth disappeared around the corner, Magnus and Sadira lingered in front of the tareks, waiting for the diversion to begin. Soon, the sorceress noticed a house agent moving toward them. She signaled their disinterest in bargaining by taking Magnus's arm and guiding him up the aisle. "While we're waiting for Raka, answer a question I've been curious about."

"If it's in my power," the windsinger promised.

"Why are you so close to Rhayn?" Sadira asked. "If I didn't know better, I'd say you're in love with her."

"Do you think I can't love because I'm of the New Races?" the windsinger demanded, an angry glimmer in his black eyes.

"I don't doubt you can," Sadira answered. "It was Rhayn I referred to. Elves are the ones who can't love."

Magnus flattened his ears. "Why would you think that?"

"Look at Faenaeyon," Sadira said. "My mother loved him until she died, yet he abandoned her into slavery."

"You're confusing love with responsibility," Magnus said.

"They're the same," Sadira objected. "When I love a man, I care about what happens to him."

"Care, perhaps," the windsinger allowed. "But you don't trap him by taking over his life. When elves love, they do it freely—with no obligations and no promises. That way, everyone can do as he chooses."

"My mother did not choose bondage!" Sadira hissed.

"She didn't choose freedom, either," the windsinger countered. "She could have escaped—or died trying."

"She had a child to think of!" the sorceress growled.

"Which explains why she chose to stay," Magnus replied. "You can't blame Faenaeyon for that. He may have loved your mother as much as he ever loved anyone—but that doesn't mean he could have taken her with him."

A deafening boom shook the emporium, then echoed through the gallery like a peal of thunder. Hundreds of bats dropped from their hiding places among the ceiling rafters and swooped toward the windows in black streams, their screeches barely distinguishable from the astonished cries of the throng below. Before the first of the swarm had reached its goal, the air began to sizzle and roar with the sound of a dozen different spells all being cast at once. Bolts of light and sprays of orange flame erupted from the main entrance, blasting pillars into bits and washing down the aisles in fiery torrents.

"Death to the slave merchants!" cried a man's angry voice.

"Death to the slave buyers!" added a woman.

Panicked screeches and cries of terror rang through the gallery. Frightened agents and buyers rushed toward Sadira and Magnus in a mad tide, those in the rear trampling those in the front. From behind them blared a clap of thunder, and, for the briefest moment, their pumping legs were silhouetted by white light. In the next instant, a swath of singed bodies fell to the floor, leaving a long, smoking furrow in the center of the crowd. At the other end stood a veiled sorcerer, the tips of his fingers glowing pinkish white.

"Slaves, rise against your masters!" cried Raka's voice, The young sorcerer spread the fingers of his hand as he prepared another spell. "The time has come to free your-selves!"

In response to the youth's cry, many slaves tried to slip their black collars over their heads, and others tugged at the greasy ropes securing them to the walls. When they could not work themselves free, Raka created a shimmer-ing sword of golden energy and began cutting their bonds. These people immediately launched themselves at those who had imprisoned them, wrapping the ends of their slave lines around the throats of nearby merchants.

The traders who escaped the angry slaves only ran faster. Magnus placed his bulk in the center of the aisle, forcing the mob to part and flow around him. Pressing herself against the windsinger's back, Sadira yelled, "Quite the diversion!"

"I should have known they'd do something like this," the windsinger answered. "The Nibenese Alliance will use any excuse to attack slave traders."

Sadira heard the agonized scream of a Shom agent who had just run past her. She spun around and saw a stolen dagger in the hands of the bony slave who had been wa-tering vines earlier. He was using the weapon to hack at the agent's flabby neck.

As the fat man fell, the slave raised his blade and rushed Sadira. The sorceress sidestepped his clumsy charge, throwing her foot out to catch his ankle and bringing the back of her fist down between his shoulder blades. The old man fell to the floor, then Sadira planted a foot on the wrist of his weapon arm. She reached down and pulled the dirk from his hand.

"Not bad," Magnus said.

"Rikus taught me," she replied, stepping away with the knife in her hand.

The man rolled over, cringing and covering his head. A terrified eye, yellow with jaundice, peered out from the crook of his elbow, but the slave did not cry out or beg for mercy.

"We're on your side," Sadira said.

The sorceress reached down and pulled the old man to his feet, then looked around to see if Dhojakt's followers had shown themselves. Here and there, a few women were calmly watching the revolt from the safety of an empty slave pen, but they had not yet done anything to reveal themselves as templars. Sadira thrust the dagger into the slave's hand, then pushed him toward the exit. "You don't have much time. Make good use of it."

The slave's toothless mouth fell open. He gave Sadira a quick bow, then turned to lash out at a woman wearing a silk sarami and a copper bracelet. A long arc of blood shot from the wound, spattering Magnus's knobby face.

Wiping the sticky fluid away from his eye, Magnus asked, "Did you have to return the knife?"

"If you'd ever been a slave, you wouldn't ask that question," Sadira said.

Without waiting for a reply, she took the windsinger by the arm and led him down the aisle. Behind them, the sounds of battle grew louder and more tumultuous.

When they neared the pillar at the end, a pair of Nibenese templars rushed around the corner, throwing off their saramis and calling upon their sorcerer-king for magic. They stopped two paces into the corridor, and one dropped something on the floor. There was a small pop and the smell of sulfur came to Sadira's nose.

A tiny sphere of fire appeared on the ground, quickly growing to the size of a kank. The woman threw her palms out before her as though pushing the flaming ball. It rolled down the aisle, picking up speed and size with each revolution. As the fiery globe passed, it left nothing behind save blackened vines, charred bodies, and scorched flagstones.

Sadira reached into the satchel containing her spell components, but Magnus caught her hand. "No," he whispered. "We're here to get Faenaeyon—not to kill templars."

The sorceress withdrew her hand, then watched as the two women walked past, following their ball down the corridor. Though her every instinct cried out for her to jump into the battle, she knew the windsinger was right.

About halfway down the corridor, the ball exploded into a fiery spray, then vanished in a puff of black smoke. Blocking the aisle stood a transparent wall of force, and through its shimmering surface Sadira could see Raka turning to flee.

"I think the time's come to get Faenaeyon," Sadira said.

As she spoke, the second templar flung her hand at the arch above Raka's head. A blue stone streaked from the woman's hand and struck the span squarely in the center. The stones vanished in a cascade of sparks, then the ceiling collapsed, showering the aisle below with stone debris.

Magnus shook his head and looked away. "What a waste," he commented sadly. "Now how will we find our way out of the city?"

"Perhaps the Alliance will send someone else," Sadira said, watching as a pair of slaves fell to their knees and began clawing at the rubble. "Besides, Raka might still be alive."

The windsinger shook his head. "How can you think that?"

The sorceress pointed at the digging slaves. "Perhaps they see something we can't."

Sadira considered taking the time to defend the slaves, but noticed that the young sorcerer's quivering force barrier still stood. It would prevent the templars from advancing any farther, at least for a short time.

"Let's get what we came for," Magnus said, pulling the sorceress around the corner.

Here, the situation was even more confused than where they had just come from. Dozens of men and women dressed in silken saramis cowered in the center of the aisle, just out of the reach of the poor wretches still bound to the wall. Scattered among the stalls were the bodies of those who had not been so careful, buyers and merchants with puffy, purple-tinged faces, swollen blue lips, and glazed eyes rolled back in their sockets. Often, the greasy cords that had strangled them were still looped tight around their necks, with the dazed, expressionless faces of their executioners hovering above their shoulders.

Halfway down the aisle, a magical rampart of golden light blocked the corridor. A dozen men carrying shields with House Shom's insignia stood before the barrier, waiting for three bare-breasted templars to dispel the wall. Through the shimmering barricade, Sadira could see the form of an elderly sorcerer staggering toward the exit.

Magnus went to Faenaeyon's stall and grabbed the slave's line. The windsinger gave the cord a mighty jerk, but neither the black line nor the stone ring holding it gave way. He pulled the rope taut, then opened his mouth and struck a deep, rumbling note that made the floor quiver. Where the stone ring was attached, the wall shuddered visibly, and the sorceress expected the bricks to shatter at any moment.

Down the aisle, the templars and guards turned at the sound of Magnus's voice. Seeing what was about to happen, they abandoned their pursuit of the sorcerer and charged toward Faenaeyon.

Sadira quickly summoned the energy for a spell. "Magnus, hurry!"

The windsinger glanced down the aisle, then twisted his lumpy lips into a scowl and stopped singing. Still holding the slave line with one hand, he formed the other into a massive fist and smashed it into the wall.

The bricks disintegrated into a spray of jagged shards, and the ring popped free. Magnus threw Faenaeyon over his shoulder, then groaned in pain and shook the fist he had used to smash the wall. Sadira waved him toward the next aisle and followed after him, moving backwards so she could keep a watch on the approaching Nibenese.

The guards were swinging their curved blades to and fro, frantically trying to clear a path through the men and women cowering before them. They succeeded only in filling the aisle with mutilated pedestrians too stunned and frightened to crawl out of the way.

One of the templars stopped and called upon her king's magic. A glowing red stone streaked from her hand, striking Magnus square in the back. The rock glanced off his hide, taking with it a swath of skin and filling the air with the stench of scorched leather. The windsinger crashed to the floor in a bellowing heap, sending Faenaeyon rolling toward the emporium's back wall.

"Magnus!" Sadira screamed. "Get up!"

He did not answer, but the sorceress did not dare take her eyes off her enemies long enough to look in his direction. Instead, as a second templar pointed a long-nailed finger at her, Sadira flung a tiny shard of crystal high into the air and whispered her incantation.

After reaching the top of its arc, the shard did not fall. Instead, it hovered in the air for an instant, then exploded into a glittering disk of solid crystal. Though Sadira knew the wafer to be no thicker than a finger, that was impossible to tell by looking at it. The circle seemed infinitely deep, and filled with sheets of gemlike color: emerald, amethyst, even flashes of diamond.

When the templar's spell struck the other side, it flared white, then divided into dazzling waves of yellow, red, and blue. Each blast of color shot off in a different direction, then quickly slowed to a stop and hung trapped within the radiant depths of the disk.

The sorceress traced a circle in the air. Spinning in a crazy maelstrom of color, the crystal flew down the corridor, absorbing everything it touched. Within moments, it was filled with the distorted, inert figures of those who had been standing in the aisle: slave buyers, house agents, guards, and the three Nibenese templars.

Sadira turned toward Magnus and saw the windsinger struggling to his knees, but, as she moved to help him, something came scraping over the wall to which Faenaeyon had been attached. She spun around and saw Dhojakt's figure appearing at the top, his eyes burning with a hateful gleam.

Sadira began summoning the energy for another spell. At the same time, Dhojakt motioned at the floor upon which she stood, closing his fist and raising it upward as if drawing something from the earth. With a series of sharp bangs, the flagstones beneath her feet cracked apart and a gaping hole opened. The sorceress cried out in alarm and stepped away, still holding her palm downward.

A cilops crawled from the fissure, swinging its oval head from side to side and flailing its antennae about wildly. Its compound eye quickly fell on Sadira and the beast opened its three sets of pincers. Blasting her with its musty breath, it shot forward.

The sorceress leaped into an empty slave pen, but was no match for the beast's speed. Catching her around the thigh, the thing lifted her into the air. A stream of hot blood spilled down her leg, and she felt the numbing sting of venom entering her veins.

"Magnus!" she yelled, panicked by the thought of being poisoned. "Help me!"

"Don't look to your big companion," scoffed Dhojakt. "He has what he came for, and now he's gone."

The sorceress glanced at the rear wall of the emporium. As the prince claimed, neither Magnus nor Faenaeyon were anywhere to be seen. Cursing the windsinger for being so fast to leave, Sadira plunged a hand into her satchel and withdrew the first thing she touched, a wad of soot-covered hemp. She almost put it back, for it was an ingredient to a spell that she could cast only on herself. Then an idea occurred to her, and the sorceress thrust her fingers down to the cilops's pincers. She slapped the hemp onto the thing's head, then grabbed an antenna and spoke her incantation.

The cilops turned as black as Dhojakt's eyes and faded to an insubstantial silhouette. Sadira slipped from between its pincers and dropped to the floor. The shadowy beast tried to attack again, but its mandibles passed through the sorceress without effect. Ignoring the impotent attacker, Sadira ripped a strip of cloth from her sarami and made a tourniquet around her savaged thigh. The bandage would prevent the poison from traveling into the rest of her body, at least for a few minutes.

"Your king didn't say you'd be so difficult to kill," Dhojakt observed, his segmented body slinking over the wall.

"You're doing this for Tithian?" Sadira gasped. She tied off her bandage and placed her hands on the flagstones, as if to push herself to her feet. Instead of trying to rise, however, she drew the energy for another spell. With her palm touching the floor directly, there would be not be even the faintest shimmer of energy to betray what she was doing.

"I do not serve that fool," Dhojakt hissed. "I have cause of my own to end your life."

"Which is?" Sadira asked.

Instead of answering, Dhojakt began to descend, his cilops's body slinking slowly over the wall.

Sadira had begun to tingle with magical energy, but not nearly enough to stop the prince. If she hoped to overcome whatever had protected him from her spells yesterday, she would need much more power. The sorceress kept her hand open and turned toward the floor. Vines began to drop from their pillars, withered and brown. She did not stop, even after they had crumbled to ash, leaving the soil beneath the emporium as lifeless as its flagstone floor.

The stream died away. Sadira feared no more energy would come, then she felt another source yielding its life. It came from outside the emporium, flowing into her body more slowly, as if the plants were reluctant to yield it. The sorceress realized that the force had to be coming from Sage's Square, where the magnificent agafari trees grew.

"No!" Dhojakt yelled, starting across the aisle. "You must not defile my father's grove!"

Sadira clenched her teeth and pulled as hard as she could. At the same time, she reached for her spell ingredients with her free hand. For an instant, it seemed the agafari grove would not yield its life to her summons—then she felt as if a thundercloud had opened. Magical energy flooded into her in such a rush that the sorceress's muscles began to burn and quiver from head to foot. She closed her hand, but the flow continued against her will, streaming into her body and making it impossible to control her own limbs.

As Dhojakt came nearer, the prince's nostrils flared angrily, and Sadira heard the hiss of his breath rushing in and out of the cavernous openings. The skin around his nose was cracked and inflamed, probably from the trap Raka had laid for him yesterday.

The prince extended the bony mandibles from beneath his lips, then grabbed Sadira by the shoulders and drew her close. The sorceress felt energy streaming from her body into his, and control of her muscles returned to her.

"I had intended to kill you mercifully," the prince spat. "But now it is necessary to punish you."

Sadira pinched a nugget of crystallized acid between her fingers. The oils of her skin triggered an instantaneous reaction, causing her to grimace as the vitriolic stuff ate at her flesh.

"Don't waste your effort," Dhojakt snarled, turning his head so that his mandibles could pierce her throat. "Your spells won't hurt me."

"This one will!"

Sadira pulled the crystal from her satchel and thrust it deep into one of Dhojakt's nostrils. As she spoke her incantation, a cloud of brown vapor billowed from his nose.

The prince screamed in agony, then flung the sorceress away.

Sadira slammed into the back wall of the slave pen so hard that it felt as though she would knock it over. Pain raged through her body, and she barely kept her head from slamming into the bricks. Still, she felt as if she were going to fall unconscious. Her vision narrowed to a dark tunnel, and Dhojakt's agonized howls began to grow distant.

The sorceress shook her head and fought to keep her eyes open. If she allowed herself to fall unconscious, she would awake in the custody of Nibenese templars—if she awoke at all. Sadira focused all her thoughts on the throbbing agony in her skull, clinging to the pain like a falling man to a rope.

Finally, Dhojakt's cries began to grow more distinct. Farther away, the sorceress could hear the sporadic explosions and hisses of magical combat. She clung to these sounds, using them to guide her back to reality.

Sadira's vision slowly returned to normal, then the sorceress struggled to her feet. The leg that the cilops had savaged exploded into numb, fiery pain. A wave of nausea rolled through Sadira's stomach, her joints began to ache, and she broke into a cold sweat. The cilops poison, she knew, was taking effect.

Across the aisle, Dhojakt lay crumpled on the floor, his many legs twitching in agony and his torso writhing about madly. He held his hands over his face and howled for help in a pained, inhuman voice.

Sadira could hardly believe he was still alive. The spell she had used had been the most powerful she knew, capable of killing an entire company of soldiers in a single instant. That the prince had survived seemed totally inconceivable, for instead of spreading the acid fog over several acres, she had concentrated it inside his breathing passages. By now, there should have been nothing left of his head except a puddle of brown ooze.

Sadira briefly considered trying to kill him again, but could not think of how to do it. Even if she had possessed a weapon, Dhojakt was as invulnerable to blades as he was to magic. As for another spell, if the death fog had not destroyed him, she did not know what could. The sorceress decided that her wisest course of action was to leave before someone came to help the prince.

As Sadira turned toward the back of the aisle, she saw a stocky figure standing there, surveying the scene. Since his face was concealed by a white scarf, the sorceress felt safe in assuming that he was a member of the Veiled Alliance.

"You can't imagine how glad I am to see you," she said, limping toward him. Instead of moving to help her, the man fled around the corner.

"Come back!" Sadira yelled, following the veiled figure.

By the time she stepped around the end pillar, the man was nowhere in sight. However, Magnus stood only a short distance up the debris-covered aisle. The windsinger was picking his way through a pile of guards that he had, apparently, finished killing just a few moments earlier. Across his shoulders lay Faenaeyon, staring blankly at the floor.

"Magnus, wait!" Sadira yelled, almost stumbling as a wave of dizziness overcame her. "I need your art!"

The windsinger paused long enough to twist around and glance at her. "Hurry." He turned forward again and stumbled down the rubble-strewn aisle at his best pace. "I'll meet you by the door."

The sorceress took a small length of twine and formed

a miniature leash, then raised it in Magnus's direction and cast another spell. The windsinger stopped in mid-stride, one three-toed foot hovering several inches off the floor.

"Didn't you hear me?" Sadira growled. "I said wait!"

THIRTEEN

The Dead Grove

Sadira limped past a pyre of blazing tree trunks and entered the shade of the covered alley, coughing violently from the fumes of burning agafari wood. It was a hot, windless morning, and the smoke of the fires hugged the ground like a cloud of dust sinking to earth. The haze in the plaza hung so thick it was impossible to breathe without choking on mordant-tasting ash, and anyone standing more than a few feet away seemed no more than a ghostly silhouette.

In spite of the fumes, Nibenese slaves labored throughout Sage's Square, felling withered trees and throwing the blackened trunks onto mountainous fires. Somewhere in the smoke, an ensemble of the city's finest ryl pipers filled the air with sorrowful notes, accompanying a morose singer lamenting the loss of the ancient grove.

"Did you find our guide?" asked Magnus.

"No," Sadira answered. Already, it was well past dawn and they had seen no sign of Raka, or anyone else sent by the Veiled Alliance. "You're certain you saw the boy escape the emporium?"

215

"Yes," the windsinger answered. "A pair of slaves freed him from the rubble as I carried Faenaeyon down the aisle. He went with them, staggering, but under his own power. After that, I don't know what happened. I was attacked by the Shom guards, and I lost sight of him."

Through the smoke filling the alley, Sadira could just make out the cape the windsinger had used to bandage his wounds. Behind him loomed Faenaeyon, stooped over to avoid hitting his head on the low ceiling. The elven chief still seemed groggy and unsteady, but had emerged from his stupor to walk on his own. After escaping the emporium, one of the first things the sorceress had done was pour half the antidote down her father's throat. Then Sadira had asked Magnus to use his magic to heal her. Fortunately, the windsinger had been able to neutralize the venom of the cilops and stop the bleeding, but the sorceress's leg remained sore enough that she found walking both difficult and painful.

Next to Faenaeyon stood Huyar, dutifully lending an arm of support to his father and chief. Rhayn was the only one absent from the group. She had gone to fetch Sadira's kank, so that the sorceress could keep up once the company left the city.

After a moment, Huyar said to Sadira, "Perhaps your friend betrayed you. It would be the wise thing, after all."

"Don't make the mistake of judging the Veiled Alliance by your own standards," Sadira replied, upset by the elf's gloating tone.

"Whether the guide betrayed you or not makes no difference," said Faenaeyon. His words came slowly and with a thick slur, for it was the first time he had spoken since emerging from his stupor. "It seems we must find our own way out of the city."

"That won't be easy," Sadira said. "I almost killed the

sorcerer-king's son yesterday. I doubt the gate guards will just let us leave."

"Even the walls of Nibenay have their cracks," Faenaeyon said, giving her a reassuring smile. "Sneaking you out of the city shall be my repayment for rescuing me."

"Thanks, but I've already negotiated my fee for that," she said, casting a meaningful glance at Huyar.

"She has?" the chief asked, looking to his son. "What?"

Huyar gulped. "I said we'd take her to the Pristine Tower."

Faenaeyon glared at him. "Then perhaps you shall be the one who takes her there."

"But I don't know where—"

"Go to Cleft Rock and follow the sunrise until you see the tower!" the chief growled. He grabbed Huyar by the neck and pulled him close. "How could you endanger the tribe by offering such a thing?"

"It was the only way she'd ask her friends to find you," Huyar said. "Besides, we don't have to keep the promise—"

"Is Faenaeyon's life worth so little to you?" demanded Sadira.

"My chief's life is as dear to me as my own," replied the elf. "But so was Gaefal's—and I won't let his death go unpunished."

"Then find out who killed your brother and avenge yourself," Sadira snapped. "But if you value Faenaeyon's life, you'll keep your promise to me."

The chief scowled and stepped toward the sorceress. "Are you threatening me?"

Sadira shook her head. "No. But I would expect that repayment for saving a chief's life is the one debt his tribe would honor."

Faenaeyon studied Sadira for several moments, then said, "First, we must escape the city. Then we'll decide what to do about the Pristine Tower and Gaefal's death." He chuckled at the sorceress, then laid a hand on her shoulder. "Whatever I decide, don't think that I will forget what you did. I admire your bravery and cunning."

Sadira shrugged off the chief's hand. Before she could tell Faenaeyon she cared more about reaching the tower than what he thought of her, Magnus interrupted.

"She inherited her courage and quick wit from her father," said the windsinger. "Isn't that so, Sadira?"

Faenaeyon narrowed one pearl-colored eye and looked Sadira over from head-to-toe. "I thought your name was Lorelei?"

The sorceress shook her head. "No. It's Sadira—Sadira of Tyr."

"Barakah's daughter?" The words were as much an exclamation as they were a question.

"I'm surprised you remember her name," the sorceress answered.

Faenaeyon's thin lips twisted into a wistful smile. "My famous daughter," he said, reaching out to stroke her henna-dyed locks. "I should have known it from the start. You have your mother's beauty."

"I wouldn't know," Sadira spat, slapping his hand away. "My memories are of a haggard, broken-hearted crone abandoned to slavery by the only man she ever loved."

Faenaeyon's mouth fell open and he seemed genuinely perplexed. "What else should I have done?" he asked. "Take her from Tyr and her own people?"

"Of course!" Sadira answered.

Now the elf looked thoroughly confused. "And then

what? Keep her as a daeg?"

He spoke the last word in a derogatory tone. A daeg was a spouse—either male or female—stolen from another tribe. Daegs lived in a state of serfdom until the chief decided they had forgotten their loyalties to their old tribe. It could be many years before a daeg was accepted as a full member of the new tribe, and sometimes they never were.

"That would have been better than what happened," Sadira spat.

"You know nothing," Faenaeyon scoffed. "Barakah was not an elf. The Sun Runners would never have accepted her as anything but a daeg, and our chief would have given you to the lirrs the instant you were born."

Overcome by anger, Sadira shoved her father as hard as she could. The big elf barely budged. Scowling angrily, he grabbed her by the arm.

"Let me go!" Sadira hissed, reaching for her satchel.

"Quiet," Faenaeyon replied, pushing her toward Magnus. With his free hand, he pulled the dagger from the sheath on Huyar's hip.

Sadira heard the clack of two weapons striking each other, then turned and saw her father parry the slash of an obsidian barong. No one wielded the heavy chopping knife; it simply danced through the air on its own. Faenaeyon made a grab for the handle, then narrowly saved his hand by dodging away as the blade flashed at his wrist.

Suddenly ignoring the weapon, the chief rushed down the alley. At the end of the dark lane stood a boyish silhouette, his fingers pointed at the floating barong. The youth waved his hand in Sadira's direction, and the heavy knife streaked toward her head.

The sorceress dropped to the street. As she rolled over

the grimy stones, her injured leg erupted into fiery agony. She cried out, then came to rest against a pair of massive feet with ivory toe-claws. The barong descended toward her neck, but Magnus's arm flashed out and smashed the black blade against the stone wall.

Sighing in relief, Sadira looked down the alley and saw Faenaeyon raising his dagger to strike at Raka. "Don't kill him!" she screamed.

The elf's blade stopped in midair and he grabbed the boy. "But he tried to murder you."

"It doesn't matter," Sadira answered, rising to her feet. "That's our guide. Bring him here."

Faenaeyon raised his peaked eyebrows as if she were mad, but did as asked. He used one hand to keep Raka's arms pinned, and held the other ready to cut the boy's throat. When they reached Sadira, the young sorcerer glared at her with undisguised loathing. His face was covered with scrapes and lumps from being trapped under the falling arch, but otherwise he seemed to have emerged unscathed.

"You promised to help us escape the city," Sadira said, returning Raka's angry stare with a look of forbearance. "Why did you try to kill me instead?"

"You betrayed me," the youth snapped. "My master has barred me from the Alliance."

"What for?" Sadira asked, shocked.

"I cannot believe you must ask," Raka replied, shaking his head angrily. "I vouched for you, and you're a defiler. We saw you casting spells yesterday."

Sadira's stomach felt as though the youth had punched her. She bit her lip and looked away. "I don't expect you to approve of my methods," she said. "But it was the only way I could stop Dhojakt. I had no choice."

"You could have died honorably," Raka sneered.

"To what end?" Sadira demanded, now growing as angry as the boy. "So the Dragon can keep terrorizing Athas?"

"That would be better than helping him to destroy it," Raka replied.

He jerked free of Faenaeyon's grasp, then grabbed Sadira by the arm and pulled her to the end of the alley. "That grove was as old as Nibenay itself," he said, pointing at the shriveled trunks of the agafari trees. "The sorcerer-king himself proclaimed it a refuge, and no defiler ever dared touch it—until Sadira of Tyr came."

"I'm sorry your trees died," Sadira said bitterly. "But stopping the Dragon is more important—or doesn't the murder of thousands of people mean anything to you?"

"Of course," Raka answered, his attitude softening. "But so do *those* lives."

Sadira shook her head. "Call me a defiler if you like, but if I must choose between people and plants, I'll take the people every time."

"I'm not talking about the trees," Raka said. He gestured at a dozen slaves struggling to throw a heavy bole on the nearest fire. "The king kept a hundred slaves to tend this grove," he said. "Once they finish clearing it, the guards will make them join their charges on the pyres."

The sorceress felt a terrible weight in her chest. "You can't blame me for that," she said. "I couldn't have known."

"You should have," Raka countered. "Someone dies whenever you defile the land. Maybe not right away, but when they're hungry for faro that used to grow there, or when they need meat and leather from lizards that grazed there once."

"That's enough," Faenaeyon said, roughly pulling

Raka back into the alley. He raised a hand to cuff the youth. "Stop preaching and—"

"Don't hurt him," Sadira said, grabbing her father's arm. "He's right."

Taking her comment as a signal to continue, Raka said, "What's worse, you're killing the future. If the land will grow no food, not only does the man die, so do his children—and all the children that would have lived there for the next thousand years."

The young sorcerer had just finished his lecture when Rhayn approached from the other end of the tunnel. "Good," called the elf. "The guide's here."

Noting that her sister did not have her mount, Sadira asked, "What about my kank? I can't go very far like this."

"It wasn't there. I'll tell you why later," said Rhayn. "But right now, we'd better go—there's a press gang coming this way."

"A press gang?" gasped Faenaeyon. "I've never seen that in Nibenay."

"The sorcerer-king's son has never been wounded before," said Raka. "He has sent his templars out to gather sacrifices to make Dhojakt well."

Magnus frowned. "No healing magic I know demands a living sacrifice."

"Sorcerer-kings have their own kinds of magic," Sadira said, turning to Raka. "Will you help us leave the city?"

When the youth shook his head, Huyar grabbed him by the throat. "You'll show us or die!"

"Then I'll die," gasped the youth. He glanced at Sadira. "I won't aid a defiler."

Sadira tried to pull Huyar's arms away. "Let him go," she said. "You won't save us by killing him."

Instead of releasing the youth, Huyar pressed his

thumbs into the boy's gullet. A terrible gurgling sound came from Raka's throat as he struggled to free himself.

The sorceress turned to her father. "This will accomplish nothing," she said.

Faenaeyon considered her plea for a moment, then nodded to Huyar. "Let him go," he said. "I think I know a way out of the city anyway."

The warrior reluctantly took his hands from the boy's throat, then pushed him away. "Go, and be happy Sadira of Tyr is a forgiving fool," he said.

From the far end of the alley came the shuffle of dozens of stumbling feet, accompanied by the cracking of whips and the harsh commands of Nibenese templars. When the youth grasped his bruised throat and started in the opposite direction, Faenaeyon caught him by the shoulder.

"Not into Sage's Square," said the chief, pointing Raka toward the press gang. "You can repay me by serving as a decoy."

"That's not why I saved him," Sadira objected, taking Raka's arm. "He'll come with us. If it comes to a fight, we'll all be better off."

The youth pulled free of the sorceress. "I'd rather take my chances with the templars than fight at a defiler's side." With that, he reached into his purse for a spell component, then ran down the alley screaming, "Death to Dhojakt!"

"Raka!" Sadira cried. "No!"

She started to follow, but Faenaeyon caught her arm and held her back. "This way, daughter," he said, carrying her into Sage's Square.

They had barely entered the smoky plaza when an olive-colored light flashed from the alley, accompanied by a sonorous hiss of air. For a moment, Raka's triumphant voice echoed through the lane, but it was abruptly cut off by the sizzle of a lightning bolt.

Ahead of Faenaeyon, a trio of huge silhouettes came rushing toward the clamor. In one hand, each of the half-giants carried a curved sword, and in the other a trident with barbed tongs. The dark circles of their eyes were fixed on Faenaeyon and his group of elves.

"If I put you down, you won't do anything foolish, will you?" whispered the chief.

"I'll be fine," Sadira answered, her voice unusually timid. Raka's last words weighed heavily on her mind, and she found herself wondering if she really could justify all the vile things she had done in the name of fighting the Dragon.

The half-giants stopped in front of Faenaeyon. "What's that noise?" demanded the leader, regarding the elf suspiciously.

"Alliance ambush," Faenaeyon answered, casting a nervous glance in the direction of the alley. "It looks like they're coming this way—probably to attack you."

"Why d'you say that?"

Faenaeyon looked in the direction of the alley again. "Haven't you heard? Sadira of Tyr's in the city," he said. "If you ask me, she's come to free the slaves, like she did in her own city."

The comment set Sadira's heart to pounding madly, but the half-giants remained oblivious to her discomfort. Instead, they studied each other with worried expressions, then the leader waved the group onward. "You keep quiet about that sorceress," he warned. "No one's supposed to know she's here."

The chief shrugged. "If that's what you want, but you hear of nothing else in the Market," he said. "Which way to the Snake Tower from here?"

The half-giant pointed toward the hazy mouth of another alley, then took his two companions and cautiously crept toward the lane where Raka had just perished. Faenaeyon led the group across the plaza, half-carrying the sorceress to prevent her limp from being too noticeable.

As they passed through the covered lane, the chief finally released Sadira's arm.

"You were a little brazen back there, weren't you?" the sorceress asked.

It was Rhayn who answered. "It's the best way," she said. "Otherwise, they think you're trying to hide something."

"We are—remember?" Sadira replied, her limp forcing her to struggle in order to keep up with the others. "And what happened to my kank? Did the liveryman have it killed?"

"I think you have it backwards," answered Rhayn. "According to his slaves, when the old man opened the gate to have someone look it over, the drone grabbed him and left. His assistants followed the thing to the palace gates, where your beast performed some tricks for the guards. After that, both the kank and the man were taken inside. Neither one's been seen since."

"Tithian!" Sadira hissed.

"What does your king have to do with this?" asked Faenaeyon.

"According to Dhojakt, Tithian's the one who told him I was in Nibenay," Sadira answered.

Magnus shook his head in bewilderment. "How?"

"Through the kank," Sadira replied. "Tithian's become a fair mindbender. I think he's been using the Way to spy on me through my mount. That's the only way he could have known I'm in Nibenay, or that I was going to the Pristine Tower."

"I thought Tithian was supposed to be a good king," said Faenaeyon. "Why would he betray you?"

"You were a better father than Tithian's been a king," Sadira retorted. "As for his betrayal, apparently he doesn't want me going to the Pristine Tower. Neither does Dhojakt."

"So perhaps you should rethink your plans," suggested Faenaeyon, ignoring the sorceress's backhanded slight. "If the son of a sorcerer-king doesn't—"

"I'm going," Sadira interrupted. "If they're so determined to keep me away, there must be good reason. I don't know what it is yet, but I've got to hurry. It won't be long before the Dragon reaches Tyr, and I want to be waiting for him."

"Then, by all means, let us hurry," Faenaeyon said, somewhat sarcastically.

The chief led the way out of the alley and into a broader street that ran along the back side of the merchant emporiums. He always moved more or less toward the mountainous bluff on the north side of the city, stopping occasionally to ask his way. Sometimes, the nervous pedestrian would refuse to answer, scurrying past with a protective hand on his purse. More often, the passerby appeared relieved that the elves had only stopped for directions and not to accost him.

The walk was hard on Sadira's injured leg. Even had she been healthy, it would have been a struggle to keep pace with the elves' long legs. Now, with them in a hurry and every step a struggle for the sorceress, it was all but impossible. Within a half hour, she had to ask them to slow down.

"Perhaps we should hide in the city for a day or two," Magnus suggested. "I can't do anything more for your leg until tomorrow, and without a kank you won't make it more than a few miles into the desert."

Sadira shook her head. "No, we must leave today. From what Raka said, the sorcerer-king's busy healing his son. When that's done, he may turn his attention to me."

"In that case, perhaps we should leave Sadira here," Huyar suggested, looking to his father. "We wouldn't want to endanger the tribe on her behalf."

"I decide when the tribe is in peril, and on whose behalf we should endanger it," Faenaeyon said, frowning at his son. "If necessary, you'll carry Sadira on your back."

"Thank you," the sorceress said. "It's nice to know you can be a man of honor."

Faenaeyon smiled insincerely. "Thank you."

"But before we leave the city, there's one thing I need to get," she added.

Her father's smile vanished. "No," he said, starting off again.

"It won't be much trouble," Sadira insisted, "and I'll need it when I reach the Pristine Tower."

Faenaeyon stopped and gave her a puzzled look. "What is it?"

"Obsidian balls," she answered. "For the shadows."

By the way the color drained from her father's face, the sorceress knew he had seen the shadows when he visited the tower. After a moment, Faenaeyon regained his composure, then asked, "Do you have any coins?"

"Of course not," Sadira answered. "You took all—"

"I have no coins, either," the elf answered. "And now is not the time to steal them. If you need obsidian, we'll trade for it on the trail, or take it from a caravan."

Before she could object, Faenaeyon motioned to Magnus and Rhayn. "See that she keeps up," he said, resuming his pace.

It was not much longer before they came to a small plaza. Across the square rose the sheer-sided bluff that bordered Nibenay's north side. Carved into the rocky face of this crag were a dozen different palaces, each at a different height above the ground. Above the mansions, a low stone wall crowned the cliff, forming the defensive fortifications that protected this part of the city.

Before the cliff, separated from it by a short distance, rose a high tower. It had been fashioned in the form of a tangle of coiled snakes, with hundreds of scale-shaped windows glistening along its exterior walls. At the base of the turret, the entrance was shaped in the form of a serpent's gaping mouth.

A meandering skywalk, also carved in the shape of a serpent's head, ran from the tower to each cliffside palace. The highest walkway ran from the floor to the city wall, behind which Sadira could barely make out the tiny forms of a half-dozen sentries scattered over a distance of many yards.

Faenaeyon led his small group to the base of the tower. As they reached the mouth of the stone serpent, a pair of mul guards stepped out to block their path. The two men were armed with curved swords of obsidian, and wore tabards bearing the crest of a black scorpion. Although neither appeared much older than Rikus, their bodies had grown soft. To Sadira, their appearance suggested that they were the pampered gladiators of a nobleman, and had been retired from combat for use as household guards.

The sorceress's father tried to walk directly between the two men, not bothering to acknowledge them. The tallest mul placed a hand on the elf's chest and shoved him back down the ramp.

"Where are you going?" the guard asked.

Faenaeyon glared at the mul. "I've business with Lord Ghandara," he said. "Not that it's any of your concern."

The two muls lowered their swords, but did not step aside. "No one told us to expect you," said the second one.

"That's because I haven't announced myself," Faenaeyon replied. He grabbed Sadira by the arm and pulled her roughly forward. "I thought perhaps he might be interested in making a purchase."

Accustomed to the role of a slave, Sadira lowered her chin and looked frightened. At the same time, she allowed her pale eyes to wander over the muls, as though unable to resist the temptation of admiring their bodies.

Her silent appeal worked well. The muls circled around her, studying her figure from every angle. "Lord Ghandara has fine tastes," said the tallest. "I'm not sure this stock is up to his standards."

Sadira lifted her chin and scowled, then bit her lip as though preventing herself from making a sharp retort. As she had hoped, the guards laughed, then stood aside. "I'll show you the way," said the tallest.

"No need to trouble yourself," answered Faenaeyon, leading his small company up the ramp. "I've been there before."

As Sadira entered the tower, she felt as though she were plunging into an enchanted well. An ambient green light suffused the air, lighting the dust on her skin like tiny gems sparkling in a thousand dazzling colors. Ahead, the corridor divided into three branches. From each puffed a hot breeze thick with the smell of mildew and rot, masked by the overly-sweet aroma of burning incense.

Faenaeyon ushered them into the right-hand corridor and started up the steep, spiraling slope. The hallway

was lined by the scale-shaped windows she had seen from
outside. By peering out the openings, she could see that
they were rapidly climbing to the top of the tower. Whenever they circled around to the north side, the view of the
plaza below was replaced by the sheer crags of the rocky
bluff. Once in a while, they passed one of the cliffside
palaces, where a pair of stern-faced sentries stood guard
over the causeway connecting their master's home to the
tower. Sometimes, it seemed to Sadira that she heard feet
walking down the corridor toward them, but only once
did they meet anyone—an old woman carrying an empty
fruit basket to market.

When she felt reasonably certain they would not be
overheard, Sadira asked, "Faenaeyon, what are we going
to do once we reach the top of the tower?"

"There'll be a pair of royal guards," the elf answered.
"I'll kill them, and we'll cross to the wall."

Sadira peered out a window. It was fifty feet to the
ground, and the sorceress could not imagine the height of
the outside wall would be any less. "Then what?"

"You'll cast the spell you used to bring the tribe across
the canyon," the chief answered. "We'll be gone before
the sentries notice us."

Sadira stopped walking. "No," she said. "To use that
spell, I'd have to defile. I won't do that again."

"You must," Faenaeyon said, continuing up the ramp.
"It's the best way."

"Then you should have asked me before bringing us
here," Sadira said.

Faenaeyon whirled on her. "I don't need to ask!" he
snapped. "I am chief, and you'll do as I say." He glared at
her for a moment, then continued up the corridor with no
further discussion.

Rhayn slipped a hand under Sadira's arm and dragged

her after the chief. Soon, the passage leveled off and curved toward the north side of the tower.

"Leave the guards to me," Faenaeyon whispered. "Magnus, you and Huyar keep the gate open. Rhayn, watch over Sadira."

A few moments later, the corridor broadened into a square foyer. To one side, a bone portcullis hung over a short passage leading to the causeway. Just behind this gate, a narrow hall opened off the main corridor and turned sharply to the right, apparently opening into a small chamber that could not be seen from the main passage. A short stretch of the causeway itself was barely visible, suspended over the empty space between the tower and the city wall.

As Sadira's father had predicted, a pair of guards stood at the portcullis. They were both full humans, wearing purple saramis, with white tabards bearing the insignia of a cilops over the top. In their hands, they held short spears and shields, both made of blue agafari wood.

The guards crossed their spears in front of the causeway. "What are you doing here?" asked one.

Faenaeyon continued to walk toward them at a leisurely pace, holding his hands well away from his dagger sheath. The guards took the precaution of leveling their spearpoints at him, though they did not seem alarmed by his innocuous approach.

"You can't come any farther," said the first guard.

The chief stopped in front of the two men and allowed them to press the tips of their spears to his chest.

"Go on and get out of—"

Faenaeyon sprang into action, thrusting his hands up between the two spears and spreading them apart. Before the guards could cry out, he grabbed them both by the backs of their necks. One after the other, he pulled their heads down and smashed their faces into his knees. The Nibenese cried out and dropped their spears, then the elf pushed them over to a wall and beat their heads against the stones until they fell unconscious.

"As I promised, a simple matter," he said, motioning the others forward.

Magnus and Huyar went into the passage and picked up the spears of the unconscious guards. Before Rhayn and Sadira stepped beneath the portcullis, however, a Nibenese templar rushed out of the side corridor. She took one look at the unconscious guards, then turned toward the causeway, already opening her mouth to call for the king's magic.

Sadira grabbed the woman's hair and jerked her head back, smashing the edge of her other hand into the templar's throat. The Nibenese gurgled in pain, then Rhayn ended her life by plunging a bone dagger into her heart.

"Not as simple as you thought," Sadira said, shaking her head at her father.

"Things have not turned out so badly," Faenaeyon said, leading the way across the causeway.

By the time the small company stepped off the bridge, the sentries scattered along the butte were rushing toward them. Faenaeyon took the spear from Magnus's hand and sent it sailing into the chest of the nearest guard, while Huyar threw his at the one approaching from the opposite direction. Seeing that the elves now had nothing but daggers, the next men in line drew obsidian short swords and rushed forward.

"Cast your spell," ordered Faenaeyon.

"I'll cast *a* spell," Sadira said, taking a small disk of wood from her satchel.

Faenaeyon ignored her and pulled the dagger he had taken earlier from Huyar. As the chief prepared to meet the first sentry, Rhayn gave her own dagger to Huyar, then took a shard of kank shell from her satchel and began preparations for own spell.

Sadira went to the wall and peered over the edge. She found herself looking out over endless acres of silver sandgrass, mottled with boulder-sized clumps of rock-holly. In the distance, laboring under the lash of a single half-giant overseer, a dozen slaves were using buckets to irrigate the king's field.

As the sorceress summoned the energy for her spell, the first of the sentries arrived and attacked. Faenaeyon killed his almost effortlessly, dodging a clumsy thrust, then twisting the sword from the guard's hand and slicing the man open with his own blade. Huyar had more trouble, dropping his dagger when he was slashed across the forearm, and finally Magnus had to intervene by knocking the sentry from the cliff.

Sadira held her disk over the edge of the wall and uttered her incantation. The wooden circle rose from her hand and hovered in midair, then slowly began to expand.

"What's that?" demanded Faenaeyon.

"It's how we'll get off the wall," Sadira explained.

A bowstring hummed and an arrow ticked into Magnus's thick hide. The windsinger cried out in pain, but positioned himself where he would serve as shield for the others.

"Cast the other spell!" Faenaeyon ordered.

"I told you I wouldn't," Sadira said, using one hand to keep her disk from drifting away as it continued to expand. "This is more dangerous, but it'll have to do."

On the side that Magnus was not protecting, a sentry knelt and fired an arrow at the group. The shaft clattered off the stones near Sadira's head, and the sorceress could see that several more guards were coming up to join the attacker.

Rhayn chose that moment to cast her spell, tossing her kank shell into the air. The shard disappeared and was replaced by a full carapace. Huyar immediately grabbed it and used it to shield the group. To both sides of them, sentries cursed, then put their bows aside and rushed forward to attack hand-to-hand.

"I think it's large enough," Sadira said, motioning Faenaeyon onto the disk. It was now the size of a large table. "Get on."

The chief glowered, but did as ordered. Rhayn and Sadira followed next, then Huyar discarded the kank shell and joined them. Magnus came last, again positioning his arrow-flecked bulk between the others and the attacking sentries. He shoved the disk away from the wall, then raised his voice in song. Within moments, a powerful wind rose, carrying the company over the king's lush fields and out into the wastes of the Athasian desert.

FOURTEEN

A New Chief

In a dirt circle that the children had carefully cleared of rocks, two elven warriors stood with their shoulders pressed together and one arm locked over the back of the other's neck. They had coated their bodies with tangy oil squeezed from fresh yara buds, shaved the hair from their heads, and stripped down to their breechcloths. Both women breathed hard, the powerful muscles of their long legs bulging with effort as they struggled to keep their feet.

The rest of the tribe stood outside the ring. The adults cheered for the warrior upon which they had wagered, while the children mimicked the contest by wrestling each other on the rocky ground. Magnus lay on his stomach at the far end of the ring. His pockmarked back was covered with a foul-smelling balm, which the elves claimed would relieve the sting of the many arrow wounds he had suffered that morning. Judging from the vacant look on his face and the gray tone of his eyes, it had accomplished its task mainly by putting him into a slumber.

Faenaeyon sat atop a boulder near Magnus, a huge flask of broy in his hand. His face was contorted into a scowl, with an angry silver light burning deep within his sunken, glazed eyes. He gnawed constantly at his fingernails, hardly seeming to notice as he ripped away strips of cuticle.

As Sadira watched her father, the taller of the two wrestlers slipped her free arm around her opponent's waist and spun in beneath the other's shoulders. "Good, Katza!" yelled Huyar, along with dozens of other tribe members. "Finish it!"

Katza, a woman with a heavily lined face and the tip of one pointed ear missing, pulled her opponent onto her back. She spun her shoulders around to finish the throw, hurling the other woman headlong toward the ground. The defender, who was a head shorter than her opponent and half again as stocky, thrust out her arms to break the fall. For a moment, it appeared she would tumble onto her back. Then, at the last instant, she brought her feet down and sprang away in a cartwheel. Landing just inside the circle, the wrestler spun around and fixed a black-eyed glower on her rival.

"Yes, Grissi!" cheered Rhayn. "Toss that kank-riding trollop into the bushes!"

Katza cast an angry glance in Rhayn's direction. Calling a full-blooded elf a kank-rider was a terrible insult, as it implied she was not fast enough to keep up with the tribe on foot. "You're next, tul'k kisser!" growled the wrestler.

"How you going to wrestle with a broken leg?" demanded Grissi, moving forward.

Although Faenaeyon had called the wrestling tournament to celebrate the escape from Nibenay, the tribe hardly seemed in a festive mood. If the chief had expected the contests to bring his warriors closer together, he had been miserably wrong. So far, every match had deteriorated into a rivalry between Rhayn and Huyar, with their supporters taking sides behind them. The rest of the tribe wagered more on which group would win the day than on the wrestlers themselves.

As Grissi neared the center of the ring, Katza slipped to the side and snapped her leg out in a vicious kick. The blow caught the shorter elf in the face, with the big toe striking the eyeball itself. Grissi's knees buckled and she reached for her eye, barely managing to keep her feet. The entire crowd gasped in astonishment. Even Faenaeyon winced, but no one cried foul.

Katza moved forward with a smug expression, reaching out to grasp her reeling opponent's arm. Grissi let her have it, apparently concentrating all her efforts on retaining her feet. The lop-eared elf pulled her stunned opponent toward her, preparing to deliver the final throw.

Just then, Grissi came alive. She retracted the arm that Katza had seized, pulling her astonished attacker along with it. Then she smashed her forehead into the bridge of Katza's nose. The cartilage shattered with a resonant crack and blood erupted from both nostrils.

As Katza reached up to cover her face, Grissi grabbed her around the neck with one arm and squatted down to slip the other between her opponent's thighs. She pulled Katza's body onto her shoulders, then, in one swift motion, she stood up and catapulted the lop-eared elf out of the circle. Five of Huyar's supporters barely managed to leap aside as Katza sailed past and crashed into a rock pile.

"I win," Grissi growled, not bothering to see if her opponent would be capable of returning to her feet. Her eye was bloodshot and rimmed with red, but it seemed to have survived intact. "Who's next?"

A young elf standing next to Huyar began to strip. "Your tricks won't fool me," he said, throwing his burnoose to the ground. "Shave my head!"

While the youth's friends prepared him for competition, the camp buzzed with the drone of elves settling old wagers and placing new ones. A pair of Katza's older children dragged their mother off to rest, but no one else paid the woman any attention.

The green-eyed woman who had tried to help Sadira during the escape from the Elven Market stepped to the sorceress's side. Sadira now knew the woman's name to be Meredyd, for one of the first things the sorceress had done after rejoining the tribe had been to thank her for her efforts.

Meredyd's lips were spread wide in an affected smile. She had a deep cleft in her long chin and a tangle of brown hair that just concealed the tips of her pointed ears. Her hips and abdomen were so swollen with pregnancy that Sadira wondered how she had found the strength to make the long run from Nibenay.

"I've noticed you have no knife," said Meredyd. She reached beneath her burnoose and withdrew a long dagger with a blade of sharpened bone. Its ivory handle had been carved in the shape of intertwined serpents, with their heads forming the pommel. "I came across this one in Nibenay," she said. "Perhaps you'd like it?"

The offer was not as generous as it seemed. At the beginning of the wrestling tournament, Faenaeyon had announced Sadira's true identity and declared her one of the Sun Runners. Everyone had acted as though he were bestowing a great honor on her, but the chief's true intentions had not been lost on the sorceress. By naming her a tribe member, he was trying to instill a sense of obligation in her that would make it easier for him to assert his authority.

Since then, Sadira had been presented with many gifts, including the new cape covering her shoulders and the soft leather boots on her feet. As the sorceress had quickly discovered, each present carried with it the obligation to voice her support of a request about to be made of Faenaeyon.

"I could use a dagger," agreed Sadira. "What do you want in return?"

Meredyd's smile grew more sincere. "You know of Esylk's daeg, Crekun?"

The sorceress nodded. Crekun was a handsome man from another tribe who had been severely injured during a battle with the Sun Runners. Esylk had put him on a litter and nursed him back to health, and he had been her slave ever since. "What do you want with Crekun?"

Meredyd's hand dropped to her swollen belly. "It would be better for this child if Crekun was a Sun Runner." With a murderous scowl on her face, she glanced toward a russet-haired woman with a brazen figure and plump lips. The target of Meredyd's animosity stood near Huyar, shaving the head of the young warrior about to challenge Grissi. "Otherwise, if it happens to resemble its father, Esylk will claim the child as her property— probably when we are near some city's slave market."

"There will be no children sold into slavery if I can help it," Sadira said, accepting the gift from Meredyd's hand.

As she sheathed the weapon, Katza's oldest son, Cyne, returned from his mother's camp bearing a skin of broy. He pushed his way to the front of the crowd, then stepped past Magnus's litter and offered the fermented kank-nectar to Faenaeyon. "My mother's arm has been broken. Therefore, I ask that Grissi wrestle her next match with one arm bound to her side." He did not even go through the customary ruse of pretending his gift was intended as anything but a bribe.

Faenaeyon hardly glanced at the youth as he took the broy. Setting the skin down at his side, the chief looked over the boy's head to the rest of the crowd.

As Sadira expected, Huyar's followers voiced their agreement with the youth's suggestion, and Rhayn's supporters opposed it. But Cyne's impatience cost him dearly with the majority of elves, who were still neutral in the conflict between Huyar and Rhayn. Irritated at his rudeness in not buying their support with gifts or promises, they also raised their voices against his proposal. Some of them even went so far as to suggest that Grissi's opponent be the one whose arm was bound.

After gauging his tribe's reaction, Faenaeyon looked back to the boy. "You heard the tribe," he said. Though his words were already slurred, he refilled his flask from the skin the youth had given him. "My thanks for the broy."

Cyne flicked his wrist and a silver coin slipped from his burnoose sleeve. Holding the disk before Faenaeyon's eyes, he said, "It's not the tribe I ask."

The chief's eyes darted to the silver and he stuck his palm beneath the boy's nose. "Is that my coin?"

"It is now," the youth said, dropping the silver into the outstretched hand. He remained standing before Faenaeyon while the chief massaged the coin's surface with his fingertips.

Finally, Faenaeyon said, "Grissi will fight with one arm bound to her side."

A disapproving murmur rustled through the camp, which Faenaeyon quickly silenced with a stern glower.

From what Sadira had gathered about tribal politics, most chiefs took bribes—but only under a suitable pretext. Her father ignored even this minor convention, however, trusting his strong arm to keep his warriors from protesting too loudly.

Cyne stepped away from the chief, sneering at Grissi triumphantly. The black-eyed woman met his gaze with a confident chuckle, then looked back to the man who had challenged her. "I'll be ready in a moment," she said, stepping over to have her arm bound. "How about you, Nefen?"

Nefen strode forward, rubbing a last handful of yara buds over his skin. "I'm waiting now."

Noticing that her father still had not taken his eyes off his new coin, Sadira whispered to Meredyd, "I hope you have a few silver up your sleeve."

The pregnant elf shook her head. "I can only hope that Esylk does not have any, either."

Grissi stepped into the ring, one arm bound to her waist, and Nefen entered from the other side. There was no formal challenge, nor any kind of declaration that the match had begun. The crowd simply quieted and the two wrestlers moved toward each other with hatred in their eyes.

Confident he could easily overpower his handicapped opponent, Nefen rushed forward. It was a bad mistake. Grissi stopped his charge with a powerful thrust kick to the stomach. As her opponent bellowed out in shock and pain, she whirled around and used her other leg to kick him again. With the momentum of the spin, this blow lifted Nefen off his feet and sent him flying out of the circle. He crashed into Esylk and they both dropped to the ground.

"That's not wrestling!" objected Huyar.

"Maybe, maybe not—but she won. That's what counts," answered Rhayn, stepping forward to unbind her champion's arm before someone suggested that it remain tied for the rest of the tournament. "Who's next?"

When no one volunteered immediately, Meredyd took advantage of the lull to step over to the boulder where Faenaeyon sat. She took a beautiful belt-purse of lacquered lizard scales from beneath her cape and held it out to the chief. He continued to stare at the coin Katza's son had given him, apparently noticing neither the pregnant elf nor her gift.

"Faenaeyon, I have something here for you to keep your coin in," she said.

The chief looked up, his eyes burning with avarice, and snatched the purse away.

Meredyd waited a moment for him to thank her, but he did not. Finally, she pressed on with her request. "It seems to me that Crekun has been Esylk's daeg long enough," she said. "Crekun should be a Sun Runner by now."

Unlike Katza's son, Meredyd had carefully prepared her case with the rest of the tribe. Close to half of the warriors present raised their voices in agreement, and many more nodded their heads. Only Huyar and a handful of Esylk's friends opposed the suggestion.

Faenaeyon responded to the chorus by lifting Meredyd's purse to his ear and shaking it. When he heard nothing inside, the chief frowned and looked at the woman who had given it to him. "It's empty."

The hopeful smile on Meredyd's lips faded. "I had intended to fill the purse with silver," she said, barely controlling her anger. "But our sudden departure from Nibenay prevented that."

Faenaeyon shrugged, then opened the bag and slipped

...is silver coin into it. "My thanks for the purse," he said, ...ying it to his belt. "But I fear Crekun has not forgotten ...is loyalties to the Sand Swimmers. He'll remain Esylk's wife for . . ." The chief let his sentence trail off while he ...yed Meredyd's swollen belly. "He'll remain Esylk's wife ...or two more months—unless you've a coin to put in my ...ew purse."

Meredyd narrowed her eyes and stared at Faenaeyon with unabashed hatred. Seeing the woman's hand drop ...oward her dagger, Sadira moved forward to prevent her ...rom doing anything foolish. The sorceress had no soon-...r stepped into the ring than Huyar followed her, with ...hayn close on his heels.

"When I was a child, my mother could speak of noth-...ng but how wisely and well you led this tribe!" Meredyd ...narled. "But now we might as well call ourselves quarry ...laves as elves—"

Sadira caught Meredyd's arm and pulled her away ...rom the boulder, almost tripping over Magnus's prone ...orm. "Come and have more broy. Perhaps the drink ...hat's loosened your tongue will put it to sleep," she said ...oudly. More quietly, she whispered, "Will getting killed ...help your child?"

Meredyd studied Sadira for a moment, her eyes flash-...ing with anger. "I won't let Esylk sell this baby!" she ...snapped.

"What my chattel produces belongs to me," said Esylk, ...pushing her way roughly to the front of the small group ...gathered near the chief.

Sadira glared at Esylk. "A child belongs to its mother," ...she said.

"Good point, Sadira," Faenaeyon said suddenly. ..."You've won me over."

Sadira glanced over her shoulder and saw that Rhayn

and Huyar now stood on opposite sides of her father. Between her thumb and forefinger, Rhayn held a small circle of shimmering yellow metal. Faenaeyon's enraptured eyes were fixed on the disk, as were those of the entire tribe—and with good reason. On Athas, not even diamonds were as scarce as gold coins.

"From this moment forward, Crekun is a Sun Runner," the chief pronounced. "Children sired by him are to be treated as children sired by any of our other warriors."

Rhayn smiled. "You are wise, my chief," she said, passing her hand over his broy and dropping the gold coin into it.

Faenaeyon's eyes widened and he drained the entire flask in one long gulp. When he finished, he took the gold coin from between his teeth and carefully polished it on his burnoose. "That's no way to treat gold," he complained, putting the coin into the purse Meredyd had given him.

"My apologies," Rhayn said. She picked up the skin of broy Cyne had provided earlier and refilled Faenaeyon's empty flask. "Drink up, father."

As Faenaeyon lifted his glass again, Sadira joined her sister. "That was unusually generous," she whispered. "Or are you just trying to upset Huyar?"

"I did what was best for the tribe," Rhayn answered, taking Sadira by the arm and leading her away from the rest of the elves. "Meredyd earned the favor of many warriors. Faenaeyon was wrong to ignore them because she had no coins."

"But a gold coin!" Sadira said. "Where did you find it?"

"I make a habit of saving things that might prove useful at crucial times," Rhayn answered, walking toward her family's fire-circle. "And now, I must ask you to give me something that you have been saving."

Rhayn touched her finger to her lips and said nothing else until they reached their destination. All of her children were still at the wrestling match, so the two women were completely alone.

"I'm not going to give you the antidote," Sadira whispered, surmising what her long-sister wanted. "I don't want Faenaeyon poisoned."

"Why not?" Rhayn demanded, opening a kank pack. "You've seen what he can be like, and I have no more coins. How will you bribe our chief when Huyar demands vengeance for Gaefal's death?"

"It doesn't matter," Sadira said. "Only Faenaeyon knows how to find the Pristine Tower."

"I'll take you to Cleft Rock," Rhayn said. "From what Magnus tells me, you can travel on alone from there."

The sorceress shook her head. "I'll take my chances with Faenaeyon."

"What makes you think he'll honor Huyar's promise?" Rhayn demanded. She pulled out the wineskin that she and Magnus had filled from the poisoned cask.

"Maybe he won't, but why wouldn't he at least take me as far as Cleft Rock?"

"Because the tribe needs money, and that well is far from any city or caravan route where we can steal it," Rhayn answered. "But don't take my word for it. Tonight is when we make requests of the chief. Make yours and see what he says."

Sadira studied the elf for a long time, trying to imagine a reason she should not do as her sister suggested. When she could think of none, she nodded and turned to go. "I will."

Rhayn caught her shoulder. "You'll need a gift," the elf said, holding out the wineskin. "Take two cups, and put the antidote in one. If Faenaeyon agrees to take you, pour his wine into the one with the antidote."

The elf did not need to say what Sadira should do if he refused. She and Rhayn prepared the gift, then the sorceress put a few drops of the antidote on her tongue—in case she found herself drinking from the cup without the antidote. They returned to the wrestling circle, Sadira carrying the wineskin over her shoulder and the two mugs in separate hands.

When Faenaeyon saw the sisters, he motioned Rhayn to his side. "Daughter!" he said, giving her a mug of broy. "Come and drink with me."

The chief touched his cup to his daughter's, then they both quaffed down the sour-smelling stuff as though it were water. When Faenaeyon lowered his flask again, Sadira stepped forward to make her request. Huyar cut her off and refilled his father's cup from his own skin.

"I'm sorry I lack a gold coin to give you, my chief," said the elf.

"So am I," answered Faenaeyon, squinting at him drunkenly.

"It pains me to see the chief of the Sun Runners with so few coins in his purse," Huyar continued, giving Sadira a sidelong glance. "It's a pity that the tribe's new sorceress did not also think to free your coins when she rescued you from the Slave Market—or perhaps she did. Could it be that Rhayn has made a gift to you of your own coin?"

"You know better than that, Huyar!" spat Rhayn. "You were with us when we escaped Nibenay. Did you see any of Faenaeyon's purses?"

"That doesn't mean they weren't there," Huyar countered. "Sadira is a powerful sorceress. It would have been a small matter for her to conceal them."

Faenaeyon scowled at Sadira. "This is true," he said, slurring his words heavily. "Did you steal my coins, woman?"

"No!" Sadira snarled. "If Huyar had the sense of a drone, he'd know that you would not have been sent to the slave market with your purses hanging from your belt. By now, your coins lie in the vault of the sorcerer-king himself." She glared at her rival, then added, "Perhaps *he* would like to go there and recover them for you?"

Faenaeyon looked to Huyar. "Would you?"

"What I would like to do and what is possible are different things," said the warrior.

"A good answer," Faenaeyon laughed. He turned his attention to Sadira, who was still holding the cups and the wineskin. "Now, what have you?"

"Wine," Sadira answered.

"Not as good as gold, but it will do," Faenaeyon answered, reaching for the mug that contained the antidote.

Sadira pulled it away. "First, I have a request."

Frowning, the chief withdrew his hand. "I trust it will not be too demanding."

"Just answer a question," Sadira replied. "Do you intend to honor Huyar's promise? The wine is my gift to you, as long as you answer truthfully."

Faenaeyon studied her with a doubtful scowl, then shrugged. "The Sun Runners have better places to go than the Pristine Tower," he said, snatching the mug he had reached for earlier—the one with the antidote. "Now, give me my wine!"

Sadira cursed under her breath, but smiled at Faenaeyon and filled the cup. Before he could drink, however, she said, "Didn't you notice that I brought two mugs?"

Faenaeyon scowled. "So?"

"I thought you'd want to share your gift with your favorite daughter," the sorceress said, gesturing at her sister. Rhayn scowled, unsure of which cup contained the antidote. Sadira smiled, hoping the gesture would reassure Rhayn, then asked, "Doesn't a gold coin deserve a fine gift in return?"

Faenaeyon smiled. "So it does," he said, passing the mug to his daughter.

Rhayn's face went white, but she accepted the wine.

*　*　*　*　*

Despite the festivities of the night before, the tribe was packed and ready to run by mid-morning. Sadira, who had sat up late studying her spellbook, was among the last to join the train. The sorceress rode one of her sister's kanks, leading Magnus's beast on her downwind side. The windsinger's back was covered with a fresh coat of balm, and she still found its pungent smell grossly offensive.

Sadira was glad that she had made Magnus tend her cilops's bite before she saw to his arrow stings. His song that morning had been so effective that she considered herself healed. The only remaining sign of her injury was a slight tightness in the muscle. If she had waited until after she spread the salve over the windsinger's back, however, she would still be in pain. The unguent had hardly touched his knobby hide before Magnus had grown so drowsy he could barely speak, much less sing.

Sadira located Rhayn near the front of the tribe, her youngest infant slung on her back and the rest of her children mounted on kanks behind her. As the sorceress rode up to join her sister, she could not help yawning.

"Why are you so tired?" Rhayn demanded.

"I was up late," Sadira answered, tapping the satchel where she kept her spellbook. "I thought it wise to learn some special enchantments, in case Dhojakt comes after us."

"A wise precaution, but it is no excuse to be tired," Rhayn countered. "I feel wonderful, and I did not sleep at all."

"Then how did you spend the night?"

Rhayn gave her sister a wry smile. "Bolstering my support," she said. "Today, the Sun Runners choose a new chief—though they may not realize what they're doing." She motioned for Sadira to dismount, then led the half-elf to a small gathering of warriors.

As they merged with the group, Sadira saw Faenaeyon stretched out on the ground. The chief lay with his sunken eyes shielded by a coarse cloth, and his tongue half-protruding from between his lips. His skin was flaxen, and sweat ran off his face in tiny rivulets. The sorceress's stomach felt queasy with guilt.

If Rhayn felt any similar emotions, she did not show them. The elf strode directly over to Huyar and pointed at the chief's sickly form. "What did you do to him?" she demanded. "Were you afraid he'd change his mind and make you keep your promise to Sadira?"

Sadira bit her lip, amazed by her sister's nerve. Rhayn's audacity reminded the sorceress of Tithian—and that frightened her, more for the Sun Runners than for herself.

Whatever Sadira's misgivings, the attack served its purpose. Huyar was immediately on the defensive. "It wasn't me," he snapped, pointing at Sadira. "This is the second time she's offered him wine, and it's the second time he's fallen sick."

Rhayn furrowed her brow thoughtfully, then glanced

at Sadira as if considering the point. For a moment, the sorceress feared her sister intended to betray her, but the elf finally looked back to Huyar and shook her head. "Then how come I'm not sick?" she asked. "I drank as much wine as Faenaeyon."

When Huyar could not provide an answer, Rhayn pointed at Faenaeyon's pallid face. "Whatever's wrong, I don't want to wait here until he recovers. We're too close to Nibenay."

"Agreed," said Huyar, his tone reasonable enough. "I thought we'd run south, toward the Altaruk trade routes."

"I say we keep your promise to Sadira," Rhayn said. She pointed east.

"Are you mad?" Huyar shrieked. "You heard what Faenaeyon said about the tower."

"We aren't going to the Pristine Tower, just to the Cleft Rock well," Rhayn answered. "From there, Sadira can find her own way."

"No," said Huyar. "There's still the matter of my brother's death."

"And Faenaeyon will pass judgment on that when he recovers—no doubt long before we reach the well," said Rhayn.

Huyar shook his head stubbornly. "I won't allow it."

"It's not for you to decide," Rhayn replied.

Grissi stepped over to the pair. "I'd say we're at an impasse." She stepped between the two and started dragging her heel through the dirt, scraping a faint line along the rocky ground. When she finished, she stepped over it and stood next to Rhayn.

A swirling cloud of dust rose from the jumbled mass as the elves pushed and shoved back and forth across the line. Within a few moments, the line Grissi had drawn was completely erased, but there was no doubt about where it had been. The tribe stood divided into two nearly equal halves, with one part behind Rhayn and the other behind Huyar. Only Sadira, Magnus, and the young children had not joined one group or another. Between the two bands was a no-man's land less than a yard wide, and both Huyar and Rhayn were busy counting the number of elves on their side of this border.

As she studied the two groups, Sadira noticed that Huyar's supporters were primarily older warriors who remembered Faenaeyon's days as a great chief. Rhayn's group included the women who traditionally supported her, but also nearly every young man in the tribe. Sadira was surprised to see so many of them on her sister's side, for during the wrestling contests the day before, many had appeared to support Huyar's champions. Apparently, Rhayn's nocturnal efforts to bolster her support had been quite remarkable.

Huyar and Rhayn finished counting at almost the same moment. They looked at one another, both with smug expressions of satisfaction on their faces.

"It seems we will go south," Huyar announced.

"No, we will go east," Rhayn countered, pointing at Sadira and then to Magnus. "You have forgotten two of our tribe."

Huyar's face went white. "They don't count!" he snapped. "Only members of the tribe old enough to run can choose."

"They are more than old enough," Rhayn said. "And they are both Sun Runners—or have you forgotten that yesterday Faenaeyon named Sadira one of us?

"But they still can't run," said one of the men standing on Rhayn's side. "Our customs our clear on this."

Many warriors from both halves of the tribe voiced

their agreement on this point. Rather than risk losing the support of anyone on her side of the line, Rhayn nodded.

Then she pointed at Faenaeyon. "He cannot run, either," she said. "He does not count."

It was Huyar's turn to yield. He did so graciously, saying, "That is fair. But now we each have the same number of warriors on our side. How are we to decide who will lead the tribe until Faenaeyon is better?"

"A race!" suggested a woman in Rhayn's group.

"No, let them wrestle," countered a man from Huyar's.

Rhayn shook her head and raised her arms to silence the crowd. "It's no secret that Huyar and I detest each other," she said. "I say we settle this once and for all. A fight to the death."

By the astonished silence that fell over the tribe, it was clear that such contests were not common occurrences among the Sun Runners.

Finally, one of the women on Rhayn's side gasped, "Why would you do that?" Though Sadira could not see who had asked the question, she recognized the voice as belonging to Meredyd.

Rhayn glanced in Sadira's direction, then said, "I only suggest what is best for the Sun Runners." She waved her hand at the two halves of the tribe. "As long as Huyar and I both remain, we will be divided as we are now. If one of us is gone, then so is the division."

Sadira realized that Rhayn was purposely giving her no choice except to use magic to guarantee victory. If Huyar won the fight, Rhayn's corpse would not even be cold before Sadira was put to death for Gaefal's murder. There was a heartless genius in her sister's plan that reminded Sadira more and more of Tithian.

After studying Rhayn for several moments, Huyar started to speak, but Sadira interrupted before he could accept the challenge. "Today, I run with the tribe," she called, sliding off the kank. "That gives me a voice in choosing our leader, does it not?"

"Yes," called Grissi.

"Only if she survives," countered Esylk. "And not just one day—I say that when she can no longer run, her voice no longer counts!"

"Agreed," Sadira said, stepping to Rhayn's side of the line. "Let's go. I must reach Cleft Rock as soon as possible."

FIFTEEN

Cleft Rock

Sadira thought she and Grissi would never stop running. Each breath carried with it a searing wave of pain, and with every jarring step a dull ache rolled through her head. Hours ago, she had lost the feeling in her blistered feet, and she barely noticed as her numb legs carried her over the rocky ground.

"Keep running," said Grissi, effortlessly trotting at the sorceress's side. "We don't have far to go."

Had she not been so fatigued, Sadira would have hit the elf. Grissi had said the same thing four evenings in a row, after the rest of the tribe had disappeared into the desert and left them to plod along by themselves.

"Don't," Sadira croaked. "You've told me that too many times before."

Even the sorceress did not recognize her own voice, for her throat was so swollen with thirst that she could hardly draw air down it.

"No, really," Grissi said, pointing at the horizon. "Can't you see them?"

Sadira lifted her eyes from the orange dust beneath her

254

feet and glanced ahead. Her shadow lay next to Grissi's, swimming over the broken ground like an oasis eel. The purple hues of dusk were just creeping up from between the rocks, while scattered across the plain were a handful of sword-length blades of grass that the kanks had neglected to crop on the way past. On the horizon, a strange, spiderweb grid of violet lines covered a gentle, dome-shaped knoll, but Sadira could see no sign of the tribe.

"Just a few more minutes and you can rest," said Grissi.

"If I don't collapse on that hill," Sadira gasped.

This time, her words were barely recognizable. Grissi took the flattened waterskin off her shoulder, then unfastened the mouth and handed it to the half-elf. "Drink," she said. "Your throat is closing up."

Sadira shot her companion an angry scowl, then accepted the skin and closed her lips around the mouth. Taking care to keep her chin down so her eyes could watch the ground, she tipped the skin up. The sorceress continued to breathe through her nose as a trickle of hot, stale water ran down her throat. Without breaking her pace, she kept the skin raised high while she drained the last few drops of precious liquid.

Once the skin was empty, she thrust it back at Grissi. "You told me an hour ago we were out of water." This time, her words were perfectly understandable.

"Never drink your last swallow of water until you're within sight of the next one," said the elf, slinging the empty skin over her shoulder.

Sadira peered again at the dark lines on the horizon. This time, it seemed she could make out the billowing crowns of hundreds of trees. "Thank the winds," she gasped. "An oasis."

"Not just any oasis. It's Cleft Rock," Grissi said, pointing toward the top of the knoll. "See?"

Sadira squinted at the distant trees. "No," she said. "What am I looking for?"

"A split rock," Grissi said. "I'll never understand how city people go through life half blind."

Sadira ignored this last comment, for the feeling was returning to her legs. Forgetting the throbbing ache in her back, she sped up to twice her previous pace. The exertion made her temples pound as though someone were driving a rockpick through them, but the sorceress did not slow down.

Soon, Sadira could see the elven camp. The warriors were scattered about the summit, gathered in dark clusters and preparing their evening meals. The children had already taken the kanks out to graze and were driving the beasts back up the hillside to tether them for the night.

"I must be getting faster," Sadira observed. "Half the tribe's usually asleep by the time I catch up."

Grissi shook her head. "You're no faster than before," she said. "But today, we did not run so far."

At last, the two women reached the bottom of the rise. As they climbed the slope, they had to fight their way through a network of troughs filled with billowing chiffon trees and thickets of spongy yellow fungus. The channels had apparently been dug by some intelligent race, for they were arranged in a series of concentric rings and were the same depth and width. Occasionally, a narrow ditch ran from one channel down to another, giving the place its weblike appearance.

When the two women climbed out of the last trough, Grissi led the way to the crest of the hill. There, a circular monolith of black granite rose out of the dusty ground. The rock stood about as high as Sadira's chest, and was as big around as a large wagon. In the center was a jagged cleft, about two yards long and barely wide enough for a child to squeeze into. From its depths came a high-pitched hum, periodically broken by a rasping gurgle and the sound of trickling water.

Rhayn, Huyar, Magnus, and several other elves stood atop the monolith, gathered around the crevice. Their eyes were fixed on a hemp rope that had been attached to a spear's shaft and dropped into the fissure. Grissi climbed onto the rock, then helped Sadira up.

"Give me something to drink," Sadira gasped, bracing her hands on her knees and trying to control her heaving ribs.

Huyar surprised the sorceress by offering his flattened waterskin. Sadira cast a wary glance at his face. Seeing no treachery in his eyes, she lifted the bladder and poured the contents into her parched mouth. A trickle of hot, fetid water ran down her throat, then the bag was empty.

Sadira thrust the skin back at Huyar. "I'm in no mood for jests," she growled. She looked to her sister, then asked, "Would you give me some fresh water?"

"What Huyar provided is all we have here," answered Rhayn. "In a minute, the children will send up more."

Sadira sat down on the warm stone, too exhausted to stand while she waited. Huyar stepped over the cleft and came to her side.

"You surprise me," he said. "I didn't think you'd last until we reached Cleft Rock."

"Most of the time, neither did I," Sadira answered, surprised by the elf's grudging congratulations. "If I had been running only for myself and not all of Tyr, I probably wouldn't have."

"How noble," the elf said, his voice dripping sarcasm. "Then all of Tyr must be as happy as you are that our father has not recovered from his illness."

"I'm not happy about Faenaeyon's condition," Sadira said, noticing that Rhayn was keeping an attentive ear turned toward their conversation.

"Come now," said Huyar. "You must admit that it served you well. We have reached Cleft Rock."

"What's your point, Huyar?" Sadira asked.

"Only this: that in the morning, you'll leave to find your tower," the warrior said. "If you can help the chief recover, there's no longer a need for you to withhold your help."

"I can think of one reason," said Rhayn, joining the pair. "The instant Faenaeyon's awake, you'll demand vengeance for Gaefal's death."

"Perhaps I was wrong about Sadira's involvement," Huyar said, flashing a smile at the half-elf. "I should thank you for trying to save his life, not blame you for his murder."

Sadira shook her head, disgusted by the elf's willingness to barter his brother's death for political advantage. "Let me see if I've got this right," she replied. "If Faenaeyon recovers, you're first in line to be the next chief. But if Faenaeyon stays in a stupor, the advantage belongs to Rhayn because she's the temporary chief?"

"This has nothing to do—"

"Don't deny it! Let's be clear about what you're saying," Sadira said. "If I'll help the chief recover, you'll let me go in peace and stop blaming me for Gaefal's death—isn't that what you're offering?"

"If you were able to help Faenaeyon, it would convince me of your goodwill toward the entire tribe, yes," said Huyar, studying the sorceress with a wary expression.

"I'm sorry, but it fell to Rhayn to keep your last promise. I don't see how I could trust you to honor this one."

Sadira smirked at the elf.

"Besides, I have her obsidian," the sorceress's sister added, as much for Sadira's benefit as Huyar's. The same day Rhayn had been named chief, the Sun Runners had come across another caravan, and she had traded two kanks for several hunks of unshaped obsidian. Sadira did not know whether the shadows would accept the pieces as a gift, but it was the best she would be able to offer.

Huyar narrowed his eyes at the sorceress. "If you think this is over, you're wrong," he spat. "The Pristine Tower is still a long—"

The warrior's threat was interrupted by a scream echoing out of the cleft. Sadira jumped to her feet and followed the elves to the fissure, then peered down into the darkness.

"Help!" cried a child. "They're—"

The voice was cut off. The only sounds coming from the cleft were the high-pitched hum and rasping gurgle that Sadira had noticed when she had first approached the fissure.

"In the name of the wind, what's wrong?" boomed Magnus.

When no one answered, Katza stepped forward. Her broken arm was still in a sling, but she seemed otherwise untroubled by the injury. "Cyne's down there!" she said. "What are we going to do?"

Sadira had already taken her satchel from Grissi's shoulder. She pulled out a handful of faro needles and began laying them out in a large square, with the rope at the center.

"Magnus, anchor that line," Sadira said, motioning at the hemp cord. "A spear shaft might support the weight of a child, but I doubt that it will hold adults."

"Then you can get us through this crack?" Katza

asked.

Sadira nodded, summoning the energy for a spell. Considering the number of trees growing on the hillside, the flow of life-force seemed surprising weak. Nevertheless, by the time Magnus had tied the rope around his waist, the sorceress was ready. Motioning for the others to stand back, she cast her enchantment.

Inside the square she had laid out, the rock turned to fluid, then slowly swirled around in a sluggish whirlpool. The current began to move faster, and as it did, the liquid changed to mist. Soon, when nothing but vapor remained inside the square, all motion ceased and there was a black cloud where rock had been a few moments earlier.

Sadira took the rope, passing it over her shoulder and around her thigh. She stepped into the mist and started to slide downward, saying, "Before you follow, wait until Magnus feels me tug on the rope."

After descending more than a dozen feet, Sadira left the dark cloud her spell had created. She found herself at the top of an immense cavern filled with steam. She could see the green outline of her rope dropping into the pink-glowing murk below, but beyond twenty yards, which was as far as her elven vision allowed her to see, there was nothing but darkness.

The sorceress pulled the rope tight across her thigh and stopped her descent, listening for any noises that might hint at what was happening below. She heard nothing but the same hum she had detected from outside, punctuated at short interludes by a strangled gurgle and the sound of trickling water.

Sadira looked up and saw a vaulted ceiling shaped from porous white stone that bore a faint resemblance to pumice. The dome had not been carved, for its contours were so softly rounded that the structure looked more grown than hewn. The entire surface seemed to glisten with tiny, pink-glowing droplets that occasionally fell free and plunged into the darkness below.

Deciding it would be wisest to see what she was getting into, Sadira pulled a wooden ball from her satchel. She pointed her palm toward the ceiling to summon the energy for a light spell, but did not feel the tingle of life-force entering her body. Instead, mottled pastel colors glowed deep within the porous stone above her hand. She pulled harder, and the stain deepened in hue and spread outward, but still no energy came to her body. Sadira gasped and closed her hand, both puzzled and frightened. The ceiling itself seemed to be absorbing the life-force she summoned, but she had never heard of any rock that could do such a thing.

The sorceress put the ball back and continued her descent into the pink haze. As she slid down the rope, the humming and the gurgling grew steadily louder and more ominous, until at last the noises completely muffled the sound of trickling water.

Within a few moments, the cavern bottom came into view. Below the sorceress rose the jagged form of a huge crystal, glowing red-hot and standing at least as high as Sadira. A thick coat of minerals crusted its exterior, while a shrill hum rose from its hollow interior. Every few seconds, a raspy sputter interrupted the buzz. A puff of steam, glowing red to her elven vision, billowed into the air.

Sadira came down next to the crystal, atop a gently sloped dome of porous rock. After disentangling herself, she tugged on the rope to signal the others to come down, then drew the dagger Meredyd had given her. She stepped away from the rope, feeling strangely blind. She could see her own body and the floor of the cavern, but the chamber was so large that its walls were beyond the range of her elven vision. Never before had she experienced quite the same sensation of standing alone in the dark.

A drop of condensation hit the top of Sadira's head, then she felt a warm trickle running down her face. She wiped the bead off her brow, then licked the water from her finger. It was the temperature of her own skin, but tasted clean and fresh.

Huyar came down the rope, followed by Grissi, Katza, and ten more elves. Except for Katza, who carried only a dagger, all were armed with longbows and bone swords.

"Where's Rhayn?" Sadira asked.

"The chief must stay with the tribe at times like this," said Grissi.

"You'll have to trust me instead," said Huyar, smirking at the sorceress. He motioned to the other elves. "Spread out and see what you can find."

It was only a moment before Katza called, "Over here! Tracks!"

Sadira and the others followed the sound of her voice, traveling a short distance down the sloping floor. Once they had come close enough to see her, they found the woman kneeling near the edge of the huge chamber. Runnels of steam condensation, glimmering pink, were running down the domed ceiling in glistening rivulets. This water was collecting in a shallow black brook that apparently ringed the entire cavern. On the opposite side of the stream opened a tiny corridor, so small that even a dwarf could not have stood upright inside it.

"What did you find?" Huyar asked.

With her good hand, Katza pointed to a few clumps of damp dirt. "Someone came out of that tunnel and into the cavern," she said. "It looks like they went back the same way."

"What race would you guess, and how many?" Sadira asked.

Grissi, who was also studying the faint trail of mud, shook her head. "Several humans—it's impossible to say how many, but their feet were too large to be our children."

"Could they be from Nibenay?" the sorceress asked. She feared that, guessing she would have to pass through this oasis, Dhojakt had sent a company of retainers to ambush her.

"They could be," Huyar said, scowling. "Let's go and see."

He waded across the black stream and crawled into the cramped tunnel, followed by the other elves. After pausing to gulp down several mouthfuls of water, Sadira brought up the rear. She followed the elves through the passage and onto a slender causeway, which crossed a chasm so narrow and deep it could only be described as an abyss. From its bowels came the gurgle of another stream, though it sounded as though the brook were a mile away.

Like her companions, the sorceress found herself gasping in wonder. From one side of the grotto came a crisp breeze, carrying on its breath the musty scent of unseen passageways and the cool touch of dew. From the other side came the whisper of a distant waterfall, though it was impossible to tell whether it was draining the abyss or falling into it.

When they reached the other end of the bridge, the trail turned left and ran along a narrow ledge. To one side lay the chasm, while the other was lined with vaulted doorways, none of which came up any higher than Sadira's chest. As she passed each one, the sorceress peered down its length. Usually, she saw nothing but twenty yards of corridor running through the same porous stone that encased the rest of the grotto.

Once in a while, though, the tunnel was short, and Sadira could see that it opened into some vast chamber. Several times, she glimpsed a magnificent arch or column rising into the darkness beyond the passageway, and once she even saw a huge room of stacked arcades.

Finally, crawling on his hands and knees, Huyar led the way into one of the side corridors. As each of the other elves followed him into the passageway, they gasped in alarm, then let out a sigh of relief and scrambled through as fast as they could.

When Sadira's turn came, she saw the reason for the elves' concern. The walls of this passageway were lined with notches that appeared to be crypts, though none could have held a person any larger than a child. Each hollow was faced with a strange sort of translucent stone that Sadira had never seen before, a little too cloudy to be glass and with a texture as smooth as ivory. In each hollow she could make out the form of a small body, and at first Sadira feared they were the elven children.

When she peered into one of the crypts more closely, the sorceress saw that the hazy figure inside was not that of a child. Rather, it seemed to be a mature man, with skin as viscid as clay, short-cropped hair, and even features. He was dressed in a plain tabard, with a small skullcap on the top of his head. Only the fact that Sadira's elven vision saw his body in a cold blue tint suggested that he was dead.

"What do you make of it?" asked Grissi, speaking from a short distance ahead. "An ancient dwarf?"

"No. From what I've heard, ancient dwarves were rugged and hairy," Sadira said. She cupped her hands around her face and pressed them against the transparent covering, trying to get a clearer view of the little man. "He looks more like a halfling!"

"Way out here in the desert?" Grissi scoffed. "Never. Halflings are mountain-dwelling savages."

The little man's eyelids fluttered open and a pair of dark pupils turned toward Sadira's face. She jerked away from the crypt, a shudder of fear running down her spine. "It moved!" she gasped, starting down the passageway. "Let's get out of here."

They crawled past a dozen more crypts, then followed the rest of the party into an intersecting tunnel. This passageway was high enough for Sadira to stand upright, but the elves could only rise if they kept their upper bodies hunched over like baazrags.

Huyar pointed down the corridor, to a sliver of rosy light spilling into the tunnel from a hole in the roof. "That's where the tracks lead," he whispered.

"What's your plan?" Sadira asked.

"If it's the Nibenese, they probably came for you," said Huyar. "If so, I'll give you to them."

"No!" hissed Grissi. "Faenaeyon named her one of the tribe. When she was the first to descend the rope in pursuit of our children, she proved it's an honor she deserves."

"Grissi's right," agreed Katza. "If you would betray her, you'd betray one of us."

Huyar bit his lips. "You couldn't think I really meant to give her over, could you?" he asked. "What I intend to do is use her as bait."

The elf outlined a simple plan that stood a good chance of success, except for a single detail that he could not have realized. Sadira pointed at the porous white stone from which the cavern had been shaped. "This rock blocks the flow of magic," she said. "I can't prepare spells until I'm outside."

"Then it will be up to us to make sure you have time enough," Huyar said, motioning at himself and the other warriors.

With that, he nocked an arrow in his bow and, moving with a sort of squatting waddle, went down the corridor. At the opening, he paused long enough to let his eyes adjust to the dusky light, then peered outside. Apparently he found no one guarding the exit, for he motioned to the others to follow him and climbed through the hole.

Only Sadira stayed behind, crouching beneath the opening and holding her spell ingredient in her hand. For a long time, she heard nothing from outside. She began to fear they had guessed wrong about who had taken the children and why.

Finally, a Nibenese woman, almost certainly a templar, called out, "Have you come for your children, elf?"

"Yes," answered Huyar. "Why did you take them from us?"

"We couldn't hope to beat your tribe to this oasis with a full company of half-giants," the woman replied, "so taking hostages seemed the surest way to get what we want."

"Which is?"

"You know the answer as well as I do," the templar replied.

"Surely, you can't want our chief badly enough to follow us into the desert," said Huyar, playing dumb. "After all, when you captured him the first time, you only sold him to the Shom slavers."

"It's not your chief we want, and you know it!" snapped the woman. "We value him no more than you do."

"What do you mean by that?" Huyar inquired, his

voice less wary than a moment earlier. "Our chief is our father."

"Oh? Does your tribe make a habit of poisoning its fathers?" asked the templar. "Or was your chief's condition when we captured him an exception?"

Sadira's stomach knotted with the dread of what might happen next. For a long time, Huyar remained silent. She began to fear he would grow so angry that he would forget about the children and return to attack her.

At last, the elf replied, "Faenaeyon may have drunk some bad wine. I assume you want the woman who served it to him?"

Although this was not the way the elf had said the conversation would go, the sorceress did not turn to leave. Even Huyar was cunning enough not to trust the templars to honor any bargain they made. No matter what Sadira had done, his best chance of recovering the children still lay in executing the plan upon which they had agreed.

The templar must have signaled her reply with a gesture, for the sorceress did not hear it. Instead, Huyar said, "Then bring the children out where we can see them. Once we know they're safe, we'll go get Sadira and meet you halfway down the hill."

"Then lay aside your bows," said the templar.

"So you can kill us?" Huyar scoffed. "As long as our children are safe, you have nothing to fear. We would not risk their lives by attacking."

"Very well, but we won't hesitate to kill them if you break your word."

There was a moment of silence, then Katza's voice demanded, "Cyne, how could you let yourself be surprised by a bunch of city-dwellers?"

The demand was Sadira's signal. She placed her spell

ingredient, a small block of granite, between her teeth
and scrambled through the opening. Even before the sorceress had climbed completely out of the hole, she began
summoning the energy for a spell.

The exit opened into a small glade surrounded by a
thicket of chiffon trees. Though dusk had completely
fallen, both Ral and Guthay already hung high in the sky.
The area was lit with a burnished amber radiance more
than bright enough by which to see.

At the edge of the small meadow were the six templars
who had brought the hostages forward. Each woman
held a child in front of her body, with a dagger pressed to
the young elf's throat. Though the children were clearly
frightened, they did not seem too panicked to follow their
elders' instructions. In fact, none of them were even
crying.

"Now!" Sadira hissed, still clenching the granite block
between her lips.

Without the slightest hesitation, the elves lifted their
bows and fired over the heads of their children. As the
astonished templars cried out, Katza yelled, "Run, children! Over here!"

By the time Sadira had pushed herself free of the hole,
five templars lay dead with arrows in their skulls. The
elves had missed only the woman holding Cyne. As the
other children bolted to freedom, the templar drew her
blade across the boy's throat. He did not die without a
fight, managing to smash an elbow into her ribs as his
lifeblood gushed out of the wound.

Screaming in rage, Katza rushed the woman with her
dagger. Before she had taken three steps, six bowstrings
hummed and a flight of arrows shot past. This time, they
did not miss their target.

Sadira took the granite block from her mouth and

threw it over the children's heads, uttering her incantation. In the same instant, a hidden Nibenese sorcerer cast a spell, and a spray of rainbow-colored lights shot from the thicket. The sorceress and her companions were momentarily blinded.

Sadira heard a series of loud crackles as her own spell took effect. Though she could not see it, she knew that a high wall of granite was sprouting from the ground where her stone had landed. The barrier had been intended to serve as a temporary shield while the elves took their children and fled into the tunnel below, but she suspected the enemy's spell would interfere with their plans.

Hearing the patter of small feet coming toward her, Sadira yelled, "Into the tunnel and back to the well chamber. Tie yourselves to the rope and tell Magnus to pull you up."

A moment of silence followed, and Sadira feared that the children would not obey. Then Huyar snapped, "Do as she says!"

As the children clambered into the hole, Sadira summoned the energy for another spell. It seemed to take forever for her vision to clear, but at last she could make out the silhouettes of the Sun Runners around her.

Only Huyar and Grissi seemed to be recovering from the spell. The others were staring into the air with blank expressions on their faces, mumbling in awe and making no effort to shake the effects of the spray of color.

Huyar grabbed the nearest warrior and began slapping him. "Wake up!" His efforts had no apparent effect on the elf.

Sadira heard the hiss of arrows flying through the air, then a half-dozen dazed elves dropped to the ground without so much as a gasp. The sorceress looked toward the wall she had created. Three Nibenese soldiers, their tabards bearing the insignia of the royal cilops, were rushing around each end of the granite barrier.

The sorceress reached for another spell component, then heard the clatter of clawed feet scrambling across a patch of rocky ground. The Nibenese unleashed another flight of arrows, and this time Grissi was among those who fell. Huyar gave up trying to wake his dazed companions and reached for his sword.

"It'll do no good!" Sadira said. "Dhojakt's coming."

"Then I hope he tears your eyes out," the elf said, jumping into the hole.

Although Huyar did not know it, it occurred to Sadira that he had done exactly the right thing. She lowered herself into the opening until only her head and shoulders were protruding from it. While keeping a watchful eye on the Nibenese, she continued to draw the energy for a spell, but did not reach for any components.

A moment later, Dhojakt came around the corner of her rock wall. In the moonlight, she could see him clearly enough to tell that his nose was swollen and purple, with a single huge lesion where there had once been two flaring nostrils.

Dhojakt's black eyes went immediately to where Sadira was hiding. The sorceress saw a hateful light flicker in the pupils, then he said, "I thought this would be the easiest way to lure you away from your protectors."

The prince pointed a finger in her direction, and Sadira allowed herself to drop into the tunnel below. Her body still tingling with the magical energy she had summoned, she turned and sprinted after the sound of Huyar's fleeing feet. A loud sputter echoed behind her, and she glanced back to see black dust billowing through the hole. Thankfully, the cloud settled to the floor and did not spread down the passageway. Within moments, flaxen rays of moonlight were once again streaming through the opening.

Sadira looked away from the hole and waited until her elven vision began to function, then ducked into the cramped aisle where she had seen the halfling. There, she stopped and listened. Huyar's footfalls had grown silent, and the only sound was the waterfall whispering in the abyss at the far end of the corridor.

A moment later, she heard the Nibenese archers enter the grotto, with the rattle of Dhojakt's many legs close behind. Intentionally dragging a foot along the floor so they would hear her moving, Sadira crawled through the passageway—being careful not to look into any of the strange crypts, lest she witness another moving halfling.

Upon reaching the end, she ducked around the corner to wait. In one hand, she held her dagger. With the other, she withdrew a small piece of hardened tree sap from her satchel. The milky nugget had been shaped to look like a lump of crystallized acid.

Soon, she heard the Nibenese soldiers crawling through the passage. As she had hoped, they were groping their way blindly. There had been no time to light torches, and, since he could not draw energy through the grotto's white stone, Dhojakt had been unable to use his magic to help them see. At the end of the line, his claws ticking impatiently as he forced his men forward, came the prince.

Sadira watched as the first three men crawled from the small tunnel, their nervous faces glowing bright red. She held perfectly still until they realized they had left the cramped corridor behind and began to rise. At that moment, she attacked, slashing her dagger across the first man's face and kicking him off the ledge in the same swift motion.

Sadira barely had to attack the second guard. He lashed out blindly with an obsidian short sword, the momentum of his swing carrying his blade toward the abyss. She stepped behind the swipe and used her shoulder to nudge him over the edge. He had not yet started to scream when she drove her dirk under the third guard's chin. The man died with an astonished gurgle, then, as she stepped away, collapsed onto the ledge.

"What's happening there?" demanded Dhojakt's angry voice. "Go!"

The fourth guard obeyed, scrambling forward over his dead comrade's body. Her body tingling with the thrill of combat and the magical energy she had summoned earlier, Sadira stepped forward again. This time the sorceress drove her blade into the hollow at the base of the man's skull.

The fifth guard froze at the exit and would not move.

"I said go!" Dhojakt screamed.

The fifth and sixth soldiers were catapulted into the abyss as the angry prince rushed forward. Dhojakt poked his head out of the passageway and looked toward Sadira.

"You've caused me enough trouble!" he spat. His bony mouthparts were fully extended, dripping venom and clacking in fury.

Sadira backed away, keeping her dagger in front of her and the hardened tree sap hidden in her other hand. Dhojakt did not even try to summon the energy for a spell, no doubt having already discovered it would not work. Instead, he seemed only too happy to leave the safety of the tunnel and follow the sorceress onto the precarious ledge.

As the prince crawled over the bodies of his two dead guards, Sadira stopped. To her right opened a dark passage. Though it offered the sorceress some small reassurance as a possible escape route, she suspected that if she needed to flee, she would not survive long enough to use it.

Dhojakt wasted no time attacking. Once he was past the dead men, he rushed forward—but not along the ledge where Sadira had expected him to approach. Instead, his centipede's body slipped up the wall, and he approached while hanging from the side of the cavern. When he reached the doorway at the sorceress's side, he stopped and reached down to grasp her.

"You should have let me kill you in Nibenay," he said. "It would have saved us both a lot of trouble and pain."

"You, perhaps, but not me," Sadira said. She thrust the tree sap toward the prince's face.

As he saw the crystal-shaped lump coming at him, Dhojakt turned away to protect his vulnerable nose. "That won't work this time, stupid girl!" he said.

Sadira spoke her incantation, but the stream that shot from her hand was not one of poisonous acid. Instead, it was a thick, gummy resin that quickly covered the prince's head and torso in a single globule. Realizing he had been tricked, Dhojakt laboriously twisted his head around to face the sorceress. As he tried to reach out for her, Sadira backed away and spoke a single command word.

The resin hardened into a milky bead, as solid as stone and just as inflexible. Beneath the amorphous globule, Sadira could barely make out the shape of the prince's outstretched arms and the mandibles protruding from his mouth. The spell had not been large enough to cover his many legs, however. He resembled a giant centipede that had suffered the misfortune of being half-encased in a giant bead of frankincense.

Sadira sheathed her dagger, then grabbed the heavy

globule and pulled. Dhojakt tried to cling to the porous wall with his clawed feet, but the weight of the milky bubble encasing his body was too much for him. With the sorceress's help, the heavy globule slowly peeled away from the stone, until at last Sadira managed to push it off the ledge.

Then, all at once, the prince's claws tore free. Dhojakt slipped over the edge and, his legs slashing at the sorceress in a desperate effort to drag her along, he disappeared into the darkness. Sadira slumped down on the ledge and listened to the prince's feet scrape along the wall of the chasm.

There was no splash or final clatter. The rasp of the prince's claws simply faded away long before it should have, with no suggestion that he had hit the canyon bottom.

The sorceress peered over the edge. She half-expected to see Dhojakt scrambling back up the cliff, but she found nothing except darkness below.

"Well done," said Huyar's voice. "Especially the dagger work against the guards."

A startled cry escaped Sadira's lips and she almost slipped over the ledge, but Huyar grasped her shoulder with a firm hand. As he pulled her to her feet, he slipped her dagger from its sheath, then pressed the blade against the small of her back.

"Let's see what you have in your satchel, shall we?"

He used his free hand to remove the bag from her shoulder, then opened it and dumped the contents on the ground. Being careful never to let the dirk leave the sorceress's back, he reached down and picked up the intricately carved vial that Magnus and Rhayn had procured in the Bard's Quarter of Nibenay.

"What's this?" the elf asked. Holding the flask next to

Sadira's face, he ran his fingers over the notes carved into its side. "The poison you used on our chief?"

"No," Sadira answered. For the moment, the truth seemed her best option—she certainly could not hope to outrun or outfight the elf. "It's the antidote."

The Wild Lands

SIXTEEN

The Wild Lands

"My own daughter!" roared Faenaeyon. "How could you?"

Sadira stood atop Cleft Rock, staring across an olive-tinged haze into the crimson disk of the rising sun. Her hands were bound behind her back, with her father pacing in front of her and Huyar standing at her side with a drawn sword. All of the other Sun Runners were gathered around the monolith, watching the proceedings in grim silence.

"I must reach the Pristine Tower," Sadira said, calmly answering her father's question.

"The tower, of course!" spat the chief. "Where the New Races are spawned—who's to say you wouldn't find the power to defy the Dragon there?" He shook his head in contempt, then waved a hand at Magnus. "Even if you were that lucky, could you bear to live with what you'll become?"

"That isn't your worry," Sadira replied. "What is your concern—or rather, should have been—is that I rescued you from the slave pens in return for a promise to guide me to the Pristine Tower."

"And when Faenaeyon wouldn't honor it, you struck a bargain with Rhayn to make her chief," concluded Huyar.

When Sadira did not answer, Faenaeyon stopped in front of her. "Is that how it happened?"

"I have no reason to tell you anything," Sadira said, looking away.

Faenaeyon grabbed her jaw and turned her head back toward him. "Tell me truly, and you shall live to see the Pristine Tower," he said. "Rhayn helped you, did she not?"

When Sadira did not answer, he pushed her down. "I thought as much," he growled, turning around to face his other daughter. "How could you? Sadira is an outsider, but you are a Sun Runner."

The elf shook her head. "Father, I didn't—"

"Rhayn, there's no use lying," said Sadira, struggling back to her feet. "Our father is no fool. He can see for himself what happened. If you tell him the truth, perhaps some good will come of it for the tribe."

Faenaeyon scowled at Sadira. "What are you saying?"

Sadira looked him in the eye. "You said that if I answered honestly, I'd live to see the Pristine Tower. Will you keep that promise—or is it like all your others?"

"I'll honor my word—though you'll rue that I did," he answered. "Now tell me what happened."

Sadira nodded. "The truth of the matter is that you don't deserve to be chief—not any more. You steal what your followers earn, you treat your warriors like slaves, and you resolve disputes by taking bribes. That's why Rhayn asked me to poison you—her idea, by the way, not mine. Sooner or later, someone else will try it again. For the sake of the Sun Runners, I hope they succeed."

Faenaeyon listened to the words with no visible emotion, then turned to his other daughter. "Is this so?"

Rhayn glared at the sorceress and started to shake her head, but Magnus stepped in front of her. "Sadira's right—there's no use denying it." He looked to the chief, then said, "You raised me in your own camp, but I also helped."

Faenaeyon closed his eyes for a moment. When he opened them again, he looked incredibly old and tired. "Perhaps there was a time when I was a better chief," he said. "But that doesn't excuse what you did. Rightfully, I should kill you all now."

"I demand it!" shouted Huyar, raising his sword. "It's clear that Gaefal saw them leaving the Bard's Quarter, and that's why they murdered him. If you don't give me justice, I'll take it."

Faenaeyon glanced at Huyar's sword with a disdainful sneer. "Did you not hear me promise Sadira that she would live to see the Pristine Tower?"

"But I must have vengeance!"

"Unless it's me you intend to attack, put your sword away," Faenaeyon growled, stepping toward the elf.

Huyar's anger changed to trepidation as he looked into Faenaeyon's gray eyes. Although he was armed, and the chief was not, he clearly did not relish the thought of pitting his skills against those of Faenaeyon. Huyar sheathed his sword. Looking at the ground, he said, "I demand—"

"You demand nothing," Faenaeyon snarled. "If you had Rhayn's courage, you'd be chief and Gaefal would be alive." He looked away from his son and ran his eyes over the rest of the tribe. "But I am still chief, and until someone comes who is strong enough to take my place, that's how it'll stay."

When no one voiced any objections to this declaration, Faenaeyon gestured at Magnus and Rhayn. "As for you two, I'll be merciful," he said. "You may choose death, or you may join Sadira on her journey to the Pristine Tower."

After glancing at Magnus, Rhayn looked back to her father. "We choose the tower, of course," she said.

Faenaeyon arched his brow in mock sorrow. "Had you been brave enough to choose death, you would have suffered less." He motioned for Rhayn and Magnus to climb onto the monolith, then pointed a long finger at the place where Huyar had thrown Sadira's belongings. "Put your satchels, weapons, and waterskins there. You shall leave the tribe as you came into it, except that I will permit you to keep the clothes you wear."

* * * * *

Sadira and her two companions knelt at the edge of a silver-green heath. The field stretched clear to the horizon, so lush and vast that nowhere did an outcropping of stone or a patch of barren earth show through the thick tangle of brush. On the horizon rose a spire of white rock, so distant that it often seemed to disappear behind the wavering bands of the afternoon haze.

Although the rock could only be the Pristine Tower, the three companions hardly seemed aware of it. Their attention was focused much nearer to their own location, on a herd of wild erdlus that had trotted into view just a few moments earlier.

As tall as elves and as plump as kanks, the featherless birds seemed completely unaware that they were being watched. They worked their way through the field at a steady pace, their serpentine necks thrashing about like whips, flinging out small round heads to snatch cones of silvery broompipe and the ivory blossoms of tall milkweed plants. Occasionally, an erdlu let out an excited squawk and scratched at the ground, then flapped its useless wings in delight as it impaled a snake on its wedge-shaped beak.

Far above the birds, drifting with the breeze, was a bell-shaped pod of slimy membrane. The floating beast was more than ten yards across, with dozens of wispy tendrils dangling from the rim of its underbelly. Inside its transparent body, a morass of blue organs pulsated at irregular intervals, occasionally giving off a bright yellow glow.

"The floater's back!" Sadira hissed, her pale eyes fixed on the strange beast. In her hand, the sorceress held a shard of quartz they had come across in the desert, and her body tingled with the magical energy she had summoned only a moment earlier.

"It must be tracking us," whispered Magnus.

"In case you haven't noticed, we've been traveling against the wind for the last day and a half," countered Rhayn. "Besides, without wings or feet, how could it follow us if it wanted to? It's at the mercy of the wind."

"The wind is everywhere," answered Magnus. "You would be surprised what's possible for those who know its secrets."

As the windsinger spoke, four ribbons of blue membrane dropped from the center of the beast's body and slipped around a feeding erdlu. The astonished bird bolted, dragging the floater through the air and squawking in panic. The rest of the flock sprang into motion, fleeing in all directions.

Instantly, Rhayn was on her feet. "Now, Sadira!" she screamed, chasing after the birds. "We can't lose them!"

Sadira pointed her quartz shard at the largest erdlu and spoke her incantation. A translucent bolt buzzed from her hand and struck the beast, scattering brown scales in all directions. Cackling in surprise, the creature took two more steps and dropped to the ground. Rhayn leaped on it immediately, placing one foot on its throat and jerking the head upward to snap the neck.

"Well done," she cried, looking back to her sister. "You saved the meat."

Sadira's attention was not focused on Rhayn. The sorceress was enraptured by the scene farther ahead, where the floater had lifted its prey off the ground and was pulling the bird toward its pulsing blue entrails. With its claws and beak, the erdlu slashed madly at the ribbons clutching it, but never managed to tear away anything more than a glob of slime.

The bird's struggles ceased entirely when it came within reach of the short tendrils rimming its captor's body. As the gossamer filaments touched the erdlu, its neck fell limp and its claws stopped slashing the air. Squawking mournfully, it rose slowly upward and passed into the floater's gelatinous body, becoming nothing more than a dark shape in the blue tangle of its killer's gut.

Suppressing a shudder, Sadira observed, "Remind me not to let that thing fly over my head."

"We've been smart to avoid it," Magnus agreed. "Still, I'd like to take a closer look. I could learn much from a being that lives in such harmony with the wind."

The windsinger's musings were interrupted by an angry cry from Rhayn. "Sadira, I need your help!"

The sorceress went over to her sister, brushing past cones of broompipe and long stems of milkweed. Underfoot, the grass was so high that her feet disappeared as she moved, and the soil from which the green blades sprang was not visible at all.

Upon reaching Rhayn's side, Sadira saw the reason for her sister's peevishness. Around the charred wound on the erdlu's flank, some of the scales were changing into downy feathers, while others were fusing together to form a sort of knobby hide similar to Magnus's. Where the beast's neck had been snapped, a writhing lump had formed beneath the yellow scales. Rhayn had torn out one of the bird's claws to use as a knife, and the resulting wound had sprouted a bud of gray fingertip.

From her earlier conversations with Faenaeyon, Sadira knew the bird would go through a transformation after being wounded. She hadn't expected it to occur so fast, or to be so gruesome.

Anxious not to prolong the misery of the last three days, the sorceress put her queasiness aside and knelt next to her sister. Since being banished from the Sun Runners with no weapons or water, the companions had barely managed to survive. They had eaten only once, sharing a single lizard that Magnus had managed to pluck from under a boulder. For water, they had spent hours digging and mashing tubers, then squeezing a few drops of bitter juice from the resulting gruel.

Therefore, after Rhayn had told her that a single erdlu could provide them all with weapons, waterskins, and meat, Sadira had readily agreed to delay their trek long enough to kill one of the birds. And now, it appeared the magic of the Pristine Tower was threatening to rob them of their prize.

"What do you want me to do?" Sadira asked.

Rhayn used the claw in her hand to cut away another talon, which she handed to Sadira. The tip of another new finger began to protrude from the fresh wound.

"We need the claws, the leg tendons and bones, the

stomach, the beak, the hardest scales—just about anything you can take off," Rhayn said. "But be careful. If you cut yourself . . ."

She let the sentence die and gestured at a tiny hand that had just slipped from beneath one of the bird's scales.

"Maybe we should have Magnus do this," Sadira suggested. "His skin's a lot tougher than ours."

Rhayn shook her head. "He'd never finish it in time. His fingers are too thick," she said. "It's better if he keeps a watch on the floater."

The elf frowned at a pair of sharp fangs that had begun to protrude from the erdlu's mouth, then fell silent and concentrated all her attention on butchering the prey. Within a few minutes, they had a large pile of bird parts that had not changed into something else: claws, scales, a pair of long leg bones, sinews, and some meat. They also had a dozen more items the two women hoped would prove useful as substitutes for the spell components they had lost with their satchels.

Rhayn tossed the erdlu's stomach onto the pile. "That will be our waterskin," she said, looking out over the heath. "Assuming we can find something to fill it with."

"You know, if this place is as dangerous as Faenaeyon says, it's unlikely all of us will make it to the tower," Sadira said. "If you and Magnus don't want to go with me—"

"We will," said Rhayn. "I didn't come this far for nothing."

"But why?" Sadira asked. "I'm doing this for the people of Tyr, but they mean nothing to you."

"Will you find the power to defy the Dragon in the Pristine Tower?" Rhayn asked, avoiding a direct answer to the question.

Sadira shrugged. "I don't know what I'll find. All I can

say for certain is that Dhojakt is going to a lot of trouble to keep me from looking."

"*Is going*? Does that mean he's still alive?" Rhayn asked, rummaging through the pile of bird parts. "Huyar said you pushed him off a cliff."

"I did, but I don't think he hit bottom," the sorceress answered. "And even if he did, that doesn't mean he died."

"I wonder what he doesn't want you to find," said Rhayn, pulling a long sinew off one of the leg bones.

"Or to become," Sadira said. "Faenaeyon raised an interesting point before banishing us. If this is where the New Races are born, who's to say the magic can't be used to give me what I want? Perhaps that's how Dhojakt became half-man and half-cilops."

Rhayn looked at the transfigured remains of the erdlu. "It doesn't strike me as something that can be controlled."

"Maybe not out here, but I've seen someone undergo a similar change," she said. "When we killed Kalak, he was in the process of changing himself into a dragon. I think he would have succeeded."

"And you believe something similar can happen in the Pristine Tower?"

Sadira shrugged. "I've heard that the original Dragon was created there," she said. "From what we've seen so far, I'd believe it."

"That's why I'm coming with you," said Rhayn. "If that can be done, then I should be able to find what I want in the tower."

Sadira raised her brow. "What's that?"

"The power to win Faenaeyon's place as chief of the tribe," Rhayn said. She looked westward, toward Cleft Rock.

"The Sun Runners will never take you back," Sadira replied. "No matter what we find."

"Don't be so sure. Elves are a practical people," said Rhayn. "They'll follow a strong chief—especially if they have no other choice."

"You wouldn't tyrannize your own tribe!" Sadira gasped.

"What I won't do is allow my children to grow up without me," said Rhayn. "They'll be treated no better than slaves in another woman's camp."

"Meredyd won't let that happen," Sadira objected. "After what you did for her—"

"By now, Meredyd has already forgotten that my gold bought her child's freedom," Rhayn spat. She sat down and, using a shard of bone for a needle, began sewing shut the bottom of the erdlu's stomach.

Sadira shook her head. "Meredyd is your friend."

Rhayn laughed. "Friendship is based on mutual need," she said. "Now that Meredyd stands to gain nothing from me, she's no longer my friend. She won't look out for my children—any more than I'd watch after hers if she had been banished."

Magnus's dulcet voice drifted across the field. Sadira looked in the direction from which it came and saw the windsinger almost a hundred yards away. He stood beneath the floater, his black eyes fixed on the thing's pulsating body. His ears twitched back and forth slowly, as if listening to some sound the sorceress could not hear, and his snout was curled into an expression of utter rapture.

"What's Magnus doing?" Sadira asked, alarmed.

The floater lowered its ribbonlike arms and allowed them to dangle a few yards above the ground. A soft warble began to play in the wind, so gentle and faint that the sorceress sensed it only as an uncertain tingle in the back of her skull.

"It looks like he's talking to it," Rhayn answered, continuing to work. "I'd leave him alone—you wouldn't want to startle the thing."

A few minutes later, the elf tied off the thread and laid the new waterskin aside. After stripping more sinew from the legs, she motioned for Sadira to sit down beside her. The two women busied themselves with making a pair of weapons, tying razor-sharp claws to the ends of the bird's thigh bones.

They were almost finished when Sadira noticed more than a dozen shadows surrounding her and Rhayn. They had vaguely human shapes, with ropey limbs, serpentine torsos, and blue embers where their eyes should have been. The sorceress looked around, searching for the beings who were casting the shadows, but found no one—even when she looked into the sky.

One of the shadows reached for the stomach Rhayn had just sewn shut. When its finger touched the waterskin, the vessel turned black and became part of the shadow itself.

"What are they?" Rhayn demanded, also staring at the dark figures surrounding them.

"Shadow people," Sadira answered, recalling Rikus's description of Umbra. She also remembered Er'Stali's account of the two dwarves who had gone to the Pristine Tower, then used obsidian to bribe the shadow people. "I think they're from the tower."

Rhayn stood, apparently less interested in where they were from than what they were doing. "Tell them to give us the waterskin back!" she said, motioning at the creatures with the lance she had been making.

"How?" Sadira asked.

When several shadows began to close around Rhayn,

the elf cast a simple spell and a beam of light sprang from her hand. She aimed it at the ground before her, trying to fend off the dark figures at her feet. If anything, her efforts only made the silhouettes grow blacker and more substantial.

One shadow stopped harassing Rhayn. Its body began to thicken and assume a solid form, then it moved into a kneeling position. When it had assumed a full, three-dimensional form, it rose to its feet. The thing stood as tall as a half-giant, towering over the elf as she towered over Sadira.

"By what right do you hunt on our lands?" it demanded, black fumes rising from the blue gash that had opened to serve as its mouth.

Instead of answering, Rhayn backed away and looked toward Magnus. When she saw that he and the floater were still singing to each other, she called, "Magnus, leave that thing alone and come here!"

When he did not seem to hear her, the shadow looked down at its fellows on the ground, then waved its hand toward the windsinger. Several of the silhouettes rushed toward Magnus, swimming through the grass like a person would swim through an oasis pond. Upon reaching the windsinger, they began circling him in a mad dance. After a few moments, they stopped and, assuming solid form, rose to a standing position.

The floater's shrill warble ceased, and it shot its ribbonlike arms down to grasp Magnus. The windsinger's song came to a strangled halt, and he cried out in pain. The beast's limbs began to retract, though instead of lifting the heavy windsinger into the air, it descended toward him. The shadow people surrounding Magnus melted back into the ground, shooting away from him as quickly as they had approached.

Rhayn screamed in alarm, then sprinted toward the windsinger. Sadira started to follow, but found her way blocked by the shadow that had been talking to her sister.

"The game on this land belongs to us," the silhouette hissed, taking Sadira's wrist. A black stain slowly spread up her arm, accompanied by a cold, numbing pain that seemed to draw the very heat from her body. "How are you going to pay for it?"

"Forgive us. We didn't know the birds belonged to anyone." Sadira pulled her arm away, but the shadow blocked her path and would not allow her to go forward. She waved a hand at the pile of erdlu flesh. "Does it look like we—"

She was interrupted as Magnus's thunderous voice rumbled across the heath, intoning a single bass note. So deep and full was the tone that Sadira could hear nothing else. She even felt the sound in her bones, a resonate vibration that made her joints rasp and her abdomen tremble.

Across the meadow, Sadira saw her sister reach Magnus's side and begin slashing at the ribbons holding him prisoner. Rhayn accomplished little, except to cover herself with slime. The windsinger shoved her away, raising his voice still louder. A searing whirlwind, full of burning sand and flying stones, roared in from the desert and entwined the windsinger and his attacker. Wild undulations rolled through the floater's body, then its blue entrails began to writhe madly about.

In the next instant, the whirlwind ripped the beast apart, flinging slimy tendrils and masses of viscid flesh in all directions. The largest part of the floater's body sailed far over the heath, where it was snatched from the air by the flick of some unseen creature's barb-covered tongue. Magnus closed his mouth and collapsed to the ground, allowing the whirlwind to dissipate as quickly as it had appeared.

Sadira sidestepped the shadow in front of her and rushed to the windsinger's side, arriving a few moments after her sister. Where the floater had gripped him, Magnus's face and arms were red and inflamed. On one of his legs was a long welt that had burst open and was slowly oozing blood.

"Magnus, heal yourself!" Sadira said, pulling a piece of slimy tentacle off his shoulder.

The windsinger nodded and began his song.

The welt did not close. Instead, the tip of a brown root sprouted from the wound. Sadira snatched Rhayn's weapon and used the erdlu claw to cut the thing off.

Magnus howled in pain, then took the lance from her hand and flung it away. "No!" he cried. "It's part of me now. I can feel it growing out of my bones."

Another root appeared from the wound. The three companions watched in horror as it grew larger and longer, until it was as big around as Sadira's wrist. Suddenly, the tip turned downward and plunged into the soil. Rhayn and Sadira grabbed the stalk and, ignoring Magnus's scream, tried to pull it free. The women were nearly jerked off their feet as the thing burrowed into the ground. Finally, when the stem had grown so large that they could no longer grasp it, the sisters gave up.

"We've got to try something else," Sadira said. "Maybe blasting it away?"

"That would be like taking off a leg, maybe worse," Magnus said, his teeth clenched in pain.

"Then what do you want us to do?" demanded Rhayn, her voice betraying her frustration.

"We could reverse the metamorphosis for you," said a deep voice.

Sadira turned around and saw that all of the shadow people had manifested themselves in solid form. They were standing several yards away, their cold blue eyes fixed on the root attaching Magnus to the ground.

"You can do that?" the sorceress asked.

"Of course," answered the shadow. "This is our land, is it not?"

Sadira and Rhayn stepped aside and waved the shadows forward. "Please do."

The group's leader shook his head. "First, there is the matter of payment," he said. "It has been more than a year since our last shipment. We had hoped you were the couriers."

"We're not, so stop wasting time and fix him," Rhayn snorted, pointing at Magnus.

The shadow shook his head. "Not without payment."

"I'll pay you!" the elf yelled, spreading her fingers to draw the energy for a spell.

Sadira laid a restraining hand on her sister's arm. To the shadows, she said, "I'm sorry, but we have no obsidian—"

"Then your friend shall remain as he is until you bring it to us," hissed the speaker.

With that, he walked over and seized the weapon that Magnus had thrown to the ground earlier. As his darkness engulfed the makeshift lance, the other shadows went over to where Sadira and Rhayn had been butchering the erdlu. They collected all of the claws, scales, and bones that the two sisters had labored so hard to harvest, then melted into the ground and swam off toward the distant tower.

"Now what?" Rhayn demanded.

"We follow them," Sadira said. "If they can reverse what happened to Magnus, I'll wager they can control the tower's magic. All we have to do is figure out a way to convince them to give us what we want."

"Leave that to me," said Rhayn. "The shadow has not been cast that can out-bargain an elf."

"And what about me?" Magnus asked.

Sadira gave him a sad look. "I don't see that we can help you by staying here," she said. "If we're successful at the tower, we'll be back with the shadow people to free you."

The windsinger nodded. "I guess that makes sense, but what about food—and water?"

Rhayn kissed Magnus on the cheek, at the same time patting the brown stalk that anchored him to the ground. "Isn't that what roots are for?"

SEVENTEEN

The Pristine Tower

Sadira slipped past the gnarled form of another bogo tree, taking care to stay well away from the dagger-sized thorns covering its trunk. As she moved, the sorceress kept a watchful eye on the burled limbs overhead. Although she and Rhayn had been in the forest less than three hours, they had already been attacked a half-dozen times by snakelike beasts lurking in the trees. The creatures liked to swing down as their prey passed beneath a branch, trying to impale their chosen victims on the barbed spines that covered their bodies.

Once Sadira was safely past the bogo tree, she turned her attention forward, expecting to see nothing but more twisted, stark boles. Instead, she was surprised to find herself at the edge of a small glade covered with clumps of ash-colored brush. Thousands of fleecy white blossoms, held aloft on long yellow stems, swayed back and forth in the hot wind.

Sadira hardly noticed the meadow. During the last day and a half, she and Rhayn had seen a dozen different fields. All had been equally beautiful, and all had concealed hazards that had to be negotiated at the peril of their lives. The sorceress was more interested in what lay at the heart of the glade.

There, a glaring needle of white stone rose into the sky, as high as a cloud and as sheer as a sculpted column. At the bottom stood an ancient gatehouse, guarding a narrow case of stairs that circled up the spire until it could no longer be distinguished as a separate feature. The pillar seemed to have no summit, at least not that Sadira could see. It simply grew smaller and smaller, until it disappeared into the sky.

"I'd say we've reached the Pristine Tower," said Rhayn, coming up behind the sorceress.

"Not yet," said Sadira, cautiously stepping into the meadow. "There's still a hundred yards to go—and that's no small distance in this place."

The two women advanced slowly, avoiding contact with the brush and its blossoms. When they could not, they carefully inspected the stems for thorns or stickers that might draw even a drop of blood. It was a slow and tedious way to travel, but with what had happened to Magnus still fresh in their memories, the women knew it was necessary.

They were about halfway across when a chorus of snorts and squeals erupted from a short distance away. Yellow canes and fleecy blossoms danced wildly as the growling creatures charged toward the sisters.

"I've got it," Rhayn said, pulling a pinch of sand from her pocket.

An instant later, several squat rodents with the bodies of weasels and the tusks of boars charged from the undergrowth. They came directly at the two women, their clawed feet spraying dirt high into the air.

Rhayn tossed the sand in their direction and spoke her

incantation. The grains began to sparkle and formed a small cloud close to the ground. The beasts rushed straight into the scintillating fog and promptly collapsed on top of each other, sound asleep.

"That's the last of my spells," Rhayn said, turning back toward the tower.

"I'm no better off," said Sadira. "We'll just have to hope for the best."

During the trek to the tower, the two women had relied on their magic to defend themselves from a myriad of creatures. Unfortunately, whenever they cast a spell, the incantation vanished from their minds. Usually, the mystic words and gestures were renewed through study, but because Faenaeyon had not let them keep their spellbooks, they could not replenish their spells.

Sadira resumed her careful approach to the tower, listening even more intently for any hint of trouble. As they neared the white spire, the sorceress saw that it was made of the same porous stone as the grotto at Cleft Rock. Although she found this puzzling, she was not particularly concerned by it. Since both she and Rhayn had exhausted their spells, there would be no need to draw magical energy through the stone.

A few tense minutes later, they reached the gatehouse. It was an ancient structure, solidly built from granite blocks and lined with the dark slits of arrow loops. Stone hinges still hung from the gate posts, and beneath the archway, the spikes of a shattered portcullis were lodged in the foyer's cracked flagstones.

When the two women stepped beneath the arch, a pair of sparkling blue eyes appeared in the darkness of an arrow slit. "Stand where you are!" ordered a voice that seemed neither male nor female.

When the sisters obeyed, a black silhouette slipped

from the arrow loop and took on the ropey form of a shadow person. It stepped forward to block their way, then asked, "Do you bring obsidian?"

"No, that will come later," answered Rhayn, taking charge of the negotiations. "For now, we have only a small gift to establish our good will, and in return we seek a favor to establish yours."

"What is your gift?" asked the shadow.

"News regarding Umbra and the obsidian mines of Family Lubar," answered Rhayn.

In preparation for the negotiations, Sadira had repeated to her sister all that Rikus and Er'Stali had told her about Maetan of Lubar's relationship to Umbra, the shadow people, and the Pristine Tower. After hearing about the obsidian caravans that Family Lubar had sent in payment for Umbra's services, Rhayn had declared she would have no trouble getting what they wanted from the shadow people.

When the silhouette expressed no interest in what she had tendered so far, Rhayn said, "We thought you might be interested in reviving the flow of obsidian caravans."

This offer met with more success. "We will hear what you have to say," the shadow replied. It drifted aside and faded back into the arrow slit.

"After you," Rhayn said, motioning Sadira forward.

The sorceress stepped past the remains of the shattered portcullis, then led the way onto the narrow stairway beyond. She found that they would need to be even more careful climbing the tower than they had been in approaching it. Although each step was only a few inches high, it was also just half as wide as Sadira's foot was long. To make matters worse, in places the staircase was so worn that it had become more of ramp, covered with a thousand years of dust and sand. The footing was so treacherous that a dune's slip face would have been easier to ascend.

"Be careful," Sadira said. "After coming so far, it would be a shame to get hurt here."

"Elves do not trip on staircases," Rhayn replied.

Sadira turned and, being especially careful of her footing, began to climb. At the same time, she asked, "Don't you think you promised too much back there?"

"What did I pledge?" Rhayn asked.

"Nothing, I guess. But it's what you implied you could do that concerns me," Sadira said. "When they discover we can't send them caravans of obsidian, they'll be angry—and where will that get us?"

"They'll be interested, and that's all we need," said Rhayn. "We may not give them obsidian at all, but we'll find out what else they want and give that to them—or make them think we're going to."

Sadira shook her head. "I hope they're not accustomed to dealing with elves," she muttered.

They continued upward for an interminable time, choosing every step with the utmost care. Sadira's thighs soon began to burn from the effort of endless climbing, while the strain of supporting her weight on the balls of her feet caused knots to form in her calves. The sorceress tried to ignore the pain and concentrate on her footing.

Occasionally, she paused to rest and took a moment to look out over the vista. There was not a sand dune or stretch of barren ground in sight. Everywhere she looked, the panorama was covered by some shade of green: silver-green broomgrass on the horizon, a ring of brown-tinged tortoise bushes closer in, and the blue-hued boughs of the bogo forest encircling the tower itself. If not for the risks involved in reaching the place, it would have been worth the climb just to see a panorama so teeming with plants.

During one of these short rests, Sadira asked, "Have you seen any sign of Dhojakt?"

Rhayn shook her head. "There are many creatures down there, but none of them seem to be following our path." She motioned for Sadira to resume the climb. "Let's go. The less time we give our culls to think, the better."

The sisters climbed the rest of the way without stopping and soon reached the summit of the spire. The staircase ended at the walls of a small bastion, built completely of alabaster and finished with an undulating cap of ivory. Beyond the open gates, a path of limestone blocks crossed an immense basin of shimmering blue water, stopping at a minaret that rose directly out of the pond. This tower was faced with white onyx and crowned by a crystal cupola, blushing pink with the radiance of the crimson sun.

After passing through the gate, Rhayn and Sadira knelt at the edge of the pool. Despite their thirst, they hesitated to drink. The water smelled brackish and foul, while the grasslike blades of some underwater plant clogged the entire basin. In the few places where they could see to the bottom, they glimpsed a rocky growth resembling the gnarled branches a myrrh tree, save that it glowed in a dozen different shades of color, from rosy pink to jade green.

Sadira scooped up a handful of water and, ignoring the fetid smell, lifted it to her lips. When she tried to swallow the horrid stuff, her throat rebelled at the briny taste and she had to spit it back into the pool.

"That water is not for drinking," said a shadow's voice.

The sisters spun around to find a dozen shadow people standing behind them. All of the silhouettes had assumed three-dimensional form, with their burning blue eyes fixed on the women.

As Sadira and Rhayn rose, the leader demanded, "Tell us of Umbra."

"Who are you?" asked Rhayn.

"I am Khidar, sachem in Umbra's absence," answered the shadow. "Tell me of Umbra."

"First, you must answer a question for us," said Rhayn.

Khidar stepped forward and grasped the elf by the throat. A stain of darkness began to creep up her chin and down over her shoulders. "There is nothing we *must* do," the shadow growled, spewing black fumes into Rhayn's face.

"And I don't have to tell you what happened to Umbra," the elf countered, answering the challenge with one of her own.

"True—you can die instead!"

The darkness continued to spread, engulfing Rhayn's entire face. Realizing that either Khidar did not understand the concept of bargaining or had no wish to, Sadira said, "Tell him!"

Her sister did not seem to hear. Instead, as blackness swallowed her head and torso, Rhayn lashed out at her captor. Her fists passed right through his body, and, when she withdrew them, they were also covered in darkness.

"We think Umbra was destroyed!" Sadira blurted. "Now let her go!"

Khidar released the elf, and the darkness drained from her body. She collapsed to the walkway, shivering and as pale as the limestone blocks on which she lay.

The leader faced Sadira. "Now that you know who is master in this keep, you may tell me more of what happened to Umbra."

Sadira studied her sister for a moment, then looked back to Khidar. "Before we continue, let me explain something to you," she said. "Rhayn and I came to the Pristine Tower because we need your help. Unless you give it to us, we'll die before we cross the meadow at the base of this spire. So, you see, your threats mean nothing to us."

"You would not find the Black such a pleasant place," Khidar hissed.

"I suspect I'd find it more to my liking than becoming a half-slug and spending the rest of my life crawling through the bogo forest," Sadira said. When the shadow did not contradict her, the sorceress continued, "Your only choice is whether to help us or not—and the same is true of us. We can tell you what we know of Umbra and the Lubar obsidian, or we can refuse."

"In which case, you'll die—"

"And be no worse off than we are now," said Rhayn, gaining control of her shivering body.

When Khidar did not try to threaten them again, Sadira said, "Let me propose this: we'll tell you what we need. If you agree to provide it, we'll tell you what we know of Umbra."

"That's no good," objected Rhayn. She rose to her feet. "How do we know they won't renege on their promise?"

"How will they know we've told the truth?" countered Sadira. "At some point, we'll have to trust each other."

"Tell us what you want," said Khidar.

"Power," replied Rhayn. "I want you to use the tower's magic to make me strong enough to become chief of my tribe."

Khidar nodded. "You shall have power in proportion to the value of what you tell us." He looked to Sadira.

"And what do you want?"

Sadira hesitated, wondering how they would react if she told them the truth. Remembering Lyanius's initial resistance to the idea of helping her defy the Dragon, she thought it would be wise to stall until she could learn more about the shadow people. Unfortunately, from what she had seen so far, they had little patience for such bartering ploys.

Fearing that she would only make matters worse by being coy, Sadira took a deep breath and said, "I want to stop the Dragon from tyrannizing my city."

Khidar moved closer, his burning blue eyes locked on Sadira's. "Surely, you don't think we can do that for you?"

"I didn't ask you to do it for me, but I know there's something in this tower that can help me do it for myself," the sorceress replied. "Otherwise, King Tithian and Prince Dhojakt wouldn't have tried so hard to prevent me from reaching it."

This seemed to satisfy the shadow. "We'll do what we can to help you," he said. "Now tell us of Umbra."

"Do you know of the war that took place between Tyr and Urik?" Sadira asked, referring to the invasion that Rikus had turned back the year before. When the shadows nodded, Sadira continued. "During that war, a great champion from Tyr, the gladiator Rikus, fought with Umbra several times. During their last battle, Umbra received a terrible wound—"

"That's impossible," interrupted Khidar. "No weapon can injure one of us!"

"Rikus's sword was special," Sadira said. "It was the Scourge of Rkard, the blade that—"

"Borys of Ebe used to kill Rkard, the last of the Kemalok Kings," finished the shadow. "The sword is one of only a few that can do what you claim—but it's been lost for centuries. Where did this Rikus find it?"

"It was given to him by a group of dwarves," Sadira answered, encouraged by Khidar's familiarity with the weapon. She purposely left the rest of the details vague, so as to honor her promise to Neeva and Caelum about not revealing the treasures of Kled. "Rikus was also wounded during the fight, and fell unconscious before he saw what became of his enemy. When he awoke, Umbra was gone—though the floor where he had fallen remained as dark and cold as night."

"Then Umbra truly did perish," said Khidar. From the relief in his voice, the sorceress guessed that he enjoyed his duties as the new leader of the shadow people. "But why haven't I been contacted to go to Urik in his place? For centuries, our people have traded our sachem's service for Family Lubar's obsidian."

"After Urik lost the war, King Hamanu destroyed the entire family as punishment for Maetan of Lubar's failure to bring him victory," Sadira replied. "If any Lubars survive, it's as quarry slaves, not masters."

"That explains much," said Khidar. "It appears we'll have to find another source for our obsidian."

"Perhaps we could come to an arrangement," said Rhayn, stepping forward.

Khidar turned his blue embers toward her face. "I was not aware that elves mined obsidian."

"Don't be vulgar," she said, offended by the mere suggestion of such a thing. "But as soon as I become chief of the Sun Runners, we'll be able to steal all you want."

"I doubt that will happen," Khidar said.

"Don't underestimate the skills of the Sun Runners."

"I don't—though I doubt any tribe of thieves could supply us with a hundred unblemished balls of obsidian each year," the shadow replied. "What I mean to say is that you'll never become their chief."

"What?" Rhayn demanded.

"I promised to give you power in proportion to what you told us," Khidar said. "You said nothing. This one did all the talking." He pointed toward Sadira. "Therefore, we'll give her what she has asked for—but not you."

"Don't try to cheat me!" Rhayn warned. She thrust her hand out over the pond. "I swear, you'll regret it."

Khidar laughed. "Your spells won't harm us."

"Maybe not, but I can ruin this garden," she spat.

To give credence to her threat, she began to draw life-force from the pond. An eddy began to swirl beneath her hand, and a column of steam formed where the energy was rising. Because the rest of the Pristine Tower was made from the same porous stone as Cleft Rock, Sadira knew that the power her sister was drawing could only come from the plants in the pool. At the rate she was going, it would take only a few seconds before the elf defiled the whole thing.

"Rhayn, no!" Sadira said, moving toward her sister.

"Do you really think they'll give you what you want?" Rhayn growled. "They're playing us against each other—and you're letting them!"

"Even if that's true, what you're doing is wrong," Sadira said. Beneath Rhayn's hand, the plants began to turn brown, and the foul stench of decay rose from the frothing water.

"Stop!" yelled Khidar.

"Why should I?" demanded the elf. "We're going to die anyway."

"It doesn't matter," Sadira said, her eyes fixed on the brown stain spreading across the pool. "This is the last time I'll ask you to stop."

"Ask all you—"

Rhayn did not have a chance to finish. Sadira dropped to a knee and spun around, using the lower part of her leg to sweep her sister's feet. With an astonished scream, the elf lost her balance and fell into the pool of brown water.

A half-dozen shadows slipped into the pond without creating so much as a ripple. They glided over to Rhayn's struggling form and clamped their hands onto her arms. As they dragged her into the pool's depths, a black shroud slowly spread over the elf's body. She turned toward Sadira and opened her mouth to scream. That was the last the sorceress saw of her sister.

For a moment, Sadira could only stare into the water, morose and somber. She did not feel guilty, however, for Rhayn had been defiling the garden. As Sadira had learned in Nibenay, not even the shadows' betrayal could justify ruining fertile soil. In exacting her petty vengeance on the shadow people today, the elf had been willing to condemn an untold number of future generations to an existence of pain and misery.

As Sadira pondered her sister's fate, an icy hand touched her shoulder. "Come, we must hurry," said Khidar's voice.

"Why? So you can betray me, too?" demanded Sadira.

"We did not betray the elf," answered Khidar. "We merely honored the word of our promise—"

"Instead of the spirit," Sadira said. She rose and looked up into the blue cinders that served as the shadow's eyes. "Would it have been so difficult to give her what she asked?"

"No, but then we couldn't have given you what you want," Khidar answered. "Would you have preferred that?"

"At least I would have reason to trust you," Sadira

answered, dodging an answer to this difficult question.

"Whether you trust us or not does not matter," the shadow said. "Now come. We must hurry, or you will change into a mindless beast and run off before we can aid you."

He pointed at the stones where sorceress's knee had dropped when she swept Rhayn off her feet. There was a faint smear of blood on the limestone. Sadira looked down and saw that she had scraped her kneecap. Already, a yellow carapace was forming around the edges of the abrasion.

As Khidar guided her toward the tower at the center of the pond, Sadira asked, "Why are you helping me—if that's really what you're doing? It would have been an easy matter to find a pretense and betray me, as you did Rhayn."

"I told you, we are honoring our agreements to the word," the shadow insisted, though his tone suggested that he was not telling her the whole truth.

Sadira stopped. "There's more to it than that." She clenched her teeth as a painful muscle spasm ran up her leg. "You have some reason for wanting me to defy the Dragon."

"What do you care?" Khidar asked. "We're willing to help you. That's all that matters."

"If I'm to stand a chance of defying the Dragon, I must learn everything I can about him and this place," Sadira answered. "Otherwise, you might as well let me die here."

"I suppose it will do no harm to tell you, and perhaps it may even help," Khidar said, starting toward the tower. "You were powerful and resourceful enough to reach the tower on your own—and that is a good portent for the struggle you've taken upon yourself."

"This is all very interesting, but it still doesn't answered my question," Sadira answered, not allowing the shadow to sidetrack her with flattery.

Khidar sighed. "How much do you already know of the Pristine Tower?"

"Enough to guess that you're taking me into the Steeple of Crystals," the sorceress began. She quickly repeated what Er'Stali had told her: that the Champions had rebelled against Rajaat, and that they had forced him to make Borys into the Dragon. Sadira and Khidar reached the Steeple of Crystals just as she came to the story of how Jo'orsh and Sa'ram had tracked Borys to the Pristine Tower.

As soon as she mentioned the dwarves' names, Khidar burst out, "May the ghosts of the little thieves never find rest!"

Sadira frowned. "What did they steal?"

"You shall see soon enough," the shadow said, holding out his hand. "You must take my arm for a moment."

The sorceress grasped his frigid hand. She had to stifle a pained cry as his touch began to draw the heat from her body, leaving her shivering with a cold agony such as she had never before experienced. Khidar stepped forward, melting into the onyx wall. He pulled Sadira after him, and a shudder of nausea ran through her body as she also passed through the barrier. A moment later, the shadow released her hand.

"Welcome to the Steeple of Crystals," he said. "It was here that Rajaat imbued his champions with the power to carry out his will, and here that the traitors forced him to make Borys into the Dragon."

At first, the sorceress could see nothing but a fierce crimson glow whirling around her like a windblown fog. When she grew accustomed to the strange light, Sadira saw that the tower housed only a single gloomy room. A dome-shaped mirror served as the floor, while sheer white walls soared high overhead to support the crystal cupola that she had seen from the walkway outside.

A shaft of pink light descended from the cupola to the center of the mirror, where a dozen obsidian spheres of various sizes had been gathered. At first, it seemed to Sadira that the balls should have rolled away, but then she noticed that they were held in place by tiny wedges of marble. Inside each globe, a wisp of blue light slowly whirled about, as if some living thing were swimming through the black glass.

"What are those?" Sadira asked. Her leg began to itch madly. When she reached down to scratch, she discovered that an articulated yellow shell had entirely encased it.

"Eggs," Khidar replied, motioning the sorceress toward the murky orbs.

As she stepped away from the wall, limping slightly, Sadira saw that there were dozens of shadow people standing along the edge of the floor-mirror. Each time they exhaled, streams of dark vapor rose from their blue mouths and drifted toward the ceiling, joining the murk that already filled the room. The sorceress did not know whether the shadows had been there all along or had only recently come into the chamber, for with their mouths and eyes closed, they would have been indistinguishable from the gloomy walls.

"We must incubate our young in isolation, transferring them from smaller balls to larger as they grow," Khidar explained, waving his shadowy hand at the obsidian globes. "Before Jo'orsh and Sa'ram came, this was not necessary. We grew them all together, inside the dark lens."

"The dark lens?" Sadira asked.

"Rajaat used the dark lens to perform his magic," he said. "Without it, we cannot make you as powerful as you would like. But if you can steal the Scourge of Rkard from this Rikus, you will have two of the three things you need to kill the Dragon."

"Could you explain this a little more clearly?" Sadira asked. "Why do I need the Scourge of Rkard?"

"Because it was forged by Rajaat," Khidar answered. "Not only is it one of the few blades that will injure the Dragon, it will protect you from his blows. No champion—even traitors—can strike someone bearing a weapon forged by Rajaat."

"I can get the sword," Sadira answered confidently. "Now, what is it that you're doing for me?"

"You will understand better after we have finished," Khidar said. "But basically, we'll open a new source of magical energy to you—one that has not been used since the days of Rajaat."

"And the third thing?" Sadira asked.

Khidar pointed halfway up the tower. "The dark lens," he said. "You'll never kill the Dragon without it."

Sadira followed the shadow's finger and saw that there was an enormous steel ring attached to the walls. In it were set seven different gems, each as large as a half-giant's head. Six bars protruded from the inner wall of this ring, supporting another steel collar centered directly above the middle of the floor. From the size of this empty band, Sadira guessed the crystal it had held to be the size of a kank. Now the setting was empty, save for the crimson shaft of light descending through it to bathe the eggs below.

"Where do I find this dark lens?" she asked, wondering how she would move it once she had located it.

"That's something you'll have to discover for yourself. We have no idea where Jo'orsh and Sa'ram went after they left the tower," he said. "Now, you'll have to endure my touch one more time." Khidar reached for the sorceress's hand. "I must take you up there, where we can focus the magic of the sun on you."

"Not yet," Sadira said, pulling away. Although she was frightened by the change occurring in her leg, the sorceress was determined to learn everything she could about the Pristine Tower and the Dragon. Besides, she assumed Khidar would be able to return her leg to normal, at least if the shadow people had been telling the truth when they offered to heal Magnus. "What do you get by helping me?"

A black cloud left Khidar's mouth. "Our reward is simple," he said. "Our race was born of the magic which made Borys into the Dragon. We're the descendants of the loyal servants of Rajaat—of the men and women whom the champions sacrificed in order to complete the betrayal of their master. When Borys dies, our race will be released from its fate."

"Thank you," Sadira said, nodding to the shadow. "Now I'm ready."

Khidar took Sadira in his arms. A terrible chill ran through her body, stinging her skin and freezing her flesh to the bone. A black stain spread outward from where the dark arms enclosed her, bringing with it an icy, deathlike numbness. The sorceress felt her knees buckle, then she collapsed into the shadow's grasp.

Khidar rose into the air, carrying Sadira's shivering body with him. Below them, the rest of the shadow people moved toward the center of the room, flitting about in a wild, rhythmic dance. Scintillating flashes of light began to shoot off the mirror, passing through the gems set into the steel ring that had once supported the dark lens.

Khidar took Sadira almost to the crystal cupola before he stopped. The sorceress saw that her body now resembled his: a black silhouette, with no hint of her wiry frame or womanly figure. Below her, a varicolored spray of light danced off the walls of the tower, rising from the gems of the lens ring to lap at her feet like flames with no heat.

As Sadira watched, the dancing rays came together in a prismatic blast of light. The eruption that followed formed itself into a simmering cloud of color, which came boiling up beneath her feet. A peal of deep, sonorous thunder rumbled from the heart of the storm. Golden rays of brilliance and black streaks of darkness flashed out to strike her, sending searing waves of pain and icy bolts of torment shooting through her body. Sadira felt herself slipping from Khidar's icy grip. As she sank into the storm of colors, she heard herself scream in agony.

When her voice echoed back to her, it was filled with jubilation and triumph.

EIGHTEEN

Song of the Lirrs

As the sun touched its crimson disk to the western horizon, Magnus raised his weary voice to join the lirrs in yet another of their morbid beast-songs. The saurian creatures were all around him, standing on their hind legs and stretching out their thorny tails to balance the weight of their scale-covered bodies. When they sang, they flared their magnificent neck fans, opening their mouths so wide that they seemed nothing but pink gullet and fangs.

Magnus had been singing with the lirr pack since shortly after midday, when they had come trotting through the field. At first, the windsinger had hoped that they would mistake him for a tree and continue on. Unfortunately, the branches that had sprouted on his upper body had begun to quiver in fear, giving him away. One of the lirrs had come over and began clawing at his trunk.

At that moment, Magnus had realized the pack would eventually devour him, but, determined not to die easily, he had cracked the creature's skull with a huge fist. The rest of the pack had immediately returned and begun circling, bellowing the eerie notes of their hunting song. It

310

was then that he had hit upon the idea of joining them.

The tactic had worked well, for his voice was more than versatile enough to duplicate the notes of their keening. The saurians had been circling him since, confused as to whether he was prey, a tree, or some kind of strange lirr. There was a limit to how long Magnus could keep stalling the predators, however, and the windsinger knew that he was fast approaching it. Already, he could hear his voice cracking with hoarseness, and before the night was finished he knew it would fail entirely.

To Magnus's relief, the lirrs suddenly stopped singing. In unison, they dropped to all fours and turned eastward, their amber eyes gleaming hungrily. An instant later, they bounded away together. Following them with his eyes, the windsinger saw that they had gone to attack a solitary figure returning from the Pristine Tower. At this distance, and in the obscure light of dusk, Magnus could not tell whether he was looking at Sadira or Rhayn.

"Watch yourself!" he yelled. "Lirrs!"

The warning came too late, for the beasts were already upon their prey. They launched themselves at her, snapping at her throat with sharp fangs and raking her abdomen with long claws. Magnus's leafy boughs shuddered with horror and he tried to avert his lidless eyes, but constrained as he was by his trunk, he could not turn far enough away to avoid seeing what followed.

To his amazement, the charging beasts did not bowl the woman over. Instead, she simply stopped walking and they slipped, clawing and snapping, off her body. Once the lirrs reached the ground, they changed tactics, savaging her legs in an attempt to topple their quarry.

The distant figure stopped and pointed a hand toward the setting sun. By the time she pulled it away, her whole body glowed with a crimson light. She kicked at the

voracious lirrs with her feet, trying to drive them away
before she unleashed her magic. This act suggested to
Magnus that he was looking at Sadira, for no elf would
have treated one of the saurians with such kindness.

When the lirrs did not avail themselves of her mercy,
the sorceress waved her hand at them. A brilliant flash of
red flared from beneath her palm. Once the spots had
faded from Magnus's eyes, he saw that the beasts had
vanished. As powerful as she had been before entering
the tower, the windsinger realized that Sadira had returned with her abilities much enhanced.

The sorceress strolled toward Magnus as though nothing had happened, and soon he could see the highlights
of her amber hair glistening in the evening light. Her
face, however, remained swathed in shadows until she
was almost upon him.

When she finally came close enough to see, the windsinger could not stop himself from gasping. Where the
lirrs had raked her, there was not even the faintest sign of
a wound. But it was not the sorceress's immunity to injury that shocked the windsinger the most. Although she
was as beautiful as ever, her skin had turned jet black.
Her eyes now had no pupils and glowed like burning embers. Whenever she exhaled, a wisp of black steam rose
from between her lips, which had changed color to match
her blue eyes.

"What's wrong, Magnus?" Sadira asked, giving him a
warm smile. "Don't you like women in black?"

"As long as you're still Sadira, I don't mind," the windsinger replied, giving her a nervous grin.

This brought a smile to the sorceress's lips. "It's me—
more or less," she said. Sadira's expression saddened,
then she added, "I'm sorry to tell you this, but Rhayn
won't be coming back."

The windsinger nodded. Choking back a lump in his throat, he said, "That's okay. It's not like I'd be going anywhere with her." He shook his branches for emphasis.

Sadira was quiet for a moment, then she asked, "Maybe you'd like to come with me, instead?"

"Don't mock me," Magnus said. "It's going to be difficult enough watching you leave."

"I'm not mocking you," Sadira answered.

With that, she moved forward and began plucking branches off the windsinger's body.

"That hurts!" Magnus objected, trying to push the sorceress's arms away. To his surprise, he found that he could not. It was not that they were strong, but they just did not yield to force. "Stop it!"

Sadira continued to pluck, ripping even large branches off his body as though they were only shoots. "I suppose you want to spend the rest of your days with leaves all over your back?" she asked, ripping the last bough off.

"That *is* what trees look like," the windsinger replied, staring sadly at the pile of limbs she had scattered about his trunk.

"Well, you're not a tree," Sadira said, laying her hands on his trunk. "You're an elf—more or less."

Deep inside his bole, Magnus felt a strange tingle where his legs had once been. He tried to move his feet and felt muscles responding to his command, though his lower body remained locked in wood.

"Brace yourself," Sadira said. "This will hurt."

"What's going to—"

Magnus's trunk erupted into flames. He screamed, sending a loud, echoing howl rolling across the field in all directions. For several moments, he writhed about madly, choking on acrid smoke and trying to bat out the fire consuming his lower half. Searing pain filled his entire body, and he began to think Sadira had decided it would be kinder to kill him than to leave him here, trapped and alone.

Then his legs came free and he fell forward, landing at the sorceress's feet. "How did you do that?" he gasped, running his hands over his still-smoking legs.

"A legacy from the shadow people," the sorceress said, holding a hand down to the windsinger. "Among other things, I've gained quite a lot of control over most forms of magic."

Magnus flattened his ears doubtfully. "What kind of nonsense—"

"It's not nonsense," Sadira responded.

To prove her point, she pulled the windsinger's immense bulk off the ground. He came up as though he weighed less than a child. His jaw dropped open and he stared at her arms in frank astonishment.

"You have the strength of a half-giant!" Magnus gasped.

"It's not strength," Sadira said. "It's the sun. As long it's above the horizon, I'm steeped in its power."

"So you've become a sun-cleric?" he asked.

Sadira shook her head. "No," she said. "The shadows explained it to me like this: the sun is the source of all life. All magic comes from life-force—whether it's drawn from plants or animals. Sorcerers get their mystical energy from plants, the Dragon gets his from animals. From now on, I'll get mine from the sun—the most powerful source of all."

Magnus remained doubtful. "The shadow people did this for you?" he asked. "It doesn't make sense that shadows would know so much about the sun."

"Who else would understand more about light?" Sadira asked. "Without light, you can't have shadow."

Instead of answering, Magnus tilted his ears forward and looked over the sorceress's shoulder. "There's something over there," he whispered.

Sadira turned around just as a sarami-swaddled body rose from the brush about fifty yards away. Even from this distance, the sorceress could see that his red nostrils were flaring with hatred, and his bulbous eyes were fixed on her face. He raised a hand and pointed it in her direction.

The sorceress shoved Magnus aside, sending him sailing through the air in a long arc.

Dhojakt's lips moved as he uttered his incantation. The glowing form of a giant owl appeared above his head, then streaked toward Sadira. Where there should have been eyes, the magical beast had orange flames, and instead of claws, it had a pair of sizzling lightning bolts.

Sadira did not even try to avoid the attack. Instead, she remained motionless and allowed the bird to swoop down upon her. When it reached striking distance, the raptor assaulted in a storm of sparks and flame, its silver talons crackling harmlessly against her skin and streams of fire shooting from its eyes and washing off her with no effect. Sadira allowed the attack to continue for a moment, then laid her hand against the raptor's body. She began to pull energy from it, much as she had once drawn the life-force of plants when she wished to cast a spell. The owl's attacks ceased and its body steadily dwindled away, until nothing at all remained of the magical bird.

Looking toward Dhojakt, Sadira turned her hand downward and expelled the energy. As it returned to the soil from which it had come, she moved toward him. "I was wondering what had become of you, Prince," she yelled.

Behind her, Magnus returned to his feet and followed

at a safe distance. "What are you doing?" he whispered. "Let's run for it—at least until we're out of sight of the tower. If he even scratches us—"

"He won't!" Sadira hissed.

As they approached, Dhojakt did not retreat. "You were fortunate at Cleft Rock," he said. "It took quite some time to work free—especially since the grotto rock made it impossible to use magic."

"I had hoped to destroy you," she answered, stopping a few paces from the prince. Magnus circled around to the side, taking care to stay well out of arm's reach. "This time I will."

"I think not," the prince replied, paying no attention to the windsinger. "Just because I didn't dare follow you into the tower doesn't mean I can't kill you now."

Sadira started to raise a hand to collect the energy for a spell, then thought better of it and let her arm drop back to her side. She wanted to know more about why Dhojakt had been afraid to follow her into the Pristine Tower.

"You're a liar," Sadira said. "If you were too weak to go to the tower, you're too weak to hurt me now."

The comment did not provoke the angry response for which the sorceress had hoped. Instead, Dhojakt gave her a confident smile. "It's not that I was too weak to enter the tower. But what good would it have done me to chase you into the midst of my father's oldest enemies? I would have been so busy fighting them that there would've been no time to kill you."

"You and your father have no reason to be enemies with the shadow people . . . or me," the sorceress said, puzzled by the prince's willingness to talk. He had never before struck her as the type who wasted much time conversing with enemies, and she did not like the fact that he was doing so now. "After all, the Dragon is as much an enemy to your father as to the shadow people."

This caused a rumble of laughter to roll from the prince's throat. "What makes you think that?"

"Even your father couldn't enjoy paying his levy every year," Sadira countered.

"No, but he does it willingly," chuckled Dhojakt. He glanced westward, to where the sun's disk had settled only halfway below the horizon. Looking back to Sadira, the prince added, "I thought the shadows would have told you—my father helped create the Dragon."

The prince had clearly intended his comment to startle Sadira, and he had succeeded. Fortunately, the sorceress was not so shocked that she had missed the significance of Dhojakt's glance toward the sun. He was trying to stall her until night fell, which suggested that he had deduced the nature of her new powers—and that could only mean that he had a thorough knowledge of the Pristine Tower.

To Dhojakt, Sadira said, "What you claim is impossible. The Champions of Rajaat changed Borys into the Dragon—"

"And when they were finished, each claimed one of the cities of Athas, and they became the sorcerer-kings," the prince finished. "My father was Gallard—"

"Bane of the Gnomes," Sadira finished, recognizing the name from her conversation with Er'Stali.

"Yes," Dhojakt replied, once again looking westward.

Sadira did not bother to follow his glance, for she had heard enough. As incredible as it seemed that the champions could survive for so many centuries, what the prince told her made sense. It explained his knowledge of the tower, the sorcerer-kings' willingness to pay the Dragon's levy, and the reason his father had sent him to stop her from reaching the tower in the first place.

Deciding she had learned all she would from the

prince, the sorceress raised a hand toward the sun. From the slowness with which energy came to her, she could tell that well past half its disk had sunk below the horizon.

"Watch yourself!" Magnus yelled.

The windsinger had barely spoken when Dhojakt flexed his two dozen legs and sprang forward. As the prince descended on Sadira, his bony mouthparts shot from between his lips and darted for her throat. The sorceress allowed the venomous mandibles to close around her neck, then staggered a single step backward as Dhojakt's heavy body slammed into her. For a moment, they stood face to face, a faint smile upon Sadira's lips as she felt her enemy's poisonous pincers trying in vain to puncture her skin.

Finally, Sadira lowered the hand that she had been holding up to the sun. "You should have listened to me," she said. "I said you were too weak to hurt me."

The sorceress slammed the heels of both palms into Dhojakt's ribs. She heard a series of muffled cracks, then the prince's mandibles released her neck and the breath shot from his lungs in an agonized bellow. The human part of his torso snapped back against the part that was cilops, smashing the back of his skull into his own carapace.

Dhojakt shook his head, then spun around to flee. Magnus came rushing out of the brush and grabbed the prince's rear segments. Bracing his massive feet against the ground, the windsinger locked his arms around Dhojakt's squirming body and did not let go.

"Hurry, Sadira!" Magnus gasped. "The sun's almost down!"

Sadira glanced over her shoulder and saw that the windsinger was right. Only a thin crescent remained above the horizon.

With his rear legs, Dhojakt scratched madly at the arms holding him. When his claws could not tear the windsinger's thick hide, he spun around and lunged toward Magnus with his pincers. Sadira slipped between the two and slapped the mandibles aside.

"Let go, Magnus," she said. "I don't want you getting hurt this close to dark."

"Don't worry about me," the windsinger objected. "If he gets away—"

"He won't!" Sadira said, holding her palm toward the narrowing crescent of the sun. "Let go!"

Magnus did as she ordered. As the sorceress expected, Dhojakt immediately tried to bolt, but she caught him by the arm and held fast. With her free hand, Sadira extended a single glowing finger toward the prince's head.

"Wait!" he cried.

"What do you take her for, a fool?" Magnus scoffed.

"No, of course not," said Dhojakt. "But there's something she should know before she attacks the Dragon. After I tell you, kill me if you like—but hear me out first."

Sadira glanced at the sun. It was no more than a sliver, its red light wavering uncertainly in the hazy sky.

"He's stalling," Magnus warned.

"No," the prince said, looking at Sadira. "Even as powerful as you've become, you'll never kill the Dragon—but by fighting him, you might be endangering Athas itself."

Sadira stopped short of touching the prince with her finger. "Explain yourself—and speak quickly!"

"The Dragon is powerful, but not as powerful as seven sorcerer-kings," Dhojakt said. "Ask yourself why they have paid his levy for so many millenniums."

The sorceress touched her finger to his face. The prince howled in pain and the air was instantly filled with the stench of charred flesh. "I don't have time for riddles," she hissed.

"They do it because the Dragon is Athas's protector," the prince said. "He needs the levy so that he remains strong enough to keep a great evil locked away."

"What evil?" Sadira demanded.

Dhojakt shook his head. "I cannot say—even to save my own life."

"Now, Sadira!" Magnus yelled.

"Who?" the sorceress demanded, pressing her finger to Dhojakt's face again. "The shadow people?"

The prince screamed in pain and flung himself to the ground. An instant later, clumps of broompipe and stems of milkweed began to wither all around him.

The glow in Sadira's finger began to fade, and the last rosy light of the evening spread across the darkening sky like a sheet of fire. Dhojakt spun around, his pincers extended and his fingers already working to cast a spell.

"Die, defiler!" Sadira screamed.

As she spoke, she spewed a cloud of dark fumes from her mouth. The vapors spread out above the prince's prone form, then coalesced into a fine mist and settled over him in a black pall. From inside came the sizzle of a misfired spell. As the murky shroud absorbed all the warmth from Dhojakt's body, there followed a series of blood-chilling screams. By the time the last glimmer of dusk had faded from the sky, all that remained of the Nibenese prince was a shadow upon the grass.

Magnus stepped to Sadira's side. "Why didn't you wait any longer to kill that thing?" he demanded, gesturing at the ground where Dhojakt had fallen. "You had at least another half-second."

"I'm sorry I pushed things so close," the sorceress answered. As the evening grew darker, her skin was losing its ebony luster and fading back to its usual coppery tone. "But it was worth the risk."

"How so?" Magnus demanded, his ears twitching uncomfortably at the changes occurring in Sadira's appearance.

"Dhojakt was right, I'm not ready to kill the Dragon," the sorceress answered. "But I am ready to stop him from sacking Tyr. Now I know his weakness."

NINETEEN

Borys

The argosy lay toppled on its side, cracked into two pieces and half-buried in rust-colored sand. The mekillots that had once pulled the huge fortress wagon remained in their harnesses, as motionless as hills and just as lifeless. Scattered for hundreds of yards around were the bodies of the outriders and their kanks, while the guards and merchants had been pulled from inside the argosy and heaped into a great pile on its shady side.

Despite the blazing heat of the day, only a faint stench of decay hung in the air. The corpses were too shriveled and desiccated to rot, for their bodily fluids had evaporated when the life-force was drawn out of them.

As she passed the scene, Sadira slowed her pace and allowed Magnus to catch her. So the windsinger could keep up, the sorceress had taken three kanks from the Silver Hand elves. Still, even though he rode his mounts in shifts, it was such a struggle for the beasts to match Sadira's pace that they often lagged behind.

When Magnus finally caught up, he asked, "The Dragon again?" Since rejoining the caravan trail at Silver spring, they had encountered a string of similar sights.

Sadira nodded. "We're getting close to Tyr, and I'd like to know how far behind we are," she asked. "Is there any way you can tell?"

Magnus shook his head. "Normally, I could hazard a guess based on how much the corpses had decomposed, but with the bodies like this . . ." The windsinger let the sentence trail off and turned his ears toward the argosy. "There's something behind those bodies," he whispered, pointing toward the corpse pile. "I think it's just an animal."

"Let's look anyway," Sadira replied.

Without waiting for Magnus to dismount, the sorceress crept over to the body heap. As she approached, she heard the sound of gnawing and slurping coming from the far side. Trying to imagine what kind of carrion eater would make such noises, she paused long enough to point a hand toward the sun and draw the energy for a spell.

Before she could step around the pile, the gnawing stopped. "Aren't you supposed to be keeping watch?" demanded a grouchy voice. "I smell something!"

"You're the one who's supposed to be watching," snarled a second speaker. "What if she comes by?"

Sadira stepped around the corpse pile to peek at the speakers. At first, she could not find them in the tangle of limbs and torsos. After a moment of searching, however, she saw a pair of disembodied heads resting on the withered flesh of a mul's leg. Both had coarse hair tied in long topknots, and the bottoms of their necks had been sewn shut with black thread. From the condition of the nearby bodies, it appeared they had been treating themselves to a gruesome feast. Although Sadira did not know the pair well, she had seen them often enough to know they were the advisors King Tithian had inherited from the sorcerer-king Kalak.

"Who are you waiting for?" she asked.

The heads spun around. "You, my dear," said one, whom Sadira recognized as Sacha. He had bloated cheeks and narrow, dark eyes. "We came out here to see you."

"Why?" Sadira demanded. Suspicious of their motives, she raised her hand to show that she was ready to defend herself.

"There's no need for threats," said Wyan, the second head. He twisted his cracked lips into the mockery of a smile and fixed his sunken eyes on the sorceress's crimson-glowing hand. "We're on your side in this."

"Why does that fail to reassure me?" asked Magnus, coming up behind Sadira.

Sacha looked at the windsinger. "Is this is a friend of yours, Sadira?" he asked, running a long, ash-colored tongue over his lips.

"He is," the sorceress replied, scowling.

"How unfortunate," sighed Wyan, glancing in distaste at the desiccated corpse upon which he had been gnawing. "I could use something fresh to drink."

"Don't even think about it," Sadira warned. "Now, tell me what you want. I'm in a hurry."

"Then you should thank us for saving you an unnecessary trip," said Wyan. "We've come to tell you that Borys is not going to Tyr—at least not right away."

"Do you take me for a fool?" Sadira demanded. The sorceress turned away and motioned to Magnus. "Come on—we've wasted too much time already."

As they started back toward the kanks, Sacha and Wyan rose into the air and floated after them. "Wait!" said Wyan. "Won't you hear us out?"

"I don't need to," snapped Sadira, not stopping. "This

is just another of Tithian's tricks. But thanks for coming—at least I know I'm not too late."

"You will be, if you insist on going to Tyr," Sacha said, drifting into Sadira's path and hovering in front of her face. "Tithian doesn't even know we're here."

The sorceress slapped the head aside, sending him soaring through the air. He did not stop moving until he had ricocheted off the shell of a dead mekillot and crashed into a nearby sand dune.

Wyan chuckled at his companion's fate. "For once, we're telling the truth," he said, being careful to maintain a safe distance. "How do you think we knew you'd be returning from the Pristine Tower?"

"The same way Tithian knew I'd be going," the sorceress replied.

"Come now—that makes no sense," said Wyan. "The kank he was using to spy on you was killed in Nibenay by Gallard himself."

Sadira stopped at the sound of the sorcerer-king's ancient name, signaling Magnus to do the same. "Where did you hear that name?"

Wyan sneered at her. "I thought that would get your attention."

"But it won't hold it for long," she warned, noting that Sacha had extricated himself from the sand dune and was cautiously drifting back toward her. "Say what you came to say—but be certain that it's worth my time. Even when I'm in a good mood, I have no patience for you two."

"We're not wasting your time," said Wyan. "The shadow people sent word to expect you."

"How?" Sadira asked. "What do you know of the shadow people?"

"That's not important now," said Sacha, returning to the group. "But our reason for coming is. Tithian told the Dragon about the help you received from Kled. Borys was furious, and now he's gone to destroy the *Book of Kings* and punish the dwarves."

The sorceress pondered Sacha's words for several moments, then stepped past the heads and motioned for Magnus to mount his kank.

"Where are we going?" the windsinger asked.

"Tyr," Sadira answered. "I'd have to be a fool to trust these two. They're the king's closest advisors," she said, waving her hand at Sacha and Wyan. "I don't know how, but Tithian's been eavesdropping on me even after I left Nibenay. He sent these two out here to divert us."

"I don't follow your logic," said Magnus.

"That's because she isn't using any!" snapped Wyan.

Sadira pointed her palm at the head. A stream of brilliant crimson light shot from her hand, and Wyan screamed in anger. "Trollop! You blinded me!"

"Quiet, or I'll make it permanent," she said. To Magnus, she explained, "Tithian is too much of a coward to defy the Dragon, so he doesn't want me to return before he pays the levy. He sent these two out here with the story about Kled, hoping the names they've so carefully mentioned would convince me to go to the village instead of Tyr."

"That is the kind of plan Tithian would think of," admitted Sacha. "But can you afford the chance that it's really what he's doing?"

Magnus turned his head so that he was looking at Sadira with just one of his black eyes. "This trick seems too complicated," he said. "Wouldn't it be easier just to make a deal with the Dragon? In return for bypassing Tyr this year, tell him about Kled and the *Book of Kings*?"

"That would make sense," said Wyan, blinking his

eyes as his temporary blindness passed. "But it's not what Tithian did. He still intends to pay the levy. By telling the Dragon about Kled, he's only trying to curry favor."

Sadira considered Magnus's point for several moments, then looked at the two heads. "I might find your story easier to believe if I knew why you had suddenly decided to betray Tithian," she said. "Surely, you don't expect me to believe you've developed a concern for the people of Tyr."

"Of course not," spat Sacha. "Let's just say that we have certain interests in common with the shadow people."

"Let's not," Sadira said. "I want to know more."

"If you must," said Wyan, rolling his sallow eyes. "You know of the rebellion against Rajaat?" he asked. When Sadira nodded, he continued, "Not all of us revolted. For our dissension, Sacha and I were beheaded."

"You were champions?" Sadira gasped.

"We still are," answered Sacha, smiling proudly. "My full title is Sacha of Arala, Curse of the Kobolds."

"And I am Lord Wyan Bodach, Pixie Blight," added the second head. "We are the last two loyal champions, and, as you can imagine, we would like nothing better than vengeance against the traitor Borys."

"If that's true, then tell me why the others rebelled," Sadira demanded.

"If you insist," Sacha growled. "The shadow people call the time of Rajaat's rule the Green Age, and with good reason. All of Athas was as lush and fertile as the halfling forests you've visited."

"But the wars took a terrible toll on the land, for we champions were not the only great sorcerers in the fight," Wyan broke in. "Every time there was a battle, hundreds of acres of land turned barren. By the time we were nearing victory—"

"You mean, by the time you had annihilated most of the nonhuman races?" Sadira interrupted.

The bitterness of her voice seemed lost on Wyan. "Precisely," he said. "By the time we were preparing to wipe the last plague of impurity from the world, much of Athas had been reduced to a desert."

"So Rajaat declared that after our victory, he would be the only sorcerer," Sacha continued. "The rest of us would have to forego the powers he had bestowed upon us. Wyan and I were more than happy to obey our master's will, but the others renounced their vows and attacked."

"And that is how Athas came to be as it is," said Wyan. "Now, will you go to Kled—or are you going to let Agis and Rikus meet the Dragon alone?"

* * * * *

"Get it out of me!" Neeva's pained voice rang out from a hut near the heart of Kled. It echoed up the orange sandstone slopes to the top of the bluff, where, with the aid of a magical spell, Sadira and her companions were eavesdropping on everything that happened in the village. "Hurry, Caelum! This hurts!"

"What's wrong with her?" demanded Wyan, hovering next to Sadira.

On the other side, Sacha asked, "Is someone torturing her?" His corpulent lips were twisted into a heinous grin.

"Have you two never heard the sound of a woman bearing a child?" Magnus asked, shaking his head at the scene below. "She couldn't have chosen a worse time."

Before Kled's gate stood Borys, his slithering tail

swished languidly about, stirring up as much dust as a whirlwind. Despite the distance and the haze, Sadira could see that the Dragon was as tall as a full giant, with a body so gaunt that he would have made an elf seem stout. He had skin the color of iron, with a chitinous hide equal parts flesh and shell, and each of his willowy legs had two knees that bent in opposite directions. His arms were almost skeletal, ending in long-clawed fingers with swollen, knobby joints. Borys's face was the most frightening aspect of his appearance, for it was no longer even remotely human. Located at the end of a serpentine neck, his head resembled that of a sharp-beaked bird, with a spiked crest of leathery skin and a pair of beady eyes so small they were hardly visible.

Before the Dragon, atop the village's modest gatehouse, were the tiny forms of two men that Sadira believed to be Rikus and Lyanius. The rest of Kled's warriors stood along the walls, arrayed in their glistening armor. From what the companions could see, they were armed with steel axes or swords, spiked bucklers, and crossbows.

On the sandstone slopes overlooking the approach to the gate, a hundred more figures stood near Borys's flank. They were all dressed in the fashion of Tyr, with long dark robes easily discernible at a distance. The fact that none of them seemed to be carrying weapons suggested they were either mindbenders or sorcerers. By the silver streak that ran down the center of his long black hair, Sadira could identify Agis standing at the head of the company.

Borys hardly seemed to notice any of this. In a sizzling voice as loud as thunder, he said, "Bring me the one known as Er'Stali, with his *Book of Kemalok Kings*, and choose half your number to die."

"It looks like we didn't get here a minute too soon," Sadira said. "Let's go."

"If you say so," Magnus said, his voice still quivering from the exhaustion of the two-day run Sadira had just pushed them through. "But it would be better if we could take a few minutes to rest—"

"I doubt we have even a few seconds," Sadira countered. As they started down the slope, she was surprised to notice Sacha and Wyan floating along behind Magnus. "I hadn't thought you would be so brave," she commented.

"When the cause serves us, we can be courageous enough," answered Sacha.

Down at the gate tower, Lyanius's ancient voice said something defiant. Unfortunately, even with the aid of her magic, the sorceress could not quite make out the words of the trembling voice. In a motion so fast she barely saw it, Borys plucked the old man from the wall and held him aloft. Lyanius screamed in anger and struggled to free himself, his fists beating against the huge finger wrapped around his chest.

The dwarven sergeant raised his arm, but he did not dare signal his warriors to loose their bolts. Even if they killed the Dragon with their first volley, the long drop to the ground would kill the *uhrnomus*. Sadira stopped. She was still too far away to use any of her combat spells, but she might be able to utter an incantation that would cushion Lyanius's fall.

"The book!" bellowed the Dragon.

Lyanius stopped struggling and stared down into Borys's nearest eye, trembling in fright.

"Why doesn't Borys just go in and take it?" asked Magnus. "He must be powerful enough."

"Easily," answered Sadira. "But he'd have to use his

magic, and he needs to save all his energy for another task more important to him."

"What?" the windsinger asked.

"To keep something locked away," she answered, pointing the tip of a red-glowing finger at Lyanius.

"You know about that?" gasped Wyan. "And you still want to deny Borys his levy?"

"Khidar and his people did not seem so terrible to me," she answered.

Lyanius stopped struggling, then looked back down to the Dragon. "No!" he yelled.

Borys's fist closed, and the *uhrnomus*'s body disappeared into a spray of blood. On the village wall, the sergeant lowered his hand. The dwarven crossbows clattered, launching a hundred steel bolts at the Dragon's chest. They struck with a hollow rattle, then fell away in an ineffectual rain of metal.

Sadira rushed down the hill, moving so fast that she left Magnus and the two heads far behind. As she ran, Borys raised one leg and stepped over the wall. Rikus lifted his sword and turned to face the Dragon, but did not move forward to attack. Instead, he suddenly lowered the blade and dropped to his stomach. Before his belly hit the roof, dozens of spells flashed from the hands of the sorcerers outside the gate. In the next instant, the air was filled with lightning bolts, streams of fire, sparkling projectiles, and more kinds of deadly magic than Sadira had ever before seen in one place.

Borys disappeared into a dazzling explosion of magical energy. Even so far from the fight, Sadira felt the ground trembling beneath her feet, and the wind was filled with the caustic stench of incendiary spells.

When the storm died away, Borys still straddled the wall. Wisps of smoke—black, gray, red, and many other colors—were rising off his mottled hide. Other than that, he showed no sign of having been injured.

Sadira continued to sprint forward, astonished by the speed with which fighting had broken out. Barely two seconds had passed since Borys had killed Lyanius, and already the defenders were fully engaged in combat. She considered the possibility of pausing long enough to cast a spell that would take her closer, but decided against doing so. At the rate things were going, by the time she stopped, uttered the incantation, and reoriented herself when she arrived, this battle might well have taken a drastic turn in a different direction.

The Dragon turned his head toward the group of sorcerers that had just attacked him. He opened his great beaklike mouth, then Sadira heard the swish of a prolonged intake of air. Agis dove away, yelling, "Take cover!"

With a deafening roar, a cone of white-hot sand blasted from Borys's mouth. He moved his head slowly from side to side, working his way down the entire hillside. As his gritty breath ignited purple spikeballs and scraped fans of goldentip from the hillside, horrid cries of agony and despair filled Sadira's ears. Men and women disintegrated into columns of greasy smoke, or had the flesh scoured from their bones by the sandy torrent.

Just as Sadira was beginning to fear the stream would consume Agis, Rikus rushed to the edge of the gate tower. With a bellow of rage, he swung his sword at Borys's stomach. The blade struck with a mighty clang, spraying blue sparks in all directions. As it sliced across the Dragon's midriff, red smoke and yellow-glowing blood spilled from the wound.

Borys closed his mouth, cutting off the terrible stream of hot sand, and glared down at his attacker. Wherever the Dragon's fiery blood fell, stones shattered and bricks dissolved into powder.

Within attacking range at last, Sadira stopped to collect the energy for a spell.

Rikus swung again, but Borys easily stepped away, then countered by slashing at the mul with four long claws. As the blow landed, there was an ear-piercing screech and a brilliant blue flash. When the light died away, Rikus was no longer standing atop the tower.

"No!" Sadira screamed.

She was about to cast her spell when the Dragon opened his mouth and hissed in anger. His long tongue darted from his beak and licked at the top of the tower for a moment, then he paused to look over the hills surrounding the village. Whatever had happened, it had apparently not been his doing.

Then Sadira saw the mul standing beneath the gate arch, where the Dragon could not see him, looking dazed and confused. Remembering that Khidar had told her no champion could strike the bearer of a weapon forged by Rajaat, the sorceress decided it would be wisest to hold her attacks until she and Rikus could join forces.

Instead, keeping an eye on both the Dragon and the mul, she went over to Agis's side. What she found made her gasp in alarm. The noble lay on the rocky ground, unconscious and barely breathing. Although he had escaped being hit by Borys's searing breath, an indirect blast of fiery sand had burned his robe away and scoured the skin off much of his face. The sorceress laid her hands on his chest, then allowed some of the energy infusing her body to flow into his. With a little luck, this would keep him alive for a little longer, but her powers did not make her a healer. For that, she needed Magnus.

Sadira rose and glanced back toward gate. Borys had

stepped completely into the village now. Dwarven warriors were swarming around his feet, ineffectually hacking at his ankles with their steel battle-axes. Paying them no more attention than Magnus would have a swarm of mosquitoes, the Dragon paused long enough to run a finger along the wound that Rikus had opened. The edges of the cut fused together, stanching the flow of yellow blood.

That done, he turned and marched through the village toward the sound of Neeva's birthing screams. The dwarven warriors followed, but succeeded only in getting themselves crushed along with whatever else happened to lie beneath the Dragon's footfalls. Seeing this, Rikus began to recover from his shock and turned to follow the battle.

Magnus's heavy footsteps finally came up behind the sorceress. Hardly turning around to address the windsinger, she pointed at Agis's inert form. "Don't let him die!"

"I'll do what I can," the windsinger replied, panting heavily. "Who is he?"

"One of my husbands," Sadira answered.

With that, she rushed toward the gate, followed by Sacha and Wyan. She caught up to Rikus just as he started to rush down the lane after Borys and the dwarves. "Rikus, wait!" she called. "You need help!"

The mul stopped and looked back. When his eyes fell on Sadira, his square jaw slackened. "What happened to you?" he gasped.

The sorceress reached over and pushed his jaw back up. "Never mind," she said. "The important thing is that I made it to the Pristine Tower and found out how to save Tyr—and Kled. Whatever you do, don't let go of the Scourge of Rkard. Together, I think we can stop the

Dragon—"

"You mean kill him!" hissed Sacha.

Rikus glanced over the sorceress's shoulder and frowned. "What are those two doing here?" he growled. "Don't tell me they're with you?"

"They're the ones who told me to come here," Sadira admitted.

"I still don't think we can trust 'em," the mul growled.

"Don't think," hissed Wyan. "That's not what your kind is bred for."

Rikus raised his sword to strike at the head, but Sadira caught his arm. "At the moment, we've got more important things to fight," she said. "Especially if Borys is going where I think he is."

With that, she led the way after the Dragon. It did not take much effort to track him. Even if his body hadn't towered far above Kled's small huts, the swath of devastation created by his passing would have made it an easy task.

When they caught up to him, the Dragon was kneeling next to a hut, his arms resting on the top of its walls and his head peering down inside. From inside came the pained groans of Neeva's labor, and no other sounds.

The entire company of dwarves was gathered around the Dragon, swinging their axes at his great body as though it were a tree. Occasionally, Borys lashed out with his tail and smashed one or two of the warriors against a stone hut, but otherwise he paid them little attention.

As Sadira and Rikus approached, Borys flicked his tongue into the hut, then said, "Come now, tell me where you have hidden this Er'Stali and his book. If you force me to use the Way, I promise your child will die with the rest of the village."

From inside the hut, Neeva's pained voice screamed,

"No!"

Sadira took one last look around, noting that Sacha and Wyan had finally yielded to their cowardly instincts and disappeared. When she saw no reason to postpone the attack, she pointed her hand at the Dragon's head, then whispered, "Now, Rikus!"

When she spoke her incantation, a streak of crimson light shot from her finger and engulfed Borys's head in a ball of radiance almost as bright as the sun itself. He bellowed in surprise and jumped to his feet, then Rikus was on him, furiously hacking and slashing at the Dragon's legs. Wound after wound opened, spattering the mul with hot yellow blood and filling the street with runnels of liquid fire. Although the heat drove the dwarves away, Rikus ignored the pain it caused him and continued to lash out at Borys.

Before preparing to cast another spell, Sadira stepped over to the hut and peered over the side. She caught a glimpse of Neeva's naked figure squatting on a bed of soft hides, her hands clenching Caelum's shoulders for support.

"Caelum, take her and run!" Sadira hissed.

"But the child is com—"

"Carry her, now!" the sorceress yelled, stepping away. As she looked back to the battle, Sadira saw the Dragon reach up and grab her sphere of light as though it were a mask, then rip it away. Instantly, she cast her next spell, firing a streak of darkness at his head. This time, Borys was ready for her and deflected the attack with a flick of his wrist. The bolt struck a hut and swaddled it in blackness. It drained into the ground, leaving nothing behind except a shadow.

Once more, Sadira raised her hand toward the sun. Rikus continued to press the attack, leaping across a small stream of boiling stone to thrust his blade toward Borys's abdomen. The Dragon, much better at defending himself now that he could see, slapped the flat of the blade aside.

"I believe that sword belongs to me," he said, gesturing at the Scourge of Rkard with one long finger.

"It's mine now," Rikus replied. He swung again, lopping off the end of the Dragon's finger.

A stream of blood shot from the wound and sprayed over Rikus's chest. The mul screamed and stumbled away, barely managing to keep his hand on his sword. Screaming in rage, Borys slashed at his attacker. Again, there was an ear-piercing shriek and a brilliant flash of blue, then Rikus was nowhere to be seen.

Guessing that the Dragon would turn his attention to her next, Sadira whispered her spell. Instantly, her hand began to vibrate with a gentle hum and glowed in a soft red color. Borys fixed his eyes on the sorceress and opened his mouth, as if to inhale.

"I wouldn't," Sadira said, raising her humming hand toward the Dragon. "My magic comes from the Pristine Tower, and you've already seen that it can affect you."

"It won't after you die," Borys snarled.

"True, but that would unleash the spell in this hand," Sadira said, cautiously bending down and touching her fingers to the street. Immediately, the cobblestones began to crack and break apart. "You could still kill me after the globes in your stomach shattered," she said. "But then, how would you collect the energy you need to keep your prison locked?"

The Dragon closed his mouth and began to shuffle slowly forward, staring at the sorceress in angry silence. Sadira rose to her feet again, but did not retreat. Despite her show of bravery, she was beginning to worry that she had made a mistake. When the sorceress and her friends had killed Kalak, they had caught him in the process of swallowing several obsidian balls as he tried to transform himself into a dragon. They had assumed that he needed the balls for the same reason there had been an obsidian pommel on Nok's cane: to convert the life-force of animals into magical energy.

If they had been mistaken in that assumption, or if Sadira was wrong about the purpose of the levy Borys collected, her error was about to become a fatal one. Still, she had little choice except to press on with her strategy, for it was the only hope she had of forcing the Dragon to leave on her terms. The sorceress stepped forward to meet Borys, reaching out to touch his chitinous body.

The Dragon stopped. "What kind of bargain do you have in mind?" he asked, keeping a wary eye fixed on the sorceress's hand.

"A simple one," she said, breathing a silent sigh of relief. "You leave Kled and Tyr alone, and we will leave you alone."

"No!" screamed Sacha, drifting into view from around the corner.

"Our agreement was that you would attack him!" added Wyan, following close behind. "Release the spell!"

Borys's eyes darted to the two heads. "Arala and Bodach. I have often wondered what became of you two after Kalak's death!" he hissed.

Sacha and Wyan stopped in back of Sadira, using her as a protective shield. "Cast the spell," urged Wyan. "It'll kill him—you'll see."

Though she did not say so aloud, the sorceress knew Wyan was lying. Destroying the globes in Borys's stomach would cripple only his ability to use his most powerful magic, but he would still be able to end her life in any

ne of a dozen other ways. Nevertheless, she thought she
night force the Dragon's hand by playing along with the
wo heads.

"How sure are you of that?" she asked. "If this doesn't
vork, you'll die with me."

"It'll work," said Sacha.

Sadira looked back to Borys. "What shall it be?"

The Dragon did not take his eyes off the two heads.
"Let me have Sacha and Wyan," he hissed.

The sorceress did not even hesitate to step aside. Be-
ore the dumfounded pair could object, one of Borys's
iands lashed out and enveloped them. "Until next year,
hen," he said, giving the sorceress a formal bow.

When Sadira did not return the gesture, Borys turned
ind started walking. As he moved away, his body grew
ranslucent and soon faded from sight altogether.

The sorceress sank to her haunches and began to trem-
ile, but she did not discharge the energy in her hand.
Never again, she suspected, would she feel safe without
he reassuring hum of this particular spell ringing in her
:ars.

For several moments, Sadira sat alone, too shocked and
:xhausted to move. The spell that she had cast to eaves-
lrop on the village was still active. Her ears were filled
vith the sounds of the battle's aftermath—Magnus's
iealing song, the moans of the wounded, and the mourn-
ul cries of those who had lost their loved ones.

One sound, she could hear above all the rest: Neeva
creaming in pain and joy as she struggled to bring her
:hild into the world. As Sadira sat listening, the shrieks
•f pain suddenly gave way to the sound of blissful laugh-
er and the wail of a newborn infant.

A moment later, Rikus rushed around the corner, his
·word still drawn. Where the Dragon's blood had

spattered him, the mul's chest and legs were covered with white blisters. "What happened?" he asked, looking around as if he expected the Dragon to pounce on him at any moment.

Sadira gave the mul a warm smile. "Why don't you tell me?" she asked. "Did Neeva have a boy or a girl?"

EPILOGUE

Far down the caravan road from Tyr, King Tithian I stood on a toppled argosy, staring into the moonlit eyes of the Dragon. Only through a practiced force of will could he keep his knees from trembling, and he was acutely conscious that the golden diadem resting on his brow had been fashioned for a head somewhat smaller than his own.

"It was Nibenay who failed to stop Sadira from finding the Pristine Tower, not me," Tithian was saying. "My only mistake was trusting them." He pointed at the two heads hanging from the Dragon's waist.

"Your mistake was in believing you could rule Tyr!" hissed Sacha.

"And in daring to think you were smarter than your slaves!" added Wyan.

The Dragon laid a single hand over the heads, pressing a finger into each of their eyes. Both Sacha and Wyan fell silent immediately.

"You may continue," snarled Borys, digging his claws in farther than truly necessary to keep the heads quiet.

"I promise you, my city will meet its levy next year," Tithian answered, forcing himself not to look at the torture being inflicted on his former advisors.

"*Your* city!" the Dragon scoffed. "Tyr belonged to Kalak, and Kalak to me. His power was my power, and you have robbed me of that."

Tithian shook his head defiantly. "No, we did you a favor. Kalak was trying to become a dragon so he could take your place."

"I'll be the judge of what favors me and what does not," the great beast snarled. "All sorcerer-kings are dragons of one kind or another, though they assume different shapes to suit their tastes. If Kalak wished to fashion himself after my form, that was his business—but he would not have dreamed of taking my place. Saying such things only shows how little you know about what you've taken upon yourself."

"Then show me," said Tithian.

The beast narrowed his great eyes. "You are too bold. I should kill you and the entire city for your impudence."

"But that would be a great waste, or you would have done it already," said Tithian. "On the other hand, if you grant me one small boon, I'll double the levy that Kalak paid."

The Dragon turned his head and regarded the king with a single black eye. "And in return? What do you want of me?"

"Nothing difficult," answered Tithian. "Just help me become a sorcerer-king."

PRISM PENTAD
Troy Denning

The adventure that began in *The Verdant Passage* & *The Crimson Legion* continues with

The Obsidian Oracle: Book Four

When Tithian, the power-hungry king of Tyr, sets off on a perilous journey into the Athasian desert, Agis follows. Tithian searches for an ancient oracle that will allow him to become an immortal sorcerer-king, but what the two men find may lead to the salvation of Athas—or its destruction.

On sale June 1993.

The Cerulean Storm: Book Five

Armed with the Obsidian Oracle, King Tithian I leads his former slaves—Rikus, Neeva, and Sadira—on a desperate mission to save the world. But when the journey into the mysterious Sea of Silt begins, old hatreds and passions prove as dangerous to the party as the enchanted fleets and terrible dust storms that batter their tiny caravan.

On sale September 1993.

HARSH NEW WORLD! HOT NEW ENGINE!

Prepare to take a *quantum leap* in computer AD&D® role-playing – on the most successful new fantasy world ever launched: the DARK SUN™ game world! *SHATTERED LANDS*, first in this next generation of adventuring, delivers state-of-the-art technology, unrivaled game design and an intricate storyline.

A harsh new world, brutal and sun-scorched, awaits the party you create. Choose from all-new races with higher levels and multiple classes.

Spectacular full-screen graphics and cinematics unfold in continuous action – you never leave the screen to go into another mode for combat, inventory and conversation.

A splendid music score and sound effects truly bring the DARK SUN game world to life!

The full-blown 16-bit engine delivers smooth animation and game play. Pick up and examine objects, interact with the physical surroundings, converse with characters, battle monsters – all with incredible richness and detail! And the point-and-click interface gives you quick and easy game play!

▶ **IBM** (SEPT.)
▶ **AMIGA** (DEC.)
▶ **MAC** (FEB. '93)

$79.95 EA.